IRENA'S
WAR

Books by James D. Shipman

TASK FORCE BAUM

IRENA'S WAR

Published by Kensington Publishing Corp.

IRENA'S WAR

JAMES D. SHIPMAN

KENSINGTON BOOKS
www.kensingtonbooks.com

KENSINGTON BOOKS are published by

Kensington Publishing Corp.
119 West 40th Street
New York, NY 10018

All Kensington titles, imprints, and distributed lines are available at special quantity discounts for bulk purchases for sales promotion, premiums, fund-raising, educational, or institutional use.

Special book excerpts or customized printings can also be created to fit specific needs. For details, write or phone the office of the Kensington Sales Manager: Kensington Publishing Corp., 119 West 40th Street, New York, NY 10018. Attn. Sales Department. Phone: 1-800-221-2647.

Kensington and the K logo Reg. U.S. Pat. & TM Off.

ISBN-13: 978-1-4967-2389-5 (ebook)
ISBN-10: 1-4967-2389-9 (ebook)

ISBN-13: 978-1-4967-2388-8
ISBN-10: 1-4967-2388-0
First Kensington Trade Paperback Printing: December 2020

10 9 8 7 6 5 4 3 2 1

Printed in the United States of America

This book is dedicated to the more than three million Jews who perished in Poland during World War II.

BASED ON A TRUE STORY

Prologue

Szucha Street No. 25
Warsaw, January 1944

The bone jutted sharply out of her thigh, a jagged peak with a bloody summit. She turned her head, afraid she would pass out if she stared at the gruesome gash any longer. She moaned, the pain coursing up her leg through her heart, stabbing her mind. She screamed, a shrill shriek of agony. The cry cut off as she gasped for air. Coughing, fluid filled her mouth. She tasted metal and salt. She spat the foul liquid, gulping for air.

"I will ask you again, Frau Sendler, where is Żegota? Who is Żegota?"

That name again. Her mind wandered through the dark alleys of consciousness. She knew that name. There was something about it, something important. She couldn't remember what. She traveled the tunnels of her mind, seeking answers, but she was exhausted and alone, pain her constant companion. She labored to move her hands, to touch the fiery laceration on her thigh, but her wrists were restrained at her waist, secured to this damnable chair.

"I don't know why you won't help me, Irena. Why you won't help yourself."

She felt pressure on the broken bone. She tried to wrench her eyes open to see what was happening, but the blinding agony barred her. Her mind exploded with fire, her head spun, and she felt the world tilting. She cried out again, louder this time. She heard words, begging, pleading. Her words.

"Just tell me the truth, Irena, and this will all end. You can have morphine. Later, we'll bring you food. Everything your heart desires. Do you think I want to do this to you? You've left me with no choice. Now I ask again, where is Żegota?"

She wanted to tell him. If she could only remember! Why wouldn't her mind work? If she could just find a pathway through the burning torment, she would tell him everything, anything. "Morphine," she whispered. That was the answer. "Give me morphine."

"Not just yet. Tell me first."

"Żegota," she said, trying to remember.

"Yes, Żegota," the voice repeated eagerly. "Give me everything."

His words were close now, right next to her ear. If only she could remember. The pain subsided a fraction. The brilliant brightness was gone, leaving the darkness again. Her mind wandered through an abyss. In the distance she saw something familiar, a name, a face. Żegota. She whispered the name out loud again.

"Yes. Tell me now. Quickly."

She tried to move her lips, but it was too late. She was falling, tumbling through the darkness.

"Irena!" She heard his screaming voice, but soon even that was fading away.

Chapter 1

War

September 24, 1939
Warsaw, Poland

Irena stared at the door. Why didn't they come? The Germans had attacked weeks ago. Surely, she'd be needed more than ever now. She took a deep breath from the cigarette she clutched, letting the smoke burn her throat. The pain calmed her. She walked to the window, scanning out of her second story window along Ludwicki Street. The road was deserted, the sidewalks, normally bustling with the noisy clamor of working class families, contained a single pedestrian hurrying under a stifling sun. She turned to the door again. She couldn't wait any longer. She would go to them. She took half a step.

"Irena, what are you doing?" called her mother from the bedroom. The voice was thin and sputtered between breaths. "Please, bring me some water."

She sighed, taking another drag on the cigarette before she crushed the burning end in an ashtray overflowing with butts. The blue smoke hung stagnant in the heat of the apartment.

Cheap shelving lined the walls, a jumble of books crammed every surface. A table stood in the middle of the room, worn and stained, covered by paperwork and plates of half-eaten food. A single framed photo rested against a lamp. She glanced at the image. Her father as a doctor near Warsaw, caring for the poor and the Jews.

"Irena? Where are you?" Her mother called out again.

She closed her eyes, drawing a deep breath. She drew back a hand that was already reaching for the door. She staggered to the kitchen, glancing in a mirror that hung over the sink. A gaunt and weary face peered back. She'd set her long auburn hair in a severe bun. Her cheeks were pale. A hint of a wrinkle crossed her temple. She possessed plain features bred from hardworking peasant stock. There was nothing extraordinary about her, she well knew, except her eyes. Her pupils burned with an icy, piercing passion. Everyone remembered her eyes.

She scanned a stack of dishes and retrieved a cup that wasn't too dirty, scraping a little food off the inside with her thumb. Irena filled it with water and hurried into the bedroom where her mother lay under a mound of blankets, her ashen hair limply splayed over the covers. Irena pressed the cup against her mother's lips and with her other hand drew her head forward so she could drink.

"Irena, the water is warm!" her mother protested, sputtering. The liquid spilled from her lips and dribbled down her chin.

"I'll get you more in a minute," she said, her eyes drawn back to the door.

"Have you had any news?"

"About what?"

"This war, of course. What else is there?"

"Radio Warsaw says we're winning on every front."

"Do you believe it?"

Irena looked out the window. "The fools in charge would

say the same thing, whether we were victors or losers." She cocked her head, listening to a dull thudding in the distance. "Do you hear that? It doesn't sound like victory."

Her mother listened for a moment. "Artillery. Is it theirs or ours?"

"Does it matter? Either way, it draws closer every day." Irena looked back down at her mother. Her skin was pale and stretched. She looked not much more than a fragile sack of bones and flesh. In her mid-fifties, she could pass for seventy. "You have to eat more, Mother."

"I don't have an appetite. Besides," she joked, "soon there won't be enough for anyone and you'll be glad to have my share."

Irena didn't answer. She was staring at the door again.

"What are you waiting for, child?" Her voice carried a hint of annoyance.

"I'm expecting a visit from the department."

Her mother scoffed. "You're not thinking of going to work?"

"My job won't go away because of a silly war. If anything, there will be more to do now than ever."

"Have you heard anything from Mietek?"

"No," she answered curtly, not wanting to think about that right now.

"I hope he's safe."

"I'm sure your wish will come true, Momma. Nothing ever happens to him."

"He's your husband."

"I'm well aware."

"I'd hoped when you saw him things might be better."

"There was never anything wrong. We are the best of friends."

She rose and hurried to the kitchen. She didn't want to talk about Mietek. She turned on the faucet, letting it run for a while this time, and filled the cup with cold water. An abrupt banging startled her. She dropped the cup and sprinted to the entryway. She unlatched the lock and twisted the knob, whipping the door open.

Ewa Rechtman was there, all smiles beneath a tumble of raven curls.

Irena rushed into her friend's arms. "You're safe. How have you been?"

"I'm doing well," she said. Her voice lilted musically. "And how are you?"

"Smothered in this tomb. I need to work. People must be starving out there."

Ewa laughed. "Always the busy one, aren't you? But there's nothing for you to do right now. Everything is shut down. The kitchens, the bakeries. The office is a desert."

Irena gasped, her breath quickening. "You've been to work?"

"Just today," said Ewa. "It's almost abandoned. No power, no phones. I expected to find you already there. Imagine my surprise that I beat Irena Sendler."

"I want to go," she said, heading toward the door.

"There's nothing to do there," said Ewa.

"There's always something." Irena wasn't sure that was true, but after weeks cooped up here, she was desperate to get out. Even for a few hours. "Let's go down together and at least see if we can learn anything."

Ewa nodded, grinning. "I knew you would say that."

Irena stepped into the hallway and paused. The water! She rushed back in and shoved a mug under the spout, the liquid sloshing violently into the cup. She rushed into the bedroom and put the cup down next to her mother.

"Irena, where are you going?"

"Work needs me."

Her mother's face creased in surprise tinged with fear. "You can't leave me. I'm too ill to rise."

"Don't exaggerate, Mother, I'll only be gone a few hours."
She was already rushing to the door.

"Irena!"

She paused, avoiding Ewa's glance. She squared her shoulders and moved on, rushing past her friend and out into the corridor. Ewa shuffled along behind her, trying to keep up. In a few moments they stepped out into the sunshine. Despite the heat, Irena reveled in the freedom; her apartment seemed a tomb. On the sidewalk they could walk side by side and Irena took Ewa's arm, helping her as she limped along beside her.

"How are your parents?" Irena asked.

"They're scared."

"Of the artillery?"

"Of the Nazis."

Irena gave her a squeeze. "Surely the rumors are propaganda. They can't be much worse than these nationalistic fascists that run Poland already."

"I hope you're right. But if the stories are true, the Germans will do worse to us than our own government ever dreamt of."

"*Our government.*" Irena spat the words. "They fabricate stories all the time. The rumors about the Germans are probably nothing more than propaganda."

Ewa stopped and turned to her friend. "And if they aren't?"

Irena shrugged. "Then we will fight them as we did at university."

Ewa laughed. "Always picking a battle, Irena, aren't you?"

"Only until the people finally have their freedom, no matter what religion, race, or class."

Ewa's face darkened. "You still believe in socialism? After the Russians attacked us?"

Irena flinched. She thought back to the news, just a week old, that the Soviet Union, the workers' paradise, had joined Germany in attacking her homeland. "I don't want to talk about Russia," she said, turning and hurrying along. She fought down the anger and distress. She wouldn't think about that right now. She reached a corner and looked back. Ewa was far behind her now, limping along with a frantic gate. She was out of breath and she took long moments to catch up.

"I'm sorry, I shouldn't have said that."

Irena composed herself, fighting to drive the fire down. She allowed Ewa a moment to recover her breath while she checked the cross street. They were halfway to her office.

She never could remember later when she first heard the planes.

The distant thudding danced with a rising buzz that consumed the quiet afternoon. They stood at the corner, mesmerized. Irena searched the heavens, scanning the sky for the source. She spotted them. Distant dots against an azure canopy. The specks grew in size and shape, assuming the form of hulking birds of prey. She hoped they might be Polish, but she knew better. She hadn't seen a friendly plane over the city since the war began. No, these were from the enemy. The planes grew closer. She knew she should drag her friend to safety, but she was so tired of hiding. She didn't want to go back to the indoors, the stifling heat and the boredom. She wanted to see, to hear, to be part of the maelstrom of events swirling around her.

The metallic birds drew overhead, dozens of them, lumbering toward the zenith of the heavens with black crosses on their wings. A whistling shriek pierced the rumble, tearing at her ears so that she feared they would burst from the pain.

A flash. The light reached her before the noise. The sound hit next, a thunderous roar. A building less than a hundred meters away disintegrated into fire and belching smoke. The street was chaos now, the scramble of humans escaping an iron death.

A building collapsed. The explosions progressed in rapid crescendos now, mixed with the screams of scrambling pedestrians fleeing the fire.

Ewa was there, pulling at her arm, her mouth moving without making any sound. She reached up with her hand and touched her ear. Pulling away, she saw the scarlet liquid soaking her fingertips. The crashing explosions continued. She felt unable to move. She wanted to stay here, to feel the fire around her.

Ewa tugged at her again. She shook her head, struggling to clear the cobwebs in her mind. Of course, her friend was right. It was death to stay in the street. She allowed herself to be led toward a nearby building. They entered and discovered stairs leading into a cellar. They scrambled down into the space below, finding it already packed, with fifty or more people crammed in the darkness and the heat. The stale reek of sweat and fear overwhelmed the space. They wormed their way into the crush of bodies and held on to each other. Irena wondered if there was any real protection here. She clung to Ewa, tighter with each explosion, waiting for the detonation that would kill them all.

Standing there, pressed against the cracked wood, Irena thought of her mother, who might never know what happened to her. She remembered her parting from Mietek. She had left things unsaid . . . She thought of her friends, her job, the future she dreamed of—everything would be gone in an instant.

Ewa's normally jubilant face was drawn and pale. "I'm frightened," she whispered. Irena read the words on her lips.

Irena held her close, stroking her hair. "We will be all right. You'll see."

"I pray to God you're right."

Irena thought of her childhood, her Catholic training. She tried to pray, but God was a distant companion abandoned long ago. "Trust *me*, we will survive this," she said finally.

A thunderous boom jolted the cellar, they were plunged into darkness, and the room swayed and rocked as if they would be ripped apart. The air was gone, she tasted smoke and dust, she choked, her eyes burning, her head swimming. She felt a hand on her wrist, tugging her toward the stairs.

* * *

The sun stabbed her eyes. She blinked, and her body jerked. Her mind spun, and she rolled onto her stomach, vomiting. She tasted bile and blood. The pavement beneath her gradually materialized. She pulled herself to her knees. She saw men, women, and children, covered in thick brown dust, lying in jumbled positions nearby. Some were starting to stir. A woman lay on her back, staring at the sky, covered in blood. Irena scanned the group, searching for Ewa. She was sitting nearby on the curb, head between her knees, rocking back and forth. Irena turned and found the building where they had sought shelter. The structure had collapsed in on itself. Fire raged, and a black cloud billowed out of the rubble. It was a miracle they had escaped in time.

Irena checked her arms and legs. She had some minor burns and cuts, but she was not seriously injured. She crawled over to Ewa and placed her hands on her friend, checking her for injuries as well. They sat there together for a long time, amidst the burning buildings, the screams, the dead and the dying— too stunned to speak or to move.

"Irena." Ewa's voice, thick with emotion, reached her through the ringing in her ears.

"Yes?"

"We should go home. Your mother might need you. My family . . ."

"Of course, you're right," she responded. She pulled herself up. Her entire body ached. Her skin felt like the top few layers had been scraped off. She reached her hand down and drew Ewa up.

"Run along now," Irena said. "Make sure everyone is safe."

"I'll come for you tomorrow," Ewa said.

"Come when you're ready."

Ewa turned and limped away as quickly as she could, a gray ghost amidst the dust and the flames. Irena watched her until she turned the corner several blocks away. She dusted herself off as best she could, turned to the right, and continued toward her office. She passed more scenes of violence and death. Whole blocks had crumbled under the German attack.

She noticed a mother with two children in her arms, sitting on the sidewalk, her eyes glazed, tears running in rivers down her cheeks. She had a hand on the head of each of them. They looked like twins, boys, no more than three. Neither was moving. Their little bodies were covered in blood. They were gone. She tried to speak to the woman, but she didn't hear, couldn't see.

Irena scurried on through the shattered streets of Warsaw. The smell of acrid smoke filled her nostrils. Her mouth was parched, tongue dry and heavy. The bombers were gone. She scanned the sky as she navigated the broken pavement but saw nothing. She knew the Germans might return in an instant. Out here exposed in the open, even a near miss would surely kill her. Her panic rose. She wanted to run home, but she steeled herself and marched on. In another kilometer she reached her office in the social welfare building on Złota Street, not far from the banks of the Vistula River.

The three-story structure appeared intact. The whole block was unscathed. The bombers apparently hadn't reached this far. She scrambled up the stairs and into the interior. As Ewa had told her, there was no power. The corridors were dark and difficult to maneuver. The building was deserted.

Inside, Irena felt a measure of safety. She searched an office and found what she was looking for: a half-empty pitcher of water. Ignoring the layer of dust floating at the top, not even bothering to skim it aside, she tipped the vessel back and gulped greedily from the contents. The water was almost as hot as the air outside, but she had never tasted better.

Refreshed, Irena stumbled back out into the dim hallway and felt her way to the stairs. If the interior of the building was dark, the stairway was blackest night. She groped around until she found the rail and pulled herself up, step by step, to the second floor. Making her way along the upstairs corridor she came to her office. The space was little more than a closet. Two desks shoved face-to-face in the space, with just enough room to pull out a chair and sit down. The walls were bare, but the desks were covered with papers. Irena stared at the familiar scene and only now her emotions overwhelmed her. She stood for long minutes, tears running down her face.

"Irena."

She was startled out of her grief by the voice of her supervisor, Jan Dobraczyński. "What are you doing here?" he asked.

She was embarrassed. She thought she was alone. There was no way to hide her tears. She wiped her cheeks with the back of her sleeve and looked up to see Jan standing over her, like a professor proctoring an exam. Spectacles crowded close-cropped iron-gray hair. Wrinkles etched like riverbanks outward from piercing eyes. Everything about him reminded her of university.

"What are you doing here?" he repeated, a hint of irritation and command in his voice.

"I came to the office."

"That's obvious. However, there is no work here right now."

"There's always something to do," she said. Taking a step toward her desk, she fumbled with the mound of documents.

"Look around, Irena," he said, motioning down the hallway. "There isn't a soul here. There is no power. The phones aren't working. People are dying outside by the hundreds. Go home to your family."

He scrutinized her more closely, his eyes widening. "My God!" he said. "Look at you. You're cut all over." He took a step forward.

"I'm fine," she said dismissively. "It's nothing." She turned toward her desk again. "I want to get the soup kitchens reopened. It's been weeks. People are starving."

She felt a hand on her forearm, holding her back. "Are you listening to me? There is no one here and nothing we can do."

She pulled away from him. "I'll get started right away."

"Irena. There is no one to man the kitchens. There's no way to communicate with them. Even if there was, where would you get the food?" His voice softened. "Look, I'm proud of you that you came in. That must've been terrifying for you. You're a brave woman, Irena, but your place is at home right now with your family. That's where all of us should be."

She turned back to him, regarding him with an arched eyebrow. "You're here."

"Not for long. I just came to grab a little paperwork and make sure the office was closed. I didn't expect to find anyone here."

"I've already talked to Ewa. I will find her. If the phones are down, we can go door to door. I only need four or five people and from there we can reach out directly to our volunteers that run the kitchens."

He looked at her, exasperated. "There's no point," he said. "There's no food."

"I have a contact with families in the countryside. I have a friend who has some wagons. He doesn't live far away from me. Once I get everything together, I'll reach out to him and get him started right away." She turned to him. "But I'll need some money."

He shook his head again. "Irena, it's not going to work."

"It will if you help me. All I'm asking for are a few zlotys. That's it. You don't have to do anything else. I just need the resources and I will take care of everything. All the risks, all the duties."

He hesitated, scratching his chin. "I don't know, Irena. If people are killed trying to assist us right now . . ."

"Then it's on me. Besides, people are dying in their homes.

What difference does it make if they are bombed in a soup kitchen instead? At least it's a good cause."

He was quiet for a moment and Irena watched him closely. She could see the objections ticking through his mind. His lips opened several times, but he did not speak. Finally, he nodded his head slightly. "Fine," he said. "But it's on your head. I'll return with the zlotys. I can't spare many."

"Whatever you have will serve."

He left her, and Irena went to work. Over the next several days she labored furiously. With Ewa's help they established a network of workers willing to assist them in getting the soup kitchens back in operation. Irena reached her contact on the edge of Warsaw and paid him all the zlotys she could spare, adding most of her savings to the pot. He contacted his friends in the countryside and purchased food. She now had provisions along with wagons to bring the precious stores back to Warsaw. She'd lined up the personnel to man the stations throughout the city. After three days everything was ready to go.

The situation in Warsaw deteriorated. The booming sound of artillery echoed ever closer. The radio blared promises of victory but the battle sites discussed by the broadcasters crept nearer to Warsaw with each passing day. The government promised the Germans would never set foot in Warsaw. They told of counterattacks and the spirited fighting of the French and British on Germany's Western Front.

Irena saw the hollow lies of these words. Large formations of men streamed into the city: wounded, without weapons, exhausted and starving. The bombers came each day now, unopposed by the Polish air force. There was violence in the streets. Looting increased as the residents of the city struggled to survive. There were few police. Civil order was breaking down.

Irena's mother begged her to stop. Several of the social workers helping voiced the same concerns, but she persisted, braving the streets of Warsaw each day, making contact with different locations, assuring the staff that supplies would be present at each point when the food arrived. Everything was set for tomorrow, September 27. She would meet the wagons coming in from the west. Ewa would direct the food distribution to the numerous kitchens while Irena ensured all the purchased goods were accounted for before the provisions were split into smaller parcels. She had hired men to stand with her, protecting the food from looters while she counted the supplies. The men would then ride, one with each wagon, to make sure the rations made it safely to the sites.

Irena slept fitfully that night. She dreamt that Mietek appeared at her door, a bloody corpse with a blank stare, a mouth open to scream but emitting no sound. She looked past him, searching. Were they all dead? The scene shifted. Gray steel monsters chased her through the smoldering streets of Warsaw. No matter where she hid, they eventually found her. She woke at dawn, exhausted and afraid. She dressed quickly in the semi-darkness, trying to be as quiet as possible, not wanting to wake her mother, to add to her burdens on this critical day.

She left her flat minutes later, rushing down the stairs and out into the street. The city was dark, deserted, a black blanket beneath a sky growing brighter as the minutes passed. She made her way down the street, heading west toward the outskirts of Warsaw. She had to hurry. Her friend would be waiting with his wagons, twelve loads brimming with sustenance for the starving children of the capital. If she was late, he might be overwhelmed, the structures picked clean by starving looters.

She reached the outskirts of Warsaw twenty minutes later. She saw the wagons ahead of her parked in the street. Her driver had placed them on the side of the road facing toward the interior of the city. A group of men stood protectively around them. A small crowd perched across the street, greedily eyeing the food. She smiled to herself, glad she had hired these bodyguards protecting her precious cargo. She searched for her friend. He should be there as well. She spotted him standing near some soldiers. He was gesturing, arms pointing toward the city. One of the soldiers, an officer, shook his head.

Irena hurried. Something was wrong. The army must have stopped him. She felt fear rising. What if they confiscated her goods? She was a patriotic Pole, toward her nation rather than its government, but she had worked too hard to secure these supplies, only to have them taken away. She crossed the last few meters, approaching the soldiers.

"I'm in charge here," she said. "What seems to be the problem?" Her friend looked up in surprise, his eyes full of fear. What was he worried about? She could handle a few arrogant men.

"What have we here, Fräulein?" the officer asked.

Too late, Irena realized her terrible mistake. In the early dawn light, she had failed to recognize the color of the uniforms. These men were not Poles, they were Germans. The enemy was here. Her supplies were lost, along with Warsaw. The Polish war was over.

Chapter 2
Endings and Beginnings

September 27, 1939
Warsaw, Poland

Irena rushed up to the cluster of German soldiers. She searched for the words in German, reaching back to her university training.

"Excuse me, Hauptmann," she said, recognizing the officer as a captain.

The soldier stopped mid-sentence, looking her way. He sized her up with his eyes and then turned back to his men, beginning to issue orders.

"Herr Hauptmann, I need to speak with you."

The captain turned to her, eyes flaring with impatience. "What is it?"

"These wagons are the property of the Polish government. I am a social worker assigned to bring this food into the city."

"I'm sorry . . . what is your name?"

She hesitated, then answered. "Irena Sendler."

"I'm sorry, Frau Sendler, but I cannot let you take this food. My soldiers are hungry."

"They may be hungry, but my people are starving!" she responded, iron in her voice.

"That may be, but the food is here, we are here. I am taking the wagons."

"You must not," insisted Irena, taking a step forward.

"Just shoot her already," said one of the other soldiers, laughing and raising a rifle. He pointed the barrel at Irena.

The captain shoved the weapon aside, sharply rebuking the soldier. He turned back to Irena. "I'm sorry, Frau Sendler, but as I said, I cannot release the supplies to you. As you can also see, it's dangerous for you to be here. Not everyone will be as understanding as me. Go home and wait a day or two. Order will be restored, and it will be safe to go out."

"My people don't have a day or two."

"Your people will get nothing from you if you're dead," he responded icily. "Now shoo." He lifted his hand and dismissed her as if she were an insect.

Irena turned, fighting back tears of frustration. The Germans were already unloading the supplies, helping themselves to the bread, fruits, and vegetables while the bodyguards looked helplessly on, arms in the air. She wanted to go to them, to demand their freedom, but she was afraid. That soldier back there moments ago wanted to kill her. If it weren't for the captain, she might be dead right this moment. She turned and rushed away, heading back into the city. The streets were already lining up with Poles, faces drawn with stunned expressions. The news was out. The Germans were here. Their beloved city had fallen.

She weaved through the crowd, heading toward her flat. She needed time to recover, to think. She was angry, the rage filled her. She had worked tirelessly for days to bring this food to the people who needed it. She'd orchestrated everything and at the moment of success the Germans had ruined everything. How dare they? Surely there was someone higher up that would decry what they had done. The Germans weren't monsters, were they? Oh, there were the stories put out by her government. Whispers of Nazi atrocities. But wasn't that just propaganda? After all, the Polish leadership had no problem spreading lies about the Jews and the socialists. She'd witnessed this first-hand.

No, the Germans were a civilized people. She would wait a few days like the captain suggested. Then she'd go and complain. She would work her way up the ladder until someone listened, then she would arrange for replacement supplies. Perhaps the situation wasn't as bad as it seemed. After all, she had all the names of the workers and the locations. All she needed was food and she could be swiftly back in operation. Working through all this she felt immediately better. She decided she didn't need to go home after all. The Germans couldn't make her do anything. Instead she stopped on the sidewalk and joined the growing crowd of onlookers, watching for the enemy to arrive.

She didn't have to wait long. In an hour they were there, long lines of marching soldiers, steel-gray boots clomping in perfect unison on the pavement as they stomped by in machine precision. Their uniforms were new, as if they'd hardly done any fighting at all. The faces were stern, grim, arrogant. The men stared forward, uninterested in these people they'd just conquered.

She stayed there for hours, watching the endless stream of soldiers marching into the city. There were tens of thousands of them, all young, strong, full of an endless energy. All she had seen of soldiers in the past month were the Polish wounded who limped through the streets, dirty, exhausted, and dejected. What a stark contrast these superhuman Germans made. These new masters.

She was pleased to see they were behaving themselves perfectly. A few soldiers were assigned to each street corner. They maintained a close watch on the crowd but there was no bullying, no lording over the people with their sudden victory. These men were like the captain, simply doing their job. Perhaps that other soldier, the one who had wanted to shoot her, was an exception. She realized he might even have been joking. She knew little of soldiers' ways.

Eventually she grew bored. One can only watch so many boots. She decided to walk to her flat. Her mother was probably hungry and would be angry at Irena for not returning to take care of her. She sighed. She'd rather go elsewhere, find her friends and coworkers, talk to them about what had transpired, learn what they'd observed. There would be time for that. She needn't stay long at home. She just wanted to get a little food and change her clothes. She would fix her mother a quick meal, give her medicine, and head back out into the city. She decided to go to Ewa's as soon as she was finished. Her friend was likely home and they could go to the office together.

As she traveled farther into the city, the crowds thinned out. She was off the main streets now and could move faster. She reached her apartment, pushing through the downstairs door and hurrying along the corridor past faded wallpaper and a single flickering light. She clambered up the narrow staircase, feeling her way along until she spotted the dim glow of the upstairs hallway. She reached her door, fumbling with a ring of keys until she found the correct one. She jiggled the lock and pushed through, hurrying to the cupboard in search of a little bread. She'd skipped her morning meal, assuming she could eat from the wagons, and she was famished.

"Irena, is that you?" her mother called urgently from the bedroom.

"Just a minute." Irena opened their meager pantry and removed a half loaf of stale bread. She unwrapped it from a brown paper container and turned the food over and over, picking off mold and throwing the discarded crumbs into a nearby pail. Inspecting the bread a final time, she bit deeply into the end, ripping off a chunk and chewing greedily. Her arms trembled, and she drew a deep breath, relishing the taste. She gulped down a little musty water from a cup, washing down the food.

"Irena?" Her mother called out again. "What are you doing in there? I need you."

She shook her head, setting the food down and turning to refill the cup. She reached back into the cupboard and removed several pills from a bottle. Tearing a third of the remaining loaf off, she hurried into the bedroom where her mother lay, waiting intently for her. Irena lowered the cup so she could drink.

"Ach!" her mother sputtered. "Warm again. I brought you into this world. Can't you do me the courtesy of running the water for half a minute before you fill the mug?"

"The water's fine," said Irena, dropping the pills into her mouth. Helping her mother drink again, she tore bits of the bread and fed them to her. Her mother consumed the scarce meal in a matter of moments.

"Is that all?" she asked.

"All for now. I'll try to bring you more tonight."

Her mother's eyes widened. "Surely you're not leaving me again?"

"The Germans are here. I have to go."

"The Germans! Then you must stay. What will happen to me?"

"Honestly, Mother," Irena said with a laugh. "Do you think the Nazis are interested in us? They've plenty to keep them busy."

Her mother shook her head in disapproval. "Your place is here with me. Your father would never have left me like this."

"I'll only be gone an hour or two."

Her mother's hands rose slightly from the sheets as if in surrender. "If you insist on leaving me, at least help me take a bath before you go."

"I'll bathe you when I get back."

"Always later!" Her mother shouted now. Her cheeks were mottled scarlet and her feet moved back and forth rapidly under the sheets. "I've been lying here in my own dirt for a week. You barely feed me, hardly take me to the toilet. I've nothing to do and nobody to help me."

Irena paused. What difference was a couple of hours? She wanted to change her clothes and leave. Her frustration consumed her. "Fine," she snapped. "A quick bath and then I'm going back out."

She helped her mother out of bed and pulled her to the bathroom. She started the water and then assisted her in removing her clothes and stepping gingerly into the bath. She counted seconds in her head while her mother slowly cleaned herself. When she reached ten minutes, she reached down and pulled the plug.

"Why did you do that?" her mother demanded.

"You've had your bath. I told you, I need to go."

Her mother turned her head away, refusing to look at Irena. "I don't even know what to say to you."

Irena pulled her up and wiped her down with a towel. "There's nothing that needs to be said. I'll see you when I get back."

She left the flat as quickly as she was able, checking her watch as she went. Two hours! She'd meant to stay for a few minutes, and now much of the day was gone. Would she even be allowed outside? If the Germans set a curfew, would she be stuck somewhere? It would serve her mother right if she was unable to return until the morning.

She reached the downstairs and stepped outside. The sun was already low in the sky. The streets were near deserted again, distant figures scurrying this way and that. At the corner of the nearest intersection she saw a lone German soldier, marching slowly back and forth, his rifle shouldered. An elderly gentleman passed him. Irena wondered if he would be stopped, but the German kept walking past, ignoring the man.

Irena started toward Ewa's and then stopped herself. If there was a curfew, she'd never make it. She felt her anger rising again. Shaking off her emotions, she turned and headed instead toward her office. She could make it there with time to spare, and if she was stuck by a curfew, there was a kitchen and a few cots on the upper floor. She could remain there in relative comfort until the morning, and work through the night as long as she was able to stay awake. As she walked she thought of the Germans and her anger increased.

She would get her supplies back! She was going to confront the Nazis and demand her provisions. This thought filled her with energy and fire. She increased her pace, plans ripping through her mind as she raced to keep up with her scheme. She thought of contacts, government officials and professors she knew with enough influence to get her an audience with the authorities, the *new* authorities, that is. Somebody would be able to help her. Once she found the right German, she would tell them her story and ask that the food be returned to her.

What difference could it make? a voice in her mind asked. *It's only one meal, perhaps two. Then they'll all be back to starving.* She shook her head. It didn't matter. She would focus on this meal. The next one was tomorrow's problem.

She neared her office, rushing up the concrete stairs and toward the door. She didn't even see the guard until she'd nearly run him over.

"*Halt!*" the soldier demanded, raising a rifle in her direction. She froze, her heart in her throat, petrified, her life at risk for the second time in a day.

"I'm sorry," she responded, searching for the words. "I work here. I just need to go into the office." She took a step forward.

"*Nein!*" the soldier shouted, raising the rifle to his shoulder. "*Es ist verboten!*"

"I don't understand," she responded, raising her arms and speaking as softly as possible, hoping to calm the German down. "I work here. This is a welfare office. What could you be guarding?"

"Orders are orders, Fräulein. Now turn and go!"

"But the curfew. Is there a curfew?"

"Go!" he screamed, and his hand drew the bolt back, cocking a bullet into place.

She turned and fled down the stairs, tears streaming from her eyes, her breath coming in short spurts. She hurried away into the growing darkness, fear and rage stalking her.

Irena stumbled to a stop a few blocks away from her office. She fought to catch her breath, the fear coursing through her. She looked down the street in both directions, searching for Germans. The streetlights were out. The darkness enveloped her. She strained her eyes, trying to see. She glimpsed shadows moving, black shapes in the blackness. They were everywhere around her. They must be Germans, perhaps searching for her. She lurched across the street, trying to see, moving away from the specters. She didn't know where to go. Ewa's flat was too far away. She'd never make it. She had to try to somehow navigate back home. Her mother's words echoed through her mind. She'd been right, she had no business going back out here. Then again, if her mother hadn't forced a delay she could have gone and returned in the daylight. Perhaps the office wouldn't even have been guarded earlier. No, she hadn't been wrong to leave, but she'd departed too late.

She crossed another street and another. The darkness was her friend now. If the streetlamps were illuminated, she would surely be caught. A figure passed her the other way, bumping into her violently. She gave out a shriek of surprise and pain, but the shape moved rapidly on. Another Pole, she realized.

She continued, feeling her way along the buildings from street to street. She couldn't see the signs posted on the side of the corner buildings, but she'd walked this route thousands of times and knew the distance by heart. She was halfway back now. She felt the panic departing, replaced by a growing calm and a determination to make it back to her building. She was already mapping out a new plan—one without access to her office. She knew where her supervisor lived, along with many of her coworkers. She would visit them tomorrow during the day, find out what the new situation was, and determine the next steps to getting her food back. She couldn't wait to tell Ewa what had happened today. They should invite Ala Golab-Grynberg to hear as well. Ala didn't work directly with them, but she would be furious.

She passed another street and another. Just a few more to go now. She reached the corner of Ludwicki Street and started to cross when she saw him. A German soldier standing right in the middle of the street. He was staring at her, although he had not raised his rifle. Her heart thundered in her chest. She was so close to home and she wasn't going to make it. She stood there for long moments, waiting for the inevitable.

He nodded his head slightly, waving for her to pass. She couldn't believe her fortune, but she wasn't about to stop and ask him why he was letting her go. She hurried past and scurried down the sidewalk, rushing along past the last couple of blocks. She was moving too fast, reckless in the darkness, but she didn't want to run into another guard, one who wouldn't show mercy. She reached the front door, pushing through into the dim corridor. The bare bulb seemed as bright as the sun after the terrifying journey through the blackness. She took a deep breath, calming herself down. She made her way upstairs to her flat, collecting her emotions. She felt a surge of joy, of triumph. She'd stayed out past curfew. She'd walked the streets where *they* now ruled the world, but they had not stopped her. She was alive.

She reached her door. She thought of her mother. Her anger rose again. Perhaps it wasn't fair, but the truth was her mother's delay had put her in the darkness, had risked her life. The bath could easily have waited, but her mother had made her feel guilty. This was not going to happen again. She squared herself, ready for a confrontation.

Irena opened the door, pushing through and marching into the flat with purpose. "Mother!" she shouted. "We need to talk right now!"

She stopped. Her mother sat on the sofa in a nightgown, a blanket draped over her shoulders. It was unusual for her to be out of bed, but that wasn't what caught her attention. Standing near her were three German soldiers, pistols in hands.

"Frau Sendler," one of them said. "We need you to come with us immediately."

She was under arrest.

Chapter 3
Captured

September 27, 1939
Warsaw, Poland

The Germans rushed Irena into a waiting car. She was shoved violently into the back seat. Soldiers wedged in on both sides of her. She couldn't move. She could see the eyes of the driver through the rearview mirror. He was watching her, smiling with a sardonic lilt of his eyebrows. Another soldier, a lieutenant, jumped into the front passenger seat, turned toward Irena, and fastened a blindfold around her eyes, jerking the knot severely. She could not see, and the cloth was secured so tightly her head felt like it would explode.

The car tore off into the night, jerking this way and that, speeding through the streets of Warsaw. She couldn't measure time like this. She felt the sway of the car, heard the rattle of the engine, a cough. She smelled stale breath, leather. She couldn't move. She was frozen by fear. Her mouth was dry and a bitter taste coated her tongue. She wanted to ask where they were going, why they had taken her, but she couldn't summon the courage to do so.

The car shuddered to a stop. Doors opened, and she heard rapid barked commands. Hands clutched her arms and tore her out of the back seat. She was led, stumbling, pushed and pulled. The guards dragged her down a flight of stairs. The floor was hard, like concrete or tile. She heard a door open and she was shoved forward. Hands forced her down. She cried out, her mind spinning, expecting to crash to the ground, but she stopped midway. A chair, she realized. Her arms were drawn back, and ropes tied around her wrists. The blindfold was torn off. She blinked as harsh light stabbed her eyes. She couldn't see for long moments.

When she focused she took in her surroundings. She sat in a bare room. A concrete floor met bare wooden walls. A single lightbulb hung from the ceiling, dangling in the air a few feet above her. There were no pictures, no table—no furniture of any kind, in fact. She was alone in the room. She tried to move her hands, but it was useless. They were secured so tightly that she could not even shift them a fraction of a centimeter. Her arms pricked with stinging needles of pain.

She sat there for what felt like hours. Her mind was a cocktail of fear and exhaustion. She heard a piercing shriek. The sound was muffled, but she knew it must be coming from a nearby room. Deep voices shouted, and the scream repeated over and over. She felt the blood pulse through her wrists, up her arms, the throb coursing to her temples with each ragged beat. The hollering continued, agonizing, minute by minute.

The door tore open. She shook and gasped, surprised by the abrupt movement. A soldier entered, carrying a wooden chair. He brought it over and placed the seat directly in front of Irena, a scarce meter away. He stood watching her for a moment, a grin on his face. He lunged at her and Irena heard herself scream. The soldier threw his head back in laughter and he left the room. She could see into the hallway now, but there was nothing to observe. Another bare wooden wall, more concrete. The space felt like a basement of some kind.

Two Germans stepped through the doorway. The first was enormous. He was two meters tall at least. His uniform fit tightly across his chest. He had a boyish, cherub-like face. His legs seemed too small to support his upper body, as if he would topple over at any moment. He could be scarcely twenty. The boy, for that's what he seemed, moved quickly to the side, making way for an officer who marched abruptly into the room.

The leader was the opposite of the young man in every way. He was middle-aged, handsome, with chiseled cheeks and peppered brown hair. He was medium height with a muscular, trim build beneath a tailored uniform. He stepped with a measured grace, his steel-gray eyes never leaving Irena as he removed his cap, handed it to the giant, and stepped to the chair directly in front of her. He sat down and began thumbing through a thin folder, his eyes moving rapidly over the contents of the file.

"Irena Sendler," he read. "Social worker. Father a socialist and well-known supporter of the Jews. Married to a Mietek Sendler but estranged. A socialist herself, she may even have communist leanings." He stared at her for a moment. "Is that true, Frau Sendler? Are you a Bolshevik?"

Irena was stunned. She took long moments to answer. "I'm sorry, sir, but how do you know any of that? How do you know anything about me? You've been here a day."

He shrugged. "We started compiling information about the Polish government months ago. We are German. We don't leave things to the last minute and we don't leave things to chance." He leaned forward. "You didn't answer my question. Are you a communist?"

She turned her head, emotions ripping through her. *The Russians had betrayed them, joined the Germans. She owed them nothing.* "No," she responded.

"Are you sure?"

"I'm very sure," she said, her voice finding strength.

"I have a report you were attempting to smuggle food into the city. Explain yourself."

How did he know that? How did he know so much about her? She was a lowly functionary, a pawn so many levels down in the organization of the Polish government that she was scarce worth taking notice of, yet this German not only knew who she was, but details about her family, and even what she was doing this morning!

"I . . ." She decided she would tell the truth. "I was organizing food from the countryside for distribution to the poor. Our welfare system was disrupted by the war, by your bombing. I was working to renew it. The wagons that were confiscated yesterday were the first shipment in weeks. Everything was going forward until your men took my food away. People will starve because of that."

His eyes pierced through her. "You? Why you? Shouldn't that decision have been made by someone higher up?"

"I obtained approval from my supervisor."

"But it was your plan. You insisted?"

"Yes."

He removed a pen from a pocket and jotted down some notes. He worked away for ten minutes, reading and rereading what he'd written. Finally, he turned the document around and showed Irena. "If this is correct, you will sign at the bottom."

She read the statement, which accurately reported what she had told him. "I can't sign," she said.

"You refuse?"

"My hands," she said, shifting her arms a fraction.

He looked down as if noticing for the first time that her arms were tied. "What's this nonsense? Peter Schwarzmann."

The giant drew a dagger from his belt and moved behind Irena. She felt a sharp tug and her hands were released. She drew her arms up, rubbing the wrists as the assistant fumbled with his oversized fingers, removing the ropes. She felt the blood return painfully to her hands; she moved them back and forth until the stinging subsided.

"You will sign," he repeated.

She looked at the document again, taking it and the pen into her hands. She noticed that in large letters at the bottom she was asserting she was not a communist. Why did he want her to sign this? She decided to ask him.

"That is not for you to worry about, Frau Sendler. I ask the questions here. Now I must respectfully request that you either sign the document or inform me that you refuse."

She hesitated a moment longer and then, seeing no reason to decline, she signed and dated the paper.

He seemed relieved that she had done so. "Good, good," he said, pulling the document back and tucking the pen into his pocket. "Frau Sendler, I am authorized to offer you a position with us."

With *us*? Was he mad? She could never work for the fascists. "I'm sorry sir, I don't know what you mean."

"Don't worry, Frau Sendler. I'm not asking anything nefarious. We must keep order, you see. All the social systems and infrastructure must be maintained. We want you to keep doing what you were doing before. Get the food distribution systems up and running again. You will have a free hand, all the food you need, and our full support."

What was he saying? She didn't know how to respond. She was delighted by the prospect of renewing the food distribution. There were tens of thousands who desperately needed sustenance. They would give her a free hand? She'd never had that with the Polish government. All the food she needed? She could do so much. But to work for the Germans? How could she agree? She would be a traitor to everything she believed, to her people, to her nation.

"I'm sorry, sir. I must refuse you. I appreciate your offer very much. But I cannot work for the Germans."

She saw a flicker of anger across his otherwise serene features. A hint of frustration perhaps. The emotion was gone so quickly she wasn't sure it had ever existed. He put his hands out as if in surrender. "You would not be working for the Germans, you would be working for Poland, the same as before. Certainly, we are here, and we will be from now on, but we want the Poles to run Poland." He reached toward her. "I'm not asking you to do anything you didn't do before. I'm asking you to do what you have always wanted to do. You can feed your people, but you can do it on your terms, and with German efficiency." His voice assumed a tinge of the scolding schoolmaster. "Really, Frau Sendler, we aren't going to go anywhere. Poland is part of Germany now, and always will be. If you want a voice in its future, if you want to work in your field, you will have to work with us. So, what will it be? Will you assume your old responsibilities?"

She did not know what to do. He was asking her to work with the fascists, something she abhorred more than anything in the world. Still, hadn't the Polish government stood far to the right? Wasn't there already anti-Semitism, anti-socialism, in every layer of the Polish system? Besides, if they were going to allow the Polish government systems to continue, wasn't she really going to be working for Poland, not for Germany? She wasn't sure. She was so tired, and her brain was clouded. She thought she would be tortured, perhaps killed. Instead, this man was offering her everything she'd wanted. A promotion to deal with food distribution for the poor all through Warsaw. On her terms, under her conditions. "I need some time to think about it," she finally responded, still not sure what she should decide.

He slapped his hands down on his trousers. "Of course, Frau Sendler. That's perfectly reasonable." He reached into his pocket again and drew out a card. "Here is my information. Take the next day and think about things. I look forward to your answer."

She stared at the card. *Hauptmann Klaus Rein, Gestapo.* She paused, not sure what to say. "That's it?"

"That's it."

"I'm free to go?"

"Of course, you are." He turned to the giant boy. "Peter. Take Frau Sendler home. Use my personal car." The assistant stood, inclining his head slightly. "I look forward to your answer." He turned and strolled out of the room, leaving her with this oversized child, who gazed down on her, grinning from ear to ear.

"Shall we go, Frau Sendler?" Even his voice was high-pitched, and he sprinted from syllable to syllable, as if his words raced each other.

"Yes, I'd like that." She rose and started to walk, but her head was spinning. She stumbled and started to fall. His strong hands grasped her, pulling her up.

"Be careful, madam," said Peter. "You've had quite a night. Let me help you." He tucked his arm through hers and guided her slowly out of the room, leading her out of the building and toward the car. As she rose out of the basement her spirits soared. She was alive, unhurt. She'd survived. She had a decision in front of her, but what was that compared to life itself? It was morning now. The sun was climbing in the eastern sky. She felt the warmth on her face, she smelled the crisp air, took in the trees, the leaves, the soft pink and gray of the buildings. She breathed in her life. No matter what, she was still here, she was alive.

"You can't say yes," said Ala. Irena sat at an outdoor café on Senatorska Street with Ala and Ewa, sipping tea and munching on sauerkraut and a mushroom pierogi. The afternoon sun was warm on her back. The tables were full of diners, chatting away and enjoying themselves as if the world had not ended yesterday. As she looked around it felt almost as if nothing had changed, with one startling difference. Some of the patrons were German soldiers, in their gray uniforms and leather jackboots, laughing, jostling the waitresses, gulping down quantities of vodka as they joked in their harsh Germanic accents.

"What difference does it make?" responded Ewa. "Aren't they the same jobs we had before?" Ewa had been contacted too, albeit in less dramatic fashion. She had simply received a notice, delivered to her flat, instructing her to return to work on October 2, the following Monday.

"There is every difference in the world," said Ala. She absently ran her hand through a tangle of dark curls. "Last week you served Poland. Tomorrow, you would be serving the Nazis."

"What will you do then?" asked Irena.

"I don't know," she said. "The hospital is supposed to be for all people. I will stay there. But I won't work with them. No matter what. Not directly anyway."

"And if they take over the hospital?" asked Ewa.

"Then I'll quit and stay home with Rami."

"Your words are admirable," said Ewa. "But you can't eat virtue. Pride won't give you shelter or keep your child alive."

"What about your husband?" asked Irena. "What does he say?"

"He's gone."

"What do you mean?" asked Irena.

"He left Warsaw. He won't serve the Germans. He knows what they will do to us, to the Jews. He's going to fight them. He headed into the forest with a few friends. He's going to try to find a group out there to start a resistance. If I didn't have Rami, I would have joined him. But I can't take a five-year-old girl out into the forest."

"That's madness," said Irena. "The war isn't even officially over yet. There are Germans everywhere. They have all the guns, food, supplies."

"Nonetheless, he's going to resist them. There are others. Freedom fighters. They are going to keep the dream of Poland alive." Ala looked intently across the table at Irena. "You should too."

"Maybe she's right," said Ewa.

"What do you mean?"

Ewa shifted in her seat, not meeting Irena's eyes. "Maybe we should refuse. Can we really work for the Germans?" Her face was flushed, and her eyes looked back and forth from Irena to Ala. "I just don't know what to do."

Irena turned on her friend. "So you're going to starve, Ewa? Fine for yourself. What about all the people depending on us? I'm not doing this for the Germans, I'm not doing it for me. I'm doing it for the people."

"Whose people?" asked Ala. "The Poles or the Jews? It's easy for you to help the Germans. They aren't after your skin. Ewa and I are different. They've made no secret of their plans for us."

"How dare you say that to me?" Irena retorted, her voice rising. "Have I ever differentiated? One Poland, Jews and Poles alike. A workers-and-peasants Poland. That's what we've dreamed about, isn't it? What we've worked for?"

"The Russians ended that dream," said Ala. "They've betrayed us to the butchers. Now we've nobody to protect us and nowhere to run. We have to fight."

"That's what I want to do," said Irena.

"No, you want to serve them."

Irena rose. "That's enough."

"Please sit down!" Ewa pleaded. "You'll attract notice."

Irena reached into her bag, pulling out a few zlotys. She dropped them on the table. "I won't create an incident, since you two are so worried about your own skins. You can both do what you want. I'm serving the Germans, am I? I'm serving the people, like I always have. If you want to hide in your flats and take care of yourselves, that's your choice. I'm going to feed our people, Poles and Jews alike!"

"Irena please," implored Ewa.

But she'd had enough. Irena stormed off, weaving between the narrow tables, trying not to attract attention to herself. She battled to control her anger. How could they be so blind? What good would it do to bury their heads in the sand? She wasn't surprised by Ala, but she hadn't expected Ewa to turn on her. She counted on her friend for assistance. She was a critical component. She would have to bring Ewa around. That would be easier without Ala.

She hurried back through the streets. It was a few hours before darkness, but she didn't want to brave the night again. She was exhausted. She'd forgone sleep so she could meet with her friends and run her plan past them. She'd expected some resistance, but not an outright refusal. She felt a moment of doubt. Was Ala right? Would she be serving the Germans? She shook her head. Ala's resistance was just one form of fighting. She admired her friend, but she knew there was truth in her own words. Refusal wouldn't feed the thousands of starving Poles. Resistance would land her without position, without means to survive herself. It might be more than that. She thought back to the barren room, the ropes, the screams. This was a new world. A reality where her life was threatened multiple times in one day. These were new masters, new rules. She was going to beat them, but in order to do so, she had to be in the game.

She reached her building a half hour later. She didn't bother checking at her office. She knew the door would be barred to her, at least for now. She would not be admitted until she had responded to Klaus, the name on the card, the man in the room.

She hurried up the stairs. Her mother must be terrified, worried sick. She felt a nagging guilt that she hadn't returned to take care of her when she was released. But she'd had too much to do. She had plans to make, and the meeting she'd set up with Ala and Ewa. She'd make it up to her mother tonight. She would make dinner, bathe her, sit and talk with her. She would stay up late and visit about the old days, about her father. Her mother would be satisfied, at least for a little while.

Irena stepped on the landing and turned toward the corridor. Her hand touched the handle to her door. She felt her body shaking. She fumbled with the keys, but she couldn't calm the tremor in her hands enough to open the door. She fell to her knees, leaning her head against the door, tears streaming down her face. *I almost died today. They could have killed me. They will kill me.* After long minutes she pulled herself up, took a few deep breaths. *I will survive. I will fight them. I will win.* She wiped her tears, opened the lock, and returned to her home.

Chapter 4
A New Poland

September 29, 1939
Glówna Train Station, Warsaw

Klaus waited at the station platform, Peter at his side. He gazed above him at the art deco architecture and to his left and right at the shops and restaurants. Glówna was designed as one of the most modern stations in Europe, with every convenience. *For all the good it did them.* He glanced at his watch again. The train was a half hour late. "Check with the attendant and find out what's going on," he said.

"It's just a delay, sir," said Peter, shrugging. "There's a war on. What can you expect?"

"I said check."

"Yes, sir."

Klaus thought he detected a hint of defiance in Peter's voice. He would have to have another talk with him. The large boyish figure ambled off toward the station doors, a wrinkled shirttail poking out from the bottom of his tunic. Klaus shook his head. He'd have a talk with Peter about that as well.

He looked at his watch again. Thirty-two minutes late. How could they rule the world with this kind of inefficiency? he wondered. The platform was deserted except for a few soldiers guarding the doorways and an elderly couple, waiting nearby. Klaus wondered who they could be there for. Poles were strictly forbidden from train travel at the present time. The man said something to the woman. He spoke German. That explained it. They must be Volksdeutsch. Poles of German ethnicity. Perhaps their son was a soldier, coming in on the train.

Klaus lost interest in them as Peter returned. "Well, what did he have to say?"

"He doesn't have any information," said Peter. "Something about cut telephone wires."

"Was that all?"

Peter hesitated.

"Well?"

"He said the train would arrive when it arrives, and to be patient."

"He did, did he?" Klaus took a step toward the door. "Let's have a chat with this gentleman."

At that moment he heard a distant whistle. He took another step toward the door but changed his mind. What matter? He turned and looked down the rail line. He could see a train in the distance, charcoal smoke billowing out of the engine like some sort of mechanical dragon. The engine was slowing down, and it took ten more minutes before the first cars passed them and the entire vehicle ground to a lurching halt.

Klaus searched up and down the line of cars, scanning the windows, excitement coursing through him.

"*Vater!*" He heard the musical voice and turned to see his little girl, Anna, auburn curls bouncing, a blur of burgundy dress and lace that latched on to his legs, hugging him and giggling in delight. He reached down, lifting her over his head, turning her around and around as she squealed in joy.

"Don't drop her, darling." He lowered her gently, setting eager eyes on his wife, Briggita. She hurried to him, a delightful vision in a gray wool dress with blonde hair spilling out of a scarlet hat. Her sapphire eyes danced, and she rushed to him, kissing him with cherry lips. He held her closely. He hadn't seen her in months. He felt the overwhelming joy of her touch. He kissed her again and then composed himself, withdrawing a handkerchief.

"I hope you didn't get lipstick on my uniform."

"She didn't, but it's all over your face," said his assistant, laughing.

"Peter, so good to see you," said Briggita, patting his mountainous arm. Klaus smiled at the contradiction. His wife barely reached the giant's chest and couldn't have weighed a third as much.

"Uncle Peter, do you have sweets for me?" asked Anna. Peter wasn't really her uncle, but she'd known him for years.

Peter composed a look of confusion and sadness, making a great show of searching his uniform. Finally, he reached into a pocket and removed a hard candy.

"For me?" she asked.

"Just for you."

She took the wrapper and greedily opened it, pulling the candy out and shoving it into her mouth. "Cinnamon!" she said. "My favorite."

"Of course. I would never forget," said Peter.

"Let's leave this place," said Klaus, looking around. "We've created enough of a storm."

"There's nobody here," teased his wife.

"That is beside the point."

Briggita sighed dramatically. "Always so serious, Klaus." She looked over at his assistant. "Peter, can you help us with the bags?"

They left the platform and loaded everything up in Klaus's

car. While Peter drove them through the streets of Warsaw, Briggita regaled them with stories of the countryside they'd seen during the day-long train trip from Böhlen. She commented on the orderly farms of Germany, and the dramatic changes once they'd crossed the border into Poland. Vehicles still burned in the fields. Villages lay in ruins.

"And Mother kept shutting the shades for all the good parts," protested Anna.

Klaus could imagine what the *good parts* were. There were still plenty of unburied bodies outside Warsaw. Well, that would be put to order shortly, like everything else. He was disturbed his daughter had seen any of these signs of war, but glad her spirits seemed undampened. Primarily he was satisfied to bask in the glow of his family's presence here. Glad to be reunited with his loved ones.

The afternoon turned to evening as they arrived at their new home, a three-story townhouse. Peter squeezed out of the driver's seat and lumbered back to the trunk, lugging the baggage out as they marched up to the front door. Klaus removed a key and brought them into the entryway.

"Oh, *mein Gott*, Klaus, how can we afford this place?" said Briggita, looking in stunned surprise at the deep cherry walls and the marble-tiled entryway.

Klaus was pleased by his wife's reaction. "Let me give you a tour," he said. He led his wife through the downstairs sitting area, kitchen, and library. She whistled again when he led her into the dining room, a twelve-seat table already set with the finest china. He watched her face fill with awe as he introduced her to their cook, maid, and butler, all Poles who were employed in this household before. They bowed and smiled, fawning over Briggita and his daughter.

He led his family through the rest of the house as the butler and Peter carried the luggage up to their respective rooms. Briggita was delighted with the master bedroom, a massive space with a large four-poster bed and double doors leading to a balcony.

"Oh, Klaus, this is too much," she said. "I've never dreamed of anything like this. And with servants. Really, darling, how can we afford this?"

"Don't worry about a thing," he assured her. "The department assigned this house to us, and the servants. We don't have to pay a *pfennig* for it. It's built into my new salary."

"How wonderful," she said. "I'm so proud of you, Klaus. Joining the Gestapo was the best decision you've ever made. Could you imagine if you'd stayed in your post as a city policeman? We'd still be in that little hovel of an apartment, and you'd probably be in the army by now."

"That wouldn't be so bad," he said, his arms around her.

"It would be a catastrophe," she said, pulling away. "You could be killed and then who would raise our wonderful Anna." She laughed. "Besides, this is so much better. We will be together every day." She turned to admire the room further, sitting on the bed and running her hands over the dressers. She pulled open a drawer. "Klaus," she said, and he heard a tremor in her voice.

"What is it?"

She pulled some clothing out, a dress, and showed them to him. "Whose things are these?"

Klaus was perturbed but not for the reasons she supposed. "It must be the last owner's. I instructed Peter to make sure everything is out."

She looked at him inquiringly for a moment, as if she didn't believe him.

"Come on, dear. We arrived in Warsaw yesterday morning. I've been up since then, no sleep, running all over the city taking care of issues. I've only walked through this place briefly before you came here. Do you really think I had time for any nonsense? And even if I had, do you truly believe me capable of such a thing?"

She looked at him for a few seconds longer and then laughed. "Of course not, dearest." She ran into his arms, kissing him and holding him tight. "Still" she said, looking down at the skirt still in her hands. "Who do you suppose owned this?"

"Who knows?" he said, shrugging as he lied to her. "They must have fled to the east. Probably communists. They went to join their friends in Russia."

"I'm sure you're right," she said. "You will have these removed, won't you? I'd hate to be reminded of this again."

"Certainly, I will. I'll have Peter arrange for everything." He did know who had lived here before, but she didn't need to worry herself about such things. It would only upset her and what was the point? This was their home now.

"I'll let you explore it then."

She looked up, a crease of concern on her forehead. "Surely you don't have to leave us already? We just got here."

"I have a little work tonight and then I'll be back. Don't worry, my love, I won't be gone too long. Tomorrow I'll take the morning off and we can go for a stroll in the park."

She smiled. "That would be lovely. Are you going to see Anna before you go?"

He shook his head. "Kiss her for me. I'll see you soon."

Peter and Klaus sat in his car in the darkness. They'd shut the motor down and cracked the windows to prevent the windshield from fogging over. The interior was growing chilly in the fall evening air. They were parked on a side street about fifty meters from a T intersection. They could see a large apartment building at the end of the street. This structure was the focus of their attention tonight.

Peter was gnawing on a sandwich, his fingers fumbling through the wrapper as he searched for crumbs. Klaus tried to ignore the racket as he examined a long ledger with his penlight. Finally, he'd had enough.

"Peter!"

"Yes, sir."

"Stop that. I can't concentrate."

"But I'm hungry."

"You can eat the sandwich, but you don't need to consume the wrapper as well."

Peter chuckled and set the package down, making yet more noise as he did so. He held the bread in both hands now and munched away happily, the smacking sounds still making a racket in the enclosed space.

"Peter!"

"I'm sorry. I'm almost done."

Klaus returned to the list, reviewing the long ledger of names. He came across a surprise about three quarters of the way down.

"Irena Sendler."

"What?"

"Why is Irena Sendler's name on this list?"

"Who is that?" asked Peter.

"That social worker. You remember the one from the cellar."

Peter shrugged. "Why do we care? She's a nobody, isn't she?"

"She's a somebody to me, Peter. I told you this morning to strike her name for now, and we would wait and see until she responds."

Peter glanced at the list, sucking on a finger. "It must have slipped my mind."

"Like removing all the clothing from the townhouse?"

"I did remove everything."

"Funny, someone must have put new things in my wife's dresser drawers then, because she found some this evening. For a moment, she accused me of having some sort of lady friend. As if I have time for that."

Klaus shined the penlight in Peter's face. Even in the darkness he could see how pale his assistant's features had become.

"I'm sorry, sir, I—"

"I don't want sorry, Peter. I want you to follow my orders. Now the next time I ask you to strike a name, you will strike a name, and the next time I ask you to remove all the clothing from a house, you will do so. You will do what I ask and do it perfectly. Do you understand?"

"Yes, sir, I'm sorry, I was just—"

"Let me guess, you were just chasing some Polish skirt."

His assistant scoffed in protest. "We just got here yesterday."

Klaus turned to his assistant, leaning in. "Don't give me that. I know you. I might not have time for that silliness, but you always manage to. You would have been looking around the moment we arrived. What is her name?"

"I don't know what you mean, sir."

"Her name, Peter."

Now the face was flushed with color. "Myrka. You should see her. She's barely eighteen, jet-black hair, a real beauty."

"Not a Jew, I hope."

Peter shook his head. "Of course not, sir."

"Don't *of course not* me. Remember the rules: You can chase all the skirt you want, *on your time, mind you*, but no Jews, and only after your duties are completed to my satisfaction. Understood?"

"Yes, sir."

"Good. I don't want to have this conversation again. We've been together a long time, Peter. I am tolerant of your weaknesses, but this is war. What was allowed in peacetime cannot be permitted now."

"I will be perfect from now on, sir, I only had the one . . ."

"Shhhh," said Klaus. "They're here." Klaus could see forms in the distance, lining up outside the apartment building. There were a dozen or so. He strained his eyes to see what was going on. Another soldier walked up to the group, pulling out a pistol and pointing to the door. The men moved out, running toward the entrance.

"Let's go," commanded Klaus. They exited the vehicle and hurried out into the night. Klaus greeted the officer who still stood on the street in front of the building. "*Guten Abend.*"

"*Guten Abend*, Herr Hauptmann. *Was machen Sie?*"

"What's the situation?" asked Klaus.

"The men just entered the building a few moments ago. They are collecting the suspects now." The officer checked his watch. "I anticipate they will be back on the street in the next ten minutes at the most."

"I ordered minimum fuss," said Klaus. "Were your men instructed to conduct the raid as efficiently as possible?"

"*Jawohl.*"

Klaus nodded his head in approval. Even as they watched, the first soldiers reappeared, escorting a middle-aged gentleman out onto the street. The man still wore his pajamas and was in his bare feet. His eyes were wide, and he was shaking, obviously stunned by the sudden appearance of Germans at his doorstep in the middle of the night.

"He's had a bit of a shake-up," joked Peter. Klaus ignored him. As additional men arrived on the scene, he watched them closely, keeping a mental count. Soon there were twelve men and two women standing on the sidewalk under guard. Fourteen. Klaus pulled out his ledger and flicked on his penlight. That was the right number for this location. He then went down the list, calling out each name and verifying that the people lined up here were in fact the same as the names on his ledger. Everything seemed to be in order. He was pleased.

The first Pole who had come out started to cough. Klaus wasn't sure if it was the cold, or some other condition, but his hacking increased until he was doubled over, gasping and barking, holding on to his knees with his hands. One of the soldiers stepped up to him and ordered him to stand up. When he did not respond, the soldier brought his rifle butt down on the man's back. The Pole gave out a great groan of pain and crumpled to the ground.

"What are you doing there?" asked Klaus, stepping forward. The soldier turned to him.

"Just helping him along."

"Stand at attention when I speak to you!" ordered Klaus.

"*Jawohl*, Herr Hauptmann."

"What is your name?"

"Obersoldat Hans Klein."

"You were ordered to treat these men properly, is that not correct?"

"*Ja*, but he wasn't listening to—"

"I don't want to hear your excuses. You will follow your orders to the letter, do you understand!"

"*Jawohl*. I'm sorry, sir."

Klaus turned to the private's officer. "This man is to be reported. He disobeyed my orders, and yours."

The officer looked like he was going to argue, but apparently thought better of it. He nodded his head without speaking.

"Help that man back to his feet."

Several soldiers sprang forward and pulled the Pole back to a standing position.

"Thank you so much, Hauptmann," the Pole said.

"Think nothing of it. The men are under orders, and orders are to be followed."

"Why are we out here?" asked the Pole.

"What is your name?" asked Klaus.

"Bronislaw Dziadosz."

Klaus consulted his ledger. "You are out here because your name is on this list. See, just here." He showed the Pole the name on the ledger.

"Why is my name on that paper?"

Klaus shrugged. "I don't know that, Herr Dziadosz. I don't make the lists, I just deal with the names on them."

"What's going to happen to us?" asked Dziadosz.

Klaus ignored him, stepping back and returning to the officer. "Everything is in order," he said. "The list is correct."

"*Jawohl,* Herr Hauptmann."

Klaus yawned. "It's late. I've got to get some sleep." He turned to his assistant. "Peter, are you ready to go?"

"What is to be done with these Poles?" the officer asked.

"Shoot them," said Klaus.

"What? Did you say shoot them?" The officer stammered the words.

"*Ja.*"

"Where?"

"Here, now."

"But sir—"

"Those are the orders," said Klaus. "Shoot them now."

"Herr Hauptmann, what are you saying?" asked Dziadosz.

"Let's go, Peter." They moved off.

"Herr Hauptmann!"

The tear of rifle fire ripped through the night and then all was silent.

Chapter 5
Irena Rising

January 1940
Warsaw, Poland

Months passed for Irena, and the news from everywhere was dire. The Germans had quickly wrapped up the war with Poland, consolidating their power. In October 1939, Hitler decreed that large portions of western Poland would be annexed directly into a Greater Germany. A rump portion of the nation, not annexed and not part of the Russian conquest, was administered as a Polish General Government by a Nazi named Hans Frank, who set up his headquarters not in Warsaw, but in a medieval castle in Kraków to the south.

The English and French were still at war with the Germans, but according to the news that they did receive, there was no real fighting going on. Their *saviors*, the nations who were supposed to protect Poland, were apparently content to sit in their trenches on the Western Front and do nothing. In the meantime, Poland suffered.

Irena had gone ahead with her program of food relief for the poor. She had convinced Ewa to work with her, along with many others. Unfortunately, Ewa was forced to quit her job, as a German decree barred all Jews from government positions, as well as jobs such as doctors, lawyers, and actors.

Despite this setback, Irena re-established the soup kitchens all over Warsaw. The Germans cooperated at least to the extent of allowing her to bring food in from the countryside, although there was never enough to truly keep the population healthy. She had bread and a trickle of vegetables, but meat, milk, and fresh eggs were difficult to obtain.

Even the wealthier citizens of Poland were suffering. Grocery stores were bare, and rationing was strictly enforced. A thriving black market assured the availability of goods to those willing to take the risk, but the Germans imposed terrible penalties on those who were caught, including in some cases, execution.

Irena thought of all this as she stood at the distribution kitchen, monitoring the handing out of provisions. They had set up one of their locations at a former Jewish store bordering Krasiński Square. From the front windows Irena could see across the square to Krasiński Palace with its arched windows and giant triangle abutments adorned with statues.

The store was packed with families. Each carried a document from the welfare department, entitling them to a certain amount of food. Irena walked up and down the line, talking with some of the people and inspecting random documents. She spent a day each week inspecting her food distribution sites.

She stopped in front of a young family queued up in the line. The father and mother were dressed in coarse workers' garb. The mother held a sleeping infant in her arms. A little girl, three or four, held the father's hand.

"Good morning," Irena said to them.

The father nodded in response.

"Can I see your paperwork?" Irena asked.

The man turned the documents over to Irena and she checked them. They were legitimate. The father had worked in a factory as a metal machinist but the Germans had closed the operation down. Another family in desperate need of social services. The number grew every day.

"Everything is in order here," Irena said, smiling.

"Thank you so much for what you're doing here," the mother said. "I don't know what we would do without you."

"Think nothing of it," said Irena. She kneeled down. "And who do we have here?" The little girl looked up at her and then blushed, turning away and wrapping her arms around her father's leg.

"This is Kaji," the father responded.

"Hello, Kaji." Irena patted her head. "I have something special for brave girls who come here with their parents." She fumbled around in her pockets and pulled out a piece of candy. "Just for you," she said, handing the treat to the girl.

Kaji's face brightened and she reached out, taking the treat and then looking up at her dad.

"Go ahead," he said, nodding.

She popped the candy in her mouth and Irena stood back up. She was moved. This family, and thousands of others, were what she had joined the social field for in the first place. The war just made the work more difficult, and more rewarding.

The mother took her hand. "Thank you again," she said, her eyes filling with tears.

"You have nothing to thank us for," said Irena. "The state should look after its people."

A few hours later Irena thought of this family as she pored through reports detailing available foodstuffs, wagons, employees, and lists of families applying to receive government aid. She sighed, examining the new applications. There were dozens of new ones every day. If she only had to deal with the needy at the pre-war level, she would have enough food to go around. The number of families had doubled in the past months, making her job nearly impossible. She squared her shoulders. She would never surrender.

Irena removed some stationery from her desk and began to write. She spent hours each day drafting letters to government officials, some Polish, some German, imploring them for workers, resources, anything that might help. Each afternoon she called these people. Twice a week she physically visited their offices, waiting sometimes half a day to obtain an appointment. In many instances, she was rejected or ignored. Undaunted, she would start over, writing, calling, visiting. She would badger them until she got what she wanted.

She had a new list today. She'd discovered another overlapping branch of authority in the German government. There were so many. The Nazis were efficient and organized, too organized in some instances. The army conducted work that the police should be doing, the civilian government overlapped with the military, and the SS seemed to have a shadow branch of everything—a state within a state. This was the new source she'd discovered. She had compiled a list of SS officials and was intending to start in on them right away.

There was a knock at her door. "Come in," said Irena absently, not looking up.

"What are you working on?" said Jan. She hadn't seen much of her supervisor over the past few months. After he'd received orders from the Germans about Irena's role, he'd left her alone for the most part. This had come at a price. Never close, he seemed to take afront at her new authority, and was distant and cold.

"Trying to find more contacts. I can't handle the influx of new families. I need more food, more transportation, more locations for distribution."

"There may be a solution to the problem, but you're not going to like it."

She looked up now, eyes narrowing. "What do you mean?"

He handed her a document he was holding in his hand. "Read this. Please understand, this is not coming from me."

She took the paper from him and scanned the contents. A fire burned through her and she boiled over. "Who is responsible for this?"

"Who knows," he said, shrugging, "but the orders didn't come from the Polish government. This came direct from the Germans."

She read the letter again. As of January 15, 1940, all Jewish families were to be stricken from the social welfare rolls. They would not be eligible for government food distribution, medical help, or any other welfare.

"How can they do this?" she asked.

Jan shrugged. "Who will stop them? Besides, we Poles have our own problems."

Irena knew well what Jan was saying. For months now, the Germans had persecuted the Polish population, primarily the educated. Doctors, lawyers, professors, businessmen and -women were arrested by the thousands. Sometimes the Germans didn't even bother carting them away and simply shot them where they stood. Irena had lost friends, teachers, and colleagues to these purges. She thought back to her meeting with Klaus and what might have happened to her if she'd refused to work with the new government. She was certain she too would have disappeared.

She thought she had fought back in her own way. She was feeding the people, keeping them going. She'd battled to keep the food coming, to increase it even, and she'd succeeded. Now thousands of the most desperate people, already bereft of their jobs and their rights, were going to lose their only means to survive.

"I won't let them get away with it," she whispered.

"Irena, there's nothing we can do. This isn't a suggestion;

this is a direct order from on high. If you ignore it, they will swat you like a fly and replace you the next day with someone who will do what they want. Besides," he said, shrugging, "these families will be all right. The Jews always take care of themselves."

"How can you say that?" demanded Irena, her anger flaring again. "What do you know of Jews? Are you friends with Jews? Did you grow up with them? Go to school with them? They will take care of themselves? How? You're speaking from prejudice. The Jews of Warsaw have no jobs. The Germans have taken all their property and their money. They have nothing left. They cannot take care of themselves!"

Jan paused. Taking a step forward, he placed a hand on her shoulder. "I know you grew up around Jewish families, that your father helped them, that he died treating them. It's not that I don't care, Irena, but you must be realistic. It's not just our choice what to do. The world as we knew it is gone. The Nazis are killing Poles by the hundreds of thousands. We are looking at the survival of our civilization. I want to protect the Jews too, but if I must choose, I choose the Poles. And we don't really have a choice. We will follow the orders, or we will die. I'm sorry, Irena, but it's as simple as that."

"I won't accept this."

"You have to. For you, for me, for all of us. Do you think your defiance would only affect you? They'll arrest all of us. You, me, the distribution workers, our whole office. All of this," he said, spreading his arms, "will be gone in a moment. And you will not have helped a single Jew in the process. Take the rest of the day off, Irena. Spend some time with your mother. Walk along the Vistula. Visit the Praga market. Do some thinking and clear your head. We can meet back tomorrow. When you've thought things through, you'll realize it's our only choice. When you're ready, I need a report outlining how many people this will affect. Remember, this will mean more food for our Polish families."

"The Jews are Poles too."

"They are and they aren't. Let's talk tomorrow."

He left and she sat there stunned, her mind spinning. She thought about ignoring his advice and digging even deeper into her work. She decided he was right, she should take the day off. She'd worked one-hundred-hour weeks since the war ended. Sometimes she labored twenty hours in a day. She was exhausted. She needed to get some rest and think about things. He was correct that she shouldn't do anything hasty. There was no sense in throwing her life away when another Pole would just step in and follow the German orders. Perhaps there was some other solution that she could not yet see?

She packed up her things and left the building. The afternoon was cold but fine, with an azure sky bereft of clouds. The sun was warm on her face and as she walked along, she started to feel better. She decided to take Jan's advice and stroll along the Vistula. She reached the river after a half hour and walked along the bank. The Poniatowski Bridge dominating the horizon to her left. There were couples out, holding hands, strolling as if there was no war, no Germany, a future without submission and slavery.

She thought of Mietek, her estranged husband. She'd received a letter from him. He was in a POW camp in Germany. He said conditions were good, but of course there was no way to know, as any correspondence would be carefully censored. She'd written him back, hoping he was well. She wanted to care for him, to be the wife he'd always wanted. A solid, faithful, hardworking Polish spouse, who stayed home, cooked, cleaned, and cared for their children. That's what he'd wanted, not a socialist who worked outside the home and talked back.

She smiled. They'd been so young when they met. A couple of kids. He was from a stable, reputable family. She was the daughter of radicals. He'd thought he could bridge that gap and for a year or two they'd managed, but then the passion had faded, and they'd lived parallel lives, he in his vocation, her with ongoing university work. When an opportunity came several years ago for him to move and take a new job, they had said their goodbyes. There was no divorce, they weren't ready for such a drastic step, but they weren't living as husband and wife anymore.

She continued her stroll, enjoying the sweet melancholy that coursed through her veins. She'd worked so hard; she'd had no time for herself. After an hour of bliss, she turned toward home. The streets were bustling with workers returning to their flats after a long day of work. There were few vehicles on the streets—only Germans traveled by car these days. The streetcars were full of Poles. The Jews were forced to walk. As she approached her home building, she realized she felt so much better. She would figure out something. She sprang up the steps to the second floor with new spirit, with renewed hope.

"Irena."

The voice startled her. She stared at a figure in the hallway. It was him. Adam Celnikier was standing there in a worn lieutenant's uniform. A Jew, they'd been friends before the war. He was a socialist like her; he even flirted with communism.

"Adam, what are you doing here?"

"I just got home," he said.

"Come in," she said. "You must be starving."

"The German army is not like anything you've ever dreamed of," said Adam, as he munched away at some bread at the table with Irena and her mother. "They move like lightning. Their infantry ride in trucks. They bring their artillery with them, along with tanks. As if that wasn't enough, when they attack, they come from above as well. Their planes work in close coordination with the infantry, diving in to strafe the lines with bullets and bombs."

He took a sip of vodka, and a bite of kielbasa. His onyx

pupils flickered in the candlelight, peering out from under a canopy of sable curly hair. "Worst of all are the Stukas—their dive bombers," he explained. "You would hear their scream and before you knew it, they were on you, eagles with fire and death in their talons. We fought them with rifles and horses. We had enough men, but they came at us from every direction, East Prussia in the north and Czechoslovakia in the south. We were poorly led, poorly equipped, and prepared for the last war, not this one. Our men fought bravely, but there was no hope. I knew from the first day that we would lose. I think we all did."

"How terrible," said Irena. Throughout the dinner she'd listened with rapt attention as Adam described his war experiences. "But you were never wounded?"

"By some miracle, I wasn't. Men were killed next to me so many times I can't even count them. Bombs exploded, killing dozens at a time. Bullets whizzed past, kicked up the dirt in front of me. I was sure I would die. God must have watched over me."

"I thought you communists didn't believe in God?" observed her mother.

"Don't be rude," snapped Irena.

Adam chuckled. "She's not being rude. She speaks the truth," he said, taking a sip of vodka. "But old habits are hard to break. I spent my youth reciting the Torah, learning Hebrew, celebrating the sabbath and Passover. I've tried hard to shed myself of the old ways, to embrace the true path, but I've failed at times. Out there in the fighting, when you're a moment from death, you want to believe more than anything that there's another world after this one. Otherwise, what a terrible waste this life is."

"Mietek is still a prisoner," said her mother, peering closely at him. "How is it that they've released you?"

"The one advantage of being a Jew," laughed Adam. "They aren't interested in keeping us in the POW camps. We might spread disease, they said. They asked about our religion on the first day of incarceration. We were only there for a few weeks and then they separated us. I thought we would be killed when they carted us out of there, but they took us to a different camp filled only with Jews. After another month, they brought us back to Warsaw and dropped us off. I've been back for a couple of weeks."

"And you just came here now?" asked Irena, feeling a fraction of anger.

"It took a few days of processing to get new papers," explained Adam. "Then I had to make sure my family was safe. Of course, you and Janina were on my mind," he said, using her mother's name.

"How is your wife?" Janina asked.

"She's doing fine. Thank you for asking. We've had our difficulties. We separated about a year ago."

Irena had heard rumors about this. She'd wanted to ask Adam, but it seemed a rude question.

"It must be nice for you young people to have the luxury of separation," Janina said, snorting. "I would do anything to have my husband back. But you two throw away spouses like chaff from the wheat."

Adam's cheeks filled with color. She thought he would say something. She hoped he would, that he would call her mother to task, explain why he was separated, defend her own separation from Mietek, but he said nothing. Instead, he sipped his vodka, looking away thoughtfully.

Janina rose, pulling herself out of the seat. "I'm tired and I'm going to bed. Thank you for coming, Adam, it was good to see you. I suppose you'll be leaving now."

"No, he will not," said Irena. "I haven't seen him for ages and we're going to stay up and visit."

Her mother stumbled and sank back into her chair. "I rose too fast," she said.

Adam rushed to her side, motioning for Irena. They walked her back into the bedroom and laid her gently on the bed.

"If you give me a few minutes, Adam, I'll help her change and then we can chat."

"Don't bother with me," said Janina. "You might as well go back out there and do whatever you're going to do. I don't know what the world's coming to. Two married people alone together without a chaperone."

"The world's changing for sure," said Adam sadly, "and all for the worse. Thank you for having me to dinner tonight." He bowed and stepped out of the room, closing the door behind him.

"What is wrong with you?" whispered Irena, eyes flashing. "I haven't seen him in months and you're going to drive him out of here with your barbs."

"Good!" her mother whispered back. "That would be the best thing for both of you. If Mietek knew you would willingly eat dinner with another man, he would die right here and now." She closed her eyes and leaned her head back, muttering to herself. "Poor boy, alone out there in some terrible camp. And his wife's at home betraying him."

"Giving some bread to an old friend is not a betrayal, Mother. Besides, he's hardly my husband anymore."

"He is your spouse under the law and before God. And he always will be."

"You're impossible," said Irena. She stood and walked out of the room, tearing the door open and slamming it behind her. Her mind was a storm of conflicting emotions. Her face must have been a mess, for Adam took one glance at her and turned away.

"I should be going," he mumbled, taking a step toward the door.

"No! Please, stay, even if just for a little while."

He hesitated and then sat back down. "As you wish."

She took the place next to him, a half meter between them. "I can't believe you're here," she said.

He smiled at her. "Me either. It's a miracle to be back in Warsaw."

"What will you do now?" she whispered. She didn't want her mother eavesdropping.

He shrugged. "Who knows? The Germans won't let me practice law anymore. The bastards have taken everything we owned, at least on paper. But they don't have it all. My father was always smart. We have zlotys, gold and silver jewelry. Enough to last the war if it doesn't take too long. My family has been buying food on the black market to supplement what they give us officially. I'll try to help. Maybe I can find work in the country?"

"You can work for me," she offered.

"For the government? Impossible."

"Not officially. A driver. We always need them. You could travel out on a wagon and pick up supplies. When you're out there, you'd be able to trade for food directly, for your family. You'd get better prices; your money would last longer."

"Wouldn't they grow suspicious? I don't have papers."

"The Germans aren't careful with food deliveries. They know about my wagons and my drivers. You'd be on official business. They hardly ever check papers and even if they did, they'd only shoo you away. Heaven knows it's been far safer to be a Jew these past few months than a Pole, particularly an educated Pole."

"So, the rumors are true. They're killing off the intelligentsia?"

She nodded.

"How many?"

Irena shrugged. He was leaning in now and she could smell him, feel his warmth. His head was close to hers.

"Tens of thousands. Maybe hundreds of thousands. Dozens of people I know have disappeared."

He moved a little closer, his eyes full of concern. Her heart beat with a rapid thud. She felt dizzy, excited, confused.

"Aren't you worried about yourself?"

"They won't touch me," she said. "I work for them."

He drew away, his eyes wide and forehead furrowed. "What do you mean, you work *for them*?" he demanded.

She was surprised by his reaction. "It's not what it sounds like. I'm just doing what I did before. But the Germans oversee it. They're in charge of everything."

"You're working for the fascists!" He shouted this time, startling her.

"Adam, quiet, people will hear." From the other room she heard her mother, calling her name, asking what was going on.

"I won't be quiet! What has happened to you?" He pointed an accusing finger. "The Irena I knew would never collaborate with the Nazis. She would die before that happened!" He started to rise.

She stood also, reaching out for him. He jerked his arm away, storming toward the door. "Please, Adam! Don't! Let me explain."

He turned on her. "There is no explanation. I won't spend a moment talking with a collaborator." She saw the betrayal and the pain in his eyes. "I thought I knew you," he said. "Obviously I was wrong."

She tried to stop him, but he pushed her away. He slammed the door shut behind him, knocking a picture off the wall. She stood with her head against the door, palms against the panels, tears erupting down her cheeks.

Chapter 6
A Confrontation

October 14, 1940
Warsaw, Poland

Irena worked by candlelight in the living room of her flat. She glanced out the window. The sky was just beginning to lighten. Her mother was asleep in the next room. She tried to be quiet, but the manual typewriter she worked from had a mind of its own. The staccato clap of the keys refused to be muted, and if she pressed too lightly, the letters did not show up properly and she was forced to start over.

She worked from a list she had handwritten. One column contained first names and the second family names. She had written down about a hundred of each. She combined the columns when she created new names, then she would trace locations on the map. The rest of the biographical information she made up as she went.

Each form had to make sense. The Germans could review records at any time. They frequently did. There had already been arrests at her office and random searches. She knew if she wasn't careful, she would be the next person the Nazis would take into custody. She finished typing the form and pulled it out of the typewriter. She reviewed the information, straining her eyes in the dim light. There were no mistakes. She had just created a family out of nothing. An Aryan Polish family. She could now use this form to set up a client file, and to apply for food welfare. When she was approved, she would assign this file to one of her Jewish families, and there would be one less starving household in Warsaw.

She'd done this hundreds of times now. Methodically, she was eradicating the loss of social welfare for the Jews of Warsaw. She worked alone; afraid she would be betrayed if she shared what she was doing with anyone else in the office. She was forced to labor in the mornings, often three or four hours before work began. She wished she could prepare these reports at the office, but it was too dangerous.

She had confided in Ewa and Ala. When Ala learned what she was doing, what sacrifices she was making, she had forgiven Irena and the rift between them was healed.

Not so Adam. She'd tried to reach out to him multiple times. She'd appeared at his door, but he refused to talk to her. She'd sent Ewa to intercede with him, but as soon as he learned that Irena was behind the visit, he'd ordered her to go away. She hoped he was safe, healthy. She wanted his forgiveness but as the weeks turned to months, she realized that might never come.

Thankfully there was still her work. The job was harder each day. The Germans were cutting back food supplies, limiting what each family could eat on a monthly basis, even if they were recipients of social welfare. Her contacts in the countryside were drying up, as the Germans demanded more of the farmers' crops and produce, forcing the Polish peasants to horde what little they could for themselves.

Still she found a way to bring the food in. She employed

more workers. Labor was almost free. Life was cheaper than food in these terrible times. She sent her workers to comb the farms. Sometimes she visited the countryside herself, talking directly to the landowners, convincing them to give just a little of their precious reserves to keep the people of Warsaw alive. She didn't mention Jews; that would have stopped them cold. Even before the war, the average Pole had little sympathy for the Jewish population. As Jan had said, *to each their own.*

She finished her work and counted the forms. She'd prepared a dozen today. Twelve more families that would survive the winter with a little luck. They would likely have to make it a lot longer than that. Everywhere the war news was bleak. The Germans had smashed the French and British in a few weeks this past summer. Rumor had it that England was already invaded, falling as quickly as France. They had no allies, no hope. This was their new world. At least the arrests seemed to have stopped. She hadn't heard of anyone seized in months, but what a price they'd already paid. The rumors were whispered from Pole to Pole: hundreds of thousands were missing from Warsaw.

She shook her head, driving the despair down. There was nothing she could do about it. She was fighting her little war, one family at a time. She packed her files into a worn leather satchel along with a canister containing her lunch, a little *barszcz* left over from the night before, and set out into the early morning streets.

She arrived at her office a half hour later. The late October morning already contained a hint of chill. She dreaded the coming winter. Coal and wood supplies were low last year, and the Germans would likely cut back even further this fall. She entered her office building gratefully, thinking of the coming months. As a government structure, so far, they had sufficient heat. She moved through the busy corridors of the first floor, nodding to a few acquaintances as she went. She bounded up the stairs and stepped into her own office.

She was startled to see two men sitting across her desk, both dressed in suits. She blinked in surprise, taking a step back, trying to understand what was going on.

"*Guten Morgen*, Frau Sendler," said the middle-aged gentleman. They were Germans. She realized she recognized the man who had greeted her, and she struggled to come up with the name. Klaus Rein. He'd worn a uniform last time she'd seen him, an SS captain. Now he wore civilian clothes. The large man with the boyish face next to him was his assistant. Peter, that was the name. He loomed half a head taller than his commander, but Klaus was the one that emanated power.

"What can I help you with?" she asked, trying to assume a nonchalant air. She hoped he did not detect the tremor in her voice.

"Sit down, please," Klaus commanded, gesturing to her desk chair. She stepped into the office and took the offered seat, moving her satchel down next to her on the floor. She kept her hands in her lap. She did not trust them on the table. She battled to stop the trembling in her fingers, squeezing them together as hard as she could. The pain drove her panic down a little.

"What can I help you with?" she repeated, as cheerfully as she could muster.

Klaus watched her with the dead eyes of a snake. His face was serene, his mouth set in the fraction of a smirk. She felt her own forced smile fade under his stare.

"We've had reports of acts of treason among the social workers in this department," Klaus announced, leaning his elbows on the desk. "Tell me who is breaking the rules, please."

Irena laughed. "What would I know about that? I'm a lowly food distributor." Her entire body buzzed with electric fear.

Klaus reached down to his right and fumbled with something, retrieving a file. He opened the folder and scanned the contents. "According to my sources, there are medical supplies going missing."

"That's not my department," responded Irena, relieved. "I

don't believe it could be true for a second, but I wouldn't know for sure."

He watched her closely, pausing for long seconds. "What about the food going to the Jews. That is your department." He said each of these last words distinctly, pausing between syllables.

"That's not possible," she asserted, shaking her head. "We keep careful records on each family. After the new laws came down, we removed all the Jews from the distribution list. So, I'm sorry, sir, but you must be incorrect." She heard shouting down the hallway, and a scuffle. "What is that?" she asked, her heart beginning to pound.

"That . . . is the sound of the medical workers who will be joining us at headquarters." He looked at her again, the smile growing on his face. "Now, Frau Sendler, you do not want to come with them, is that correct?"

She was frozen, terrified. She couldn't answer, but she managed to nod her head.

"I asked you to work for us because I believed you were ambitious. I admired your efforts to bring food into the city, even as our armies closed in on Warsaw. Since then you've done admirably, extracting supplies out of those selfish Poles after we'd already picked them to the bone." He reached out a gloved hand and placed it on her wrist. "Oh yes, Irena, I've been watching."

"I—"

"You've done well, better than I'd even hoped. But then these disturbing reports began to filter in. It's one thing to squeeze the farmers, it's quite another to feed the Jews."

"I haven't fed any Jews," she responded, keeping her eyes on his. She hoped her face was calm and stony as she tried to imagine it. She forced herself to take calm, measured breaths. Her life depended on this.

Finally, he shrugged, smiling again. "Excellent, Frau Sendler, you pass the test."

"Test?"

"I don't really have information about you. But I can't afford to be wrong." He rose to his feet, as did Peter. He put his hand out, reaching for hers. She gave it to him, and he pressed her hand, holding it, not letting go. "Keep up the good work, Irena."

"I will, sir." She smiled, feeling the relief wash over her. Klaus turned and walked toward the door. He stopped at the threshold. "Oh, one more thing."

"What is that?" she asked, the piercing fear returning.

"We have to conduct random checks. Part of the job, you understand. Could you give your satchel to Peter, please?"

"My what?"

"Your bag, the thing you brought in this morning. The object you set at your feet instead of on the desk. See, it's a funny thing, but I've learned in the past year that when people are breaking the rules, they tend to bring their dirty laundry home with them. I'm confident we won't find anything," he said, his voice soft as silk, "but I'll feel better if we see what Irena likes to take from work. I have to attend to that other matter down the hall." He turned to Peter. "If you'd be so kind as to search her satchel. Bring anything of interest with you." He nodded to Irena and left.

"Don't worry about him," said Peter, dropping heavily back into a seat. "He's not so bad. He likes you; you know?"

"But he just said—"

"He's a police officer, his whole life. He's suspicious of everyone." Peter yawned, his girth spilling over the back of the chair as he stretched. "You don't have any tea, do you?"

She was confused. Tea? Her life was on the edge of a knife and this slob wanted tea. "I'm sorry, I don't. How long have you known Captain Rein?" She wanted to keep him talking. As she did so she leaned slightly to the left, trying to ease her hand down toward her bag.

"Ages. He hired me right out of school. My dad didn't want

me in the army. Too big a target, he said. He's probably right. I wanted to be a pilot, or a tank commander, but I don't think I'd fit." Peter laughed to himself, stretching his arms again. "I'm so tired today. Are you sure you don't have any tea? How about coffee?"

"I'm . . . I'm sorry, I could make you some in a few minutes. We have tea in our cafeteria."

He shook his head. "I wish I had time for that, but Klaus is always on the run. I'm surprised he's not back here right now, yelling at me to hurry."

She was almost there. Her hand was on the bag now. She was fumbling for the zipper. She found it and started to pull but the bag moved with her, sliding across the floor. She needed both hands!

"I guess I'd better take a look at that bag."

She froze. She was so close! She just needed another minute or two. "Of course," she said. "Let me get it for you." She turned and quickly unzipped the bag, trying to keep the sound as quiet as possible. She turned back to him. "Do you have a girlfriend here?"

He smiled, blushing slightly. "I've had a few. Polish women are so different from Germans. They are appreciative of the little things, cigarettes, champagne." He smiled. "I love all women."

She reached her hand into the bag, fumbling with the contents, trying to remove the file. She touched her lunch, some makeup, finally she felt it, a sharp corner. The files!

"I bet they love you too, a strapping young man," she said, trying awkwardly to flirt with this giant. She'd never been very good at it, but her words seemed to have the desired effect. He beamed at her.

"Some of them do," he said.

She tugged at the folder, pulling on it. Halfway out it stuck, caught on something. She reached down a little to get a better grip.

"I better get that satchel," he said, half rising. "Do you have it there, please?"

"Tell me about your current girlfriend."

"I'm sorry. The satchel."

She could scream in frustration. She'd had the damned thing! If it hadn't stuck. If this dolt would have answered one more question, she would be saved. She reached over with both hands and pulled the bag up onto the desk, shoving the folder down in again as she did so.

"Here we are," Peter said, taking the bag in both hands. He reached in with his fat fingers and began pulling out the contents, placing each item on the desk. He removed the makeup first, looking the individual pieces over curiously as if he was a child. "I've never really seen this stuff up close," he said, turning a lipstick container over and over in his hand. "You women are so mysterious. Why would you bother with all this work? Not that I mind."

He pulled out the file, opening the contents and reading the first page. "What's this?" he asked, his face suddenly serious.

"Those are applications for relief," she said as dismissively as she could muster. "From Polish families who are in need."

"I probably need to show this to Klaus," said Peter. "I don't understand this stuff, but he likes to look at paperwork, that's for sure." He set the file down on the desk and reached in again, drawing out her lunch. He unscrewed the tin and gave the contents a sniff. "Soup?" he asked.

She nodded, feeling wretched again. Klaus would surely investigate the families listed in her folder. A visit to any of these very real addresses would reveal that whoever lived there had names different from her list. That would be true for each and every file. She might have been able to explain one mistake, but twelve? That was impossible.

"I'm starved," he said. "We left early this morning. I didn't have time for *Frühstück*."

"Do you want some?" she asked. She reached into her drawer and extracted a spoon. She could see his eyes widen.

"That would be lovely, Frau Sendler."

She handed the silverware to him and he started in immediately, slurping contentedly. "Mmmmmm," he said, sitting back again, his eyes closed. "I don't know if it's only because I'm so hungry, but it tastes the best I've had."

"I'm glad you're enjoying it," she said. She reached into a drawer and grabbed a stack of forms. Without hesitating she opened the file, removed the counterfeit documents, replacing them deftly with a stack of other biographical forms. Authentic ones.

"What are you doing?" he asked, noticing the stack of documents in her hand as he opened his eyes for another bit.

"Oh, I . . ." Her mind scrambled for an answer. "I thought you might like a few more for review."

He smiled at this and reached for another spoonful. "That's kind of you, but this should be plenty. I cannot believe how wonderful this tastes. You must be a magician in the kitchen." He stared at her for a moment, eyes brimming. "Does your magic extend to other parts of the house, I wonder?"

She smiled back, revolted by this fat overgrown child, but terrified to make any mistake. "That's a topic for a later time."

He laughed and took another spoonful, then patted his wide stomach. "Well, that does it for me, Frau Sendler, I must be on my way." He picked up the folders and started to leave.

"Do you want the rest?" she asked, picking up the container.

"You're too kind," he responded, taking the tin like an eager child at Christmas. "Thank you again and I hope to see you soon."

"Of course," she said, forcing another smile.

He turned and left, bowing his way out of the office. She sat there for long moments before the shaking returned. She waited another half hour, afraid to move, then she rose and darted from the office, fleeing for her home.

Klaus and Peter returned to her office the next day. She hadn't expected that. A fresh set of forms rested in a new bag she'd brought. Klaus didn't leave this time. He demanded the satchel, his eyes never leaving her. She handed it over and he searched the contents, quickly removing her file. He opened the folder, his eyes brimming with excitement, then he turned to her again. *He knew. He already knew.*

She gasped, her eyes opening. She was in total darkness, lying in bed.

"What is it?" her mother asked groggily. "Another dream?"

Irena turned on a lamp. She rolled out of bed and opened the curtains. It was already light out. She looked at the clock. She was supposed to start work an hour ago. She shook her head. *Not today. I'll go tomorrow.*

"Are you all right?" her mother asked, pulling herself up. "Let me get you something to eat, you've hardly had a bite in three days."

Three days. It seemed a year. She hadn't moved from her bed except to go to the bathroom in all this time. Her mother rose, heading into the kitchen. Irena's incapacity seemed to drive her mother back to a semblance of health. She'd made all her meals, serving her tea and toast, which Irena refused. She rolled over, turning away, letting her thoughts wander.

She'd been a moment from death. If Peter had opened his eyes and seen her change out those forms, he would have arrested her in an instant. Nobody came back from the Gestapo. Well, that wasn't entirely true, but few did, and those sorry souls were forever broken in body and soul.

She'd known she was taking risks. She'd been so proud of herself. She wasn't working for the Nazis, she was defying them! She was rubbing their nose in it by taking care of their greatest ideological enemies. The system was so simple. No-body checked on these names or the addresses. After all, the families collected the food at her distribution centers. So long as they had the proper paperwork, they could take their por-tion. She'd been so careful not to tell anyone. Only Ewa and Ala knew, and they were Jews themselves. That wasn't quite true, she thought. She'd had Ewa tell Adam as well. But he was Jewish also, and he hated the fascists more than anyone.

She'd enjoyed the game, but this was too far. It was one thing to feel the excitement, the danger. It was another to face death a split second away. She was in too deep, she realized, and she wasn't sure she could get out of it. The forms she'd given to Peter were legitimate, but would that satisfy Klaus? She re-membered those dead eyes, how closely he'd watched her. No, he would check on her, dig deeper, she would be caught. It might be too late already.

Her mother brought her some tea and toast on a tray. "Here you are, my dear."

"No, thank you."

"You have to eat. You've hardly touched anything for days."

She rolled over and sat up, propping a pillow behind her back. Accepting the tray, she took a nibble off the toast before setting it down. Her stomach turned and she feared she would throw up. She took a deep breath and drank a sip of tea, hoping it would settle her stomach.

"Have you thought about what I said?" her mother asked.

"I have."

"Well?"

"You want me to give all of this up? Flee with you to the un-known?"

"Otwock isn't the unknown, Irena. We know more people there than here. We have friends there."

She thought of the spa town twenty kilometers southeast of Warsaw. She'd been raised there on the banks of the Vistula. Her father had died in the little town. The memories of her youth had been pleasant, until the center of her life was taken away from her. When they'd moved she'd sworn she'd never return.

"What difference would it make?" Irena asked, trying to set aside the pain of the past. "If they track down what I've done, they'll find me, here or there."

"You're right, my dear. It's correct to worry about that. But there are other ways to hide. We have connections in Otwock who could help us. We might be able to obtain false papers and hide with one of the families."

"Mother, you're talking about Jewish families, aren't you? What good would that do us?"

"Plenty of good. Look at the last year. They've stripped the Jews of a few rights, but they've largely left them alone. The real victims have been us, the Poles. It's far safer if we are mistaken for Jews."

She felt the battle burning within her. She didn't want to leave her position, her passion, helping people. She'd accomplished so much, even without her little act of defiance. But she felt the net closing in. She knew what would happen if she was caught. It would be the end of her, the end of everything.

"Perhaps you're right, Mother."

Janina's face brightened. "Of course, I'm right," she said. "I knew you would come around. Let's not wait another day. We could be packed and on the road by noon. If we leave by then, we could reach Otwock today."

Irena laughed. "Now who is being unrealistic? You can't walk to the bathroom on most days. Now you want to march twenty kilometers at one go? If we are going to accomplish this, Mother, we'll need a wagon."

Her mother sat down, holding her hand, fire in her eyes. "But you have connections, don't you, my dear. You have all those drivers who bring produce from the countryside. One of them will take us, won't they?"

"Perhaps," she agreed. "Yes, I'm sure I could arrange it. But not today."

"Tomorrow then," her mother pressed.

Irena hesitated, unsure what she wanted to do.

"Irena, we must. If you stay here, you will die."

She knew her mother was right. "Tomorrow then."

Janina fell into her arms. "I love you so much, Irena. You've made the right choice. You've saved us."

There was an abrupt knock at the door. Her mother gasped. "Oh my God!"

Irena held on to Janina, not knowing what to do. *How had they found out so quickly?* There was another rap on the door, sharper this time. There was nothing they could do, they were on the second floor and there was no back entrance. If they jumped out the window, they would break their legs on the pavement below, probably they'd be killed. She drew herself out of the bed, pulling away from her mother, who still sought to hold on to her. "Let go, there's nothing we can do."

The sharp bang on the door erupted a third time. She took a step toward the handle, then another. She felt the panic rising, the terror she'd only felt twice before: on the first day of the war and again just three days ago. She unlatched the lock and pulled the door open, waiting for the Gestapo to burst inside.

To her surprise there were not men waiting beyond, but women. Ewa and Ala were there. "Thank God you're here," said Ewa, "we've been scared to death."

Irena opened the door farther and let them in. She felt dizzy and she stumbled over to the sofa, lowering herself down.

"Are you all right?" asked Ala, concern on her face. "You look pale, terrible."

"You just startled me. Give me a moment, I'll be fine."

"Get her some water, Ewa," commanded Ala. Irena buried her head in her hands, taking deep breaths. She felt a nudge on her arm and looked up. Ewa was there, smiling, compassionate, holding a cup.

"Thank you," she said, drinking some of the liquid. The cool water calmed her down a little.

"Why are you here?" she asked.

"Ewa heard from a friend at the office what happened. When you didn't show up the last few days, they feared the worst, that you had been arrested. Jan was going to come and visit you, but I told him we would check on you instead. He was grateful, he's terrified for his own life. There've been arrests at the office."

"I know, I was there. Who was it?"

"Wojciech and Stanislaw," said Ewa.

"Are they safe?"

Ewa shook her head. "They never came back. You know how it is. They probably never will. Jan thought the same might have happened to you. He said the Gestapo met with you."

"They did, but I survived it, by a breath." She related in detail her meeting with Klaus and Peter. Ewa and Ala listened with amazement. When she was finished, Ewa hugged her, holding her for long moments.

"Thank God," said Ewa, finally, letting her go. "You've been incredibly brave. There are so many families that are alive today because of you." Her friend leaned forward. "I hear things are breaking down at the office. If you don't return soon, someone else will take over. Unless you're very lucky, it won't take the new person long to figure out something is wrong with the paperwork. When are you coming back?"

"I'm not coming back."

"What are you talking about?" asked Ala, her voice tinged with a hint of iron.

"The Germans are on to me. It's only a matter of time now before they figure out what's really going on. When they do, they'll arrest me."

"But you switched the paperwork," objected Ala. "They'll check those families and see that you're doing your job. You should be safe."

"You don't know this Klaus," said Irena. "He's a blood-hound. I can see it in his eyes. He knows I'm lying. He won't stop until he catches me."

"You don't know that for sure, Irena," said Ala. "There are thousands of families depending on you. If you leave, they will lose their food allotments, they will starve."

"Jewish families," interrupted Janina. "They aren't supposed to be receiving this food in the first place. You can't ask my daughter to keep breaking the law, to risk her life for them."

"German laws!" said Ala, her voice rising. She turned to Irena. "I was angry at you when you said you would work for the Germans. I thought you'd gone mad. When I found out what you were doing, I swallowed my foolishness and came back to you. You were right and I was wrong," Ala admitted. "You've done some real good for these people. Don't you realize that this is bigger than you now?"

"It's my life, Ala."

"Is yours more important than thousands of others?"

"It won't make any difference," her mother said. "If she's caught, the Jews will lose their food anyway. We have to take care of ourselves."

"Is that your decision?" Ala asked.

Irena hesitated before answering. "I don't think I have a choice."

"Everyone has a choice. A choice to live in fear or die a hero."

"I already lost a husband saving the Jews," said Janina. "You have no right to ask me to lose a daughter as well!"

"Quiet, Mother!" insisted Irena. "The neighbors."

"I don't care a damn about them!" her mother screamed. "I'm not going to let these people talk you out of it. We're going tomorrow to safety." She turned on Ala and Ewa. "If you love my daughter, you will let her go. She's done enough for you."

Ewa started to say something but Ala interrupted her. "In this world, it's not enough. In the German world, the sacrifice of one life is merited when many others will live. You cannot abandon us."

She started to respond but she was jolted by a sharp knock at the door. *Who on earth could that be? Nobody else would come here.* They all froze. Irena rose, stepping toward the door.

"Don't open it," whispered her mother. "Maybe they will leave."

"They never go away," responded Irena, opening the door. She gasped, taking a step back into the room. He was here.

Chapter 7
Closing In

October 1940
Warsaw, Poland

Klaus sat on the sofa of the downstairs parlor, his hands sifting through the documents. He set the paperwork aside for a moment as Briggita brought him a tray of tea and some cookies. She'd made the baked goods from scratch. He smiled at her, showing his appreciation. She was so thoughtful.

She stepped away and he carefully lifted the kettle, tipping the rich auburn liquid into the saucer. He held his breath, concentrating, watching the surface of the tea rising until it was a centimeter from the brim. He set the kettle down and took up the sugar, measuring out a teaspoon. He carefully scraped off the top of the spoon, assuring an exact measure. He turned the fine white grains into the liquid and then poured an equal amount of cream. He stirred the contents slowly in full revolutions, counting to twenty. He set the spoon down and lifted the saucer, taking a sip. He breathed in satisfaction. It was perfect.

"What are you working on?" Briggita asked.

"Just some paperwork," he muttered absently.

"Can't you put it aside? We want to spend some time with you, don't we, Anna?"

"*Ja, Vater,*" said Anna, looking up from a large oriental rug where she was playing with a doll. "Come and play with me."

He took another sip of his tea and laughed, setting the documents aside. "Fine. I surrender." He rolled off the sofa and landed on the floor hard. "Ouch," he grimaced, "I'm getting too old for this kind of thing."

Briggita laughed. "Nonsense. You're in better shape than most of the younger men you work with. Look at Peter."

"Mountains don't count," he responded.

"Truly. Though, Klaus, I'm worried about him. He's bigger each time I see him."

"He'll be fine." Klaus made a show of rubbing his chin, as if considering the matter further. "But perhaps you're right. I know," he said finally, considering the matter. "Peter should re-qualify for his sports badges."

"That would serve him right," laughed Briggita.

"Daddy, you're not paying attention to me," protested Anna. "Come and have tea with Hannah and me."

"Oh, it's teatime is it? Well, let me get the tray then."

"Not real tea!" she shouted, rolling over onto her knees and picking her doll Hannah off the carpet. "Pretend."

The phone rang. "What is it now?" Briggita said.

"Please answer it," said Klaus.

"Do I have to? Can't we have one evening to ourselves?"

"I would love that, my dear, and we will soon, I promise. It's just this city and this war. There are a million details and so much left undone."

"But it's been more than a year."

"I thought we'd be finished by now, but it's like a string hanging off a carpet, the more I pull, the more fabric becomes undone."

Briggita answered the phone. "It's Peter," she said, holding the phone out. She refused to look at him.

Klaus pulled himself to his knees and then rose. He felt the soreness in his joints. *I am getting too old for this.* He took the receiver. "*Ja*, Peter."

He listened for a few minutes, asking questions, and he hung up. He turned to Anna. "I'm sorry, my dear, but I have to leave for a little while."

"But, Daddy, you promised you would have tea with Hannah and me!"

His heart fell. He hated to disappoint his little girl. He saw the sadness in Briggita too. This job was too much on them. He was gone most nights until they went to bed, and often he'd left in the morning before they arose. He made a mental note to request some leave. A few weeks off would fix everything. Of course, that would have to wait a few months at least. They would have more work soon, not less.

"Goodbye, my love," he said to Briggita. She still looked away, her head giving him the slightest of nods. He turned and walked out of the house. He would have to worry about his home life later. Duty called.

"Where are we headed?" asked Klaus, squinting through the windshield into the night.

"Ludwicki Street," answered Peter.

"Are you sure we have the right address?"

"I double-checked it."

"And the evidence?" asked Klaus.

"I've looked it over and over. I missed some of the details the first time through. The fabrications are very subtle."

"You're certain then?"

"Without any question."

"So be it." Klaus pulled out his penlight and reviewed the list in his folder. He read the names of the two social workers they already had in custody, along with half a dozen other government workers they'd arrested on the same day. "Any progress on the questioning?"

"Yes, sir," nodded Peter. "Some solid information, particularly from Stanislaw."

"What about Wojciech? He seemed weak."

"Dead," said Peter.

"What do you mean *dead*?"

"Our interrogator was a little too enthusiastic with his questioning. He caved in his chest with an iron bar. Collapsed both lungs. They filled with liquid and that was the end."

"I'm not happy with that," said Klaus. "There was no order terminating his life."

"That's a formality," chuckled Peter. "Before or after, you know they'll sign the warrant."

"That's sloppy and it's against the rules," said Klaus. "I want that interrogator pulled off the team."

"Why, sir? He's one of our best."

"He broke the rules," said Klaus. "I won't have it. Replace him. Tomorrow."

"Very well."

Klaus reviewed the list. "I want two more days of questioning, then they are to be shot. *After* a warrant is produced."

"All of them?"

Klaus thought about the question. "No, leave Stanislaw. But not intact. I want the message to get back to *that* department."

"I think they'll understand things pretty well by the time we're done," said Peter.

"They need to. We have much bigger things coming up." Klaus thought for a second. "I'm not sure a few bruises will suffice. Take a hand. His writing one."

Peter nodded. "That should get their attention. On to bigger issues: When are we starting?"

"Tomorrow."

"So soon? I don't want more work right now. Did I tell you about Zotia, my newest conquest?"

Klaus shook his head. "When are you going to settle down and start a family?"

"I don't need a family," responded Peter. "I have yours."

"Briggita's worried about you."

"Why?"

"She's noticed you've gained weight."

Peter laughed. "Is that all?"

"I'm worried too. You're way past regulation."

"They wouldn't touch me with you in charge."

"That's not the only issue. It's not good for you. I'm ordering you on a diet, starting tomorrow. No desserts, no second servings, and most of all, no alcohol."

"But sir—"

"No arguments. Thirty days. I want your uniform fitting by Christmas. The *original* one you brought to Poland. In three months, you will retake your physical qualification tests. And you will pass them. Do you understand me?"

"Yes, sir." Peter grew quiet.

Klaus smiled to himself. His assistant needed to be reined in now and again. He would have to keep a close watch on him; Peter lacked the discipline to stick to the requirements by himself and would cheat outrageously if Klaus didn't prod him on. He would secure the services of this new girlfriend as a spy. A few zlotys and some cigarettes should do it. If he broke the rules, which he inevitably would, Klaus would confront him, both assuring he kept on his program and continuing the myth of Klaus's omniscience.

"Are we almost there?" Klaus asked.

"Just about, it should be just around the corner. Damned rain."

Klaus strained his eyes in the darkness. The wipers were barely keeping up with the downpour and spread grease across the windshield. The rubber made a horrid squeaking noise as it went. "Get those wipers replaced tomorrow as well, Peter. These should have been tested during the dry season."

"I'm sure I did, sir."

Klaus was sure he hadn't. "Is that it?" he asked, pointing at a building ahead to the right.

"I think so, although they all look the same to me."

Klaus pressed his face against the passenger window, trying to make out the numbers above the door. He checked his file. This was the right place. He nodded to Peter. The giant turned off the vehicle and reached for the door, but Klaus stopped him. "I'll handle this one alone."

"But, sir, I'm supposed to—"

"That's an order."

"Very well."

Klaus stepped out of the vehicle and moved toward the doorway. He thought about the soreness he'd felt rolling to the ground earlier. He couldn't afford to get soft. He would handle this arrest alone. Besides, there was little real danger here . . .

He made his way upstairs to the second floor of the building. He removed his penlight on the way up the stairs, checking the file again to make sure he had the correct apartment. He made it to the second floor and walked about halfway down the corridor. He stood outside the door for a few moments. There were voices inside. He drew his Walther 9mm and checked the ammunition, flicking the safety off. He knocked sharply.

Chapter 8
He's Here

October 1940
Warsaw, Poland

Irena stood frozen as he stepped into the room. She heard gasps of surprise behind her as well. She knew she should do something, anything, but she felt immobilized.

He stared at her, his face an impenetrable mask. She breathed deeply, closed her eyes and ran forward, throwing her arms around him, burying her face in his chest.

Adam tensed for a long moment and then she felt his hands on her back, patting her softly, holding her tight. "You're here," she whispered. "You're finally here."

"Ewa told me what happened," he said. "I wasn't sure if I should come. If I'd be welcome here. But when she came again this morning and told me you'd disappeared from work, I knew I had to make sure you were all right."

"I'm not all right. At least—I haven't been. I'm much better now." She looked up at him. "Have you forgiven me then?"

He pulled away, looking down at her. He fumbled for words

before he responded. "There was nothing to forgive. I've felt the fool all these months. You did what you thought you had to do, and you were right, you've done far more for my people working alongside the Germans than anything anyone I know has performed." His voice was tinged with bitterness and he looked away, struggling with the words.

She held him closer, pulling his attention back to her. "Don't worry about that now. I'm so happy you're here."

"What does it matter," said Ala. "You're quitting."

Adam drew back. "What do you mean?" he asked Irena's friend.

"Ask her. Irena's decided her own life is more important than everyone else's."

Adam turned to Irena. She felt the happiness drain out of her. "What is she saying?"

"The Gestapo is investigating me, Adam. It may be already too late. My mother has contacts outside of the city." She couldn't meet his eyes. "We are . . . we are considering leaving tomorrow."

His eyes narrowed. "How can you do that?" he asked. "You're helping so many people."

"Apparently that doesn't matter anymore," said Ala. "Now that her own skin is on the line."

"Now be fair," Ewa interjected, stepping over to Irena and putting her arm around her. "Your life isn't at risk. You don't know what you would do when the time comes."

"I won't run," said Ala firmly, eyes never leaving Irena. "I will stay, and I will fight."

"It doesn't matter what you will do!" said Janina. "We are leaving tomorrow and that's the end of it."

Adam stared at Irena, his eyes clouded, a stunned expression frozen on his face. He shook his head. "I just don't understand," he whispered. "How do our own lives matter in the cause of the people?" He looked as if he was going to say more, but he turned and moved toward the door.

"Wait!" said Irena. "I haven't made up my mind!"

"Yes, you have!" said Janina. "We are going!"

Irena turned on her mother, her anger flaring. "I will make my own decision, Mother! I need some time to think." She turned to Adam. "Will you walk with me?"

He stared down at her, a hand absently reaching across his suit coat to scratch at his opposite elbow. "What is the point?"

"Please, Adam. I want to talk to you."

"Irena," her mother insisted. "We don't have time for this."

"I'm going," she said. "I'll be back soon."

She retrieved her coat off the hook and moved to the door, Adam following her. They left the building and walked along together toward the Vistula. Crossing the river at the Kierbedź Bridge, they walked through the Praga market square, and then found a garden. They strolled along the paths, looking at the trees and the dormant plants. For a long time neither of them spoke.

"So, you're leaving," he said finally, still walking.

She reached out and took his arm, pulling him to a stop. They faced each other. She watched him for long seconds, her eyes locked with his. "They're going to kill me, Adam."

"Do you know that?"

She shook her head. She told him the whole story. A half hour passed as they stood there, next to the path, and she outlined everything that had happened. He listened intently, interrupting only to ask a point of clarity here and there. When she was finished, he was thoughtful.

"I understand now," he said. "I didn't know what happened."

"So you think I should go?" she asked.

"No. I don't."

"You think I'm a coward then?" She felt her anger rising, mixed with humiliation that he saw her that way.

"No. You're very brave." He turned, looking away, his face troubled. "I don't want you to go for selfish reasons."

"What do you mean?"

"I need you in Warsaw, Irena. I need your strength, your hope. You're a bright light in the darkness. I feel my own courage fading."

"We haven't spoken in months."

"I've thought about you often. It's not your fault we haven't spent any time together. It's mine. When you told me you were working under the Germans, I was angry. You have to remember, I'd just returned from our humiliating fight with them. Worse than that, I was reeling from the Russians' betrayal. I'm still trying to understand how they could have stabbed us in the back."

"I am too," she said. "Of all the things I could ever have imagined, I would never have believed our socialist brothers and sisters would sell us out to the fascists."

He turned back to her, his face lit with intensity. "We have to build our own world, Irena, right here in Poland. I believed that Russia would come and help us one day, but now I realize they are corrupted, that they've lost their way. If we are going to create the future we want, we must do it right here, right now."

"That's what I want too," she said, stepping closer to him. "But the Germans are here. They may never leave. What can we do?"

"Nothing lasts forever. We must fight them. Not with armies in the field, now is not the time. We must battle them by sabotaging their factories, by organizing the people, gathering arms, shielding the remaining intelligentsia, and," he said, looking down at her, "by protecting the Jews."

"I've done everything I can to help them."

"Yes, you have, and you should be proud of that. But the question at this point, Irena, is not what you have done, it's what you are willing to do from today forward. Not when it's easy, not when the Germans are oblivious to you, but when everything is at stake."

"I'll stay," she said, making her decision. "You're right. I must keep going. There's more than just my life at risk, it's the future of our nation."

He pulled her close, holding her. She escaped into his arms, her fears melting away. She was part of something bigger, something with Adam. She would take the risk with Klaus. After all, she had no proof that he was still even looking for her. That might be the end of their investigation. They must be spread thin, dealing with the whole city. If she left with her mother, there was every chance that the interest in her would increase, not subside, and that the Germans would track her down to Otwock, false identification or no. No, she was safer here, in control of her own destiny. Close to her friends.

She remembered those months at the university in the law program. He would argue with his professors on fine points of social justice. Adam was radical, even then. So different from Mietek. Her husband wanted everything to stay the same in Poland forever. Hard work, faith in God, a family and children. One path from cradle to grave. Not Adam. He wanted a Poland for all the people, not just the elite. Jews and Poles, worker and farmer. Everyone would have a place in the new order.

They'd spent time together, first in groups, then alone. Sometimes he angered her. He had little patience for contrary opinions. They would quarrel and might not speak for days, but she found herself drawn back to him.

She was not allowed to continue in the program. Women had no business studying law, the university officials told her. She transferred back to social work and their paths diverged. They kept in contact as they were able, an occasional social event, a chance meeting. They were never alone again. As time went by, she'd expected him to fade from her mind, at least for the image to blur. To her surprise, he never had. He'd burned brightly all these years and now he was here in front of her. She would stay now, no matter what.

"Tell me what you've been doing these past months," she asked him, as they continued their walk through the gardens.

"There's not much of a story," he answered, looking away.

"But it's been so long."

"What's there to do for a Jew?" he snapped, stepping ahead of her. She scrambled to keep up.

"What do you mean?"

"I can't do a thing. That's what I mean! You've told me all about your work, the problems, the hours, the risks. Don't you realize I'd trade everything, gamble everything, just for the privilege of something productive to do?" He stopped and turned to her. His cheeks were rimmed with scarlet and his breath came in short gasps. "You Poles complain about your difficult lives. What do you know about it? We Jews have no jobs, no money, no food. They've taken everything away from us. And for what? Because of religion? Hell, many of us gave that garbage up long ago. No, because of some foolish notion of our race. As if you can group all the Jews into one lump of a people."

He turned and faced the Vistula as it rippled by in the distance. "What do I have in common with most of the Jews? The mass of them can't even speak Polish. They sit in their little communities, rattling away in Yiddish, dirt poor, observing the old ways and keeping everyone else at arm's length. The Poles hate them for it, but do they go after the poor? No! *Your* countrymen targeted the few Jews that have made something of themselves, the doctors and lawyers and business owners. As if there was some special quality to being a Jew that gives an unfair advantage!"

"I've never felt—"

"And if it wasn't bad enough under *your* government, they failed utterly to protect us from the Germans. Now we have these bastards in charge. They hate us even more. They've taken everything away from me, Irena! What have I done these many months?" he shouted. "I've sat in my damned apartment, reading books, pacing, raving at the walls. I can't practice law. Hell, they wouldn't even let me be a clerk or a police officer. I'm wasting away while you go to work each day, making decisions, changing lives, doing something." He pointed a finger at her. "You're worried about your skin because you've fed a few Jews. At least you can work, at least you can eat! Think about us!"

"But you've been better off than we have," whispered Irena.

"How can you say that?"

"They've left you alone. They've been arresting and killing us. Many Poles in the last year have wished they were Jews. Look at your war service: When it was over, they sent you home. Poor Mietek—"

"Of course, I forgot about your husband," he said bitterly. He started to turn away. "It's time to head back."

"Don't do this," Irena pleaded, taking his arm. He made to pull away, but she held on to him, pulling him closer again. "Why are you mad about Mietek? We are separated."

"But the bond remains," he said. "Truly, we should return." He started to walk away from her, and she hurried to keep up. "Adam, please!"

"What do we have here?" asked a new voice. "A couple of Jewish lovebirds flying loose in the park?"

They both froze. The words were in German. Irena looked

up and saw a group of Wehrmacht soldiers. There must have been a dozen of them. They didn't have weapons with them, but they were in full uniform.

"I'm not a Jew," said Irena.

"Come on now," said the leader, a sergeant who appeared no more than twenty. "Look at your boyfriend there," he said, pointing at Adam. "Hooked nose. Curly dark brown hair. He's a Jew, all right." The other men laughed. Irena moved close to Adam as the soldiers fanned out, surrounding them.

"We are going home," Irena said.

"Not just yet you aren't. Give me your papers," the sergeant demanded.

Adam handed his over. Irena fumbled for her identification but realized in the emotional whirlwind at the apartment, she'd left her documents behind.

The sergeant examined Adam's and then turned to her. "I don't have mine," she said.

"Out on the streets without papers? I could have you arrested right now," the soldier stated. He turned to Adam. "I was right, you are a couple of Jews. You know you're not allowed in the park, correct? What are you doing here?"

"The regulations do not ban us from the park," Adam responded robotically. "We are banned from the benches. That is all."

The sergeant rubbed his chin as if considering what Adam said. He turned to his friends. "Well, gents, what do you think? Should these Jews be wandering about in here?"

"*Nein, nein,*" came the responses amidst laughter.

"What shall we do with them?" the sergeant asked.

"You said they were lovebirds, but I don't see any wings," said one of the soldiers. "If they can't fly, perhaps they can hop."

"Excellent suggestion, Helmut." The sergeant turned to Irena and Adam. "Squat down until your hands touch the pavement."

Adam started to comply, but Irena interjected. "We're not

going to do that," she said. "I'm not a Jew, and like Adam told you, it's not illegal for him to be here."

The sergeant stepped forward. "Please squat down," he whispered. At the same moment he slapped her hard with the back of his hand. She flew backward, knocked to the ground. The world spun and a burning fire ripped through her face. She heard blows and Adam hit the pavement next to her.

"Now then," the sergeant repeated. "If you'd be so kind as to assume a squatting position."

Irena erupted with anger. She wanted to scream, to kick, to fight them. But she knew there was no point. There were a dozen of them. And Adam was here. Full of humiliation, she rolled over on her knees and then drew herself up with her feet under her, assuming the position the sergeant wanted. She saw out of the corner of her eye that Adam had done the same.

"Now, hop, hop, hop," ordered the sergeant.

She hopped forward on her legs a few meters, then moved to stand but hands pushed her down. She repeated the movement again and again. The soldiers followed, surrounding them, hooting and shoving them. Her legs burned. Her eyes were on fire from salty tears, obscuring her view. The torture went on and on.

"That's enough now!" ordered the sergeant. She struggled to rise but she couldn't force her exhausted legs to function. She fell over on her side. Rough hands clutched her and ripped her to her feet.

"You are compliant little Jews," said the sergeant. "Have you learned your lesson about polluting our parks?"

Irena refused to answer. The sergeant stepped close to her. She could smell his fetid breath, laced with the reek of alcohol. "I asked you if you've learned your lesson, or do you need some more training?"

"I've learned my lesson," she whispered.

"*Gut!*" responded the sergeant. He bowed to her in mock

respect, then waved the back of his hand at them dismissively. "Go away now, little Jews. But don't come back here ever again."

The soldiers turned, laughing, and marched back into the park, leaving Adam and Irena.

They stood for long moments without speaking. Irena was shaking in anger and humiliation. She felt violated, unclean.

"Do you still say it's better to be a Jew?" Adam asked finally.

"How dare you say that right now!" she retorted. "I'm slapped and beaten, and the only thing you can ask me is if you've made your point? What's become of you? You were righteous in your socialist beliefs, ready to take on the world, proud, strong, brilliant. Now all you can do is tell me how difficult your world is? That your life is harder than mine."

"Isn't it?" he retorted hotly. "You saw what just happened to us. I see that kind of thing every day. Do you? Do you have to hop to your office? The building where you get to work?"

"Please, Adam. Don't. I'm trying to understand. I believe you that things have been difficult. But you're not the only person who is suffering."

He turned away from her. "Let's go back."

"Adam, talk to me!"

But he wouldn't. He shuffled off ahead of her, strolling rapidly. She was a foot shorter than him and she labored on her stinging legs to keep up. She called to him several times, but he would not slow down. The minutes passed and they neared her building. There was nothing she could do for now.

As they reached her home, she noticed people standing in front of a poster tacked to the front of the structure near the downstairs entryway. They moved off and Adam paused to read it. He threw his hands up and turned to her. "There," he said, pointing to the poster. "You Poles have had it tough, have you? Here's what is happening to us."

She stepped up to the poster and read it, shocked by the

words. *All Jews must relocate to a Jewish district within Warsaw immediately.* Irena glanced at the area described; it was the poorest part of Warsaw, not far from her office. She knew it well. The area circumscribed was small, less than twenty blocks. Her mind reeled. There must be a half million Jews in Warsaw with all the forced transfers. They would never fit into the space. The Germans had spoken. There would be a ghetto.

Chapter 9
A World Away

November 1940
Warsaw, Poland

Irena knocked at the apartment door. There was no answer.
She took a deep breath, swallowing her anxiety. She knocked
again, louder this time. There was still no response. She considered leaving. A part of her wanted to flee, to avoid the conflict
she was sure was coming. But she had to move forward. She
rapped her knuckles harshly against the door, loudly banging.

"All right, all right," came a voice. "Give me a moment."

The door opened. Adam stood before her, his face unshaven,
eyes splotchy, his hair greasy and disheveled. He looked like he
hadn't bathed or slept in days. "Oh, it's you," he said, turning
away and stumbling back into the room. He didn't invite her to
join him, but he didn't slam the door either. He seemed broken,
as if he didn't care anymore.

She entered the apartment and was shocked by what she saw
there. Clothes were piled up in every corner and on the sofa.
Plates of half-eaten food clogged the coffee table and the near-

by kitchen. Books were stacked on the floor, others opened facedown and strewn throughout the apartment. The rank, stale smell of perspiration permeated the space.

"What's happened in here?" she asked.

"What difference does it make to you?"

"What do you mean?"

"I can't take any of this with me." He motioned to the items inside the flat.

She stepped farther into the apartment, dragging objects out of her way to make a pathway. "Have you secured housing?"

"Why bother?"

"The best locations are already taken. If you don't hurry, you'll be left with—"

He scoffed. "With nothing? All the best is already scooped up? Yes, by my rich brothers and sisters. I've heard all about it. They took all the flats up and down Sienna Street, leaving the scraps for everyone else. The world never changes."

"This is no time to play at politics, Adam. What about your parents? Your extended family?"

"What about my wife?" he retorted. "Oh, she's been here just like you. She wants to make sure her family is taken care of along with mine. Everyone wants their little nest feathered. But why should we take the best locations while the people suffer? I won't do it."

"This isn't a communist paradise, Adam. This is survival. I have contacts. I located a unit that's available. It won't last long, but it's big enough for you, with space for your family nearby . . . for her family."

He looked up with a wry expression. "You're concerned about my wife now? How thoughtful of you."

"What's wrong with you, Adam? I'm trying to help."

"I don't need your help!" he shouted.

"What are you going to do then!" she screamed back at him.

"What can I do? They won't let me take my books with me.

I've already lost everything else in this world. Now I'm losing my home, my last identity! They're shoving us into a sty like pigs. I'm telling you, Irena, it's the last stop before the slaughter-house!"

She stepped toward him. "Adam. You don't have a choice. They'll kill you. You must go. You have more than just these things," she whispered, her hand extended in a sweep around the room. "You have your family. You have me."

"I don't know," he whispered, refusing to meet her glance. "I don't know what to do." He sat down on the sofa.

She took a risk, knowing he might reject her. She sat down next to him and pulled his head into her lap. At first he resisted, but then he put his arms around her waist and his head against her stomach. She felt his shoulders convulse and he sobbed qui-etly. She stroked his hair, his neck, letting him release the emo-tion.

After a time, he calmed down. He stayed in that position, head resting against her abdomen, eyes facing out in the room. She enjoyed the sensation of his closeness. She felt the electric-ity coursing through her. But she forced down her excitement, focusing on him.

Eventually he started to talk, sharing stories of his combat experience. He'd railed against his officers, against the incom-petence of the government. In secret, he'd held communist meetings with the men. He'd talked about a future where nei-ther Germans nor the right-wing Polish government would dominate them. Where the poor, the Jews, the workers and farmers would own everything, and share alike according to the needs of the people.

The other officers had got wind of what he was doing. They'd threatened to arrest him, but there was no time. They were al-ready fighting, already losing. The officers died too fast to prosecute him. Adam had hoped this might be the start of a revolution, the old world falling away to give birth to the new.

But that dream would have to wait. They'd replaced one set of right-wing masters for another. If they wanted the Poland of his dreams, of Irena's, they must take their nation back from the Germans.

"I don't care about communism, or fascism, or any 'isms' right now," Irena whispered. "The only thing I want in this world is to be here, now."

He laughed. "Yes, Irena. And I too. But we can't stay here forever. Outside those walls the world still waits. And we can't ignore it."

"Then you will move?"

"I have to. I know that. I just haven't been able to accept it." He looked up at her. "Thank you for coming. For talking to me. You help me to see things clearly. I'll move. In all the misery before us, at least I'll live in a space that you picked out for me."

Irena wanted to stay like this. She felt warm and safe. She'd never touched Adam like this. She didn't want to move, but she knew she had to. She had pressing matters at work. She reluctantly left him and returned to her office on Złota Street. She was fortunate, her workplace was near the new ghetto. She'd be able to see Adam whenever she wanted, although she wasn't sure what that would be like. He would have his whole family there. *She* would be there. Irena shook her head. She wouldn't think about that right now. Nothing was going to ruin her day today.

She walked along the streets, her coat pressed up against the cold. She could hardly feel the biting cold. She thought of his head in her lap, his warmth and his smell.

She didn't see them coming. The two well-dressed men approached her rapidly from either side. They seized her arms and dragged her toward a nearby car. She screamed for help. There were others on the street, but they only watched, terror on their faces. Irena was shoved into the back of the car and the men jumped in on either side of her. She felt a hard object shoved into her ribs. The vehicle tore off violently and ripped through the streets of Warsaw. She tried to hold on to her emotions, but she gasped, and tears tumbled down her face. She thought of Adam, of her mother, her friends. Nobody would ever know what happened to her.

She tried to speak, but the object was pressed hard into her stomach. A pistol barrel, she realized. She closed her eyes, trying to stifle her tears. She steeled herself for what she knew was coming. She was so afraid of torture. How would she be able to endure it for long? She didn't want to betray the Jewish families or those social workers who turned a blind eye to what she was doing. A part of her hoped they would shoot her in the back of the head when she arrived wherever they were going. She'd never know what had happened and her secrets would be safe. But the Germans didn't operate that way. They took what they needed first, and death was only granted as a mercy at the end.

The car slowed down, and she opened her eyes. She didn't recognize the part of the city they were in. They'd pulled up in front of a nondescript building. A solitary man stood out front, also wearing an overcoat. He motioned at the car and the men inside threw open the doors, dragging her out and marching her swiftly to the entrance. She was rushed down a corridor and into a room with a chair and a table. She was shoved down into the chair. A bright light shone down from above, directly into her eyes. The other side of the room was lost in shadow. The men turned and stormed out of the space, leaving Irena as quickly as they'd confronted her. She was alone, or so she thought.

"Why are you helping the Jews?" The voice came out of the darkness, soft and metallic, a man's voice. She strained her eyes to see who was there, but the shadows defeated her. She leaned forward.

"Stay where you are," said a raspy whisper.

She leaned back, not moving, not knowing what to do.

"I asked you why you're helping the Jews?"

"I'm not doing anything."

"Don't lie to me, Irena. I know everything about you. I've been watching you for a very long time. We can play games if you wish, but I don't think you'd enjoy them very much. Tell me why you're helping them."

The man spoke Polish. In her terror, she hadn't realized that at first. Who was this? Some German who'd learned the language with a perfect accent, or was this a Pole who'd sold out to the Nazis? How should she respond? She decided to ask a question in return. "And how am I helping them?"

"You feed them. False papers. Thousands. Now I've indulged you, Irena, you must indulge me. Why do you feed the Jews? Is it that fool of a boy you're fawning over? Or is it something else?"

She felt an icy hand on her heart. They knew about Adam. There was no hope. They'd kill her and he'd be next. She decided there was no point in lying. "I grew up with them. They are people, just like the Poles and the Germans."

"People just like us," the voice repeated. "Interesting answer. You haven't been listening to the Nazi propaganda, I take it. And who am I?"

"You're a German or a collaborator. You're an enemy of Poland!" Her anger spilled over. She knew she was moments from torture. She was exhausted and afraid. This game was almost worse than being beaten. Let them get started on her . . .

The voice chuckled. Long moments passed. "Oh, Irena. You amuse me. Today is your lucky day. I'm not a German, and I'm certainly no collaborator. No, my dear, you've come afoul of the resistance."

The resistance! Her hope surged. Unless this was some right-wing group. There were many fighting for Polish freedom; some of them were socialists like she was, but others wanted a return to nationalist Poland.

"Don't worry," said the voice as if it could read her mind. "I'm not talking about our fascist countrymen. No, Irena, we're just like your father, just like you. Like I said, we've been watching you for a long time."

She felt relief, but with it, a rising anger. "Then why did you abduct me?"

"We can't be too careful. Our members and our safe houses are secret. Even after all this time of investigating you, I can't say we trust you completely. But we've decided to help you."

"What do you mean?"

"You have a big problem. The problem that made you leave your boyfriend's apartment today to head back to work."

"He's not my boyfriend," she said.

"That issue is immaterial to us. What we care about is your problem. You do have one. Don't you?"

How could they know that? How closely had she been watched? The reality was, she *did* have an issue at work.

"All the Jews are being forced into the ghetto," he stated, showing how much they understood about what she'd been doing. "Your paperwork won't work for them anymore. Their movements will be restricted, if not outright prohibited. They can't travel to your food distribution centers anymore, and you can't bring food into the ghetto for them, because there won't be any Aryans living there, and the Jews are not allowed welfare distributions. Have I hit the problem on the head?"

She nodded, amazed by his knowledge of what she was doing. "Yes, but how do you—"

"We can help you. We are setting up networks even now. If you can keep the food coming to the current centers, we will have alternative *families* who will pick up the food at those locations. We'll take the food from there and smuggle it into the ghetto."

"How will you do that?" she asked. "Who will be involved?"

"I'm sorry, Irena, but you'll have to leave that to us. We're still not entirely sure about you. There may come a time when we'll give you more information, but for now, I need to know if you will help us. Will you keep your food distributions coming to the same locations for the Jewish families?"

What should she do? What if he was lying, if he was a German or a spy after all? What difference did it make? she realized. If he was working for the Germans then she was already compromised, and her life was over. She had to trust him. "Yes," she said finally. "I will do as you've asked."

"Excellent," said the voice.

"And who are you?" she asked.

The voice laughed again. "Like I told you. We don't trust you. Perhaps some other time."

"How will I get ahold of you?" she asked.

"You won't. You do what we've asked for now, and we'll see how things develop. If we need you, we know where to find you. At your boyfriend's if nowhere else . . . For now, I will bid you farewell."

She heard the door opening behind her and she looked over her shoulder to see the same men entering the room. "Wait!" she said.

"What is it?"

"I have one request of you."

A few days later, Irena walked through the streets of the new Jewish ghetto. The sidewalks were crammed full of people, many with arms loaded down with baggage. There was hardly room to move. She'd never seen more humans together in one place in all her life. She walked along Sienna Street and turned on Marianska. She thought about Ewa, who lived nearby. She hadn't seen her in several weeks and she really should stop by to visit, but she didn't have time today. She made a mental note to come back tomorrow and check in on her friend.

She moved on through the south part of the ghetto until she

reached Chłodna Street. She waited at a gate for long minutes as Aryan Polish traffic passed back and forth. Finally, the Germans lifted the gate and allowed the Jewish pedestrians to cross from the little ghetto to the big ghetto. She reached Leszno a few blocks later and then moved north past Nowolipki, Dzielna, and Pawia until she reached Gęsia Street. She kept moving north on Smocza until she arrived at the northern border of the Jewish Quarter. She had traveled the length of the ghetto because she wanted to get a feel for what the Jewish population was going to experience here. The conditions were bad, but not terrible. Certainly, they were overcrowded by every definition of the word. But with enough food and proper sanitation, they should be able to get by.

Having walked the ghetto, she headed toward Adam's apartment. As she grew closer, she could feel her excitement rise until she could barely contain it. He'd invited her to help him organize things before his family arrived tomorrow. They'd be alone together all day. A day of talking, working together. She thought of the last time they'd been together, his head in her lap. She couldn't help but smile. He was brilliant, radical, fiery—all the missing parts she'd never had with Mietek. She knew she fulfilled the same for him. He'd told her all about faithful, simple, dull Regina. She sounded like a mirror image of her own Mietek. Stable, hardworking, but hardly alive with the passion that burned in Adam and her.

Irena reached his apartment building and climbed the three floors as quickly as she could. He opened the door. She saw his face light up when he saw her and she blushed, pleased with his reaction. He invited her in, and they enjoyed some tea, talking about little things. She watched his face, basking in his presence.

After a little while they went to work. He'd only brought a few belongings, what he'd been able to cart over in a wheelbarrow he'd borrowed from a neighbor. He had his clothes and a handful of books he'd not been able to part with. All of them had socialist, even communist themes. She flipped through one of them. He'd made notes in the margins and she was fascinated by his thoughts, what was important to him. He wanted everything she desired. A free, equal Poland, where everyone had enough to eat, justice before the law, and an opportunity to serve the greater good. There would be no rich, no powerful. Everyone would have an equal share of what was produced. Surely this was what God had intended when he'd made the world—if there was a God. She may have lost her religious beliefs long ago, but she'd never let go of her father's dream for a socialist Poland. She'd embraced it with every fiber of her being. Mietek had never understood that. Never understood her. But now she was spending time with someone who shared her passions, her hopes for the world.

She dreamed of that future. Somehow, they would drive the Germans from their land. Adam would serve in the government as an attorney, perhaps even more—a leader. She would go back to her social work, but now everyone would receive food, medical care, education. They would be heroes for their work during the war. Irena had run the food distribution for Warsaw; why not for all of Poland in the new system? They would labor together, have children, raise them in the new paradise. Everything was possible now, if they could only endure to the end. What about Mietek and Regina? she wondered to herself. She shrugged. There was no need to worry about that right now.

He looked up from a bag he was sorting through. She must have had a strange look on her face because he laughed. "What are you thinking about?"

"The future."

"And what does the future look like?"

"Perfection."

He smiled. "Perfection sounds delightful. But how do we rid ourselves of these pesky Germans?"

She laughed. "I haven't figured that part out yet."

"Let me know when you do."

She turned serious. She realized she had an opening. She wanted to broach her plan. "If there is going to be a future, we have to survive."

"I know that," he said.

"I'm worried about you. I'm worried about this place they've sent you to."

He looked around. "It's no paradise, but we should get by."

"It's not the now I'm concerned with. What if this is just the first part of the plan? What if once they get you here, they decide to take other actions? You said yourself this was the first step to the slaughterhouse."

"That might happen," he conceded. "But not for a little while at least. There will be time for us to consider things."

"I don't know if there will be. I have something I want to ask you to do."

He lifted his head, his eyes thoughtful. "What is it?"

She hesitated. She knew she was taking a risk here. "I have papers for you. False papers. They name you as an Aryan. I want you to get your family settled here and then I want you to leave."

He pulled himself to his feet. She could see the discoloration in his cheeks. "What do you mean? Are you saying I should abandon my family? How can I do that? And you want me to hide as an Aryan?" He scoffed. "Have you looked at me? I wouldn't last a day. One can't look more Jewish than me."

"You don't have to be out there in the open for the world to see," she said, taking a step toward him with hands out, attempting to calm him. "There are places to hide. I have connections."

He stepped back, turned away, and paced the room. "You want me to spend the rest of this war, no matter how long it lasts, in hiding? It's been bad enough when I couldn't work. Now you want me to stay inside, crammed into a cupboard, dependent on others? Waiting for the day the Nazis come for me? I can do much better here, no matter what happens. Besides, I'm not going to abandon my family."

"It's not your family you're worried about," retorted Irena accusingly. "You don't want to leave *her*." She knew she wasn't playing fairly but she didn't care.

Adam sputtered and threw his arms in the air. "That's right, Irena. You've figured it all out. I'm sacrificing everything to be close to Regina." His voice dripped with sarcasm.

"I'm sorry," she said. "I shouldn't have said that."

He stepped forward and put his hands on her shoulders. She was facing away from him. She felt a flash of fire and her ears buzzed. He rubbed her shoulders gently. She closed her eyes, basking in his touch.

"I'm not mad," he said. "We both have our own problems with our spouses. That's one of the things I appreciate about you. You understand."

She turned around and faced him, taking a step forward. "I do understand," she said.

He pulled her to him and held her. She buried her face in his chest. "I know you do," he whispered. "I'm so grateful for you."

An hour before dark she left him, promising to come back in the morning and help his family move in. She'd dreaded meeting his wife again, but now she didn't care. As she walked home, she had another idea: She would talk to him again about the false papers, in front of his family. Perhaps they would be willing to convince him it was the best course of action.

The next morning, she rose early, made breakfast for her mother, and headed out with a basket of food toward the ghetto. She was a few blocks away when she realized something was different. There was a crowd standing out in front. She hurried along, panic rising. Then she realized what it was. The road was blocked by a wall that had apparently sprang up from the very ground in the middle of the night. Even as she watched, workers scurried over every inch of the structure, laying additional bricks over layers of grout. The barrier was already five feet tall. They were sealing off the ghetto!

She hurried forward and rushed along the wall, seeking any way in. She walked for kilometers but could find nothing. She finally reached an opening where the Germans were constructing a gate. There were soldiers with machine pistols guarding the opening. She put her head down and moved away, continuing to seek a way in. Hours later, exhausted, she reached her starting point. Except for a few closely guarded gates, the ghetto was closed to the world. She couldn't get in, and Adam couldn't get out. Five hundred thousand Jews were locked off from the rest of Warsaw. She sat on the curb and buried her head in her knees, sobbing. He was lost to her.

Chapter 10

A Problem of Calories

November 1940
Warsaw Ghetto, Poland

Peter drove Klaus through the swarming streets of the new ghetto. The top was down, and his breath steamed through the air. Everywhere people were jostling for room. There were already beggars, children mostly, although nobody approached them.

Klaus was angry. He pressed his emotions in, maintaining a stony visage. He could not believe the mess he was in now. The authorities had slopped this district together almost as an afterthought. He'd seen policy after policy related to the Jews, which were quickly started and just as rapidly abandoned. Apparently, someone at the top had decided to dump the problem on the Polish General Government. Eager leaders from all parts of Germany, France, the Netherlands, Czechoslovakia, and Austria were now shoving their Jewish populations onto trains and shipping them into Poland, where they were unceremoniously dumped at stations and left for Hans Frank and the SS leadership to deal with.

Frank had summoned Klaus to Kraków less than a week ago and given him a "promotion" to run the Jewish Quarter in Warsaw. He'd declined, but at the end of the day he was not given a choice. After sitting down to review the details of the operation, he was appalled by the lack of organization. He was presented the map, a plan for walling off the quarter, a woefully inadequate budget for security and food, and not much else. Since the appointment he'd worked twenty hours a day to implement the orders. He'd managed to wall off the ghetto on time, but the hasty requisition of supplies without proper bids had cost him dearly. Now he had five hundred thousand screaming Jews shoved into a teeming cauldron, and no idea how to deal with them.

One stroke of brilliance Klaus had come up with was to dump many of the problems on the Jews themselves. He formed a Jewish council called the Judenrat, placing a president in charge named Czerniaków, a former engineer and senator. The Judenrat was responsible for housing assignments, food distribution, medical assistance, sanitation, essentially all the elements of life inside the ghetto.

This left the problem of security and food to Klaus. After the cost of the wall, his budget was inadequate for what he needed to provide. He helped the security issue by forcing the Poles to provide policemen as auxiliaries to assist his German force. He also required the Judenrat to create a force of Jewish policeman. They weren't given any weapons except batons, and their authority extended strictly to the Jewish population, but he was thus able to draw on a significant pool of manpower to police the interior of the ghetto.

This left the problem of food. Headquarters allocated six hundred calories per day, per person, to the ghetto. Klaus wondered why they bothered. A person could not live on six hundred calories a day. This was another botched decision at the administrative level. What was their goal for these Jews? If they wanted to keep them alive, for the purpose of providing a labor force, then they would need at least twice that many daily calories, three times if it was heavy labor. If they were trying to eliminate the population, well . . .

His issue was he wanted to expand his security detail of good German forces. While he was satisfied he had enough of the auxiliary forces, Polish and Jewish, they were, at the end of the day, enemies, not friends. He needed enough men he could truly rely on, and he didn't have the money for them.

Peter stopped the car in front of the offices of the Judenrat on Grzybowska Street. They stepped out of the vehicle and marched into the building, Peter in the lead. The sidewalk on the outside and the building within were packed with people, but the crowd parted like the Red Sea before the two SS men in their crisp green uniforms.

They moved quickly to the president's office. They strode past his secretary, who stood and protested. They ignored her, and Peter tore open the door without knocking. They stormed in and found Czerniaków at his desk, surrounded by a group of elderly gentlemen. The president looked up, anger registering on his face to be rapidly replaced by fear as he saw who had entered.

"Get out," ordered Klaus to the assembled men.

"This is our council," protested Czerniaków, rising from his desk. He started to introduce the other Judenrat members.

"I don't care what their names are," said Klaus. "I want them out."

The men stood, with shock and confusion registering in their faces. One or two of them looked as if they were about to say something, but nobody did. Klaus waited. He wasn't going to ask again. Eventually the council shuffled out of the office, avoiding his eyes. When the last one had left, Peter closed the door. Klaus moved to a chair in front of the desk and sat down. Czerniaków moved back behind his desk.

"You can stand," said Klaus.

He saw the color in the president's face but the man didn't defy him. *Good,* he thought. Absolute authority over the Judenrat was essential.

"How goes the organization?" he asked.

"As well as can be expected, Herr Sturmbannführer," he answered, using Klaus's new rank. The heavier responsibility had come with a promotion from captain to major, the one positive of this disaster.

"The conditions in here are unacceptable," said Klaus. "There are people crawling all over the sidewalks like ants in an anthill. I want order and I want it now."

"But, sir. You can't expect miracles. The walls were a surprise, and it just happened."

"I expect that you will administer this district efficiently, or I will find somebody who will. There is a war on. Changes come rapidly. You should have anticipated the need for a wall. We want to *protect* the population, after all."

"Yes, sir. We . . . appreciate the gesture. I'm not criticizing the change; I'm merely pointing out that we are still getting organized in here. Many people arrived in the past few days, and there is a backlog in housing assignments. To be frank, we are out of space. If we could just have a few more blocks."

"You have more than enough room right now," said Klaus. "The authorities already extended the quarter, adding all of the blocks south of Chłodna. You should be grateful."

Czerniaków raised his arms to his chest, hands out toward Klaus. "I'm sorry, sir, if I've given you the wrong impression. Of course, we are grateful for the extra space, and for the protection of the wall."

Klaus stood. "I will be back in two days. When I return, I expect to be greeted by order. I want guards at the door. I want people coming here with appointments only. I want the streets patrolled, no beggars, no milling about. If when I come back in two days this has not occurred, you will be replaced and taken into protective custody. Am I clear?"

Czerniaków's face paled until it matched the color of Klaus's snow-white shirt. "I . . . I understand, Herr Sturmbannführer."

"I'm glad. I would hate to have to take measures into my own hands. I suspect your custody would not be pleasant. Although I assure you it would be brief."

Klaus moved toward the door.

"*Auf Wiedersehen*," Czerniaków called out. Klaus ignored him and followed Peter back to the car.

"You frightened the hell out of him," observed his assistant, chuckling.

"I hope so," said Klaus. "I need his cooperation, not his corpse. If I start killing off the leaders, nobody will want the job, and my duties here will be more difficult. I need him cowed, but I need him alive. For now."

"I still don't know why you took this job on," said Peter. "Things were busy enough before."

"I had little choice. Besides," he noted, glancing at Peter's new uniform, "we both earned promotions."

"Mine is thanks to you, sir, as always."

"You've lost some weight," said Klaus approvingly. "You followed my directions."

Peter laughed. "I had little choice."

"You're a good young man. You have a future if you keep at it."

"Everything I have, I owe to you."

"You're a big part of things, Peter. There will be a time, though, when you will have to pick one loyalty."

"What do you mean, sir? I've never betrayed you."

"You keep part of your life in your pants," said Klaus. "Because of it, you're sloppy and unclear in your purpose."

Peter laughed. "You're always pushing me about this."

"I'm serious this time. You lack discipline. I worry about what might happen to you if you're not careful."

"It's just a little bit of fun with the ladies."

"It's time to settle down, Peter."

"Is that an order?"

"You know I can't force you to make that decision, but I want you to think closely about what I've said. You have a duty as a German to settle down with a nice woman. A German woman. Start a family. Have some children. We have to have the next generation of strong young Aryans if we are going to be masters of Europe."

"Do you believe all of that propaganda?" Peter asked. "About our superior race and our right to rule the world?"

"It doesn't matter what I believe," said Klaus. "It's the law. And if you don't believe it, you had better learn to at least follow it. Your life may depend someday on being able to say no."

They left the ghetto and headed back into Aryan Warsaw. They were quiet for a long time as they moved through the streets toward his home. "Stop at the Gogolewski cake shop," Klaus ordered. Peter pulled over and Klaus stepped into the store. The shop was empty except for a Polish husband and wife who took one look at Klaus and retreated out the door. The shopkeeper's face was pale, and he moved to the counter cautiously.

"May I help you, sir?"

"It's my daughter's birthday tonight. I need a cake for the party, and a selection of other pastries."

The shopkeeper packaged up some *drożdżówka* and *paczki*, cutting little portions off with shaking hands for Klaus to sample. They picked out an enormous quantity of the pastries and a full-sized cake. Klaus ensured that the treats were meticulously packaged, insisting that several damaged pieces be removed. He looked over the contents, walking back and forth and inspecting each box for several minutes. When he was sure all was in order, he nodded to the owner.

The storekeeper assisted him in loading everything in the trunk, and Klaus paid with cash, leaving a generous tip as well. Soon he was back in the car and they were headed toward his home.

"What did you get Anna for her party?" Peter asked.

"I don't know everything," responded Klaus. "Briggita took care of much of the shopping. I did select a pony for her. It's time she learned to ride."

"How wonderful," said Peter. "Every little girl should learn to ride a pony."

"Every German girl, at least."

They arrived at his home a few minutes later. Peter parked the car and they hurried inside while his servants scrambled out to unload the desserts. The house was already full of guests, almost a hundred people, including government officials, SS officers, and their families. The dining room table was piled with every conceivable dish. Briggita had hired extra servants and they navigated through the crowd, pouring champagne.

"Klaus, you're here, thank *Gott*," his wife shouted from across the room. She made her way through the throng and kissed him on both cheeks. "Save me from them," she whispered.

He laughed, knowing she didn't enjoy this sort of thing. "Remember, my dear, this is for Anna, not for us."

"This is worse than a war," she said. "I hope I survive it."

He kissed her and together they spent the next several hours mingling with the crowd. Klaus fielded endless questions about the new ghetto, the conditions there, and most importantly, from the viewpoint of the questioners, what opportunities there might be to make money or advance their careers in the new arrangement. Klaus made no commitments this night, but he arranged appointments for several people to come see him. These connections could come in handy in the future.

He was enjoying himself. Unlike Briggita, he had no fear of social engagements. He was amused at how popular he'd suddenly become, how interesting his job was now that it had the potential to benefit others.

Finally, it was time for the cake and pastries, followed by the opening of presents. Anna sat on the floor near the fireplace in the front room, surrounded by other children and at least fifty gifts. She tore each open with delight. There were dresses, coats, dolls, silk scarves, and a rocking chair made of mahogany. When she opened the card telling her about her new pony, she squealed in delight and ran to Klaus, jumping in his arms.

The party drew to a close. Klaus and Briggita stood at the door, shaking hands and bidding the guests farewell. Several reminded him of their upcoming appointments, and how much they looked forward to working with him. Near midnight, the last guest departed, and they were left alone with their daughter and the sounds of servants cleaning up.

Klaus and Briggita sat down on the floor near their daughter, who was surrounded by a pile of presents.

"Did you have a nice birthday?" Briggita asked.

"The most wonderful ever," she said.

"Do you like the pony?" Klaus asked.

"Yes, *Vater*! When will I see it?"

"Tomorrow perhaps," said Klaus. "I could take the morning off and show you."

Her face curled in a grimace.

"What's wrong, my dear, don't you want to go in the morning?"

"Yes, yes, it's just that my stomach hurts," she said, clutching at her middle.

"You ate too much cake," her mother said reprovingly.

"It was so good."

"Off to bed, now," said Klaus. "You're up way past your bedtime."

With her mother's help Anna rose and staggered up the

stairs, clutching one of her new dolls. Klaus took a seat by the fire, contented and exhausted. He'd had a busy day. As the servants moved about, he lit his pipe, his one vice.

He couldn't help but reflect on the stark difference between this birthday party and all the previous ones. They'd lived a modest, middle-class life. Their friends were police, clerks, mechanics. Now here they were in this luxurious home, fawned over by the elite of German society while his daughter received expensive gifts and a pony to ride. He couldn't help but smile to himself.

Puffing away with pleasure, he realized he knew the solution to his ghetto problem. He thought it through for a few minutes and nodded in approval to himself. It was perfect.

Tomorrow he would contact headquarters at Kraków and inform them that he was setting the calories per person in the ghetto at three hundred per day. This would give him plenty of money for more German guards. The decision had an additional benefit. The population would decrease quickly, making his job that much easier. It was also humane to the population, who would not linger on for a year or more, suffering from gradual starvation. If headquarters wanted more calories, they could tell him and he would comply, but if they did, he would press for more money and staff. He hoped his decision might force them to reconsider their strategy as well. Did they want slaves or corpses?

He leaned back and closed his eyes, taking another deep puff on his pipe. His mind was at peace now, after days of working through what seemed an impossible solution. He thought of taking another piece of cake, but his stomach hurt a little as well. He'd already eaten too much.

Chapter 11

Crossing the Rubicon

January 1941
Warsaw, Poland

Irena went through the motions of making breakfast before she left for the office. Her mother sat at the kitchen table, sipping tea and thumbing through the newspaper. Irena was slicing up cold cuts and some cheese. The rations were meager and barely kept them fed, but she was able to bring home a little from the wagons here and there, and they did much better than most of the population of Warsaw.

Of course, this only included the Aryan Poles. What about the Jews? What about Adam? She thought of him this morning as she'd thought of him daily these past two months. Every weekend she walked the perimeter of the wall, hoping there would be an open gate, some way to enter the ghetto freely. She also sometimes rode the trolley that bizarrely still ran through the middle of the Jewish district, but nobody was allowed to get on or get off. She'd kept a close look out in the crowd for Adam, but she'd never seen him. She was desperate for news, any word, about him. She also hoped her friends Ala and Ewa were alive and safe.

She'd pressed at work for a pass into the ghetto. A few Poles from the department were allowed in for various reasons, including medical inspections. However, her area of expertise was food distribution, and this was now in the hands of the Germans. She'd put in for a transfer to the medical department, but so far she'd heard nothing about whether it would be approved. She doubted it would be. What did she know about medicine? She had no education or work experience in the field.

So, the months had passed, crawling by with agonizing slowness as she tried and failed to get into the ghetto. She had hoped she would hear from the resistance. If she knew how to get ahold of them, she could press to use their contacts to secure her a pass. She didn't know if that was even possible, but they seemed all knowing and must have resources she did not possess herself. Unfortunately, they had not given her any means to reach them. She would have to wait until they contacted her again.

"Are you still pining after that Jew?" her mother asked her, pulling her abruptly out of her thoughts.

"Mother, watch your mouth," she said irritably.

"It's been months now. They closed off that wall and there isn't anyone that's going to come out of there. The Jews are done in this country. You should be thankful, when they cut you off it saved your life. You aren't breaking the rules anymore so they've no reason to arrest you. They've saved your soul too. You are a married woman, after all."

"There's nothing going on between Adam and me," retorted Irena. "And Mietek and I are separated, as you well know."

"Separated isn't divorced," quipped Janina. "And you'll find no bishop to annul your marriage. You're stuck, and you'll stay stuck." Her mother's lips curled into a self-satisfied smirk.

"I wouldn't need a bishop, only the courts."

"You don't mean you'd go against your faith? To marry a Jew? What's become of you?"

"I might ask the same of you," Irena snapped, dropping her mother's plate down so hard on the table that it bounced. "Where is your passion for the cause? For our socialist future?"

Janina shrugged. "Those were your father's dreams, not mine. They died with him, as did my future. All I have now is my faith, and these scraps of food you give me."

"I give you everything I have," Irena barked in response. "Do you know what would happen to me if I was caught taking this extra food? They'd line me up against a wall."

"Fine words," her mother responded. "You'll risk everything for a bunch of strangers—people who aren't even our kind, but it's too much to ask to do a little for your own flesh and blood."

Irena rose. "This conversation grows tedious." She strode to the door, snatching her coat from the rack. "I'll be home this evening. I'll try to bring something home for dinner."

"Don't bother," her mother said. "I wouldn't want you to take the risk. I'd rather starve."

Irena stormed out into the snow and the cold. As if she didn't have enough to worry about! She bottled her anger. She wouldn't give her mother the dignity of adding to her worries.

She arrived at her office. When she reached her desk there was a note asking her to visit Jan as soon as she arrived. She felt a surge of excitement. This must be about the transfer she'd requested. She removed her coat and took the note, climbing up to the third floor and down the hallway to the corner office occupied by her supervisor. His secretary greeted her and then knocked at the door, informing him that Irena was here to see him. She was ushered in immediately.

Jan looked a decade older. He'd lost weight and his forehead and temples were lined with fatigue. Irena knew that even more than her, he'd fought for more than a year now to try to hold together a fragile system of social welfare with ever decreasing resources and constant changes from the Germans. Worse yet, the Nazis had raided the department multiple times and arrested some of his best people. Irena was surprised he hadn't been taken himself, as the Germans thrived on collective responsibility.

"Irena, how nice to see you," he said.

"Thank you. What can I do for you?"

He picked up a file and flipped through it. She recognized her application for transfer. "Do you want to tell me about this?" he asked.

"Certainly," she responded. "I have been thinking about things, and I believe it's time for a change. I know food is a priority, but disease is an even bigger problem. I was hoping I might be able to help our department more if I'm identifying outbreaks and assisting in containing and preventing them."

"Nonsense, Irena," responded Jan, eyes watching her over his glasses. "I know exactly what you are doing. You want a way into that ghetto, and you figure this is your ticket."

She acted surprised. "Why would I want into the ghetto? There's nothing for me there."

"Do you take me entirely for a fool!" he retorted, his voice rising. He leaned forward. "Now listen to me, Irena, I know all about the game you were playing with the Jews. The false records, the food shipments."

She was taken aback. He knew? She tried to deny it. "I never—"

"Don't lie to me! I know exactly what you were doing and how you were doing it. It was a miracle you weren't arrested when we were raided. I thought you'd doomed yourself and likely me too. But you're a clever one, Irena. You managed to mask your little deception so even the Germans couldn't sniff you out. But that's over now. The Jews were cut off when they sealed that damned ghetto. I'm not going to let you risk your own life, and the lives of our department, by letting you have access to them again."

"But sir—"

"Silence! There is no argument I'm going to listen to. We have enough problems out here among our own people. God knows there isn't enough food, enough medicine. These damned Germans want to exterminate us! I'm no anti-Semite, Irena, but they are not our own people, and it will be a miracle if we survive another winter under the Nazis, without spreading ourselves still thinner by trying to help those poor Jewish souls."

"If I did go into the ghetto, it would only be a little—"

"There is no little to spare. I'm talking about the survival of our race. If I had the resources, I would help them, but I don't, and I can't risk more of my people trying to give them something that I don't have to provide. Now look at me, Irena."

She was flustered but she met his eyes.

"I want your word that you will focus on your duties. You're the best I have at food distribution. I want you to put all your energy into those contacts in the country. Bring me more food, more wagons. Find me more families to feed—Polish families. I need your help to get our people through this crisis. Will you help me? Will you give yourself fully to our cause?"

"I'll have to think about it," she said finally.

"You do that, Irena. Think long and hard, because if you refuse, I must remove you from your position. I don't know if anybody else can give me what you have, but I can't let you kill us all. If the Germans close us down, and they've been damned near doing it for months now, then our people will get nothing. Thousands of families will starve. Polish families. And it will be on your head!"

"I understand, sir. Is that all?"

"Yes, that's all." He stood. "Please, Irena. I don't want you to go. We need you. Poland needs you. Let the Jews take care of themselves. Their fate is with the Germans, not with us." He took her hand, his eyes compassionate and friendly.

"Thank you, sir, I'll give you my decision by the end of the day."

She stormed out of the office, ignoring the secretary as she left. When she'd departed, she sprinted to the women's bathroom. Ripping open a stall door, she fell to her knees, vomiting violently into the bowl.

How could he do this to her? He was going to fire her? For what? Trying to save people's lives? What difference did it make if they were Poles or Jews? They were all citizens of Poland. They were all under the Nazi yoke! Why couldn't he see with open eyes? The Germans planned to kill them all, to grind them into dust so they could make a new world for the Germans alone. If the Poles let the Jews die, Adam, Ewa, and Ala, they were simply hastening their own destruction. She couldn't let that happen. But what could she do? He wanted her commitment. She didn't care about that. They were just words. But if he'd already known what she was doing, then he must have ways of tracking her. And he'd watch her twice as closely now!

There was nothing she could do. The resistance had asked her to keep feeding the Jews, but several months had passed now since she'd been able to do so. She was clearly far down on their list of priorities. She was going to have to sit back and do her job and wait for something to change. In the meantime, Adam was behind those walls. So were Ala and Ewa. Who knew what was happening to them!

She shook her head, wiping the tears from her cheeks. She wouldn't do it. She wasn't going to wait and see. With new resolve, she turned and headed back upstairs. She stormed past Jan's secretary and burst through the door, slamming it behind her.

"What's the meaning of this?" he demanded, his face a mask of fury.

"You are going to get me into the ghetto."

He sputtered and his face flushed. "I can't believe you, Irena," he said, reaching for his phone. "I see I have no choice but to terminate—"

"You're going to do what I ask if you cherish your safety."

He lowered the phone, his eyes widening. "Are you threatening me?" He rose from his desk. "Get out!" he demanded.

She ignored his order. "I have connections. With the resistance. They want me helping the Jews. If I don't have a pass by the end of the week, I am going to go to them, and I can't vouch for what they will do to you."

He shook his head in disbelief. "You've lost your mind, Irena. You're threatening me with the Polish resistance? You're damned lucky I don't report you to the Germans right now! Get out of my office! You're dismissed from your post!"

She fled back to her office in shock. He'd called her bluff. Now she had nothing, no access to the ghetto and not even her job. She reached her desk and began collecting her personal belongings.

She heard a knock at the door. Jan was there. He refused to look at her. Reaching out, he handed her a document. "What is this?" she asked.

"Your pass," he said. His voice was mechanical and emotionless. "I'm naming you an inspector for communicable diseases in the Jewish Quarter. You will begin your duties immediately."

Irena couldn't believe it. "Thank you, sir! You have no idea how—"

"Don't thank me, Irena," he said, his voice a menacing whisper. "If you're caught doing anything wrong, it will be on you. You'll get no help from me or this office, do you understand?"

"Yes, sir."

"And if you ever threaten me again, you'll lose your job that day, whatever the consequences."

"I understand, sir."

Jan marched out without another word. She felt the sting of his rebuke, but it was nothing compared to her sweet elation. She had won! What's more, she was going to the ghetto! It was too late today, but she would be there first thing in the morning. She had official license to visit every day, from now on. She would see Adam by this time tomorrow! She'd abandoned her faith long ago, but she found herself head down, thanking the universe, or God, or fate, for bringing this miracle to her.

Irena stood at the corner of Gęsia and Smocza streets, frozen in stunned silence. Snow covered the pavement, four or five centimeters thick. Frozen drifts of a meter or more hugged the buildings. Everywhere she looked she saw suffering she'd never encountered in her life. The first thing she'd noticed on arriving in the ghetto was the density of the population. She remembered how packed the quarter had felt before the wall went up, but it was now far worse. There were people everywhere, shoulder to shoulder, pushing past each other, sometimes violently, as they scrambled through the snow and the cold wherever they were going. Each person wore the star of David now, a blue star on a white background in a cloth square, on the upper right arm.

A few meters away from Irena, a mother and her child sat in one of the drifts. They were clad in rags. The child was barefoot in the snow. The little girl's eye sockets were sucked in so deeply she looked like a living skeleton. Neither could move or seemed to have the strength to beg. The only way Irena could tell they were alive was the shallow rise and fall of breath beneath their thin shawls.

She approached them and reached out, dropping the few zlotys she had with her into the open hand of the mother. She didn't even have the strength to close her fingers around the money. The crumpled notes lay there for a few seconds, and then blew off in the wind, to be picked up by a mob of desperate pedestrians that fought over this pitiful scrap of currency. A man rushed forward, arms swinging, knocking people out of his way until he grabbed the zlotys. He laughed maniacally and sat down, notes grasped firmly in his hands, gibbering to himself.

There were starving people everywhere as she walked along. Worse yet were the dead. Every block there was at least one body lying on the pavement, naked except for newspapers covering them along with a thin layer of snow. The pedestrians ignored these corpses as if they didn't exist, but Irena could not stop staring at them.

There were police and soldiers everywhere as well: Germans, Polish in their blue uniforms, and the Jewish police with their yellow Stars of David on their caps. Irena noticed that the Jewish police looked well fed, and not affected by the terrible conditions as much as the rest of the population.

Here and there she observed civilians who also seemed to be getting along well. She spotted a family crossing Gęsia near Zamenhofa. The father led the mother and two young children through the crowd. They were dressed in warm furs and hats. They wore gloves and boots. They held their heads high, as if they were above the crowd, beyond it. Irena wondered how this family had managed to maintain their health and their position amidst the chaos of the ghetto.

"Help me." A young man stepped in front of her, his hand out. "Spare some zlotys."

"I don't have any," Irena responded, starting to move around him. He blocked her.

"Your zlotys."

"I told you, I don't have any. I gave them away."

He grabbed her wrist, squeezing and twisting. She gasped at the pain. She searched this way and that, but nobody was paying any attention to them.

"Your zlotys now."

"Irena!" She heard a familiar voice and turned to see Ala hurrying up to her. Her friend wore a heavy blue wool coat and a white nurse's hat. Her eyes flashed steel. She screamed at the young man in Yiddish. Irena caught some of the words but didn't understand everything that was said. The youth hesitated, responding with a few words but he was cut off by Ala, who pressed in, grabbing Irena's arm as if she were a possession and pulling her away. The young tough held on for a moment more before releasing her and disappearing into the crowd.

"Ala, thank God you're here."

"What are you doing in the ghetto?" her friend demanded. "You have to be careful. He could have picked you to the bone."

"I have an epidemic pass," Irena responded.

"What do you know about disease?" Ala asked in surprise. "You're a food distribution expert."

"It was the only way I could get back in."

Ala laughed at this and threw her arms around Irena, holding her close for a few moments. "Well, I'm glad you're here. Whatever the reason. I'm on my way to see Ewa, will you join me?"

"Ewa?" Irena's spirit soared. "She's okay?"

"She's alive, at least. She's helping Dr. Korczak at the orphanage. I'll show you." Ala turned and marched down the sidewalk, weaving in and out of the mass that pressed around her. Irena followed, falling behind at first until she learned how to maneuver in the crowded space.

"Look at you," Irena said, her eyes running the outline of Ala's uniform. "You're a nurse still?"

Ala smiled grimly. "*The* nurse in a way. They've named me chief nurse of the ghetto."

"Congratulations."

Her friend scoffed. "It's hardly a privilege. We have plenty of doctors and nurses but hardly a drop of medicine. There are five hundred thousand Jews wedged in here. Disease is rampant—although the greatest killer is starvation. The Germans don't give us a tenth of what we need to survive. The Judenrat keeps pushing for more food, but the Germans refuse. Something about shortages due to the war effort. Is it the same in Aryan Poland?"

Irena shook her head. "They've cut back, but nothing like this. We can't get meat generally, and hardly any eggs, but there's plenty of vegetables and bread. What you can't get with your ration card you can find on the black market, if you're careful."

"It's the same here but worse. A fraction of the families have enough wealth or connections; they get a better share of the rations, or buy what they need on the market. There is smuggling everywhere."

Irena was surprised. "Smuggling into the ghetto? Even with the wall?"

"Hundreds do it every day. The Germans hunt them, usually shooting them on the spot. But there are too many. Look, just there," she said, pointing at a streetcar passing in front of them. As Irena watched, the car slowed down. A young man on the trolley threw several sacks toward the crowd, where they were caught by waiting people with arms outstretched. These men turned and ran off into the masses. Irena observed a German policeman across the street who had watched the whole thing. He nodded to the man on the trolley and then turned around, ignoring the crime.

"That German looked the other way."

"Yes. He's probably in the pay of the smuggler."

"I would never believe a German would accept a bribe," said Irena.

"Oh, they're human enough, at least some of them. And thank God for that. Without the smuggled food we'd all already be dead. But the distribution is uneven. As always, the wealthy and powerful prosper and the poor suffer and die."

"It's not fair."

"True enough, Irena, but it's the way of things. Let's go."

They continued, making their way toward the southern section of the ghetto, the "little ghetto." Finally, they arrived at a large building at 16 Sienna Street. The orphanage was a five-story limestone structure with steps leading up to the first floor. Dozens of windows faced the street and Irena could see faces poking out from behind curtains, watching them as they climbed the stairs into the entranceway.

"This is Dr. Korczak's orphanage. He has two hundred children here," explained Ala.

"So many?"

"If he had room, there would be a thousand more. Countless parents have died from the cold and the lack of food. There are more orphans every day."

They climbed the stairs and entered the building. There was a large reception area. Children were everywhere, sitting at tables with puzzles, the little ones on the floor in a circle, playing with toys. Multiple doors lined the walls.

"They lead to other parts of the building," Ala explained. "There are offices too, for the staff. We have our own small clinic here. I try to keep at least one nurse on duty seven days a week."

"Is there enough food?"

Ala nodded. "Usually. Dr. Korczak has quite the reputation. He's a special project of the Judenrat. There are also donations from influential families. The children here do as well as anyone does in the ghetto. It's the ones on the street who suffer the worst."

Children came up to Ala, hugging her and laughing. They knew her here, Irena realized. She was about to comment on this when a door opened, and she saw a familiar face. Ewa was there, accompanied by Dr. Korczak, whom she had met before, and another woman she thought she recognized, but couldn't place. Ewa flew into her arms. Irena laughed, holding her friend, then turned to greet Dr. Korczak.

The orphanage director was a thin waif of a man in an impeccable woolen suit. His round glasses rested on the bridge of his nose, adding weight to his dignity. His eyes brimmed with intelligence and a balancing dose of sadness. "Irena, it's been so long. I hope you've been well. How did you find your way into our lovely ghetto? Are you coming to help us?"

"Dr. Korczak," she said, taking his hand warmly. "It's so wonderful to see you."

"How did you get in?"

"I have an epidemic pass from the welfare department."

"Well, we have plenty of diseases for you," he joked. "Typhus, typhoid, diphtheria. Our German friends have created a cauldron of infection."

"I will be coming every day from now on," Irena promised. "If there is anything I can do for you."

"And who is this?" asked the other woman.

"Let me introduce you," said Ala. There seemed to be an odd strain to her voice as she said this. "Irena, this is my cousin by marriage, Dwojra Grynberg. But you may know her as Wiera Gran."

"The famous singer?" asked Irena.

"I don't know about all of that," said Wiera, raven hair flowing out of a rose-colored cloche with a wide tan ribbon. She arched an eyebrow and flashed a wry smile, emphasized by her high cheekbones. "Besides," she said. "Nobody is famous in the ghetto."

"You're too modest," said Ala. "Wiera is still in high demand, even in this hell. She performs daily at the Café Sztuka on Leszno Street."

"There are cafés in the ghetto?" asked Irena in surprise.

"Like I said," explained Ala. "The wealthy and powerful still prosper. They demand their entertainments, and Wiera is happy to indulge them. Aren't you, Cousin?"

"Now let's not be rude," retorted Wiera. "To each their own skill. You were a nurse before the war and now you're the lead nurse here. I was a singer. What should I do? Try to be a nurse? I'd kill all my patients." She laughed. "I'm trying to survive, just like you."

"She does more than survive," interjected Ewa. "She gives heavily to the orphanage. Without people like Wiera, we would have been shut down long ago."

Irena saw Dr. Korczak nod in agreement. "Yes indeed, Wiera has been a tremendous friend to us."

"And now I shall be your friend," she said to Irena, her eyes softening. "If there is any way I can help you."

"Thank you so much," she replied.

"Ewa, why don't you take a break and visit with your friends here," said Dr. Korczak. "I have a little more business with Wiera, then we can meet after lunchtime and go over some logistics." He turned to Irena. "So wonderful to see you."

"You as well," she said. "I look forward to learning how I can help you."

"I'm sure you will be of wonderful assistance." He bowed and turned to leave.

Wiera turned to Irena. "I look forward to seeing you again. I've heard wonderful things about you from my cousin. You must come visit me soon."

"I will," Irena responded.

"Snake," hissed Ala as her cousin walked out of earshot.

"Why do you hate her so much?" Irena asked.

"She's never been any good," said Ala. "Always the self-promoter and schemer. Now she makes money on the backs of our people. Not to mention her connections. She consorts with the worst of the ghetto, and with the Germans."

"You don't know that," said Ewa. "Those are rumors. Look

what she does here. Without her help, these children would starve. You're doing your part, Ala, and she's doing hers."

"Believe your illusions if you wish. I won't give her a grain of trust." Ala turned to Irena. "Now, enough unpleasantness, what shall we do? Would you like to see my hospital? A tour of the ghetto? How do we make our long-lost friend welcome in our humble Jewish Quarter?"

"Adam."

Ala smiled. "How did I know you would say that. I'm surprised the topic hasn't come up sooner."

"Do you know where he is?"

"He doesn't leave his home, by all accounts," said Ewa.

"Can we visit him?"

"Certainly," said Ala. "It's not so far."

The three of them left the orphanage and marched back out onto the swarming streets. As they walked along, Ewa and Ala filled her in on stories of the ghetto: the food, the smuggling, the raids and killings, the starving children, the disease and death. She tried to listen, but her mind was focused on Adam. She hadn't seen him in so long. Now she would finally be reunited with him. They'd left on difficult terms last time, but she was sure that all would be forgiven when she was face-to-face with him.

They made their way through the streets as quickly as they could, weaving through the throng. Irena noticed that Ala received many greetings, and respectful bows. Her friend was a person of importance here, she realized, and clearly well respected.

Finally, they reached Adam's street. About midway down the block they found a nondescript three-story building. They entered the dimly lit corridor and climbed the two flights of stairs to the top floor. There was a stale stench to the hallway, a stagnant reek like wet laundry left too long in a washer. Irena could feel her heart thumping in her chest. Blood rushed to her ears. What would she say to him? She tried to fight down the emotions. She was with her friends and would not be able to show everything she wanted.

"Here we are," Ala said, finding a door about halfway down. She knocked lightly and waited a minute. There was no answer. She rapped the wood harder. She heard shuffling inside. The door opened a crack. Irena saw Adam's eyes staring out in fear. The door closed and there was a rustling inside as he fumbled with the latch. He opened again and he was there. Her Adam.

Her elation froze into anguish. He was pale, ill, so thin his skin was transparent. He stared at them with a dull expression as if he didn't recognize them. His back was hunched over and his breath rattled in his chest. He was dying.

Chapter 12
New Ventures

January 1941
Warsaw Ghetto, Poland

Irena rushed into the apartment. Adam slumped to the floor even as she reached for him. She stood frozen, unsure what to do, but Ala was already there, taking his vitals with expert hands. "He's starving," she said. "But that's not the problem. Severe dehydration. We've got to get him medical care right away."

"Will he be all right?" Irena asked.

Ala looked up. "It's too early to tell. We must get fluids into him immediately. Ewa, get to the hospital as quickly as you can and find some help. We need a cart and some help to carry him."

"I'll go with you," offered Irena.

"No, I need you here with me."

Ewa nodded and raced down the hallway.

Irena turned back to Ala and Adam. "What do we do?" she asked.

"Get me some water," Ala ordered. Irena rushed into the

apartment, wading through the litter of clothes and crumpled papers until she reached the sink. She fumbled for a cup and twisted the faucet. Nothing came out.

"It's not working!" she shouted.

"Go to the neighbors."

Irena sprinted out of the apartment and down the hallway. She beat on the first door she came to, but nobody answered. Moving to the next apartment she repeated the violent knocking. This time somebody answered, a pair of terrified eyes peering from behind the crack in the door.

"I need water," Irena screamed, trying to force the door open. The chain prevented her from entering.

The eyes behind the door stared at her for a moment and then the head nodded. The door opened and she saw an elderly gentleman was there, his wife hiding behind him. She ran into the flat and moved to the sink.

"Don't bother," the man said behind her. "It hasn't worked in months."

"What then?" she demanded, frantic and angry.

He hobbled to the kitchen counter and retrieved a metal pitcher. He approached her cautiously, as if she would attack him, and poured some water into her cup. The liquid was discolored and smelled rusty, but she didn't care. She thanked him and turned, moving as quickly as she could toward the door without spilling the liquid.

It seemed an eternity to move down the hallway without losing the precious water. She finally made it and turned back into Adam's apartment. He still lay on the floor. Ala cradled his head in her lap. She looked up in relief when she saw Irena return. "Hurry," she pleaded.

Irena bent down and carefully offered the cup. "Help me tip his head back," Ala ordered.

Irena moved behind Adam and lifted his neck. Ala shoved her fingers into his mouth and pulled the lips apart, forcing his mouth open. She pressed the cup against his lips and tipped a little water in. Adam sputtered and coughed. Some of the liquid dripped out of his mouth.

"He's not taking it," said Irena. "Give him the rest."

Ala shook her head. "He took a little. In a minute, I'll give him another sip. You can't give him a bunch at one time. His body can't handle it. He must be reintroduced slowly. What he needs is an IV, but we must wait for that. This will help a bit until they get here."

"Is he going to make it?" Irena repeated.

"I don't know. He's very weak and it doesn't look like he's eaten in a week." She looked up, giving Irena a reassuring look. "Don't you worry though. He's young and he was healthy before. There's an excellent chance he'll be fine, once we get some fluids into him."

Irena felt a hot cocktail of emotion wash over her. She heard footsteps clambering on the stairwell and along the corridor. Help was here. Ewa appeared in the doorway along with a couple of men. They held a canvas stretcher supported by two thick wooden poles.

Irena moved out of the way as the men went to work, laying the stretcher onto the floor and pulling Adam gently into place. With a grunt they lifted him and maneuvered out of the apartment. The hallway was too narrow, and they had to angle Adam sharply to get him through. His arm fell out of the stretcher and wedged against the doorframe. Adam gave out a groan of pain.

"Stop!" screamed Irena. She moved forward and disentangled him, pulling his arm back into place. "Now you can go."

With Ala in the lead, they lumbered along the hallway and down the stairs. The men huffed and puffed as they carried Adam awkwardly down the narrow stairwell. Finally, they reached the street and were able to increase their speed, Ala shouting at bystanders to move out of the way.

They were a mile or more from the hospital, and each moment was agony for Irena. Adam shivered under a thick blanket and his head lolled back and forth. "Hurry!" she demanded.

"We're going as fast as we can," retorted one of the men. "If you think you can do better, you're welcome to take an end."

"Don't worry," assured Ewa. "He's going to be all right. We're nearly there. Look."

Irena saw that they'd reached a building with a large red cross embossed crudely on a plywood sign tacked over the door. A nurse and a doctor stood at the top of the entryway, holding the doors open and motioning for Ewa. Two orderlies rushed out and down the stairs, taking over the handles of the stretcher. The stretcher bearers doubled over, breathing heavily as the orderlies rushed up the stairs and into the hospital. Irena and Ewa followed as Adam was transferred onto a rolling table and whisked down the hallway and through a set of double doors. Ala turned at the entrance and blocked Irena, her hands held up. "Stay here," she ordered. "The staff needs some time."

Irena tried to push past her, but Ala refused to budge. "You would only be in the way. Let me do my job. I'll come for you as soon as I can."

Irena resisted for a few moments longer, but Ewa reached up from behind and held her arms. She struggled for a second and then nodded and stepped back. Ala rushed through the doors and they were left there alone in the vacant corridor, the hallway suddenly quiet and dark.

Irena felt the tears welling up and she collapsed on the hard floor, her breath coming in sobs. Ewa was there, kneeling down, a hand on her back, whispering words of compassion. She wept hot tears, letting out all the frustration of the last few months. She'd waited so long to see him. Week after week of uncertainty and fear. Now she had made it into the ghetto only to find him on the verge of death. Had they found him in time? Had she risked her life obtaining this pass only to lose him forever?

She lay there for a long time, slowly pulling herself together. The cold, hard floor felt good, drawing her back to reality. She clung to the surface, her face pressed against the tiles, her breath coming in ragged spurts. After a half hour she was sufficiently recovered to sit up. She felt better. She could face what would happen next. She had friends here, companions who loved her and supported her no matter what the result.

"That's right," Ewa echoed, as if she could read her thoughts. "Everything will be all right. No matter what."

"Thank you for being here for me," Irena said.

"Always and forever, my friend. Now let's sit somewhere a little more comfortable." Ewa drew Irena up and led her to the waiting room. There were seats and some newspapers strewn about a worn cardboard table. Irena scanned the headlines. Rubbish. The papers told of German victories over the English. The lead story predicted the capitulation of the lone remaining German enemy at any time. There was no way to know whether the stories were true or not, as the Germans carefully censored the information released to the Polish population, but she wouldn't be surprised if it did turn out to be accurate. The vaunted French and English allies had done nothing to help them during the war or to ease their suffering in the past year. Then the Germans had invaded and defeated the French almost as quickly as they had the Poles. The English couldn't possibly last much longer. The superhuman Germans would reign supreme through all of Europe.

They sat there for hours as the afternoon light dimmed into evening. Ewa periodically talked to Irena, trying to engage her in conversation, but she could only nod or give short responses, her mind lost in fear for Adam and despair at the condition of her nation, her city, and her friends. The door opened periodically and she would look up, hope in her heart, but again and again these interruptions were medical staff coming and going.

Finally, Ala appeared in the doorway. She looked exhausted but she was smiling. "It's going to be okay," she said.

"Thank God," said Irena. "Can I see him now?"

Ala nodded and motioned for her to follow. Irena rushed after her. Her friend led her back down the hallway and through the double doors. They walked farther along, eventually coming to a door about two thirds of the way down a second corridor. "He's in here," said Ala. "You can visit for a few minutes, but that's all," she said sternly. "Then come see me. We have some things to discuss."

Irena sprinted past her and into the room. Adam was there in a hospital bed. An IV was attached to a tall metal hanger, a tube extending down into a needle in Adam's right hand. He was awake. He looked drawn and exhausted, but he was smiling and there was life in his eyes again. "Hello. Irena."

She rushed to his side and threw her arms around him.

"Careful," he whispered, chuckling to himself. "You'll detach me, and we'll have to start all over again."

"Thank God you're safe," she whispered.

He reached up and took her hand. She felt electricity sizzle through her entire body. "Thanks to you."

"What's happened to you? Where's your family? How did they let this happen to you?"

"They live one building over," Adam responded. "I haven't visited them much. It's my fault they've stopped trying to see me. They had no idea things had got so bad."

"How can they be excused?"

"It's my own responsibility. I've shunned them. Since the wall went up I've . . . well, let's just say I haven't been myself. My family tried to help. But I wouldn't let them. Even my—"

"Don't say your *wife*."

"That's what she is. Even if we are separated. Yes, Irena, even she has tried to help me, but I've refused. I turned into myself, reading my few remaining books, trying to understand what is going on." His eyes turned the color of molten coal. "I've been angry. Furious at the fools in charge of this country for letting us down. At the Germans, the Russians. Even at you." He pulled his hand away.

"At me? How can that be?"

"You've spent the last months in Aryan Poland, still living some kind of life. We've been here starving, dying. The world has forgotten us."

"I haven't," she insisted, grabbing his hand again. "Every day I fought to get back in here. It took me this long to obtain a pass. You know I would have come on the first day if I could."

He hesitated and then nodded. "I know that. But you must understand, when you are here, in the heart of despair, it's easy to blame everyone, even those you know care about you. Anyone who isn't in the same crucible as yourself."

"I'm here now."

"Yes, but you have a pass. You can come and go."

"Don't say that. I'm doing everything I can."

"I know you are. I'm just so bitter." He closed his eyes. "Perhaps I'm angriest at myself."

"But why?"

"Look at your friend Ala. At Ewa. They are fighting, working, helping our people. All I've done is brood and weep. I've sat in my apartment letting other people do the fighting for me."

"You didn't have a choice. Look how weak you are."

The door opened. "Irena, your time is up."

She felt her frustration overwhelm her. "Just another minute," she pleaded.

Ala looked at her with understanding. "Just one more then." The door closed.

"Tell me you are not angry with me."

"I'm not. Just with myself."

"Stop talking like that. You must concentrate on getting well, then we will get through this together."

"You'll keep coming back?"

"Every day. I can come and go now as I please."

He took her hand again. "I'd like that. When you are near, the darkness seems to fade away a little."

"I have to go. Ala is just outside the door, I'm sure, counting the seconds."

"You have a good friend there," said Adam. "She's a savior in the ghetto. Ewa too."

"You wait. When you're better, you'll do the same."

He closed his eyes again. "Perhaps."

She reached down and touched her lips to his cheek. He was warm again and the touch of his skin sent a chill down her spine. "I'll be back tomorrow. Get some rest."

She let herself out as quietly as possible. Sure enough, Ala was waiting just outside the doorway.

"Will he be okay?" Irena asked.

"It appears so. For now."

"What do you mean?"

"He needs more than water. The crisis has passed but he needs food, Irena, a steady supply."

"Won't his family take care of him?"

"You don't understand how critical the situation is here. They may be doing about the same as him, or even worse. People are dying every day, Irena, by the hundreds."

"But they were wealthy. Can't they buy food?"

"For a time, perhaps. Who knows? The black-market items are sold at exorbitant prices. A single loaf of bread might cost a month of pre-war wages. Even the wealthy are running out of money."

"But you said people are still thriving."

"The smugglers themselves, and the collaborators with the

Germans. Some people in the Judenrat. The peddlers. Everyone else is dying—slow or quick."

"You seem to be doing okay," observed Irena. She regretted the words as soon as she said them.

A flash of anger passed Ala's eyes. "Gifts from friends and families for my work. All of it obtained honestly. Ewa is in the same boat. There is enough food at the orphanage to keep the workers alive and relatively healthy. We are the lucky ones."

"Of course. I didn't think otherwise for a moment. Please forgive my hasty words. It's been an unbelievable day."

Ala placed a hand on her shoulder. "I'm not angry and I understand. The ghetto is a shock for anyone not used to it."

"What can I do to help him?"

"You can bring him food."

"How could I manage that?"

"You are inspecting every day, correct? You have a pass? You can smuggle some bread in."

"Smuggle? But what if they search me?"

Ala looked at her grimly. "It's hard to say. They might simply take it. They might arrest you. Or—"

"Or they might shoot me then and there."

Ala nodded. "It's a risk. I'm not telling you that you should do it. But you're asking how you could help him."

"Can't I just bring in zlotys?"

"You don't have enough money to begin to buy food in here. Out in Aryan Poland, bread is still relatively cheap, is it not?"

Irena nodded.

"Then you must buy the food on the outside and bring it in."

When they rejoined Ewa she was horrified at Ala's proposal.

"You're signing her up for a death sentence," Ewa protested.

"Do you have another solution? Can you spare food from the orphanage for him?" asked Ala.

Ewa shook her head. "Not unless he worked there."

"It's the same at the hospital. We might give him a little, but we can't bring him enough to keep him healthy over time. If you want to save Adam, you're going to have to bring him food yourself. Once he's back to normal health, we might be able to find him work. But for the next month or so, he needs your help."

Ewa seemed to think it over and finally nodded. "I don't like it, but she's right. You're his best chance to survive."

Irena didn't hesitate. "I'll do it. I'll bring him what he needs, whatever the risk."

"Do you care about him so much?" asked Ewa.

"Don't ask her that," said Ala. "In these times, everyone has a right to decide what they are willing to risk their life for."

The next morning Irena rose early. In the darkness, she made a sandwich for her mother and left it on a plate near the bed. Sneaking out into the early morning, she made her way through the streets of Aryan Poland. She saw everything around her with new eyes. She felt ashamed. She'd felt sorry for herself for so long. She'd sulked because Poland was under German occupation. She couldn't buy new clothes or enjoy all the food and drinks she might want to have. She resented the German soldiers, the arrogant searches, the lack of coal and warmth.

Now she realized she was living in paradise. Aryan Warsaw was a heaven on earth compared to the ghetto. Nobody was dying out here—well, not many. Certainly, thousands had perished during the purges, but the Germans had forgotten the Poles in their newfound focus on the Jews. Food was adequate if not abundant here. The streets were empty, with room to stroll and breathe. She chastised herself for her moping and her attitude. She promised she would never complain again. She would live for her Jewish friends, for Adam. She would sacrifice for them, risk her life for them.

She stopped by a bakery and slid some zlotys over the counter. She'd pulled these notes from their emergency savings. There wasn't much left. She realized if she was going to keep Adam alive, she would have to come up with some kind of solution for money. Perhaps the resistance could help? She felt her frustration rise again. Why hadn't they given her a way to contact them? What was the point of her helping if they wouldn't assist her in return?

She shook these thoughts from her head. She had enough to worry about today. She ordered three loaves of bread and a little cheese. The baker wrapped the food up and she tucked the paper sack into the bottom of an oversized purse she'd brought. She placed her scarf and some papers over the top. The baker was watching her closely, his eyebrows raised. She turned and fled the store, not wanting to answer any questions. She would need to pack her bag somewhere else from now on, she realized. Best to pick another baker as well. This one seemed far too curious about what she was doing.

She walked along the street again, her heart in her throat. She was getting near the Twarda Street gate of the ghetto. She checked her purse to make sure her pass and papers were on top. The last thing she could afford was for some helpful policeman to start digging through her possessions, looking for her documents.

She reached the gate and joined the line to enter. There were a few people in front of her. The gate consisted of a narrow-arched entryway constructed into the wall. There were larger gates, some capable of allowing a car or wagon to enter, but she hoped that a smaller one might have fewer guards and attract less attention.

The entrance was guarded by two German soldiers. One stood slightly behind with his rifle in his hands, resting at his waist. The other perched at the entrance, barking questions and reviewing papers. There was also a Polish policeman, a "blue" who was standing slightly behind, a black baton in his hands. The German waved the first person in line through, then another. Despite the cold she was stifling in her clothing. She was sure she looked guilty and would be arrested on the spot. She tried to make her face as calm as possible but how could one tell what one really looked like to others?

Another person made it through, then another. Finally, she was standing before the guard. He was young, perhaps no more than twenty. He eyed her up and down, his face a set mask. "Where are your papers?" he demanded.

She fumbled for her bag and drew out her identification documents and the pass. He looked at the contents for a few moments and looked up at her, eyeing her suspiciously.

"What's in the bag?" he demanded.

Oh no. This is what she was afraid of. "Nothing," she stammered. "Just some notebooks and an extra scarf. I'm supposed to be taking notes on the number and type of diseases in the ghetto."

The guard took a step back. "You're exposed to diseases all day?"

"Yes," she responded.

The other guard laughed. "You should check her bag. Maybe you'll find some typhus inside."

The first soldier stared at her for another moment, as if considering what to do. He jerked his thumb, waving her past, looking beyond her at the next person.

Irena stumbled rapidly into the ghetto. She tried to remain calm, but her entire body erupted in excitement. She'd made it! She'd survived! She was defying the Germans, beating them at the game of life and death!

Once she was immersed into the crowd, she hurried along toward the hospital. She swam upstream through the throng, pushing her way through as she'd seen Ala do. Gone was the hesitancy, the gawking of yesterday that had pointed her out to everyone in the ghetto as a newcomer, a sucker, a target. Today she moved with purpose, confident, knowing she had beat the Germans and that she would defy hunger and save Adam. She arrived at the hospital a half hour later, found Ala, and made her way toward Adam's room.

"How's he doing today?" she asked.

"Much better. He seems greatly revived by the IV, and by seeing you."

Irena blushed. "I know he's married and so am I, but—"

"You don't have to explain anything to me. I meant what I said yesterday. Besides, you and Mietek haven't lived as husband and wife in years."

Irena stopped at the door, grabbing Ala's hand and giving it a squeeze. "Thank you for understanding. Although, frankly, there isn't anything going on between us."

Ala raised an eyebrow but didn't respond to that last statement. "Think nothing of it. Now let's go get Adam healthy." She turned the handle and entered the room. Adam was there and as Ala had said, he looked greatly recovered today. His skin had lost its pallor and he looked this way and that, his eyes attentive and his movements firm. He smiled when he saw Irena.

She went to him and bent down, holding him for a moment. His hands were warm on her back. She didn't want to let go but Ala was there, and she pulled away, turning to busy herself with her bag as she fought down the buzzing thrill coursing through her mind. She pulled out the package and unwrapped the contents. Adam took one of the loafs and greedily stuffed the bread into his mouth.

"Not too fast!" Ala ordered. "A little at a time." She picked up the other two loaves and all the cheese. "He can have one loaf for now but that's it."

"But he's starving," Irena protested.

"It's the same as the water," said Ala, chewing on a curl of her hair. "When the body reaches this point, it has to be introduced to food again slowly, otherwise his whole system will shut down, he'll end up with dysentery, and he'll be worse off than he was before."

Irena nodded, not understanding. "I'm so glad you're here."

"Of course. He can eat this over the next few days."

"That might be just as well."

Ala looked up. "What do you mean?"

"You were right about the cost. Food is not too much on the Aryan side. Still, I don't have any real savings. A few more days and I'll be out."

Ala thought about that for a moment and then she handed Irena one loaf and half the cheese.

"What do you want me to do with this?"

"Sell it."

"Where?"

"Anywhere. Keep an eye out for the Germans, but if you pull this out on the street, you'll have fifty offers before you can get a word out."

Irena felt a hot flush in her cheeks. "I'm not good at selling."

Ala laughed. "You won't have to say a word, my dear. Just listen to the offers and take the highest one. But make sure it's cash to you right then and there. Don't let them walk off to get the money, and don't go anywhere with anyone. You make them count out the money to you right then, before you hand over the food. Then you turn and walk right out of the ghetto. Don't linger for a moment. Others will be watching for you."

"Don't tell me they would attack—"

"You remember what happened yesterday? Trust nobody."

"But these people are Jews, your people."

"They are people. That's just it. They are starving and desperate. If you're going to survive, Irena, you must forget your former life. Forget Poland before the war, even Poland before the ghetto. Remember that money and food are everything. It may save your life."

Irena nodded. "I'll go after a while."

Ala smiled with understanding. "Of course, but not too long. Same as yesterday, he needs his rest."

Irena spent an hour with Adam and then stepped out into the street. She felt nervous, almost worse than entering the gate. She laughed at herself. She'd always been terrified of selling. She was a social worker and had no experience in such things. *I'd rather risk my life with the Germans than offer bread to a starving crowd.* If it wasn't for Adam, she would have refused. But she didn't have the money for the food he would need in the long run. There was no choice in the matter.

She moved a few hundred meters away from the hospital, keeping an eye out for Germans. If anything went wrong, she didn't want to be associated with Ala, or with Adam. She watched for a time and when she was satisfied there were no Nazis around, she reached into her purse, pulling the loaf and the cheese out. Instantly she was hemmed in from all directions. Children and mothers stared in awe at the food, as if she'd conjured them from magic. She heard the pleas from all around her, but she forced herself to ignore them, to shove her compassion and sorrow down and to focus on the other voices, the ones calling out numbers. She was stunned at the offers: five hundred zlotys, a thousand, two thousand. She turned to the man who made the last offer, a middle-aged person in a business suit and hat.

"Sold," she said.

He shoved his way forward, reaching his hand out.

"Your money first," she said, remembering Ala's advice.

He reached into his pocket and pulled out a wad of cash. Irena had never seen so many zlotys in one place before. He counted out the notes and handed them to her, his hands high in the air above grasping fingers. She took the currency and a thought struck her. "For the loaf only."

"No, for the cheese and the bread."

Everything inside her screamed to agree but she held back, feeling brave and determined. "No. Only the bread."

"Another thousand for the cheese," he said finally.

"Agreed." She took the extra zlotys and handed him the food. She stuffed the money into her pocket and retreated as quickly as she could, away from the exchange. She expected to hear a whistle, the sound of the police closing in, but there was nothing. She strode away, her heart pounding, knowing she might be followed by Jews willing to rob or even kill her. She weaved through the masses and eventually reached one of the gates. She passed through, showing the contents of her bag without even being asked, the zlotys safe in her pocket. Another few minutes and she was free. She rushed out into the empty streets of Aryan Warsaw, her veins coursing with elation. She had made it! She'd survived. She'd brought Adam food and what was more, she'd sold on the black market and had more money in her hands now than she'd ever had in her entire life.

Over the coming weeks she repeated this miracle day after day. She purchased bread and cheese along with cakes and pastries, stuffing all the items into her bag. She made her way through the same gate. The guard barely talked to her now, keeping his distance because of her association with disease. She brought food to Adam and sold some for more money, repeating the cycle. She was making more zlotys than she'd ever dreamed of. She used some of it to improve her life at home. She bought better food on the black market. Her mother's health improved along with Adam's. But the majority she brought back into the ghetto, donating heavily to the orphanage and the hospital. Each day she also brought extra food, giving some to the starving children on the street, to the desperate mothers, seeking some miracle to keep their family alive for another day; or to Rubinstein the clown, an elderly beggar who made his money pulling faces at the Germans, at risk of his life.

Over time, she became another institution in the ghetto, like

Ala, a person known to the population. Another little savior helping them hold hell and death away for at least another day.

"Hold a moment, please." The voice caught her by surprise. She'd grown so used to seeing the same German each day at the gate that she'd hurried through. She looked up. A German officer was there. Older, perhaps thirty. He towered over her, pale blue eyes glaring at her. "Your papers, please."

She fumbled for her documents. Fortunately, they were right on top in her bag. She handed them to the lieutenant. "I inspect facilities to look for disease," she explained.

He examined the documents, reading them carefully. She relaxed. Everything was in order.

"What's in the bag?" The question caught her off guard.

"Just . . . ah, my notebooks," she stammered.

The officer stared at her bulging bag, full of bread and foodstuffs.

"That doesn't look like only some notebooks. Open your bag for me."

"But, sir, the diseases."

"I don't care about that right now. Open up your bag."

She hesitated. She looked over and saw a familiar face. It was the other guard. He was at his post just behind the gate, as usual. She saw recognition in his eyes and something else. Was it sympathy? She prayed for a miracle, that he might step forward and help her, but he was a private, a nobody.

"Open the bag!" the officer shouted.

She pulled the two ends of the satchel apart and showed him the contents; her papers and her shawl were on top.

He stared into the bag for a moment and then he reached out, pulling it from her. "Let go," he demanded. She still held on, petrified by fear. "Let go this instant or I'll have you shot!" he snapped.

She relented. She felt dizzy. She hung her head, staring at the ground. Hoping for anything, anyone, to save her. She heard the officer sifting through the contents, and he gave out a loud murmur of triumph. "Look at this," he said, talking to the other guard. "Notebooks indeed. There are ten loaves of bread in here, and sausages. This Jew-loving bitch eats better than we do."

She turned to leave, hoping against hope he would let her go, but she felt his hands on her in an instant. "Not so fast. You will have to answer for these."

She turned to look at the young guard again, but his face was set in a frown now. There was nothing he could do. He raised his rifle, covering her while the officer ran his hands up and down her body. In any moment he would find the zlotys. She would be arrested, or worse—he might shoot her on the spot. The world was closing in on her.

Chapter 13

Kaji

January 1941
Warsaw Ghetto, Poland

The officer pulled Irena through the gate, shouting at the guard to secure the entrance and close the gate to anyone else. She tried to resist but his hands held her in an iron vise. Tears stung her vision. Her sight was a blur, her mind a fog. She closed her eyes, waiting for the bullet.

"Lieutenant, what do you have there?" She heard a woman's voice, a vaguely familiar one.

"Stay away," ordered the lieutenant. "This is none of your business."

"Everything in the ghetto is my business," the woman said, laughing. "Including you."

"Who the hell are you?"

"Don't you recognize me, Lieutenant? I've seen you at your table, up front, every night for the past month."

"Wiera Gran?" the lieutenant asked. Irena was stunned. She wiped her eyes with the back of her sleeve and strained them, the scene before her slowly coming into focus. The lieutenant still had her by the arm, but he was facing away from her now and toward a beautiful woman a few feet away. The young guard was looking at her as well, clearly transfixed.

"That's right," she confirmed.

"It's nice to see you," the lieutenant confirmed. "But I have business right now."

"What kind of business is that?"

"This woman is a smuggler."

Wiera glanced at the bread. "A smuggler, over that? It looks like a picnic to me. Why don't you let her go and talk to me instead?"

The lieutenant stammered. "I have a job to do."

Wiera laughed. "We all have jobs to do. Look, I know this woman. I asked her to bring me some loaves for the café. We're a little short. You wouldn't want to starve tonight, would you?"

The lieutenant looked back at Irena. "Is that true?"

Irena was confused, but she played along. "Yes."

"Why didn't you tell me?"

"You didn't give me a chance to respond."

"You said you had notebooks in there."

"I do, but I also had this food for the café."

"Why should we worry about that?" Wiera said, stepping up to hook her arm through the lieutenant's. "Why don't you let her take her things and we can have a little walk. I know you like Mozart. I've seen you request it. But you've never told me why."

The officer hesitated, his face filling with color. He looked back and forth at the two women. Finally, he handed Irena's bag back to her. "Get going," he ordered. "And next time tell me up front what you have."

"Yes, sir," she said, turning to hurry off. When she made it to the safety of the crowd, she turned around. The officer was not watching her. He was several hundred meters down the wall, walking arm in arm with Wiera, as if they were taking a stroll through the park.

Irena hurried to the hospital. When she arrived, she did not go to see Adam immediately, as was her habit. Instead she sought out Ala. She was still shaking when she found her friend.

"What is it?" Ala asked, recognizing immediately that something was wrong. Irena told her what had happened.

"It's a miracle you survived," Ala said finally. She shook her head. "I don't understand it. Wiera risked her life for you." She stared at the floor for a few moments. "Perhaps I've misjudged her."

"It's hard to recognize friend from foe in these times."

"True enough, although I trust you entirely."

Irena managed a weak laugh. "You do now. Remember, it wasn't so long ago you thought I was a German collaborator."

"I never thought you would betray us to the Germans. I just thought you shouldn't work for them. I was a fool, and that's long in the past."

Irena still felt the fear coursing through her. She'd stood a hair's breadth from arrest or worse. "I can't keep doing this, Ala."

Her friend smiled and took her hand. "I don't think you have to. Adam is almost back to full health. I have even better news on that front. Ewa has found him work in the orphanage. He's going to be hired as a teacher."

"That's the perfect job for him—well, a professor would be the best of all, but anything to use his mind. He has so much in that head of his." Irena looked at her watch. "I'd better go see our convalescent."

"You won't find him here."

"What?"

"He was discharged this morning. He said he was going to go home and rest today. He's starting with Dr. Korczak tomorrow."

Irena kissed Ala on the cheek. "Thank you. Thank you for everything you've done."

"No, thank you, Irena. You're the one who saved him. In the ghetto, it's one life at a time."

A half hour later, Irena stood at the open door of Adam's apartment. She was amazed at the change in him. He had gained some weight and he looked young and strong in his shirt and tie. The old fire danced in his eyes as he brought her into his room. The apartment itself was transformed. When she'd been here last there was garbage everywhere, but now the interior was clean, with books and papers stacked neatly and a warm fire at a simple hearth.

"All this in just one day?" she asked.

"I knew someone might be stopping by, so I had preparations to make."

She blushed. "Have you seen your family?"

"Not yet. But I will. They visited me in the hospital a few times."

"And your wife?" She felt a surge of jealousy as she muttered the question.

He looked away. "Once."

"Everything looks in order," she said stiffly. "I'm glad you've recovered." She turned to leave but a hand on her wrist stopped her.

"Don't go," he said. "Sit and have some tea."

She acquiesced and stepped farther into the apartment, taking a seat on his sofa in the middle of the room. She sat there for a few minutes, battling her emotions while he busied himself at the counter, boiling water and preparing the tea.

She knew she wasn't being fair. He was married and his wife had a right to see him. Irena was married too. Besides, they were separated just like Mietek and her. But he'd brought his wife near him in the ghetto, along with his wife's family and his. Didn't that show something more? She tried to imagine if the roles were reversed. What if she was in the ghetto and Mietek was nearby? What if his family was in need? She would have done the same, she realized. No matter what their marital situation was, she would move the world to save his life.

"Here you go," he said, stepping around a low table and taking a seat next to her. He set down a small platter with a teapot and two cups. "I'm afraid we will have to miss the sandwiches. I don't have any provisions."

"I do," she remembered. She reached into her bag and retrieved the loaves of bread, the sausages and cheese. "We should enjoy these. They nearly cost me everything today."

"What do you mean?" he asked, concern carving deep creases in his forehead.

She told him about the gate, the near arrest, and Wiera's intervention.

"I told Ala that Wiera was a good person," he said finally. "I don't know why she dislikes her so much. I've wondered if it's the attention she gets."

"Ala's not like that."

Adam nodded. "Who knows what gets Ala upset? Still, Wiera has done nothing to create mistrust."

"Well, she does sing at that café, with the informers and Gestapo agents."

"Anyone with money goes to the Café Sztuka," responded Adam dismissively. "That doesn't make them all traitors. Besides, she's not a patron, she's an employee. If a singer wishes to eat, they must go to the audience. The paying crowd. They don't get to choose the content."

She watched him as he tore up the bread and crafted crude sandwiches with his hands. He was so much like the old Adam: witty and alive. She took a plate with a little food and a cup of the tea. She didn't feel hungry, but she played along, sipping the hot liquid and munching away at the meal. Her eyes never left him as he told her about the new job and what it would entail.

He would be teaching the classics to the children. Book by book they would explore the world—the real one, not this hell crafted by the Germans to deny these same children a future.

"I'll prepare them for the after. For the time when these bastards are defeated and gone. We'll have a whole new generation of Irenas and Adams."

"What about socialism and Marxism? Will you teach them that too? Not everyone in the orphanage might approve of that," she teased.

He laughed. "Perhaps a little crumb here and there. We can't raise another generation of right-wing fascists, that's for certain. That's one thing the Germans have done well. They've cured our people of their yearning for nationalism."

"At least for a generation," said Irena. "But people soon forget."

He set his tea down and took her hand, turning toward her. She felt the excitement coursing through her. He watched her for long moments, his eyes taking in every part of her face as his thumb traced designs on the back of her hand.

"I haven't thanked you. You saved my life, Irena."

She blushed. "Ala saved your life. I just brought you a little to eat."

"Nonsense. You risked your own life to save mine. I was at the end of things, I will tell you. I'd given up in mind and body. You brought me back. Not just the food, but the risks you took for me. You inspired me to come back to this life and to not just exist, but to fight for others."

He leaned forward and pressed his lips against her cheek. She felt his warm touch and she leaned against him. He held her there for long minutes. She closed her eyes, feeling his heat, his nearness. Enjoying every part of him. There was a loud knock at the door. She didn't want to let go but he pulled away, standing and making his way to the door. He opened it to find his mother there. Gray straggly hair raining down her shoulders. Her eyes scanning the room until they rested on Irena.

"Mother, so nice to see you. Do you remember Irena Sendler?"

Her mother stared at her for a moment and then nodded dismissively. "When did you get back?" she asked, returning her eyes to Adam.

"Just this morning."

"And you didn't even bother to come see your momma?"

"I wanted to get things straightened up here."

His mother glanced at Irena again. "I see that."

"Now now, none of that."

"I just don't understand you, Adam," she protested. "The whole family's been worried sick. *Your wife* has been fraught with concern. Then when you're finally well, you don't even bother to come see us."

"I was on my way."

"Ten minutes," she commanded. "I'll start a meal. We must have a celebration. Not that we have any food to rejoice with."

"I do," said Irena, reaching into her bag. "Look. I have bread, cheese, a little sausage."

"No, thank you," his mother responded, refusing to look at her. "We will manage just fine on our own."

"Momma, don't be like that."

"Ten minutes," she repeated. "I'll let your wife know you are on your way." She turned without looking at Irena again and marched off.

Adam shuffled back to Irena, starting to sit down, but she rose, stepping away from him. "Don't," he whispered.

"You have your family to attend to. And your wife."

He stepped toward her, arms out. "Please, Irena. She's just happy I'm home."

"I understand," she responded, laboring to push down the boiling emotions. "I'm so happy you are recovered. She's right. You should be with family right now."

He dropped his arms, his eyes still searching hers. "Will you come tomorrow? Visit me at the orphanage?"

"I don't know. I have my own duties."

"Please come by, I need encouragement on my first day of work!"

"Very well." She reached down, removing the food from her bag and placing it on the table.

"You should keep that," he said.

She shook her head. "It's too dangerous. Besides, you'll need it. Take it to your celebration feast. Your mother won't protest once I'm gone."

"Irena. Don't be angry with her. She's never accepted that Regina and I do not live as husband and wife."

Irena thought of her own mother. Would she have acted any differently? "You're right," she said at last. "Mothers cling to their own dreams for their children." She stepped forward and kissed him lightly on the cheek. "Tomorrow then," she said.

"Tomorrow."

She left the apartment and stepped out into the frozen, desperate streets of the ghetto. The bitter air stung the tears in her eyes as she battled through the throng, trying to ignore the desperate pleas for help as she made her way to the nearest gate and out of the Jewish Quarter.

Her emotions were in tattered rags. She was happy for Adam and proud of herself for her part in saving him. But she'd almost lost everything in the effort. She was amazed that this emotion didn't dominate, however. Her deepest feelings were anger at his mother and jealousy of his wife. She knew intellectually that they were separated, but there was the irony. His wife, who he claimed he didn't care about, was just a building away, with a mother nearby pushing him to reconcile. At the same time she and Adam were separated by a wall.

Her thoughts were interrupted by a quiet voice begging her for food. It took her a moment to realize she was already outside the wall. She looked over and saw a young girl about four years old, standing at the entrance to an alley. Big brown eyes stared out beneath raven hair. She was Jewish. No doubt about it. Irena looked around, getting her bearings. She was in Chłodna Street, just across from the ghetto wall. She took a couple of steps toward the little girl, who cringed backward into the alley, but did not run away. For some reason, she looked vaguely familiar to her.

"Who are you?" Irena asked.

The girl didn't answer but raised her hands, her heart in her eyes.

Irena took a step farther. "Are you from the ghetto?" she asked, pointing with her head toward the wall. She couldn't help thinking there was something familiar about her.

The little girl hesitated, then nodded.

"What is your name?"

"Kaji," she said.

"Where are your mother and father?"

Kaji didn't answer and Irena saw tears welling in her eyes.

"Are they gone?" Irena asked.

She nodded. "My brother too."

That was it! She had met this little girl in the food distribution line this past year. She remembered her family. They were all dead now. She felt her heart sink. "How did you get out of the ghetto?" she asked.

"There's a hole near the bottom of the wall," she said. "It's very small but I can crawl through."

"What are you doing out here?" But Irena already knew the answer. There was no point standing in the ghetto, trying to beg from the beggars. In Aryan Warsaw there was at least a chance of getting some food or money from a passing Pole. Irena reached into her pocket and pulled out a handful of banknotes. There were several hundred zlotys. A small fortune in prewar days. She handed them to Kaji.

The little girl took the money, bursting into tears, but she didn't let go of Irena. "Take me with you," she begged. "Please. Take me away."

"I can't," said Irena. "There are Germans everywhere. You have no papers. No records. They would arrest you and take you to a terrible place."

"No place is worse than here."

Irena was at a loss for what to do. She'd walked past thousands of children like this in the ghetto. The girl was not her problem, any more than all these children were her concern. There was nothing she could do for this child. She would do more harm than good if she took her.

"I'm sorry. I can't help you," she said. Her heart broke as she muttered the words. She reached back into her pocket and took out the rest of her money, reaching her hand out to Kaji. "Take the rest," she pleaded. "That's all I can do."

"I don't want that," Kaji said, refusing to look at Irena. "I want to go away."

Irena put the money away. "I'm sorry, I just can't." She turned and started to depart, Kaji's hysterical cries threatening to crush her. A few meters away she stopped and turned back. She could not do this. She felt responsible. She'd met this family, a little unit of humanity that the Germans had eliminated, except for this lone survivor. She motioned for Kaji to join her. "Come on," she said.

Kaji ran to her, throwing her arms around her. "Thank you, thank you!" she cried.

"You must be quiet!" Irena warned. She looked around. There was a woman just down the street who had stopped and was staring at them. She was in real danger here. "Come with me," she said, turning away from the woman. She picked Kaji up and marched quickly away, turning the corner and moving as rapidly as possible away from the ghetto. Where was she going to go? What would she do with this little girl?

Kaji clung to her as she moved. She hardly weighed a thing, but Irena felt her own breath coming in deep huffs as she labored to escape from the ghetto walls. She moved a block away then another, her mind a blank. Finally, she stopped, a kilometer or so from the Jewish Quarter on a deserted street corner. The little girl's head was buried in her shoulder. She rocked her back and forth, humming a little tune as she considered what to do. Finally, she decided.

Two weeks later Irena sat in the smoke-filled environs of the Café Sztuka, sipping vodka. "To my friend Irena," said Ala, sitting across from her with glass raised. "For keeping us alive." She whispered these last words.

Irena understood her caution. Looking around, there were half a dozen uniformed German officers sitting at tables sprinkled through the little café. Some sat together, others were eating and drinking with prominent Jewish businessmen. "That one there," said Ala, pointing out an elderly gentleman near the front. "He helps the Judenrat. He ran a clock-making factory before the war." She leaned forward. "It's rumored he's selling smugglers to the Germans at ten thousand zlotys apiece."

"That can't be true," said Irena. "Who would sell out their own people?"

"Look around," said Ala. "This place is full of them."

Irena didn't need to see the people here to take in the surreal world of the café. Besides the vodka there was champagne at their table, along with caviar and fresh fish. She thought of the thousands of starving children standing around within a few hundred meters of the restaurant. But here in the middle of this hell was an oasis of milk and honey.

"Look who's performing now," said Ala, jerking her head toward the stage. Irena turned. Wiera was at the stage with Władysław Szpilman near her on the piano. She recognized him immediately. He was famous before the war too. Władysław's fingers danced over the ivory and Wiera joined him, her voice waltzing through the space, enveloping them all.

"She's wonderfully talented," said Irena. "I've never heard her in person."

"She's certainly talented at singing. Among other things."

"You still think she's collaborating?" asked Irena.

"I don't know," said Ala, taking a sip of champagne. "I want to believe that she's a good person. I always have. But she rubs me the wrong way. I don't know why." She leaned forward again. "That's not what I wanted to talk to you about. Tell me about Kaji."

Irena filled with joy as she thought of the little girl. "She's still at my office," she explained.

"Why don't you take her home?"

"It's too risky without papers. We have nosy neighbors. Besides, once I brought her there, I wouldn't be able to see her during the day. As it is, I can spend my whole working week with her. She's such a precious little thing. And so brave. She sleeps in that cold dark building every night by herself."

"Aren't you worried she'll be discovered? There are so many people in your building."

"She stays down in the basement during the day. We keep our records down there and I've carved out the perfect hiding space behind some cabinets and boxes. I can come down and see her many times each day."

"What about the weekends?"

Irena laughed. "Have I ever taken many days off? The weekends are best of all. There's nobody there and I can bring Kaji upstairs. With a little caution we can spend the entire day together."

Ala's face grew concerned. "Irena, what are you going to do with her? She can't stay at the office forever."

"Do with who?" came a voice behind her. Irena jerked in surprise but realized with relief that it was only Wiera. "Have a seat," she said.

Wiera sat down between them. "I get a little break now," she said, ignoring the looks of a half dozen men at different tables trying desperately to get her attention. "How better than to spend it with two of my favorite girls."

"I haven't been able to thank you for saving my life," Irena whispered, taking Wiera's hand.

"I hardly did that," said the singer, laughing. "A pretty thing like you? At the worst you might have received a slap on the wrist, or more likely one on the rear. Who isn't smuggling in a few luxuries these days?"

Irena shook her head. "You didn't see his eyes," she responded. "He was out for me."

Wiera poured herself some vodka and quaffed the liquid down, her face grimacing for a moment. "Let's talk about more pleasant things. Who are you hiding in your office?" she asked, winking. "Is it a handsome man?"

Ala's eyes flashed a warning but Irena ignored her. She told Wiera all about Kaji.

"You found her the same day I saw you? It was a lucky one indeed. She sounds delightful! I wish I could get out of this rat trap and come to see the two of you."

"I'm sure your connections would let you out," said Ala.

Wiera turned to her cousin by marriage, her face growing cold. "What connections would those be?"

Ala shrugged. "Look around."

The singer sighed. "I've told you a dozen times, Cousin, I don't have those kinds of contacts. I work here, nothing more."

"I'm supposed to believe that?" said Ala. "There's twenty Germans in this room who would sell their soul to sit at this table with you."

"Ala," interjected Irena.

"That's all right," said Wiera. "I can defend myself." She turned back to Ala. "You refer to the unfortunate circumstances I find myself in. I am a performer, Ala, nothing more. I can't choose my audience. The curse of fame, something I've never wanted, is people out there who come to know you through your art, believe you know them in return. The whole sordid mess breeds a familiarity that is both distasteful and misplaced."

"So you are a helpless victim in all this?"

"Entirely."

Ala raised her glass. "To my helpless victim cousin then." Her voice was laced with sarcasm.

Wiera set her own glass down and rose, turning to Irena. "Thank you for coming today," she said.

"I'm sorry," Irena said, starting to rise.

"Don't be," Wiera said. "You trust me, don't you?"

Irena thought about that for a moment and then answered. "I do."

"That's enough for me." The singer smiled down at her for a moment and then turned to Ala. "Goodbye, dear cousin."

"Goodbye." Ala kept her eyes on her drink.

"I'll see you soon, Irena," said Wiera, and turned to walk swiftly away.

"Why do you have to be so rude to her!" demanded Irena.

"Keep your voice down," whispered Ala, glancing this way and that.

"I'll do better than that," said Irena. She rose and pushed in her chair. "Thank you for the meal, Ala. I think I'll show myself out."

"Irena, don't . . ."

But she was already stepping away, weaving through the closely set tables until she found the doorway. She marched out into the streets and headed toward the ghetto gate. She'd planned to visit Adam today at the orphanage, but she was too angry. Why couldn't her friend see past her own prejudices? Wiera had saved her life and had only been kind to her. She was clearly a woman stuck in her circumstances. If she were a nurse and Ala was the performer, would they not simply be in identical but opposite roles?

She shook the thoughts from her head. She wouldn't worry about this right now. She wanted to see Kaji. She left the ghetto and strode through the relatively barren streets of Aryan Warsaw. On the way she stopped at a cake shop and purchased a little bread and some pastries. She counted her zlotys. She was running low again now that she'd stopped smuggling food into the ghetto. The extra cost of food for Kaji was another problem. She and her mother had hardly made it, even without another mouth to feed. She didn't care, she would figure out what to do somehow.

As she moved toward her office, she considered the bigger question Ala had been preparing to ask her. What was she going to do with Kaji in the long run? She had been working through that question ever since she took her to the office. She knew she couldn't keep her at work in the long run. Somebody would start asking questions. She was surprised there hadn't been a problem yet, despite her precautions. There were simply too many people in the building, and not all of them could be trusted. She couldn't take Kaji home either. She knew that. Someone in the building would eventually turn them in.

She had to do something, and she had to do it soon. But she still had no idea what. As she reached her work building the problems melted away. She could tackle these problems later. For now, she would have the day with her Kaji. Today was Saturday and she would have the building practically to herself. She could bring the little girl up to her office and they could spend the time together.

She unlocked the front door, closing it behind her, and she rushed down to the basement. Kaji was there in the hiding space, a tiny area Irena had fashioned with stacks of boxes in the very back of the file area. Kaji was asleep and she gently woke her. The little girl threw her arms around Irena's neck, practically pulling her over. Irena laughed and picked her up, holding her close.

"How's my little girl?" she asked.

"It was scary here last night," she answered. "There were shadows and noises everywhere."

"You say that every night," said Irena, laughing. "But you're my brave little girl."

"When can I come home with you?" Kaji asked. She made this inquiry every day they were together and it crushed Irena's heart, for she knew the answer.

"I don't know, my dear. I'm trying to figure out what to do with you, but I'm still not certain."

"You have to bring me to your house. I want you to be my mother from now on," she pleaded.

Irena wanted more than anything to make Kaji her daughter. She didn't know what to do. "Don't worry, my dear. I'll think of something."

She carried Kaji upstairs to her office and set her in the seat across from her desk. While Kaji told her all about her morning, Irena busied herself with preparing an afternoon meal for the two of them. She glanced over as she was cutting up the bread. She smiled to herself, noting Kaji's flushed, healthy cheeks and bright eyes. She had gained a little weight over the past week. She had more energy and was excited and lively, like a four-year-old girl should be.

Irena wondered again what might have happened to her parents. She'd asked her, but Kaji always started crying, and she didn't want to press her too far. She'd tried to learn something about her family, to see if there was anyone in the ghetto she should contact, but Kaji didn't even know her last name.

She handed her a small vanilla cake and the bread. Kaji grabbed the cake, licking the frosting and shoving the pastry in her mouth before Irena could stop her.

"You're supposed to eat the bread first!" Irena protested, laughing with her. "The cake is for after."

"So you've finally brought your little surprise upstairs," said a woman's voice. Irena jolted in her seat and looked up. It was Maria Kulska, a cigarette dangling from a twisted grin. She stood at the doorway, swimming in a faded dress, watching Irena with a sardonic flare in her eyes. The social worker reached slowly up and took the cigarette between thumb and finger, taking a deep drag before pulling it out of her mouth. Irena did not know her well. She worked in another department and they'd rarely spoke.

"Maria, you startled me. Have you met . . . my niece."

"That's not your niece," said Maria, her words exhaling lazily through a cloud of smoke. "That's the Jew girl you've been hiding in the basement."

"What are you talking about?" Irena's heart froze at the words. "I'm not hiding—"

"There's no point in lying, Irena," said Maria, taking another puff. "Half the office knows about it. Did you think you could hide a whole person in our office and get away with it?" She looked down at Kaji, pinching her cheek roughly. "Even such a little one."

"What's wrong?" Kaji asked, wincing from the pain and responding to the tension in the air.

"Nothing, darling," said Maria. "I'm just having a little talk with Irena here."

"What are you going to do?" Irena asked.

"I'm not going to do anything. But you are going to have to do something before you get us all arrested. And you'll have to do it fast." She finished her cigarette and dropped it on the floor, crushing the burning butt with her shoe.

"I'm trying."

Maria looked over her shoulder. "You better try harder. This secret won't keep much longer."

"Are you going to turn me in?"

Maria reached down into her pocket and retrieved another cigarette. She raised it to her lips, lighting the end and taking a deep breath. "Handle the problem."

Irena heard footsteps, to her horror. Maria turned her head down the hallway and then back their way. She pursed her lips. "It looks like you're out of time."

A man appeared in the doorway. It was Jan Dobraczyński,

her boss. He stared at Irena and then at Kaji, his eyes narrowing. "So, this is the little girl you've been hiding?" he demanded.

"Why are you here on a weekend?" Irena asked.

"I came to investigate a rumor I'd heard. A story about you hiding a Jewish child at our office. I see it's true."

"She's not a Jew, she's my niece." Irena knew the words were hollow even as they left her mouth.

"Don't lie to me, Sendler. I warned you when I gave you that pass that there would be no more problems, but here you are defying me again. This is the last time." He turned and marched away. Maria still stood in the doorway, a cynical smile on her lips.

"Time's up."

Chapter 14

Eyes from the Mountaintop

February 1941
Warsaw Ghetto, Poland

Klaus and Peter sat on the trolley next to Colonel Hans Wagner. The streetcar rolled slowly through the ghetto and the colonel craned his neck back and forth, watching with deep interest as Klaus explained the layout and conditions in the ghetto.

"What about those bodies over there?" asked Wagner, gesturing toward a pile of corpses on the sidewalk near an intersection. "Aren't you in danger of disease?"

"The cold keeps the problem at bay," said Klaus. "Besides, that is merely a collection point. The Jews provide their own disposition teams throughout the city. They will collect these units in the next hour or two and transport them to the cemetery."

The colonel nodded. "Very efficient. You say you have a

Jewish police force as well?" Wagner raised a peppered eyebrow. "They are actually willing to guard themselves?"

Klaus nodded. "Hunger is the ultimate incentive. They receive much better rations for themselves and their families. Of course, we don't trust them with wall security or any major investigations of wrongdoing, but they serve a role in watching and reporting. Without them I would need double the force to patrol and secure the ghetto."

"Excellent," said the colonel, making some notes in a small leather notebook he held. He blew on his fingers as he wrote. "Damned cold out here, isn't it?"

"We won't be much longer," said Klaus. "I just wanted you to see the situation up close. It's so hard to get a real feel of things on a ledger."

"I admit it gives me a new perspective."

The Germans were the only occupants of the back streetcar. The forward unit was full of Poles, crammed together and keeping their faces away from the second car. As Klaus watched them for a moment, he noted that the trolley was slowing down. *Oh no, not now.* He rose and moved toward the adjacent trolley, but it was too late. As he watched, a young man jumped off, a burlap sack over his shoulder, and sprinted into the crowd.

"What the hell was that?" demanded the colonel.

"An unfortunate reality of the ghetto," explained Klaus.

"Was that man smuggling food in?"

Klaus nodded.

"And he got away with it?"

"You have to understand, Colonel, there are hundreds of them, perhaps thousands. We catch a dozen a day, but another dozen rise to take their place."

Wagner was silent the rest of the way on the tour and in the car ride back to their headquarters. They settled into chairs in Klaus's office as servants scurried around serving lunch.

"Well, what did you think of our operation?" asked Peter.

The colonel set his sandwich down. "I don't think much about it, to be honest."

Klaus was shocked. "Surely this can't be about that smuggler."

"Not about *that* smuggler in particular," said the colonel. "But about smuggling in general. I was sent here by Hans Frank to look over your operation. Word has reached him about the black market in the Warsaw ghetto."

"How could we avoid it?" demanded Klaus. "Three hundred calories a day? There are bound to be rule breakers."

"You picked that number, not us." The colonel retrieved a pipe and stuffed some tobacco inside, tamping it down with the end of his thumb. Some of the flakes flicked off the end of the pipe and tumbled to the floor. He lit the pipe and took a couple puffs. "Now don't get me wrong, Klaus, we're pleased with what you've done."

Klaus looked at the mess on his carpet. He took a deep breath and returned to the subject. "But you're upset with the smuggling?"

"Herr Frank doesn't care a bit about a little black marketeering. If the Jews want to prolong their lives for a few months, so be it. We'll get all of them in the end." The colonel took a final puff and tapped the end of his pipe on his dish, expelling ash onto the porcelain. "His concern is the defiance. They are getting away with thumbing their noses at us. This encourages not only the other Jews but much worse, the Poles. We have enough of a resistance problem already, we don't need to give them further hope."

"So, it's the Poles you're really after?" asked Klaus, reaching out with a handkerchief to remove the ashes from the colonel's dish.

"Just so. We need to crack down on them."

"What do you propose?"

"You're a policeman," said the colonel. "I'm surprised I need to tell you. Do some police work. Catch them in the act. A few high-profile arrests should give us just what we need to tamp down their ardor. I want real proof though," he said. "Don't give them a reason to complain. If you have solid evidence and you hit them hard in a few places, we should have a break—at least for a few months." Wagner wiped his forehead with the back of his sleeve. "I've worked myself up," he joked. "First too cold, now too hot. I think I'm getting too old for all of this."

"Aren't we all, Colonel," said Klaus.

"Well, the two of us, at least. What about young Peter here?"

"He's certainly doing fine," said Klaus. "He's worked his way through half the women of Warsaw."

"No Jews though, correct?" asked Wagner abruptly.

"No, sir," answered Peter. "I always follow the rules."

"Good," said the colonel, rising. Klaus and Peter scrambled to their feet, saluting the inspector with a crisp *Heil Hitler*. "I'll leave you to it then. Remember, catch them in the act. Bring Frank some Poles to execute, and all will be well."

"*Jawohl*," said Klaus.

The colonel departed, leaving Peter and Klaus to settle back into their seats. "What the hell was that all about?" demanded Peter.

"Bureaucratic garbage, that's what it is," said Klaus thoughtfully. He picked up his phone and gave an order. He set the receiver down and looked back up at Peter. "*Stop the smuggling. Make an example.* What a bunch of nonsense. We have contained five hundred thousand Jews and done it under budget. But they ignore all of that and focus on the one problem we have. The same issue being reported by every damned ghetto in Poland!"

"What are we going to do about it?" asked Peter.

"We're going to give them some arrests," said Klaus, still stalking the room. "The question is, where and how?"

"We can crack down on the gates," suggested Peter. "Add extra guards and more random patrols in the quarter."

Klaus shook his head. "They don't want the Jews. They want the Poles." Klaus paused, rubbing his chin. "But which Poles? I've killed just about every leader in this city already. Who do they want me to get? And why does he want proof? As if anyone will care when this is over. How about the half million Poles we already killed? What were their crimes? A university degree?"

There was a knock at the door. "Not now!" shouted Klaus.

"I'm sorry to bother you, sir, but there is someone here to see you. Someone you are going to want to meet with."

"Can't this wait?"

"I don't think so, sir."

"Fine." He rose. "I'll attend to this." He turned to the attendant at the door. "Sweep up that tobacco. That pig has no manners." He turned back to his assistant. "I'll be back in a few minutes, Peter. I want you to draw up a list of potential Polish targets. And cancel my afternoon meetings. This takes top priority now."

An hour later Klaus returned. He stepped into the office and sat down without saying a word.

Peter looked up. "I have some preliminary concepts, sir. I think we should start with the police force. They have access to the ghetto and—"

"Forget that."

"What, sir? I'm telling you that they—"

"I said forget it." Klaus leaned back, smiling. "I have everything I need."

"What are you talking about?"

Klaus leaned forward. "Our visitor had some very interesting news about the social welfare building." He leaned forward. "Now here's what we are going to do."

Chapter 15
Betrayed

February 1941
Warsaw, Poland

Irena sat in her office, her mind racing. Maria had departed, leaving her alone with her problem and her fears. Jan knew about Kaji! Half the office knew! It was only a matter of time now until she would be betrayed. She didn't know what to do. First things first, she had to talk to Jan. He was the biggest threat right now for immediate action. She handed Kaji another cake and stepped around the desk, kissing the little girl on top of the head.

"I have to leave for a few minutes, and I want you to promise to stay right here."

"Where are you going?" Kaji asked anxiously. "Don't leave me alone again."

"I'm not going away," said Irena. "I just need to speak with the man who just visited us."

"He seemed mad," said Kaji, screwing up her face. "I don't like him."

"He's not mad," said Irena. "Everything is going to be fine. Here," she said, pulling over some paper and a pen. "When you're finished eating you can draw."

"What should I make?" she asked.

Irena stopped at the door. She could hardly force herself to think. "Um . . . draw a picture of me."

Kaji squealed in delight. "Okay, I will!"

Irena sprinted down the hallway and up the stairs to Jan's office. When she reached it, she was horrified to see the door was closed. She pounded on the opaque glass window but there was no answer. She tried the door. Locked. Panic knifed through her. Jan had left. *He's gone to turn me in*, she thought. She shook her head. She couldn't jump to conclusions. He might even be somewhere else in the building. She moved quickly through the top floor and then down to the second and the first. The building was empty. Not only was Jan gone, but Maria was missing too. What was she going to do?

Lwów. The word popped into her head out of nowhere. Of course! She'd heard the story of a Catholic parish that burned down in the city of Lwów. All the birth records were gone, which meant that any birth certificate registered to the parish in Lwów would be untraceable. They had certificates here in the building. They were kept in a file cabinet in Jan's office. If she could get ahold of one of these documents, she could doctor the form and then Kaji would have official papers. She could take her home, and nobody would be the wiser.

She checked her watch. Jan had left her office no more than an hour ago. Maria had disappeared a few minutes later. If either had run to the police, she still should have a little time before anyone would arrive. All she had to do was get into the office, grab one of the certificates, fill it out quickly, and get Kaji out of the building before anyone arrived. She rushed back to the second floor and checked on her own office. Kaji was still there, happily drawing. She wanted Irena to stop and look at the picture she was drawing, but Irena told her she would return in a few minutes and she bolted down the hallway and back up to Jan's office.

How was she going to get into the office? Perhaps her key would work. Her key opened several locks in the building, including the bathroom, the front door, the file room, and her own office. Perhaps it would work for Jan's door as well. She removed the ring from a pocket in her skirt and shoved it into the keyhole. It fit perfectly and she smiled in relief. She turned the key. Nothing happened. The key wouldn't budge. She tried both directions but although it fit the hole, it was not cut to open the lock.

She looked around desperately. Could she break the window? There was a broom closet a few doors down. She started that direction and then stopped herself, willing her mind to slow down. No, she couldn't force her way in. If she did, Jan would know someone had taken something from his office. He would eventually put the pieces together and figure out what she'd done. She couldn't risk it.

She returned to the door, removing a pin from her hair. She'd read about lock pickers, but she had no idea how it worked. She placed the sharp end into the keyhole and moved the metal pin around, trying to force the lock open. She tried for long moments, checking her watch again and again. Finally, with a scream of frustration she ripped the pin out and threw it down the hallway. Tears were coming now. Another twenty minutes had passed. Jan could be back with the police any moment. What was she going to do?

She raced back down the hallway and returned to her office. Kaji was there, the picture complete. She held it up for Irena to see. Irena forced a smile, trying to hold back the tears. Kaji was in danger and there was nothing she could do about it. She scrambled for any idea, anything she could do to get into that office. A locksmith! The idea hit her like a thunderbolt. Of course! She just had to find someone to open the door. She would pretend it was her own office. She had a key to the front door. There would be no reason for her to worry about arousing his suspicion.

"I'm going to have to leave for a few more minutes, Kaji."

"But today is our day!" she protested. "You promised to spend all of it with me!"

"I know. I'll make it up to you. Make another drawing and I'll be back before you finish."

Kaji was unhappy but there was nothing for it. Irena turned and rushed back out of the office, heading toward the door. She reached the exit just as Maria returned. The woman jerked in surprise when she saw her, a strange look on her face.

"Where've you been?" demanded Irena.

"None of your damned business, that's where," snapped Maria. "Have you taken care of your problem yet?"

"She's not a problem, she's a little girl."

"She's a Jewish little girl," responded Maria. "So she's a big problem, no?"

"I have to go," said Irena, pushing past her. Maria caught her by the arm and their eyes met.

"I would hurry if I were you."

Irena scrambled down the stairs and on to the street. She had in mind where to go, a little key shop she passed on the way to work every day. She was sure she'd seen a locksmith sign on the door. She rushed down the sidewalk, half running, pushing past pedestrians out for a weekend stroll. Her heartbeat thumped in her ears as fear and anxiety pumped through her body. The shop was halfway between her work and home. She normally took about fifteen minutes to reach this point, but today she arrived in less than eight.

The store was closed. She knew it immediately from the darkened windows. She tried the door anyway, but it was locked.

She looked this way and that. What was she going to do? She asked a passerby if they knew where another shop was. The woman didn't. She tried a second person and a third. Finally, she stopped an elderly gentleman who directed her toward a store a kilometer or so away. She started in that direction, checking her watch as she hurried through an intersection. She'd already been gone a half hour. She moved as quickly as she could, but her feet were failing her. Her breath sputtered out in ragged huffs, making foggy clouds of frozen steam as she passed down the sidewalk.

She reached the next store about ten minutes later. Closed again. She checked her watch. Forty-five minutes since she'd left. If she was betrayed, the Germans might have already come and gone. She thought back to Maria's words. To her expression. She couldn't worry about that right now. She repeated the same process, stopping people on the street and asking if they knew of any locksmiths. She finally found a lead to a third store. This one was closer. Just a few hundred meters away. She shambled toward it, noting the failing light. If she didn't find someone soon it would be curfew and she would be forced to either return home or spend the night helplessly with Kaji at the office.

She arrived at the store. This one was open. She stepped inside and spotted a middle-aged Pole of slight build, iron-gray closely cropped hair, and a thick salt-and-pepper mustache. He was moving some items off the counter. "I'm sorry, we're closing," he said offhandedly, not looking up.

"No, you can't be!" shouted Irena, rushing up to the counter and leaning over it, fighting to catch her breath.

"Have to," he said, looking her over now with curiosity. "Curfew's not far off."

"I have to get into my office! It's an emergency."

He gave her a surprised look. "There are no emergencies getting into an office. I'm open on Monday and I can help you first thing. Good evening."

He started to turn but she reached over the counter and grabbed his arm. He turned in surprise. "Please. I'm begging you. I need your help."

He hesitated. "How far away?"

"Not far," she said.

"Very well. Let me get my things."

She waited impatiently while he gathered his tools. "Please hurry," she implored him.

"I'm ready," he said. "I can't imagine what you need to get into an office for that would create this kind of crisis."

She didn't answer him but instead took off out of the store, scrambling down the sidewalk toward her building.

"Wait up, miss!"

She heard him calling, but she kept her pace, knowing she might already be too late. She turned the corner a few minutes later and froze. There were multiple cars parked out front at odd angles. There was only one reason a jumble of vehicles would be stopped outside her office.

"There you are," said the locksmith, huffing and puffing as he caught her. "Running a race, are you? Now where is your office? You said it was close."

She pointed toward her building, unable to speak. He looked up and his face turned a ghostly white. "Now, miss, I don't know what kind of trouble you're mixed up in, but I know what those cars mean. I'm sorry, but I can't help you." He backed away and then turned, springing into an awkward jog. She let him go. She knew there was no point now. She stared at the cars for a few moments longer. She thought about leaving, but what was the point? They'd simply arrest her at home. And besides, Kaji was inside. She took a couple of deep breaths and then moved toward the entryway.

A German stood at the door, covered in a dark hat and overcoat. He eyed her but said nothing, allowing her to pass. She found this even more ominous. She made her way down the hallway and up the stairs. She turned a corner and there they were, a huddle of figures standing at the entrance to her office.

An officer stepped out of the office and turned, looking in her direction. It was Klaus. "Ah, Frau Sendler. I haven't seen you in some time. Won't you come this way?" He motioned for her to join him in her office. She had no choice but to obey.

As she moved toward the door, she saw a flash of light down the hallway. Maria was there, match in hand, lighting a cigarette and watching her with impassive eyes, that half grin frozen on her lips.

She entered the office and was surprised to see several Germans sitting at the seats across from her desk. She scanned the room quickly, but she couldn't find Kaji. They must have already taken her away, she realized.

"Please have a seat, Frau Sendler."

Irena took her chair, looking around in confusion.

Klaus watched her for a few seconds. She recognized his assistant, Peter, as well, who was standing behind his commander with a slight grin on his face. He gave her a wink.

"Where is she?" Klaus asked.

Irena paused before answering him. *They didn't have her?* "Where is who?" she asked.

"The Jew you're hiding."

"I . . . I don't know what you're talking about."

"Don't play games with me, Frau Sendler. I know you're hiding a Jewish girl in this building. Now you can lead me to her, or we will tear this place apart, and find her for you."

"I don't know what you're talking about." She wondered where Kaji was. Had she gone back down to the basement? If so, they would find her in the next few minutes.

"Have it your way." Klaus turned to Peter. "Search the building and find the girl."

The hulking assistant left with the other two seated men. Irena heard him giving orders in the hallway and then footsteps moving in many directions as the search began. Klaus took a seat across from her, staring at her without saying a word. She tried to meet his gaze, but she couldn't keep up the courage and she looked away. She battled to fight down the fear. She didn't want to give him the satisfaction.

"Why don't you tell me where the little Jew girl is?" Klaus asked. "Really, Irena, I already know she's here. If you tell me, I'll put in a good word for you with the authorities. I know you think every arrest ends with a grave, but there are other alternatives. If you admit the truth now, you might come out of this alive."

She didn't respond but she looked up. What did he mean, *alternatives*?

"That's right. We have friends here, there, everywhere. You think you're being a patriot by hiding a Jew? You're only hurting your own people. But if you turn her over now, and agree to help us in the future, I'll see to it that you're returned home in the morning, alive and in one piece."

He was offering her life back to her. That and perhaps more. Protection, freedom from worry. All if she simply turned Kaji in. A simple thing to do.

"Don't worry about her," said Klaus, as if reading her thoughts. "Do you think we would harm her? I just want to return her to her rightful place. You have friends in that Jewish orphanage, don't you? Dr. Korczak, is it? Isn't she better off there than out here among the vultures where she might be killed or even worse? You know your fellow Poles can't be trusted."

She knew what he was talking about. Poles who held Jews ransom for everything they owned. They would extort the family in hiding, demanding protection money and exorbitant prices for food. Once they'd paid out all they had, the Poles would turn them over to the Gestapo, gleaning one final reward. This scum did not constitute more than a tiny minority of the Polish population, but they did exist and they were a shame on the nation's conscience.

"I see you know what I'm talking about." Klaus leaned forward. "Won't you help me then? You can walk her to the ghetto with me. Afterward we'll have a little chat. I have a few other ideas of ways you can help me. Nothing terrible, mind you. I just want to know how your department really works. Who the players are. In exchange, I would be very grateful."

She heard shouts and steps on the next floor down. They'd be in the basement soon. She had to decide. She could take Kaji to safety herself and save her life in the process. She looked at Klaus; his eyes pleaded with her to accept. She desperately wanted to. She was terrified of torture and she knew within an hour she might be experiencing that very thing. She took a deep breath, her mind reeling. But she couldn't. Something stopped her. "I don't know what you're talking about."

"That's very disappointing, Irena," said Klaus, sitting back. "I thought I'd made a better choice when I selected you for this position. By the sounds of the search, I suspect they are nearing the basement. When they retrieve the child, you and I will chat further." He rose and stepped toward the door. "Last chance," he said.

"I have nothing to say."

He squared his shoulders and stepped out. She sat there in the semidarkness, listening to the sounds of the search, waiting for the scream from Kaji that would tell her she was caught. The moments ticked by one after another, each seeming to take an eternity.

Long hours later, or was it mere minutes? Klaus appeared back in the doorway. "Nothing," he said, his voice shaking with anger. "Nothing. Where did you hide her?" he demanded.

"There is no her," said Irena, not believing Kaji had escaped. "There never was. Whoever is giving you information is lying to you."

Klaus looked at her for long moments. He took a half step into the office but then stopped himself. "All right, Frau Sendler. You can play your little game with me. I will find this brat and when I do, I'll personally attend to your questioning. Remember," he said, his eyes flashing fire, "you had your chance." The Nazi stormed out of her office. She heard the loud clapping of boots on the tiled hallway floor for a few more minutes, then all was silence.

She sat back in her chair and closed her eyes. Her body started to shake uncontrollably, and her eyes filled with tears. By some miracle she was still here, still alive. But where was Kaji?

"I see God still protects you." She looked up. Maria was there, cigarette in hand, leaning against the doorway.

"You turned me into the Germans!" Irena shouted accusingly.

"Not me, darling. But someone surely did."

"I don't believe you."

Maria scoffed. "I don't care what you believe. Perhaps what you should be thinking about is where your little Jewish brat has gone?"

"What did you do with her?" Irena demanded, rising out of her chair and preparing to throw herself at Maria.

"I didn't have anything to do with it."

"Where is she?" Irena demanded.

"Jan took her."

"What do you mean?"

"He came back about half an hour ago and he took Kaji with him."

Irena felt relief wash over her. Kaji was safe. "Where did he take her?"

"The only place he could. Where you should have taken her right from the start. Back to the ghetto."

"Why would he do that?"

"Because unlike you, he's not a fool. Unlike you, he's not prepared to sacrifice us all just for one little girl." Maria took a puff of her cigarette. "You should praise him, not condemn him. He saved you, and all of us."

Irena stood for long moments, her hands clenched. She wanted to strike Maria, but the words hit home. There was truth in them. Irena had risked all their lives to save one. Perhaps Maria was right. Perhaps Jan was. But one other overriding thought consumed her. She'd been betrayed by someone, and she swore to herself she would find out who.

Chapter 16
Escape

July 1942
Warsaw Ghetto, Poland

Irena waited in the long line to enter the ghetto. The July heat was stifling, and she sweated profusely. Although she thought she might pass out from the burning, humid sun, the moisture on her face masked the fear raging through her heart. Today was the day she'd planned so many months for.

The search at the gate was perfunctory. She knew the primary guard well, having walked through this entrance hundreds of times. He barely glanced at her documents and she didn't even have to slow down as she passed through the entrance. She walked quickly into the crowd, losing herself in the business of the Jewish Quarter. The familiar sights and sounds greeted her: the begging, the pleas for help, mixed with the black-market salesmen and -women hawking some bread or flour they'd secured on the Aryan side of Warsaw.

She made her way toward Sienna Street, reaching the wooden footbridge over Chłodna Street that separated the big ghetto from the little one. The Judenrat had ordered the bridge constructed a few months after the ghetto was created so that traffic on Chłodna would not have to be interrupted by the passage of the Jews from one section of the ghetto to the other. As she walked along, she thought about the streetcars that used to operate here. She had planned to use them, but the Germans had ceased their operation through the ghetto as part of their crackdown on smuggling.

There was a glut of foot traffic at the bridge, a common occurrence. She waited her turn, climbing slowly, one step at a time, up to the platform and then swayed with the rest of the crowd as the shuffled across to the little ghetto. She walked the last couple of blocks to Sienna Street and found her destination: Dr. Korczak's orphanage.

She entered the building. Adam was already waiting. He put his arms around her and held her briefly. She felt her whole body begin to tremble, a mixture of pleasure and fear.

"Hush now," he whispered. "Everything is going to be all right. Today is the day." His words echoed her own.

"Is everything ready?" she asked.

"Yes."

"You've talked to Ala?"

"This morning."

"Let's go then," said Irena. Adam turned and she followed him through the entrance and past a set of double doors into a long corridor. Adam stopped at the last door on the left. "Are you ready?" he asked.

Irena steeled herself. "I've worked so hard to prepare this. I am ready."

Adam opened the door. They entered a sparse room with a single bed. A small desk and chair rested in the corner. There were a few books, a tiny closet with a smattering of hangers. Ewa was there, sitting on the edge of the bed, smiling up at her, holding a little girl's hand.

"Kaji. I'm here."

Kaji looked up and squealed with delight. She threw herself in Irena's arms, holding her close. "Is today the day?" she echoed.

"It is. Do you remember everything I told you?"

Kaji nodded.

"Good. We must follow all the steps exactly like I instructed. You have to be a very brave girl today, do you understand?"

"Yes. Ewa made me practice." Kaji lay back straight as a board. She closed her eyes and held her breath. "Just like this."

"That's perfect," Irena said. She turned to Ewa. "Thank you for everything."

"Of course, my sister. Anything for you."

Adam checked his watch. "It's time, we need to go."

Irena nodded and took Kaji's hand. Ewa gave her a hug and a kiss on the head. "I'll see you again soon, little one."

"Goodbye, Aunt Ewa."

Ewa's eyes filled with tears. "Goodbye, dearest Kaji."

Irena led Kaji out of the door and they followed Adam as he left the orphanage and made his way through the streets of the ghetto. They passed the wooden bridge without incident and marched on slowly through the stifling heat of the ghetto toward the hospital. When they arrived, Ala was already standing at the entrance, waiting for them.

"You're here," she said.

Adam laughed. "Of course we are. We haven't done anything dangerous yet. Nobody wants to stop a Jew from walking *through* the ghetto."

"That's true," said Ala, smiling. "Still, I'm so nervous." She looked down at Kaji and took her face in her hands. "Are you ready, my dear?"

"Why does everyone keep asking me that?" said Kaji.

"It's an important day," said Ala. "Perhaps the most important in your whole life."

"Aunt Ewa taught me what to do. I'm ready."

"Is everything prepared?" asked Irena.

"Yes," said Ala. "Follow me."

They made their way through the halls of the hospital. Ala looked this way and that, making sure that nobody was paying them too much attention. They went down a flight of stairs, reaching the basement. They arrived at a heavy metal door with signs warning against entrance.

"It's in here," Ala said. She paused a moment and then pulled on the heavy latch. The door swung open and they entered a large tiled room with stark white walls. Several metal tables sat in the middle of the room, built on rollers with a slight incline. There was a counter with a long line of cabinets. The counter contained several trays of metal instruments.

"The morgue," Ala explained. "We store the dead here and our doctors perform the occasional autopsy. Not that we really need to know what anyone is dying from. Disease or starvation mixed in with the occasional bullet to the head. Take your pick."

Irena held Kaji's hands tightly. She was worried that the room would scare the little girl, but she didn't seem to understand where they were. Ala looked at them for a moment and then turned, moving toward another door at the far end.

"This is the loading room," she said, opening the door into a second smaller space. This area contained bunks on both sides and a long metal corrugated gate at the far end. The bunks were full of corpses on both sides, lined to the ceiling.

"What do we do now?" asked Irena, shielding Kaji's eyes from the stacked pile of dead.

"We wait for the cart," said Ala. "I told them to be here at noon." She checked her watch. "It's a little after right now. They shouldn't be long."

Irena felt a squeeze on her hand, and she looked down and smiled. She thought back to that terrible night when she thought she'd lost Kaji forever.

After talking to Jan, she'd rushed to the ghetto. Night was falling and she risked arrest, but she didn't care. She had to make sure Kaji was safe. The guard at the gate had argued with her. "It's too late to go into the ghetto today," he'd said.

But she insisted there was an emergency outbreak of typhoid fever and at last he'd relented. She'd made her way into the streets, desperately calling for Kaji. She'd searched for more than an hour, even as night was falling and the streets were emptying. She was risking everything. Her pass let her into the ghetto and gave her a certain amount of protection, but murder came easily in the Jewish Quarter, and a German might shoot first and ask questions later, particularly in the twilight conditions when she was just another body moving through the streets.

Finally, darkness had fallen. She'd given up, the tears streaming freely down her face. She'd made her way to Ala's flat, which was not too far, with the idea of spending the night. She'd start the search again in the morning. She started to wonder if Jan had deceived her, and perhaps had simply taken Kaji straightaway to the police.

She was making her way toward her friend's apartment when she'd heard a feeble voice calling out in the darkness. She'd recognized the sound and turned, straining her eyes to see through the blackness. There she was. Kaji was hiding in an alleyway. It reminded her of when she'd found her outside the ghetto, peeking around the corner of another dark alley. Irena rushed to her and picked her up. Kaji had buried her head into Irena's chest, sobbing. Irena had calmed her with words of encouragement as she rushed through the darkness. The danger had not passed. They were outside past curfew, subject to death if they were caught. Miraculously they'd made it to Ala's flat and safety.

The next day Irena had taken Kaji to Dr. Korczak's orphanage and enrolled her. In the months since then, Ewa and Adam had kept a close eye on her and made sure she'd wanted for nothing. Irena had visited her every day, bringing her food and warm clothing to make sure she was safe. She'd taken up her smuggling again, using a different gate and bringing in food and supplies not only for Kaji but for the other children at the orphanage. She'd risked her life every day, but there was another reason to do so now, not just to defy the Germans or to help Adam, but to save the life of her little girl.

Over the months they had grown closer, until she thought of Kaji as a daughter. She'd worked to construct a plan so she could get Kaji out of the ghetto and bring her to safety. She'd gained her own mother's support to have her come and live with them. She'd built up her savings by selling a little of the food in the ghetto until she had reserves to support three people at their home. Finally, and most difficult, she'd snuck into Jan's office and removed a stack of the precious birth certificates, and using an original she'd found from the Lwów parish, she'd forged a fake document for Kaji.

In the meantime, Ewa and Adam had worked with Kaji, teaching her a little Latin and the main Catholic prayers. Once on the outside, Kaji's life might depend on her ability to recite some of the Catholic rites to a suspicious policeman or neighbor. Jews were hiding everywhere in Aryan Poland, and the Gestapo was increasingly cracking down.

After months of preparation, they'd developed a plan to get Kaji out of the ghetto and smuggle her to Irena's apartment in safety. Now, as they waited for the cart in this frozen corpse-filled cellar, Irena hoped everything would go as they had planned.

Minutes passed. Kaji was shivering now in the cold of the freezer and starting to complain. Ala kept looking at her watch. A half hour passed, then an hour. "Something is wrong," she said finally. "They should have been here a long time ago."

"We can't stay here indefinitely," said Irena. "Look at poor Kaji. She's freezing."

"Let's go back upstairs," said Ala. "I'll get lunch together for us and then I'll check into things and find out what went wrong."

They left the morgue and marched upstairs to the kitchen. Ala set a little table and laid out some bread and cheese for them to eat. When they were set she left to find out what had happened to the cart.

"It's not going to happen today, is it?" asked Kaji. Irena could see the sadness and the fear in her eyes.

"That's not necessarily true," said Irena. "It's just a little delay. Eat your bread and don't you worry about things. Ala will take care of everything."

"That's right," said Adam, placing his hand on Kaji's shoulders. "We'll get you out of here today, Kaji."

"Promise?"

"I promise," he said.

Irena hoped Adam could keep that commitment to her.

They waited another half hour, now too warm again in the humid heat. Irena checked her watch over and over, the minutes ticking relentlessly by. When she thought she couldn't wait another second, Ala appeared, her face pale.

"What happened?" Irena asked.

"Janek is down with a fever," she said. "He's at home in his apartment, unable to move. He said there will be no cart today. Perhaps not tomorrow either."

"What are we going to do?" asked Irena.

"We wait."

Kaji started to cry. "I don't want to wait anymore," she said. "I want to go today."

"Isn't there something we could do?" asked Adam.

Ala shrugged her shoulders. "It's Janek's cart. He and his men operate the corpse removal from the hospital. He knows the routes, the guards. I don't see what we can do about it."

"I'm sorry, my dear. We will have to wait until tomorrow," said Irena. "Perhaps the next day."

Kaji's cries turned to weeping. "I don't want to wait another day." She turned to Adam. "You promised."

"Don't be silly," said Irena. "It's not Adam's fault. We are just going to have to wait until Janek is better."

"Why can't I take the cart out?" asked Adam.

"You don't know where you're going. And you'd raise suspicion at the gate," said Ala.

"Not just me," said Adam. "I could go with Janek's crew. If I'm just one of the men on the cart, the Germans wouldn't necessarily be suspicious. Isn't that true?"

"I'm not sure he would allow it," said Ala.

"Couldn't we try?" asked Adam. "Look at her. She's waited long enough. Let's get her out."

Ala paused, considering it. "I guess it wouldn't hurt to ask."

Irena was joyous. She hugged Ala. "Thank you. Thank you, my friend!"

Ala smiled. "You're welcome. Now stay here and keep yourselves warm. I'll be back as soon as I can."

They waited in the kitchen for another hour, the time trickling by. Ala returned and from her expression Irena knew the answer was bad news.

"He refuses," her friend said.

"Why won't he trust us?" asked Adam.

"He said it's for your own good. He said the Germans would never let Adam through. He's had the same crew for more than a year. They would stop them, search the cart. It's too much risk. He said he would be ready tomorrow. Same time, same plan."

"Let me talk to him," said Adam, starting toward the door.

"No," said Irena. "He's right. If his absence increases the risk even a little bit, it's not worth it. It's only one more day."

"No!" said Kaji. "I don't want to stay here any longer."

"I know," said Irena, holding her. "But it's just until tomorrow. Besides, I'll stay tonight with you in the ghetto. I'll sleep in the same bed with you. We can stay up late, and I'll tell you stories from when I was a little girl, just like you."

Kaji's face brightened. "I would like that," she said finally.

"Good, it's a bargain."

They spent the long afternoon and evening together in the orphanage. Ewa and Adam lingered, sitting with them by the fire. True to her word, Irena told Kaji stories about growing up in Otwock, the resort town south of Warsaw on the Vistula. The Jewish families she played with. How the poor would come to her father for medical care and he took care of them no matter what, taking perhaps a chicken in payment or a day's labor from the family. She spoke proudly of her father, his charity, his socialist beliefs, his dreams for a better Poland—a nation for everyone, rich and poor, Jew and gentile.

The night moved on and Ewa went upstairs to bed. Adam stayed with them, stoking the fire. Kaji eventually fell asleep, her head in Irena's lap.

"I thought she'd be home with me by now," said Irena.

"She will be by this time tomorrow."

"If she's still alive."

"The plan is a good one," he said, taking her hand and running his fingers over her palm.

"All plans are good until they fail."

"Why the gloom?" he asked. "You're ever the optimist."

"There's so much at stake."

"I know. But don't you worry. I know these men. Ala trusts them. Besides, the Germans want nothing to do with the dead. She'll be safe." He moved closer and she rested her head against his shoulder, closing her eyes. He was warm and comforting. He stroked her hair and she felt herself relax, her fears melting away in his protective arms.

"When are you coming out?" she asked.

He chuckled. "Have you looked at me?" he said. "My features scream Jew to anyone who would bother looking."

"Some Poles look like Jews," she said. "You speak Polish perfectly and you know enough German to get by. I can get you the papers you need to survive out there."

"And where would I go? I don't think your neighbors will believe you gained a niece and a cousin all at the same time."

"I'm working on a place."

He stroked her hair and he was silent for a few minutes. "I still have the same problems, my dear. My family is here. I can't simply abandon them. Besides, the war is coming to an end. Surely once the Russians are defeated, the Germans will be busy with their new empire. Perhaps they will forget us?"

"That's wishful thinking, you know that."

"Only time will tell. For now, all I can think about is getting Kaji out of here and safely to your home. After that, we can talk about the future."

"Our future?"

"All futures."

She fell asleep before she realized it. She awoke the next morning, still lying on the hard wooden floor near the fireplace. Kaji was snuggled up against her, fast asleep. Adam was sitting in a chair a meter away, his head pressed against the cushions. She checked her watch; it was nearly nine in the morning.

She pulled herself up and moved away from Kaji, careful not to wake her. She moved to the chair and pressed her lips against Adam's head. "Time to wake," she whispered. He stretched in the chair and opened his eyes, blinking them a few times and looking around as if he was surprised by his surroundings. "That's right," he said finally. "There was a delay. I dreamt our little operation had gone off without a hitch, and Kaji was already in Aryan Warsaw."

"That's a good omen," Irena said. "Let's hope that everything goes today as planned."

They ate breakfast and then spent the morning in the main hall of the orphanage. Kaji played with some of her friends while Ewa, Adam, and Irena waited impatiently for the time to slowly pass. At eleven thirty they departed and returned to the hospital. Ala was waiting for them, just like the day before.

"Is everything set?" Irena asked.

"Yes," said Ala. "He's already here."

Feeling relieved, Irena trailed her friend as she led them again through the hospital and down to the morgue. They entered the adjoining room. This time the outside door was already open and the cart was there, backed up to the entrance. Irena tried to ignore the stacked bodies lining the bottom. Janek was there, looking around nervously.

"Is she ready?" he asked.

"All right, Kaji, just like we practiced," said Irena. "And remember, you must remain perfectly still, and entirely quiet. Your life depends on it."

Kaji nodded. "What if the Germans find me?" she asked.

"Don't you worry about that," said Irena. "You just do what we've practiced and everything will turn out all right."

Janek reached a hand out and took Kaji's arm. He pulled her up into the cart and helped her to lie down on the row of bodies, near the middle. Irena's heart broke. How could she do this to her little girl? Still, she had to get her out of the ghetto and to safety. This was the best way. As she watched, barely able to breathe, Janek and his men carried additional bodies onto the cart, stacking them next to Kaji and then above her. They placed wooden slats on the bodies to her left and right, and then lay another corpse directly above her. The slats prevented the body from crushing her. They then filled in the rest of the cart until there were several more layers above Kaji.

"Can you breathe?" Irena asked. "Are you okay in there?"

"Yes," Kaji responded. "But I'm scared."

"You'll be fine," Irena said, her voice breaking. "You're my brave little girl."

"She's going to be okay," said Janek. "In an hour she'll be on the Aryan side and safe forever."

"Take care of her. No matter what."

"I will," Janek said.

The cart departed. Irena watched them move slowly away. She didn't move until they were out of sight.

"You should be going," Adam said.

"I wish you could go with me."

"Someday, my dear."

She pulled Ala and Adam in and held them tight. "Thank you. Thank you both. I'll see you tomorrow."

"Don't come back for a few days," ordered Ala. "Spend some time with Kaji. You deserve it."

"Okay, I will," said Irena. She relished the thought of a few days off. She would take Kaji shopping and buy her a new dress. They could walk in the park. Kaji had never known a normal life, and Irena was going to give her one.

These dreams waltzed through her mind as she departed the hospital and made her way through the gate and into Aryan Warsaw. She walked back to her apartment, arriving there a little after one. She made her mother lunch and then they sat together, waiting for the knock on the door that would signal the beginning of a new life for both of them. They sat at their kitchen table as the minutes dragged by.

"I'm proud of you," her mother said. "Saving a life is a marvelous thing."

"Even a Jewish life?" Irena asked.

"A child is a child. And I've never hated the Jews, Irena."

"You've certainly acted like it."

Her mother put a hand on hers. "Your father died from a disease he contracted taking care of a Jewish family."

"That wasn't their fault. He was just doing his job."

"You're right, but I suppose I did blame them in some way. It's a difficult life to live when your husband dies and you're still young. I lost my future that day, and your future too."

"I miss him too, Mother. But I didn't give up my future. My life is just what I wanted."

"Including your marriage?"

"Mietek is a good man. But I never loved him. I don't think he ever really loved me either. We liked and respected each other, but there was never much in the way of romantic feeling."

"And you think you have that with Adam?"

"We aren't romantic, Mother."

"If you aren't, you will be."

"I don't know that. I thought we would be by now, but something always holds us back."

"If it comes to that—"

"I know, Mother. Thank you."

An hour passed and then another. Irena could feel the fear growing inside her. Something was wrong. She waited until three, her eyes constantly scanning her watch. Finally, she could wait no longer. "I'm going back," she said.

"No, stay here," her mother responded. "They are probably just delayed a bit."

Irena shook her head. "It's something else. I know it."

She headed to the door and back out onto the street. She rushed toward the ghetto, her heart full of fear. They were caught. Her little girl was arrested, or perhaps dead. She knew this had been too much of a risk. Too many things could go wrong. She arrived at the wall and endured the endless wait at the gate. She pushed her way through, almost forgetting to show her papers, and rushed to the orphanage. Ewa and Adam were waiting for her.

"What's happened?" she demanded.

"She's here," said Ewa. "Everything is okay."

Irena breathed a deep sigh of relief. "Why didn't they take her out?"

"The ghetto is sealed off," said Adam. "They aren't letting anyone out right now, corpses or no."

"But why?"

"Nobody knows," he said.

"I do," said a voice. Irena turned. Dr. Korczak was there. His face was pale, and a deep sadness creased his face. He held a crumpled paper in his hand.

"What is it?" she asked.

"They are taking us away," he said, handing her the paper. "They want six thousand of us tomorrow for relocation to the east. And six thousand each day thereafter. We are to assemble at an Umschlagplatz—a place of gathering."

She took the paper from him and held it in trembling hands. Six thousand by tomorrow. The ghetto was sealed, and they were taking the Jews away.

Chapter 17

The Dance of the Umschlagplatz

July 1942
Warsaw Ghetto, Poland

Irena sat in Dr. Korczak's office with the doctor, Ewa, and Adam. Two weeks had passed since the announcement of relocation. Each day, the Germans rounded up thousands of Jews and herded them to the train platform at the corner of Stawki and Dzika streets. The Germans were cruel. They didn't perform the collection work themselves. They had given the Jewish police officers a quota. They must produce so many Jews a day for relocation or their own family would be taken. Adam Czerniaków, the president of the Judenrat, had committed suicide in protest. This decision was a cry of desperation, brave in its own way, but it had done nothing to stop the Germans in their relentless quest to rid the ghetto of the Jews.

"The Umschlagplatz is a hell in and of itself," said Dr. Korczak. "There is no food, no water. Sometimes families wait there for days in the heat, without shelter."

"I've heard worse than that," said Adam, pulling on a cigarette. "There are Ukrainians there. Vicious killers hired by the SS. They take our women to the upstairs of an adjacent building and rape them. Sometimes they fire into the crowd from the windows of this building, killing people at random."

"God have mercy on them all," said Ewa, bowing her head in prayer.

"There are rumors of where the trains are headed," said Irena.

"What rumors?" asked Ewa.

"They say the trains are traveling toward a single track near the town of Treblinka. The cars go this way, full of people, and return empty. Nobody comes back."

"That could mean lots of things," said Dr. Korczak. "If they are relocating our people to camps there, they wouldn't be bringing anyone back, would they?"

"Do you believe they are just moving us east, Doctor?" asked Adam.

Dr. Korczak stared into the distance for a moment. "That's what I want desperately to believe. But no. I don't know what is waiting for us out there, but I doubt it is better than what we have here. The Germans are out to destroy us. Whether it's slave labor, or something worse, it cannot be good that they are removing us from this population center."

"Agreed," said Adam. "But what can we do about it?"

"We can fight," said Ewa. "Our people are organizing."

"Are you kidding?" asked Adam. "What does *our resistance* have? A couple pistols and a grenade or two? They will slaughter us in half an hour."

"Perhaps," said Dr. Korczak. "But Ewa is right. We should fight them. At least some of us should. I must stay with the children."

"No!" said Irena. "You're wrong, Ewa. There is nothing to

fight them with. I want to get you all out. Find hiding places for you. I have those birth certificates."

"Hundreds of them?" asked Dr. Korczak. "Even if that were true, you could not get us all out of the ghetto."

"Not all at once," said Irena. "But a few at a time."

"Even if you could, where would they go?"

"I've been working on that," said Irena. "I've heard from my friends in the resistance. They are locating safe houses. I have one already—Maria."

"Maria?" said Adam, scoffing. "Since when? I thought you suspected her of turning Kaji in to the Germans."

"I don't know that," said Irena. "We've spent a lot of time together in the months since then. She's offered to hide some-one for me. I hope I can trust her."

"You should get Adam out if you can," said Dr. Korczak. "Ewa and Kaji too. If you can do more, that would be wonder-ful. But at least save those three."

"I won't leave you," said Ewa to the doctor. "As long as you are here, I will stay too."

The doctor looked over at Ewa and smiled. "That's very kind of you Ewa. You are a darling young woman. But young woman you are, and I'm an old man with not too many years ahead of me. If Irena can arrange it, I want you to go. With as many children as you can manage as well." His eyes filled with tears. "I'd like to think at the end of the day that I'd saved at least a few of them."

"It's settled then," said Irena. "I'll secure housing, documents, and a way out. Once I do, I'll take Adam, Ewa, and Kaji." She turned to Ewa. "I'm going to get Ala and Rami out too."

Ewa shook her head. "She'll never leave."

"I have to try. She should do it for her daughter if for noth-ing else."

Dr. Korczak rose and they stood up to join him. "I approve of the plan," he said. "After that, if you are able to take some more of my children, I give them to you." He stepped forward and took her hand, wearing a sad smile. "Please, Irena, save as many as you can."

"You've already saved them," she said, stepping up to kiss him on the cheek. "You brought life to them. This oasis in the midst of hell."

"You're too kind," he said. "I've done what little I could for them. I hope you can do more."

"I will do everything I can," she promised.

The meeting ended and Adam accompanied her as she left the orphanage.

"Where are you going now?" he asked.

"To the hospital. I want to speak with Ala."

"I agree with Ewa," said Adam. "You're wasting your time. She will refuse you."

"We shall see," said Irena. "Will you come with me?"

He took a step toward her and then stopped. "I have classes to teach," he said. "But can you visit me later?"

"Here?"

"Yes. Three hours past midday?"

She checked her watch. "I'd love to."

She turned and made her way to the hospital. She arrived a half hour later and inquired about Ala. She found to her surprise that she wasn't there.

"You must go to the Umschlagplatz," a nurse told her.

"Why there?" Irena asked in alarm.

"She's set up a little clinic there with Nachum Remba."

"Why?"

"She's saving people from the trains."

Irena rushed out and headed north on Smocza. She arrived a few minutes later at the gathering place. The road was cluttered with luggage, clothes, shoes, the trappings of thousands who had already gone. She checked her purse, making sure of her papers. If she was mistaken as a Jew she could be whisked away on a train before she had a chance to explain who she was. She had avoided this place since the announcement. She felt fear rising as she grew closer. She didn't want to see what was happening here, but she had to find her friend.

The Umschlagplatz was a huge rectangular courtyard surrounded by a towering wall. There was a six-story brick building looming over one of the sides, with many broken windows. The courtyard was full of families, all sitting against the walls or in the middle of the stone ground, their luggage surrounding them. In the front of the courtyard, a rail line stood. The square was crawling with Germans, Jewish policemen, and Ukrainians. Several were eyeing Irena with interest.

In a corner of the platform she spotted Ala. Her friend had set up a temporary shelter. Two long rows of bodies lay in lines on the platform concrete. Ala was kneeling on the ground, her hands running over an elderly woman who was looking up at her and smiling. Irena recognized Nachum Remba too. He was a Judenrat clerk, but here he was moving among the wounded as if he was a nurse or a doctor.

"Ala!" she called as she grew closer. Her friend looked up with a concerned expression and waved Irena over.

"What are you doing here?" she whispered. "This is a very dangerous place."

"I can ask the same of you," said Irena. "You shouldn't be here."

"I've set up a clinic to take care of the sick and the wounded," she said. "Look at these poor souls. Three women were raped today, then shot. Two of them are here, wounded and still alive. I have no medicine, little water, nothing to work with."

"Then why are you here?"

"Look at that train," said Ala, gesturing at a nearby engine sitting on the tracks, attached to a dozen cattle cars. "Do you know where they are taking people?"

"I've heard rumors. All of them bad."

204 James D. Shipman

"It's a death sentence to get into one of those cars. Nachum and I are doing what we can to save a few people here."

"That's what I came to talk to you about," said Irena, steeling herself for the conversation. "Saving some people."

Ala looked up, her interest piqued. "Go on."

"I told you I have false birth certificates. I can get other documentation from the department. I want to get you and Rami out of the ghetto."

Ala returned to her work. "That's not necessary."

"Not necessary? You just said what's happening out there!" Irena said, pointing back toward the waiting train. "Six thousand a day, Ala. In three months, there won't be a soul left here."

"I'm the chief nurse of the ghetto. Assigned by the Judenrat. I'll be exempt. For a while at least."

"And then what?" said Irena, stepping forward to grab Ala's arm and pull her up so she was facing her. "What do you think will happen when there's nobody left to nurse?"

"I have a duty to these people, Irena. You of all people should know that. I won't save myself and sacrifice all of them."

"What about Rami? At least let me save her?"

Ala hesitated and her eyes filled with tears. "No. Not now, not yet."

"Will you at least consider your child? I will make sure she is safe."

Ala turned away and returned to her work.

"Ala."

Her friend responded with the slightest of nods.

"I'll get to work immediately. You don't have to decide now. But I'll have the paperwork ready."

"Thank you," Ala whispered. She looked up at one of the Germans, watching them from a few meters away. "You'd best leave before they question you."

Irena walked away from the platform, showing her paper-work to a German guard who attempted to stop her. He waved her past. As she departed the Umschlagplatz she made her decision. She would prepare documents for Rami *and* Ala. She would convince her friend to leave the ghetto somehow.

Irena returned to the orphanage. She was struck by the now deserted streets of the ghetto. For a year and a half, she had navigated these streets, fighting through the smugglers, the beggars, and the pressing throng. Now it was as if the city was abandoned. Occasionally she would glimpse a head at a window. At one intersection a young woman sprinted across the street and dashed into an alley. Otherwise, there was little evidence that nearly a half million people still lived here.

She arrived back at Dr. Korczak's building just past three o'clock. She found Adam waiting for her in the main area near the entranceway, sitting at a table with some tea. She sat down and he poured her a cup, along with a little bread. They sat that way for a long time, neither speaking, sitting close to each other and sipping their drinks.

"I'm not going," he said finally.

"What do you mean?" she asked.

"Look around us, Irena," he said, gesturing with his hands at the little clumps of children playing with toys.

"You can't save them," she said.

"I can share their journey."

She took his hand and squeezed hard. He jolted in surprise and looked up at her. "It won't do them any good. They have Dr. Korczak here. He will take care of them. I have to get you to safety."

"What did Ala say?"

Irena hesitated. "She's still deciding."

Adam laughed. "You're a bad liar, my dear. She turned you down, didn't she?"

"She wants me to prepare paperwork for Rami. I'm going to do it for both of them."

"She'll never leave. She's a cornerstone in the ghetto. She'll sacrifice everything for her people. Why should I do less?"

"Because I love you," Irena said, whispering those electric words she'd yearned to say to him for so long. "Because I can't imagine a world without you. Kaji will need a mother *and* a father." She held his hand with both of hers now. "We can have our own children as well. A future. But not if you die out there in the east somewhere."

He looked at her for long moments. "I love you too. I've loved you for years. But that doesn't change our condition, Irena. How can I use love to justify leaving all these children? How about my family? What is to happen to them?"

"Listen to me," said Irena, soaking up his words. "You aren't facing the truth. They are going to kill all of you. Do you hear me? There is no coming back from those trains. The Germans are out to destroy you. If I could save your family, and all these children, and everyone in the ghetto, I would do it. But I can't. The time has come when we must make impossible choices. Does everyone die or do we try to save as many as we can?"

"Why do I deserve to live?" he muttered, his eyes brooding.

"It's not a matter of deserve," said Irena. "None of these poor children deserve to die. Nobody in this ghetto does. But the hard reality is most of them will be gone in a few months. The question is not whether you deserve it. The question is whether you will take your chance to avoid the fate of this ghetto."

"I don't know, Irena," he said, shaking his head. "I just don't know what to say to you about that. I need time to think."

"I know it's a terrible decision. Don't worry about it right now. It will take some days to prepare things. I just want your permission to put the paperwork together."

"I can agree to that at least," he said. "What about Ewa?"

"I'm going to do the same for her. When the time comes, I'll convince all of you to go, if it's the last thing I do."

"All right," he said. "Lay the groundwork. I must admit I'm afraid to die. But I don't know if I can live with myself if I leave here without all of them."

"We'll cross that street when we must, my darling," she whispered. "I love you."

"I love you too."

Irena left the orphanage and the ghetto, heading back toward her office nearby. She had not expected this to be easy, but nobody had really declined at this point. She would prepare all the paperwork and work on the details of an escape plan. She knew that would be the hardest part of all. It was not the documents that were the real problem, it was going to be the escape from the ghetto.

But first problems first. She squared her shoulders and marched into her building, heading directly upstairs to the director's office. She knocked and entered. Jan was there. He looked up in annoyance. "What is it now, Irena?"

Irena slammed the door behind her. "It's time to choose sides," she said.

"What in the hell are you talking about?" he demanded, his face a mottled scarlet.

"I want birth certificates. I want identification paperwork. I want you to sign everything that's necessary for three adults and two children, to show they are legally Aryan Poles."

"You're mad," he said, starting to rise. "I've warned you again and again, Irena, but this is the end."

"I want the paperwork in the next forty-eight hours."

"Or what? What are you going to do?"

"I'm going to make sure you receive the justice you deserve. I know it was you who turned Kaji in to the Germans. You've been working with them all along. This is your last chance to prove yourself a Pole and a patriot. If you don't, then I'm turning you in to the resistance. And they can decide what to do with you."

His face was white hot with anger now. "You accuse me of working with the Germans?" he shouted. "I would never betray my country. As for *your* resistance," he shouted, pointing a finger at her, "you can tell that band of Bolsheviks to go to hell! They aren't the only people fighting. I have my own connections, Irena. Freedom fighters who want to return our nation to the Catholic, democratic nation that existed before these bastards arrived."

"I remember well what existed before the war," said Irena. "Your regulations forcing Jews to sit in different parts of the hall at our university. Your laws that favored the wealthy and kept the poor weak and downtrodden. I don't give a damn about your Catholic Poland. But when this thing is over, there will be an accounting for everyone's actions. You have a chance to save lives, Jan. These are real people who will die without your help. That's not socialism or communism. That's called being a human. I don't care anymore what the risks are. I don't care if the Germans are watching. You say you've never helped them? I don't believe you. But even if you're telling the truth, that's not good enough. It's time to help your fellow man!"

"Get out!" he shouted. "Get out of my office right now and don't you dare speak about this again to me or to anyone here. Do you understand me?"

"It's not going to be that easy," she said, rising. "Think about your future. I want those five documents in two days."

She opened the door and slammed it hard. She stormed out of the building, her emotions hot. She'd just risked everything. If he was working for the Gestapo, she had sealed her fate for good. She stood on the sidewalk for a few minutes, gathering her emotions. She checked her watch; it was nearly five. She should go home and make some dinner for her and her mother.

She would need to stop by the market on the way; she had nothing at the apartment to make.

She crossed the street and headed toward a little store she knew along the way. She wondered what Jan was thinking, what he would do now. She heard footsteps behind her. Someone grabbed her wrist. "Irena Sendler," said a gruff voice. "You're coming with us."

Chapter 18
A New Plan

July 1942
Warsaw, Poland

"Who are you?" she whispered.

"We're with the resistance," the man answered. "Get in the car."

She breathed a sigh of relief and stepped into the open door of a waiting vehicle. The driver sped off into the streets.

"It's about time you contacted me again," she said. "I've needed your help badly."

"We weren't sure we could trust you."

"And now you do?"

"Enough to arrange this meeting, at least."

"Where are we going?"

"All your questions will be answered in a few minutes."

She rode along quietly for the next half hour. They traveled east, crossing the Vistula into the Praga district. The vehicle finally halted before a nondescript building. "In there," the man said, gesturing at the front door.

"Aren't you coming with me?" she asked.

"This meeting is for you, not for me."

She stepped out of the car and up toward the entrance. A flicker of fear rose in her mind. What if this wasn't the resistance? What if this was some kind of Gestapo trick? Or perhaps, even worse, what if Jan had called one of the right-wing resistance groups? The Konfederacja Narodu, for instance. There was infighting among the right- and left-wing groups, even some killing.

There was nothing she could do, she realized. She couldn't run, the car was still here. She would have to enter the building and face whatever was in front of her. She climbed the stairs and opened the door. Another man waited for her there, wearing a long leather trench coat. He looked like a Volksdeutscher, a Pole of German descent. He nodded to her and opened a door to his right. She entered the room and realized she'd been here before. She was safe.

The man was seated at the table. A couple of guards behind him stood in the shadows. "Irena, so nice to see you again."

She nodded. Now that she was here and she knew she wasn't in any danger, she felt her anger rising.

"What is it?" he asked, as his eyes searched her features.

"I've needed your help badly," she said. "You promised to help me, but you've done nothing. You've sat back while I risked my life, while thousands have suffered in the ghetto. You left me no way to contact you. What is the point of a resistance if it sits back and watches!" She shouted this last sentence.

"We had to find out if we could trust you," he said, echoing the words of the man in the car.

"And meanwhile so much horror has happened."

"We've been very busy, Irena. Don't be so self-centered as to believe you are our only project. In the time since we saw you that second time, we've purchased hundreds of weapons. We've carried out political assassinations, bribed officials, saved hundreds of Jews both inside and outside the ghetto. And we've observed your movements with great curiosity. There are some who still believe you may be a German spy."

"How is that possible?" she asked.

"Your association with Jan Dobraczyński, for example. And Wiera Gran."

"My association with Jan? He hates me. I had to threaten him with violence from your organization. An organization I couldn't even contact. In order to prevent him from firing me. As for Wiera, she saved my life."

"Yes, we're aware of that. Curious."

"What do you know about her?"

"Plenty. But it is all rumors. We haven't made up our minds about her. We have made up our minds about Jan. At the best he's a right-wing fanatic. At the worst, he's a collaborator with the Gestapo."

"I threatened him today."

The man leaned forward, curiosity creasing his features. "Tell me."

She explained the confrontation with Jan in detail.

"Interesting. Tell me more about this paperwork, the birth certificates. How does it all fit together?"

She explained the burning of the parish in Lwów, how an untraceable birth certificate could lead to additional documents, all that would allow a Jew to live in Aryan Warsaw. If they could get out of the ghetto, and if they could find a safe house to live in.

"And you have plans to help these five Jews escape. How would you get them out?"

"I haven't worked that out yet," she said. She explained the previous plan to take Kaji out of the ghetto in a corpse cart.

"We have other routes out of the ghetto. Have you tried the All Saints Church?"

"The what?"

"Now what kind of Catholic are you, Irena?" the man asked

sarcastically. "The All Saints Church is in the ghetto. The church serves Jews in the ghetto who have converted. But that's not what is interesting. There is a curious geographical reality about the church. One side opens to the ghetto. But there is a second entrance into Aryan Warsaw."

"That cannot be true," said Irena. "Why would the Germans allow it?"

"They threw up these barriers in a few days. There were bound to be loopholes."

"If that's true," Irena said, doubting it even though he said it, "then why don't Jews just walk through the church and escape?"

"The church is watched. It's risky to try to escape that way. Besides, without paperwork, what good would it do them? They would be arrested in Aryan Warsaw, or worse, subjected to the blackmail and betrayal of traitorous Poles."

"Could I get my people out that way?" she asked.

"You might. But that's not what I brought you here to talk about."

"What then?"

"We want you to do more."

"More?"

"We've heard you had connections to paperwork. That you were working to get people out of the ghetto. We want to expand your operation."

"How?"

"If you can furnish the documents, we can get them out of the ghetto. We also have safe houses all over the city. People who can be trusted. We can place them in locations where they at least have a fighting chance to survive."

"I want to bring all of Dr. Korczak's orphans out," she said. "And all of his staff."

The man pursed his lips, shaking his head slightly. He coughed hoarsely into a handkerchief before he responded. "Children are tricky. They do not listen well to instructions. When you're escaping, snap decisions can be life or death."

"I will help you," said Irena. "But the orphanage first."

There was a pause. "I'll consider it."

"I need to be able to contact you from now on."

"Agreed."

"How will I do it?"

"Maria Kulska."

"What?" Irena said with surprise.

"She's our agent in your department."

"I thought she was a German spy, at least at first."

The man laughed. "She does have a difficult personality. But she's trustworthy. When you need us, contact her. She's been watching you for a long time. And protecting you."

"Who are you?" Irena asked suddenly.

Another pause. "My name is Julian Grobelny. Our organization is called Żegota. And from now on, your code name is Jolanta."

The next two days passed in a blur while Irena made preliminary plans to get her friends and Kaji out of the ghetto, and deeper plans for a mass removal of the orphanage.

Her first order of business was to visit the All Saints Church. Her first trip to the structure was awe inspiring. Built in the seventeenth century, the church displayed two tall spires rising over a central entryway.

She spent hours over the next couple of days, praying in the pews, watching people come and go, getting used to the patterns of the priests, keeping a lookout for Germans, both in uniform and without. She took mental notes, trying to figure out the optimal time of day to bring her friends through.

It became obvious from the start that it would be no easy task. There was often a German guard at the entrance to the Aryan side. He would check the papers of each person who came out of the sanctuary and left by the Polish side of the church. This was not an insurmountable problem, so long as she secured her proper paperwork. However, she did not know this man. Did he pay close attention to who came in? Did he watch who entered from the ghetto side? If so, paperwork or no, they would be caught.

There was also the problem of the worshippers themselves. Were any of them spies? Gestapo? How about the priests? Were they collaborating with the Germans? One thing became patently obvious to Irena. While she might with some luck sneak her small party of five through this route, there was no chance they could move the entire orphanage with hundreds of children through here. Still, Julian had said that was Żegota's problem, not hers. She, Jolanta, was to focus on obtaining the paperwork.

Jolanta. She thought of her code name and couldn't help but chuckle to herself. It sounded like something out of some bad spy novel. Still, she couldn't help but feel a little proud of herself. She was a soldier now, for the socialist cause. She was attempting to save the lives of others, to craft a new, free Poland for Poles and Jews alike. She thought of her father. She hoped he was watching her from on high. The image made her immensely happy.

After two days of observation, she felt she knew enough about the church to attempt an escape. She would never be able to handle all the variables. Now for the difficult part. She hadn't seen Jan since their confrontation in his office when she'd demanded he produce the paperwork she needed. Now she must return to him and see whether he had come through for her, refused, or worse yet, set her up for arrest.

Irena stepped into his office. Jan was there on the telephone. He motioned for her to sit down. A good sign, she hoped. He talked for a few more minutes and then hung up. He looked up, his face unreadable.

"What is it?" he asked.

"You know why I'm here."

"Oh yes. The paperwork you've demanded. The rules you want me to break that put all of us in jeopardy."

"You know this is bigger than that at this point."

He nodded. "I don't like you, Irena. I don't like your politics and your actions. I think you're doing this for yourself, for your own ego, rather than for the Jews, the Poles, or anyone else."

"You don't have to like me," she responded, hot emotions swirling through her mind. "You just have to help me."

He reached into his desk drawer and pulled out a folder. "Five sets," he said. "All with valid stamps and my signature. You can fill in the blanks."

She took them. "Thank you," she said. "I need hundreds more. Soon."

He looked at her in surprise. "What are you talking about?"

"I can't tell you much," she said. "There is a plan afoot to bring out the entire population of Dr. Korczak's orphanage."

Jan whistled. "That would be something. But it sounds impossible. How would you do it?"

"I don't have to worry about the logistics," she said. "I just need the paperwork. Can you provide them?"

He hesitated. "Look, Irena, giving you five sets of these is dangerous enough. But hundreds? Someone's going to get caught and they will be coming to me for answers." He shook his head. "That's asking too much."

"There's no such thing as too much when lives are on the line," she responded.

"You're right," he said after a moment. "If they come for me then they come for me. But hundreds," he said, raising his hands as if overwhelmed by the prospect. "It will take weeks."

"That's all right," said Irena. "We have a little time. My people are working out their plan. I just need to make sure when the time is right, you'll be ready."

"I'll do everything I can."

"Thank you," she said, rising to leave.

"Just be careful, Irena. You can't just throw this together. If you make a mistake, we both will die."

Irena returned to her office. Maria was there, sitting across from her desk. Irena hadn't had time to talk to her yet since she'd found out about her role with the resistance.

"I guess I owe you an apology," she said finally. "I had no idea you were part of—"

"I'm not part of anything that needs to be discussed here," snapped Maria.

Irena stared at her for long moments. "Well, I'm sorry I misjudged you."

"I don't need your apology," she said, but Irena saw a softening in her eyes. "Just tell me what the plan is. And keep your voice down, for God's sake."

An hour later Irena was in the ghetto. Today would be the day. Now she had to convince her friends to leave with her. She traveled first to the Umschlagplatz. Ala was there, still working in her little corner of the platform, with the rows of bodies pleading for medical attention, for water, or just to die.

"Hello, Irena," said Ala, not looking up.

"I have the paperwork," whispered Irena.

Ala turned to her, her face a surprise. She looked like she was going to say something, and then she stopped herself and returned to her work.

"I'm going to take you out today. You, Rami, Adam, Kaji, and Ewa. Will you come?"

"I told you, I have work that must be done."

"Nachum is here," said Irena, pointing to the man who stooped over another body a few meters away. "He can carry on without you."

Ala shook her head. "I cannot leave him. I refuse to leave *them*."

"Rami then. Will you let me take Rami?"

Ala kept her head down, refusing to look at Irena. "We're protected."

"Look, Ala, we've been through this before. You can't survive here forever. Now is your chance to get out. Maybe your only chance."

Ala rose, turning to Irena. She took Irena's hands in her own. She smiled and it seemed to Irena that the sun shone behind her, a glimmering shimmer as if she was an angel. "Their lives are bigger than mine. I'm happy for you, Irena. Take your Adam and your Kaji out. Ewa too. I have to stay here, and I cannot bear to be parted from my Rami."

Irena realized Ala would not come with her. She'd expected this but she'd had to try. She wasn't going to give up. "There are plans for more. For something bigger. Can I ask again later?"

Ala laughed. "You never give up, do you? Yes, my darling friend. You can ask again later. But now I must get back to work. They need me here. Go make your happiness, Irena."

They embraced and Irena left her, tears streaming down her face. Ala was so brave. She was sacrificing everything for these people. Irena would not give up on her. She would get her out in the next round or the next. If need be, she might ask Żegota to abduct Ala. Poland would need women like her when all of this was over.

She walked the long kilometers back to the orphanage. She was drenched in sweat from the oppressive heat. This summer seemed hotter than any she could ever remember. Just when the suffering of the Jews in this ghetto did not seem like it could get any worse. It was as if nature itself had turned on them.

She finally arrived at Dr. Korczak's, already exhausted from a day walking the length and breadth of the ghetto in the scorching heat. Adam and Ewa were waiting for her, along with Kaji. She rushed forward and picked the little girl up, kissing her cheeks over and over. She was surprised by her weight. She was getting older and bigger. "Pretty soon I won't be able to pick you up at all anymore," she joked. "Kaji, go play with the others. I need to talk to Uncle Adam and Aunt Ewa."

While Kaji ran over to join a game some of the other children were playing, Irena sat down at the table. "I have the documents," she whispered.

"Can I see them?" Adam asked.

Irena reached down into her bag and pulled out the folder. She slid the paperwork over to Adam. "Be careful nobody notices," she said.

Adam opened the folder and scanned the documents, reading each page carefully. When he was finished, he slid the materials back to Irena. "They are perfect," he said at last. "How do you know the signature for Jan is close enough?"

"I didn't forge his signature," said Irena. "He signed these."

"Then he knows what you're doing?" Ewa asked in alarm. "I thought you believed he's a collaborator."

"He may be," said Irena. "But he's afraid of my contacts. He will not betray me." *I pray he won't betray me.* "So you're both going, correct?"

"I told you I have to stay with Dr. K," said Ewa.

"And he told you to leave."

"I won't leave him. His work here is too important."

"There are plenty of adults to assist him. We've been through this, Ewa. This is your chance."

"Did you ask Ala?" she inquired.

Irena did not answer.

"She said no, didn't she?"

"Ala has connections here that you will never have," said Irena. "She is protected. You are not."

"That's not why she stays." Ewa stood up. "I'm sorry, Irena, but I must refuse. You know I love you more than anything. I want to go with you, just for your sake. But I cannot. I made my commitment to this orphanage, to the doctor. I will not leave them."

Irena tried to stop her, but Ewa turned and walked away. She would have followed her, but Adam was still here. She sat back down.

"I'm not going either," said Adam.

"Don't be a fool," she said. "I have everything you need right here."

"How can I go while they remain behind? How can I leave my family? And these children."

"What about our family?" asked Irena. "What about Kaji and me? Will you give all of that up? Will you sacrifice your life?"

"Ala and Ewa have refused you," he repeated. His face was a ghostly white and he would not look at her.

"I don't care what they've decided," Irena said. "Besides, there are plans to take out everyone."

"What?" he said, looking up with interest.

She told him of Żegota, Jan, the new paperwork that would be ready in a couple of weeks.

"No problem, then," he said. "We can all go out together."

"I don't want to wait for that," she said. "I want Kaji out now. And you. I've waited long enough."

He hesitated. He was fumbling, unsure of himself. "You know I'm right," she insisted. "Please, Adam. I need you. We can leave right now. I have a way out, through the All Saints Church." She explained her plan, her days of observation.

"You want to leave this moment?"

"Yes. I want you to get up, take Kaji's hand and mine, and save your life."

He looked at her for long moments, then turned his eyes downward. "I'm sorry," he said. "They would not join you. How can I?"

She felt her heart sink. Still, there was a chance later. "But you will come out with the orphans, right?"

"Of course, I will. That's all I want."

"Okay then," she said, partially relieved. She stood up and

walked around to him. Putting her arms around his neck, she kissed his head briefly. "I love you," she whispered.

"I love you too. Are you going to take Kaji?"

"Yes."

"Right now?"

"Yes."

"You must be careful. In the name of everything holy, you must protect her."

"I will, my darling."

She squeezed his shoulder and then stepped away from him. "Kaji, come to me," she ordered.

"Not now," Kaji protested. "I'm in the middle of a game."

Irena stepped over to Kaji and reached down, taking her by the arm. "Now."

Kaji rose, still grumbling about the interruption to her play time. Irena chastised her for disobeying, although she was secretly pleased. How wonderful to be innocent, to worry only about your game being ruined when the world was crashing in around you.

She led Kaji out of the room toward the main entrance. Before she stepped through the door, she turned. Adam was still there, watching them. He gave her a little wave. She waved back and then led Kaji into the street.

On the walk to the All Saints Church, she kept an eye out for Germans or the Jewish police. The last thing she needed right now was to be confronted and sent to the Umschlagplatz. She had Kaji wait behind a building at each corner until she knew that the streets were clear.

"I'm hot," Kaji complained. "I'm thirsty too."

"We'll get water in just a little bit," she said. "Now remember what I said about this church. Remember what Aunt Ewa taught you? Can you make the cross for me?"

Kaji made the gesture.

"That's perfect, my dear. And the prayers?" Kaji nodded.

"Good girl. Now we are going to be entering the church in just a few minutes. I need you to do exactly what I tell you. Do you understand?"

Kaji nodded.

"What are you two doing here?" She looked up. Wiera was standing there, her hands full of shopping bags. She was smiling and hurrying up to greet them.

"Hello, Wiera," Irena said. "We are just going for a walk."

"In this heat?" she said, motioning with her arms as she lifted her bags in the air.

"Watch me," Kaji said, making the sign of the cross. "See how good I do it?"

"You did that perfectly," said Wiera, looking up knowingly at Irena. "You must be going for a very long walk."

Irena was horrified, but there was nothing she could do. Besides, she could trust Wiera, couldn't she? She motioned for the singer to come closer and she whispered in her ear. "We're leaving, today."

Wiera looked around her, her eyes finally setting on the All Saints Church. "I understand," she said. She put her hands on Kaji's head. "I pray for you both. Is there anything I can do to help?"

Irena shook her head. "Your prayers are enough."

"Irena!" She heard the voice but couldn't believe it. Adam was there, half running down the street after them. His face was pouring sweat.

"Are you coming with us?" she asked.

"Yes." He looked over at Wiera. "Are you coming out too?" he asked.

Wiera smiled. "I didn't know there were invitations. But no, at least not yet."

Adam looked confused. "Then . . ."

"Just a happy coincidence," she said. She stepped forward

and kissed Adam on the cheek. "The best of fortune for all of you." She gestured at her bags. "I have to go. These are getting terribly heavy."

They said their farewells to Wiera and then Irena turned to Adam. She was so excited he was here. "Why did you change your mind?" she asked.

"I don't want to talk about it," he said. He took Kaji's hand. "Let's go."

"Do you need to tell your family?" she asked.

"I left them a note," he said. "It's better that way."

She felt the elation flowing through her. This was her family. What she'd always dreamed of. A few more steps and they'd be in the church. In an hour they would be through and on the Aryan side, ready to start their new life.

"Is that it?" Adam asked, gesturing toward All Saints.

"Yes."

"And you're sure this is going to work?"

"I'm positive." *This must work.*

"Okay," he said, taking her hand as well. "Let's go."

They stepped into the All Saints Church. Irena led them to some holy water, and she dipped her fingers, angling herself so they could both watch her. She made the sign of the cross with her hands and then stood while Adam and Kaji repeated the gesture.

"Follow me," she whispered. They made their way up the aisle of the sanctuary. Irena kneeled at one of the pews, making the sign of the cross again. She stepped into the aisle and Adam and Kaji followed her, again repeating her gestures. Irena lowered her head in prayer. She stayed that way for a few minutes, willing her heart to slow down so she could concentrate. When she felt a little calmer, she opened her eyes a crack and tilted her head, looking slowly to the left and the right. The sanctuary contained twenty or so other people, some in groups, some sitting alone. They all had their heads down in prayer. A priest stood at the front of the sanctuary, moving objects around in preparation for a later Mass.

"What are we doing next?" Adam whispered.

"We wait here," she responded. "Keep your head down and pretend to pray."

"I'm not pretending."

She kept her eyes closed, thinking through their next steps. The priest had seen them enter from the ghetto side. She could not risk him calling them out if they headed toward the Aryan entrance. She waited another ten minutes. The priest stepped to a door near the front of the sanctuary and went inside.

"Now," she whispered, turning to move away. Adam and Kaji followed her. She moved slowly, not wanting to draw attention to them. She drew deep breaths, keeping her eyes forward. *You're supposed to be here*, she thought to herself. *You came to pray and now you're going home with your family to Polish Warsaw.* The door was a few meters away. The shouts of alarm she expected any moment did not come. They were going to make it.

"Irena!"

She froze. Peter was there. His hulking form filling up the entrance to the church. He was flashing his clumsy smile. "I haven't seen you in so long. How pretty you look!" He turned to Adam, looking him up and down. "And who is this?"

"I don't know him," she said, fumbling for an answer. "We're not together."

Peter eyed Adam closely, still blocking the entrance. He turned back to Irena, stepping forward and leaving a little space for Adam to pass him. "Who is the little one?"

"This is Kaji," Irena said, trying to play along. Adam looked back at her, but she ignored him. If she made eye contact with him Peter would instantly know, and he would be arrested. She saw him hesitate out of the corner of her eye for a few moments longer, and then he moved past. *Thank God*, she thought. *At least he is safe.*

"Where do you live, little Kaji?" Peter asked.

"I live with Dr. Korczak," she answered brightly. Irena felt her heart sink.

"Dr. Korczak?" said Peter, his face darkening. "So she's a Jew?"

"Yes," said Irena. "I brought her here. I'm . . . I'm trying to introduce her to the true faith."

Peter laughed. "That won't do her any good," he said, reaching out to muss Kaji's hair. "The converts still have to stay in the ghetto."

"I know. But it can't do her any harm."

He smiled. "You're a good woman, Irena Sendler. I've wondered for a long time if you might join me for a drink?" He took a step closer, his smile deepening.

"I'm . . . I'm a married woman, Peter."

"That doesn't bother me," he said. "Your husband is a prisoner, is he not?"

"He is. I . . . I just couldn't."

Peter feigned disappointment and he bowed. "Well, it doesn't hurt to ask. At least let me escort you back to the orphanage. It's getting dark out there and you could get into trouble."

Irena could have screamed in frustration. There was nothing she could do but agree to accompany him. Peter strolled along with her through the church and back out into the ghetto. He waltzed down the middle of the street as if they were on a Sunday stroll, yammering about inane topics as if there was no war, no ghetto, and they weren't enemies.

They reached the orphanage a few minutes later. Irena dismissed Kaji back inside and turned to Peter.

"Are you sure you won't reconsider?" he asked.

"I can't," she said. "But thank you for walking us here. I appreciate it," she lied. She didn't want Peter angry with her, and you never knew if a favor might come in handy later. There was no reason to burn a bridge even if he'd ruined her plans.

He took her hand and kissed the back of it. "Perhaps you will change your mind sometime. I like strong women," he said, his eyes twinkling. She didn't answer. "Well, good night, Frau Sendler. I must be going; I'll be late for Mass."

He turned and strolled away, whistling and swinging his keys in his fingers as if he didn't have a care in the world. Irena watched him go and then slunk down to the pavement, burying her head in her hands. She'd failed again. Well, she realized, not entirely. Adam was gone, and with any luck he'd reached safety. She had more time to save Kaji. She would just have to come up with another plan.

Chapter 19
New Friends

July 1942
Warsaw, Poland

Klaus remembered when he'd met Briggita. It was late 1932. He was twenty-eight and unemployed. He'd lost his job working at a grocery store as a clerk, the only position he'd been able to find in depression-riddled Germany. He was sitting in a café, drinking coffee and reading a newspaper when she walked in with a couple of friends. They sat down at a nearby table. He'd not been able to take his eyes off her. After a few minutes she'd noticed him. She turned quickly away, but throughout their meal she'd glanced now and again at him, starting to blush each time. He'd waited until they were finished and then stepped up to the table and introduced himself. He asked her if she would stay and have another coffee with him. To the obvious surprise of her friends, she agreed.

They'd spent the rest of the evening in that little run-down café, drinking coffee, talking and laughing. She told him about her family, how her father had lost his business and was struggling to find work. About her dreams to become a famous painter, but she lacked the funds for any more training, or even supplies. He told her of his desire to join the army, a hope that was dashed because of the strict 100,000-man limit on the German army imposed by the French and the English after the last world war.

They began to court, much to the disappointment of her family. They considered themselves above him. He didn't care and neither did she. She was his shining star. Everything changed after she met him. They were married barely six months later. She brought him to the Nazi party. She was a fervent believer in the new Germany espoused by the freshly appointed chancellor, Adolf Hitler. Their nation would no longer be the kicking toy of their old enemies. There would be jobs again, industry, food, vacations. Everything they'd lost in this terrible post-war environment.

Klaus impressed the local leader. He was loyal, hardworking, and sharp. He was made a police officer in the city force. The commander didn't like it, he wasn't a Nazi, but he had little choice. Klaus rose quickly in the ranks. After a few months of walking the streets, he was assigned as a detective, then a commander of detectives. As the years passed, his pay increased. They moved to a larger apartment, then they saved enough to buy a flat of their own. Their little girl was born. Everything seemed set.

Then the war began. A new opportunity came. An SS officer appeared one day at the department, looking for Klaus. They'd heard of his reputation as a fair and competent officer. His party record was impeccable. If he wanted, he could join their ranks as an officer and a member of the national police. He would have important duties in the newly occupied territories. He'd accepted, and they'd relocated to Warsaw, moving into a home and living a lifestyle they'd never dreamed of.

Here the hard realities of the new order set in. Preparing a new Poland with German masters was difficult. The people were stubborn, rebellious. Unable to govern themselves, they resented control by the Germans. Klaus had worked hard to follow the rules laid down by Hitler, to the letter.

"Are you already awake?" his wife asked in the darkness.

"I have been, for a little while."

She moved closer to him, resting her head on his chest. "Go back to sleep, darling," he said. "It's still a few hours until you have to get up."

He put his hands on her head, stroking her hair lightly. She murmured, enjoying his touch. In a few minutes, her breathing was deeper and regular again. He pulled himself slowly away, rising out of the bed and quietly dressing in the darkness. He eased himself out of the room and tiptoed down the hall. Klaus opened another door, peering into his daughter's room. She was there, sleeping, safe. He lowered his head, saying a little prayer for his family.

Peter was already out front, the car running. Klaus stepped in and accepted a cup of tea out of a canteen Peter brought each morning. He looked over at his assistant's bloodshot eyes and noted the slight grimace as he turned his head.

"Another rough night?" he asked.

"I'm fine," Peter mumbled.

"Yes, I can see that. I see you're putting weight back on again also, my friend. It's time you lay off things."

"I'll pick up my exercise."

"You should do more than that. Take a few months off. You have plenty of war left, to sleep with the remaining female population of the city."

Peter laughed. "Where are we going?"

"We have a meeting."

"Right now?"

"That's correct. Take me to Długa Street."

Peter lurched the car into motion. The streets were deserted, and they made good time. Klaus sipped at his tea, trying to keep himself awake. He was exhausted from another night of bad sleep. *You will not think of such things*, he admonished himself. *You have a job to do and you will do it*. "Who was it last night?" he asked, deciding a little conversation would help him stay alert.

"You wouldn't believe me if I told you."

"Indulge me."

"I can't reveal my information," said Peter, obviously enjoying this little game. "But you would recognize the name."

"A celebrity then?"

"Of sorts."

"A solid Aryan woman, I hope?"

"Mm-hmm."

"I'm telling you, Peter. You need to find a good German woman and settle down. All of this tom-catting is going to be the end of you."

"There's plenty of time for that when the war is over."

"That should be in short order," observed Klaus. "Our armies have pushed deep into southern Russia."

"It's not all good news," said Peter. "The British stopped us in Egypt."

"A minor setback. Besides, that's a sideshow. If we didn't have all our forces fighting the communists, the English wouldn't last a week against us."

"And the Americans?"

"Bah. They won't be ready to fight for years. If they ever get ready. I'm telling you, Peter, a few more months and the fighting in Russia will be over. Once the Soviets quit, the rest of them will make a deal. They can't go on without the Russians."

"You're probably right," said Peter. "Hell, you're always right."

"I'm glad you're starting to understand that," said Klaus. "Now take my advice and cut the womanizing for a few months.

Let's say the first of the year. If you do, I'll put you up for another promotion."

"I don't have anywhere to go," said Peter.

"I will recommend you for lieutenant."

"Promotion to officer?" said Peter, musing out loud. "That would be worth a few months of clean living."

"I'm glad you think so," said Klaus, laughing. "Now let's see if you can do it."

"Coming up on the address you gave me," said Peter.

"Good. Stop here," Klaus said.

"You're going in alone?"

"Their rules, not mine."

Peter stopped the car and Klaus stepped out. He looked up and down the street, looking for any open curtains, cars on the street, people hiding in shadows. There was nothing to see. He stepped up to the building and gave a knock at the front door. He heard a voice inside. "It's unlocked."

He turned the knob and pulled open the door. He stepped into a hallway. "It's the door to the right," said the voice. He opened this door too, and entered a large room shrouded in darkness. "That's far enough."

"What's with all the secrecy?" Klaus asked.

"You're not exactly popular in Warsaw. I can't be seen meeting with you."

"What do you have for me?"

"There's an operation afoot to smuggle children out of the ghetto."

This perked Klaus's attention. "What kind of operation?"

"It's run by Żegota."

Klaus had never heard the name before. "Who or what is Żegota?"

"Your worst enemy."

Klaus couldn't help but laugh. "I doubt that. These little

groups crop up now and again. It's all a bunch of secret meetings and handshakes. They hardly ever come to anything."

"This group is different. They have deep pockets and deeper connections."

"Tell me everything."

"I don't know everything. But I know they have an operation planned very soon."

"An operation to do what?"

"To smuggle Dr. Korczak's orphans out of the ghetto."

Klaus whistled in astonishment. "There are hundreds of kids there. They could never manage it. And even if they could, where would they go?"

"I don't have all the details yet. But I will soon."

"How soon?"

"In the next few days."

"And what is your price?"

"Fifty thousand zlotys."

"That's it?"

"I will tell you the rest when I have the information you want."

"Fair enough," said Klaus, turning to leave.

"That's not all."

He turned back. "What else?"

"They have friends on the inside."

Chapter 20

A Desperate Chance

August 1942
Warsaw, Poland

Irena knocked at the door. She checked her watch. It was almost curfew. She'd taken a terrible risk coming here. What if they weren't home, if they'd stayed the night somewhere else tonight? After all, the rendezvous had only been a few hours ago. If it had even gone off. Perhaps this had gone awry as well.

There was no answer. She breathed deeply to herself. She must not panic. She knocked again. This time she heard shuffling inside. "Who is it?" came a voice.

"Irena."

She heard the rustling of latches and the door opened. Maria was there.

"Is he here?"

"Yes, just like I promised."

She rushed through the door and found Adam sitting at the table.

"My God!" he said. "Are you all right?"

"Keep it down!" demanded Maria. "We can't arouse the suspicions of the neighbors."

He rose and rushed into her arms. He kissed her on the cheeks and then the lips. She felt her heart flutter. He'd never done that before.

Maria cleared her throat and looked at her watch. "I hate to do this to the two of you, but I remembered that my friend upstairs has been a little depressed lately. I'm going to visit with her and probably spend the night. Will you two be all right on your own?" She had a sly grin on her face as she said this.

Irena blushed. "Yes. We'll be fine. Thank you, Maria." Her friend departed and she turned to Adam.

"Is Kaji safe?" he asked.

Irena nodded. "Yes. She's back at the orphanage."

"And I'm out here . . ." he said, his voice trailing off. He disengaged and walked to the window, staring out.

"She's safe. That's all that matters for now. I can get her out with the rest. It will only be a couple of weeks."

"And what if you can't? What if Ewa, and Kaji, and all the rest never leave the ghetto? What about Ala? I shouldn't have listened to you," he said, covering his face with his hands. "I'm a coward. I've left them all to fight and die while I run and hide."

"That's nonsense," said Irena. "You came out because I asked you to. Kaji would be here right now with us, if it wasn't for fate. And there is no harm. We weren't arrested. She's back where we know she will be okay until the paperwork and the plan from Żegota comes through."

"How do you know you can even trust them?" he demanded. "Jan could be working for the Germans. It's quite a coincidence that this Peter shows up today just as we are trying to leave. Didn't you say he's a drunk and a womanizer? But he still finds time to attend Mass? Isn't it obvious? You were be-trayed."

"That can't be true," said Irena. "Jan had no idea I would use the church today."

"They could be checking every day!" he shouted. "Some-times, Irena, you are incredibly naïve about the world."

"And what should I do? Nothing? Sit back with my books and brood about the way the world should be? Not everyone can hide in their apartment. Someone must get out there and try. No matter how messy, how reckless." She knew immedi-ately she shouldn't have said these words, but she'd had too much of a scare today, and her precious Kaji was still in the ghetto. "I'm sorry," she said. "I didn't mean that."

"Get out!" he shouted. "Get out of here right now! You forced me to leave when I didn't want to. Then when I get here, you call me a coward and say you're the only one brave enough to do anything. Get out!"

"Please, Adam, don't say that," she said. "We have a night to ourselves tonight."

"I don't want to touch you," he said, turning away.

She stepped up to him, putting her hands on his shoulders. He jerked away. "I mean it, Irena. Leave here now."

She stood behind him, wanting to reach out again. She didn't want to leave. "Adam, we've never been alone together like this. We have a whole night . . ."

"Go."

There was nothing she could do. All her plans and dreams had fallen apart today. She stormed out of the apartment, down the stairs, and into the darkness of the Warsaw streets. She was risking her life outside after curfew, but for this one night, she didn't care. She was tired of fighting. If the Germans wanted her, they could have her. She stumbled out into the darkness, despair and the black night enveloping her.

*   *   *

Weeks passed. She tried to see Adam again, but he refused. She buried herself in her work, visiting the ghetto, spending time with Kaji, and coordinating with the resistance and Jan as the paperwork progressed.

"It's finished," the director said, coming into her office late in the afternoon. "It's taken all of my effort, but I have two hundred and fifty documents prepared. How on earth will you get them into the ghetto?"

"I won't need to," said Irena. "We can't sneak the children out through one of the gates or through the church."

"Then how will they get out?"

"That's what I'm going to go and find out," she responded.

"How do you contact them?" he asked.

"I'm sorry, Jan, I can't tell you that."

"Still don't trust me," he said with a wry grin. "Fair enough. But remember what I went through to get you this."

"I know it. And I'll be forever grateful. I may not approve of everything you stand for, but you're a good man, Jan. You've done a good thing here."

"I just pray it doesn't come back to bite me, and you as well."

"That's a chance we have to take."

"Agreed."

She thanked him again and then departed, walking excitedly down to Maria's office. She found her friend with her feet up on her desk, smoking and thumbing through a pre-war fashion magazine.

"The paperwork is ready," Irena said.

Maria took a deep drag, dropping the magazine down. "All right. I'll let Julian know."

"Has he asked about me?"

"Julian?"

"Of course not. I mean Adam."

"Who knows. He's moody, that one. He's been spending all his days with his nose in my books. He eats on his own and stays in his bedroom."

"Is he okay?"

"Physically, he's fine. Although he picks at his food. I've had to get after him a time or two. Like we can afford to waste anything in these times! Whatever is wrong with him, it's up here," said Maria, pointing a finger at her head.

"I should come see him," Irena said.

Maria removed her cigarette. "I wouldn't. When he does talk, it's about you."

"What does he say?"

"Never mind that. Just know it isn't good. You need to wait for him to cool off."

"When will you know the escape plan?" Irena asked, changing subjects. She tried hard to keep her face a mask, but she was churning on the inside.

"Before the end of the day, I would think."

"That quickly?"

"They knew the documents were coming. They've been busy."

"Let me know immediately, will you?"

"Of course, what do you think, I'm crazy?"

Irena returned to her office. Perhaps Maria was crazy, or worse, a double agent. Now why did that thought go through her head? If she was, Irena had trusted her not only with all the orphans, including her Kaji, but Adam as well. What terrible times they lived in, when you had to trust people you weren't sure you could rely on, and everything depended on you being correct.

She spent the rest of the day at her desk, trying to get some paperwork done. The minutes crawled by. She couldn't focus. It was nearly five when Maria appeared at the doorway. She stepped in and closed the door.

"Are they ready?" she asked.

"Yes, they are."

"When?"

"Two days from now."

"How?"

"They're going to get them out by the sewers."

Irena was revolted. She imagined hours, perhaps a day or two, stuck down below the streets in a river of feces and urine. "The children won't be able to take that."

"They'll do better than the adults, you'll see."

"I can't go with them down there," said Irena.

Maria looked at her, a smile crossing her face. "When it gets tough, you'll abandon the little ones, will you?"

Irena didn't answer for a moment. "No, you're right. I'll go with them."

"Have a good time," said Maria. "You wouldn't catch me dead down there." She turned to leave. "I told Jan."

"What?" asked Irena, alarmed. "Why would you do that?"

"You trust him, don't you? He must know when and where we need the paperwork delivered. There are crates of it."

"You shouldn't have said anything to him."

"Well, you should have made that clear," she snapped. "What am I?" she asked, arms in the air. "A mind reader? Go get your brats." She stormed out of the office.

Irena checked her watch. It was a little after five. She calculated walking times and the start of the curfew. She had just enough time to visit the orphanage. She rushed out of the office and headed to the ghetto. She reached Dr. Korczak's a little before six. She tracked down Ewa and brought her to the doctor's office.

"It's on," she said. "In two days, we will leave."

"How will we get out?" Dr. Korczak asked.

"Through the sewers."

He flinched. "Terrible. But perhaps foolproof. I trust they've found places for everyone on the other side?"

"I didn't have a chance to ask them directly," Irena said. "But they wouldn't go forward without that detail sorted out."

The doctor slumped back in his chair, closing his eyes for a moment. Irena saw a tear run down his face. "Finally. A miracle. We will save these poor children."

"You have to come," Irena said. "Ewa too. Everyone is coming."

"So long as they bring all the children, I will come," said the doctor. "But if one is left behind, I will stay with them."

"You're the bravest person I've ever met," said Irena.

"You're forgetting Ala," said Ewa.

"Ah yes, Ala," said Irena, smiling. "Well, you're in very good company at least."

"Will she come with us?" asked Ewa.

"I don't know. I'm going to try again tomorrow. She wavered last time when I told her I was going to get the entire orphanage out. I hope at least she'll let me bring out Rami."

"She'll come with her or not at all, I'd say."

Irena turned in surprise. Wiera Gran was standing in the hallway, hands on the door. "What are you doing here?" Irena asked.

"Just visiting the doctor with a donation. So, you're getting the little ones out? How about me?"

"I wouldn't think you would need any help escaping the ghetto. With your—"

"Connections? Yes, everyone thinks I have all these contacts among the Germans. They might like a pretty face, but they've little use for me as a person, or me for them. No, I will need your help as well someday, Irena. They've already shut down the café."

"Where is Władysław?"

"They found him a job in a factory. He's safe for now. But me. Nobody seems to want to make sure that I'm all right."

"Don't worry, Wiera. I'll arrange for you to get out, and a safe place to hide. I owe you one, remember."

Wiera smiled. "I knew I could depend on you." She stepped forward, dropping a paper bag on the desk. Dr. Korczak opened it; it was full of zlotys. "That's the end of it, I'm afraid," she said. "Use it how you think best," she said. She nodded at Ewa and turned back to Irena. "I'll be in contact soon. Please, anything you can do. And perhaps I can work on Ala as well. She's stubborn as a mule. But then you already know that, don't you?"

Everything was set. Irena left the ghetto and checked her watch. She could make it home, or, if she hurried, there was just enough time to . . .

A half hour later Maria opened her door. She smiled her cynical grin. "I don't know why, but I was expecting you. Come on in. Mr. Brooding is in his room."

Irena stepped into the apartment and moved tentatively to the door to Adam's room. She knocked cautiously.

"What is it?"

She opened the door. Adam was lying on the bed, a book in his hand. He had a day's growth of beard on his face. His eyes were red and bleary. He looked up at her without expression. "It's you."

"I have all of the paperwork," she said. "I'm going to get them out."

His face brightened at this and he looked up. "So, you've done it," he said finally. "When?"

"Two days."

"Will Ala come?"

"I don't know. I'm going to see her tomorrow. But I have two hundred and fifty documents. Enough for the doctor and all the children."

"Oh, Irena, you're really going to make this happen." He raised his arms and she knelt down to him, falling into his embrace. He kissed her on the neck, the cheek, on the lips. "I'm so sorry I've doubted you. I'll never doubt you again."

Irena flushed. "You don't have to say those things."

"Yes, I do."

"I see you two have finally made up," said Maria, feigning a yawn. "I think I'll visit my friend's apartment. She needs some company. I don't think I'll be coming back. Remember," she said sarcastically. "Don't make a racket."

Irena smiled appreciatively at her friend. "Thank you."

"Don't mention it. Just get to it, you two, for God's sake." Maria turned and closed the door behind her. A moment later they heard the front door open and close. They were alone and would be until the morning.

Adam moved closer and took Irena's hand. She shivered under his touch. He walked to the outlet and turned off the light. He kissed her, first gently, then more deeply. She threw her arms around him, letting him envelop her.

She burned with desire. She'd yearned for this moment since the moment she'd met him. He moved with skill, taking his time, exploring every part of her. She'd never experienced anything like this.

She lay against him afterward, a dim light illuminating his chest and arms above the blankets. She clung to him. She felt so alive. She thought of Mietek and his robotic fumbling in the bedroom—the last chore of his day.

She'd never known it could be like this. This might be the only time. Tomorrow she could be dead. Adam could be discovered and arrested. Now that she truly had him, she felt a new fear—not just the risk for her, or for him, but for them.

"That was delightful," he said, chuckling a little.

"Indeed," she said, resting her head on his chest.

"Why did we wait all these years, Irena?"

"Too many obligations."

"But the foundation has crumbled to rubble."

"Is that why you're with me? Because you have nothing left?" she asked, starting to pull away.

"I'm with you, finally, because I can't wait any longer. Because I don't know how much longer we have. Because I've wanted you since the moment I saw you."

Her body lit up with electricity. His words echoed her own. *Since the moment I saw you.* She turned toward him and kissed his neck.

"I hope everything goes well tomorrow," he said.

"Shut your mouth," she said, kissing his lips. "That's not what I want to talk about right now."

He returned the kiss violently, moving his hands down her back.

She woke in Adam's arms. She felt his warmth, admired his naked form in the early morning light. She was happier than she could ever remember having been. She moved closer to him, kissing his neck, holding him close. He groaned and rolled over, still asleep. She smiled, laughing to herself. She finally had her Adam, and in the next few hours she would have her Kaji too. She rose and dressed quietly in the darkness. She tiptoed out of the room and made her way to the door. The flat was still in darkness. She wanted to find Maria to thank her but it was early, and she wasn't sure which flat her friend had gone to. *I'll come by and thank her tonight. I'll bring Kaji with me.* She can visit with Maria and perhaps Irena could even snatch a few minutes alone again with Adam.

Daydreaming, she traveled home through the early morning streets of Warsaw. The air was already hot, promising a stifling day. She crossed the Vistula and moved on toward her flat, arriving in a little less than an hour. She peeled off her clothing and took a bath, immersing herself in the warm water. She closed her eyes, imagining her day. She'd buy a cake and some special food, perhaps even some meat. They would celebrate tonight.

On the way to the ghetto she stopped at the bakery on Długa Street, piling a basket full of bread and cheeses. She wanted to bring some food to Ewa and Dr. Korczak.

A half hour later, Irena arrived at the orphanage. She was grateful to finally be there. The bag was heavy and the heat stifling. She couldn't wait to sit down with Kaji and give her the news. She would be home with her that very night. There would be no risks this time. She would ride out in an official vehicle, with documentation and a pass. No German guard would dare interfere with her.

She stepped through the door and realized immediately that something was wrong. The great entryway was empty. Toys were strewn all over the floor as if the children had just left the room abruptly. Irena rushed down the hallways, calling for Kaji, for Ewa, for anyone. But nobody answered. She rushed to Kaji's room and threw open the door. The room was empty, all her clothes were there, and the bed was made.

She sprinted back down the hallway. Where on earth had everyone gone? And then it struck her. *Oh no, it can't be. Not the children! Not today!* She rushed out of the building and back down the street. Her heart felt like it would burst out of her chest, but she kept running, slowing down only now and again when she couldn't run any longer. She crossed the wooden bridge, shoving people out of her way, and turned north on Smocza Street.

In the distance she could see a large crowd moving down the road, marching toward the Umschlagplatz. They were too far away to gauge whether the children were among them. Irena stood for a few moments, catching her breath, and then she began jogging again, the mass jarring up and down in her vision and growing slowly into a more recognizable form. In less than a minute she knew. She could see the smaller forms at the back of the line. A large group of children. Dr. Korczak's orphanage was marching to the Umschlagplatz.

She was already exhausted, but she broke into a run, screaming. Her voice was drowned out by the clamor of the mass moving toward the Umschlagplatz. She drew nearer. The heat beat down on her mercilessly. She was within a hundred meters of them now. She scanned the children, searching desperately for Kaji. To her right a group of German soldiers stood in a group, joking and pointing at her. Her mind was ripping through scene after scene of chaos. She couldn't see, couldn't think.

She reached the tail end of the column. She could see Dr. Korczak at the head, dressed impeccably in a gray wool suit. He held the hand of a child on each side of him.

"Irena!" She heard the shout. She turned to her left and Ewa was there. "My God, Irena," she said, pulling close to hold her.

"Where is Kaji?" she demanded.

"I don't know," Ewa said. "I looked for her, but the Germans came so fast."

"Move along!" ordered a German guard, prodding Irena in the back with the barrel of his gun.

They stumbled forward, shambling with the children, whose cries and pleas were ignored by the Polish police, the Germans, even the Jewish officials. *What kind of world is this?* Irena wondered. She moved forward into the crowd, searching desperately for Kaji. Ahead there was a little girl with jet-black hair and a shirt she thought she recognized. She rushed forward, screaming her name, and lifted her into her arms. The face was strange. She was mistaken. This was not Kaji. The girl shouted and pushed away, fighting her. Irena set her down and moved on, tears streaming down her face.

They were approaching the Umschlagplatz; Irena could see the tall wall in the distance. As they drew closer, she saw the platform was already full of families crammed into the space, waiting for their turn to load onto the trains.

Dr. Korczak reached the gates at the head of the column and stepped to the side, touching the hands of his children as they passed. His face was calm, and he smiled, as if they were on a field trip to the museum. Irena watched him until she drew near, then she rushed up to him. "Dr. Korczak, what are you doing!" she demanded.

"Stop it!" he hissed, not changing the serene blank on his face. "Look at the children. We must remain calm."

Up close she saw the pain in his eyes. She saw the truth. He knew where they were going, and what was going to happen. He was keeping his composure for the children's sake. As much as she'd always respected this man, she'd never admired him as much as she did in this moment. But she had to know. "Kaji, have you seen Kaji?"

He didn't respond, as if he hadn't heard her.

"Doctor," she repeated. "Have you seen my little girl?"

"What?" he said, turning toward her. "Kaji? No, I haven't seen her."

A wild hope filled Irena. Perhaps she had hidden or run away. She had told Kaji to do so if she ever was gathered up and taken to this place. She searched through the children again, her eyes moving over them like a lighthouse beacon sweeping out to sea. *She's not here.*

Irena turned to Ewa. "She's not with us."

"I'm so thankful," said Ewa.

"Come with me," Irena pleaded.

Ewa hesitated, looking over at Dr. Korczak.

"I can't, Irena."

"Please, you must. There's nothing left here for you to do."

Ewa shook her head. "You're wrong. There is one journey left. The children need me."

Irena took her arm. "You can't help them any longer. Come with me right now. We can still get away."

"Irena. Irena Sendler?" She heard the voice and her blood froze. She turned and there was Klaus, a few meters away, standing with a group of officers. "What are you doing there? Come here this instant."

"Run, Ewa. Turn and run."

"They'll shoot me."

"If you board that train, you're gone forever. If you run, there's a chance."

Her friend looked at Dr. Korczak again then turned to Irena and smiled. "Go find Kaji, my friend. God bless you." She turned and walked toward the Umschlagplatz.

"Frau Sendler. Come here!" Klaus ordered her.

Irena thought about disobeying, but what was the point? Ewa had made up her mind. She turned and waded through the passing children until she reached Klaus.

"What are you doing in here?" he demanded.

"I was walking with my friend," Irena said, her voice faltering. "I know Dr. Korczak, I know these children."

He stared at her for a moment. "I see."

"Is there nothing you can do for them?" she asked.

He shook his head. "Nothing. If I turned them around, they would have to come tomorrow, or the next day. They have a place prepared for them in the east."

"I've heard about that place," said Irena, hate in her voice.

He looked surprised at that, but he quickly recovered. "Yes, I've heard those rumors too. Place your mind at ease. We are not monsters."

"You are more than monsters."

He stared at her, his expression blank. "That's quite enough, Frau Sendler. You have no business here. Do you want to join them? If not, you'd best be on your way."

She nodded and turned, moving away from the platform. A

train was already there, and the cattle car doors were open. As she departed, she could see the children being helped up into the cars. She saw Dr. Korczak, standing at the entrance of one of the openings, reaching down to help one of the little ones inside. Next to him was Kaji, dressed in a beautiful white lace dress Irena had brought her, staring out at the crowd.

"No!" Irena screamed. She rushed back toward the entrance, but one of the guards stepped in front of her, barring her way.

"No!" she repeated, falling to her knees, her mind dizzy and her screams in her ears.

"What are you doing, Frau Sendler?" Klaus asked.

"My little girl is on that train."

"What little girl?" he demanded sharply. He turned toward his men. "Guards, seize her!"

"Irena, what are you doing?" In the fog of her grief she heard Ala's voice.

"I apologize," said Ala to Klaus, rushing up to stand in front of Irena. She was wearing her official head nurse uniform. "Irena has been ill. She may have caught something."

Klaus turned to the nurse. "Out of my way," he ordered.

"Please, sir. Irena has typhus. She's been exposed during one of her inspections. She wandered out of the hospital and must have walked here."

Klaus took a step back. "She has typhus?"

"Yes, sir."

Klaus hesitated. "You'd better get her out of here immediately. And yourself as well."

"*Jawohl*, Herr Sturmbannführer." She tugged on Irena, whispering in Polish. "We have to go right now. Your life depends on it."

"I don't care," Irena whispered, half to herself. "Kaji is on that train."

Ala tugged hard on Irena, pulling her to her feet. "You have to help me," she said. "I can't hold you like this much longer."

Irena thought of charging the Germans and letting them shoot her. She wanted to join the train, or to just die. But Ala kept pulling her away. With an animal shriek she turned and stumbled away, allowing Ala to lead her down the block. They turned a corner and Irena collapsed, burying her face in the pavement. "They've taken my little girl. She's gone. She's gone forever."

She felt a dizzy blackness overwhelming her, and soon there was only darkness.

Chapter 21
Tea in Hell

August 7, 1942
Treblinka, Poland

Klaus did his best to ignore the endless chatter from the engineer. His seat was uncomfortable, crammed into the space near the train's driver. Peter sat next to him. The area was intensely hot, adding to the scorching heat of the August afternoon. The train shimmied and rattled. All of this was bad enough, but the engineer was an incessant chatterer, rambling on about his job and the importance of transportation to the war effort.

Klaus didn't need to be here. He was beginning to regret his decision to come, but he wanted to see the entire process from beginning to end. He had learned long ago that understanding all aspects of an operation, not just the elements he was responsible for, helped him to improve efficiencies, and gave him an advantage over others in the same department, who were often not as thorough as he was.

The engineer continued. "You don't know the troubles that we encounter," the man said. "We are constantly called on by multiple departments for transportation at the same time. Everyone thinks their project should be first, and nobody is sure who is really in charge at the top. Besides the Führer, of course. So I'm stuck taking what I consider to be the most important projects. I was in Russia for a long time. But I didn't like it. Different gauge of rail and everything. Did you know that? Damn train doesn't feel natural on it. I was more than happy when a job came up in Poland. This is a milk run. Just seventy-five kilometers in and back. No bombers, no tanks, no attacks on my train. And we don't even have to help unload it."

"That's quite enough," said Klaus, reaching the end of his patience.

"Well, I see I have another high-and-mighty officer on board," the man said, almost under his breath. "Never mind then, I'll just do my job. Nobody appreciates us."

"You heard the major," said Peter. "Quiet your mouth." He turned his head away from the man, giving Klaus a wink.

The engineer finally shut up and Klaus felt his pounding headache begin to dissipate slightly. He stared out at the countryside for a few minutes. The landscape was dotted with little farms, the houses a light yellow color with low thatched roofs. The structures were foreign to him, so different than the tidy farms near his home in Germany. The Poles lived so close to the fatherland, but they were so different. Perhaps that is why they had often been enemies.

"How much farther?" he asked.

"Oh, now you want to talk to me."

"Just answer the question," ordered Peter.

"Not too far now," the engineer said, pointing. "See just ahead, we veer off on that rail line."

The train slowed gradually and lurched as it shifted lines at a rail spur. A worn sign near the track said "Treblinka." Once the train completed the shift, it picked up speed again.

"Not much longer now," said the engineer after a few minutes. "Look ahead, there's the camp coming up just past those trees."

Klaus stood, holding on to a metal bar for balance. He leaned forward, straining his eyes. In the distance the forest parted, and he could make out a long rectangular wooden structure on the right. It was a train station with one tapering gable in the middle. The sign at the station said Obermajden in large letters and indicated that Białystok was the next stop and Walkowysk was the terminus.

The train slowed down, and it took another ten minutes before they were at a complete stop. Then Klaus and Peter stepped off the train. They were met by a delegation of SS in crisp dress uniforms, led by the camp commander, SS Obersturmführer Irmfried Eberl. The commander was perhaps a touch over thirty, with a handsome face and a short mustache clipped in the Hitler style.

"*Guten Nachmittag*, Herr Sturmbannführer," he said, greeting Klaus in crisp German, albeit with an Austrian accent.

"*Heil* Hitler," Klaus said in return, giving a salute.

"We're excited to have you," said the lieutenant. "We haven't had many visitors yet."

"Thank you for having us, Doctor," he responded, remembering Eberl was a physician. "You've only been in operation for a couple of months, correct?"

"Less than that, actually," said Eberl. "We're still learning as we go. But I'm excited about the progress we've made. Would you like to have some refreshments now?"

"I'd like to see your operation," Klaus said in response.

"Excellent."

Eberl turned to one of his men and gave a command. The soldier turned and yelled toward a group of SS clustered a few meters away. They rushed forward, ripping open the cattle car doors. The cars were jam-packed with people, terrified expressions on their faces, huddled together with no room to move.

"*Raus!*" The scream came up and down the line, ordering the Jews to step out of the cars. Klaus noticed men running forward past the SS to assist them.

"Who are those people?" he asked.

"Jews," said Eberl dismissively. "We use them to assist with the luggage and get everyone moving on their way."

"Isn't that dangerous?" asked Klaus. "With what they are witnessing?"

Eberl laughed. "Don't worry about them. They don't last long. Every couple of weeks we select a new group, and these ones go up the chimney. That way there are no tales to tell."

The unloading took almost an hour. Klaus recognized Dr. Korczak amidst the crowd. He stepped down from the cattle car with a four- or five-year-old girl in a white dress in his arms. He turned to Eberl. "What's next?" he asked. The unloading was lasting longer than he'd expected and his headache had returned with a vengeance.

"We have the processing center itself," said Eberl. "I have set up some tables and chairs nearby, so we have a good view. Would you like to go there now, or watch the rest of the unloading?"

"Let's go to the viewing area," Klaus said. They started in that direction, moving past the long line of Jews already queued up and moving down a long narrow pathway with barbed wire. The path was well raked and the two-meter fencing on either side was covered in greenery.

"That's the Himmelstrasse," said Eberl. "The road to heaven! It's a little joke, but they are under too much stress to understand the humor of it."

Klaus heard an audible groan and he looked over at Peter. His assistant was green faced, and he was grimacing in obvious pain. "What are you doing?" he whispered.

"I'm . . . I'm sorry, sir. This is a lot to take in."

"No stomach for this kind of thing, eh?" asked Eberl.

"I'm fine. I'll be fine," said Peter.

"Why don't you wait in the train," said Klaus. "You don't need to be here for all of this."

Peter nodded gratefully and turned to leave, moving rapidly back toward the engine compartment.

"Not much of a man, is he?" said Eberl. "My boys handle this just fine."

"He's a good man," snapped Klaus. "I don't need your commentary about my staff. Just show me the process."

"Yes, sir," said Eberl, his face blanched. "It's just this way."

They stepped around the barbed wire trail and out into an open part of the camp. They walked for another hundred meters and approached a long set of portable tables with about twenty chairs, all facing a long barnlike structure about fifty meters distant. This structure was painted light brown on the lower half and the gable contained a large star of David. The table was set with a white cloth, china, and silverware. There were four silver tea sets and five trays laden with meats, cheeses, and bread.

Eberl gestured to a couple of seats in the middle of the table and Klaus sat down to his right. The rest of the officers and men in Eberl's group took their seats and a group of servants hastened up, pouring tea and serving an afternoon meal. Klaus waived off any food, gesturing to his cup. A soldier poured some tea for him. "Sugar and milk?" the soldier asked.

"Just sugar," Klaus said.

The soldier looked around on the table for a few moments. He moved up and down the line, finally returning to Klaus. "I'm sorry, sir, there doesn't seem to be any sugar here. I can go get you some."

"Yes please," said Klaus in irritation.

"Are you enjoying yourself?" Eberl asked.

"What's next?" Klaus said, ignoring the question.

"I just want to make sure you are comfortable."

"I am fine, Lieutenant. What is the next step in the process?"

"Look over to those buildings," said Eberl, gesturing to

some structures near the barn that looked like barracks. "Ah, here they come now."

A line of Jews was being herded out of the barracks. They were naked, and even from here Klaus could see their fear and misery.

"Why bring them out naked in public?" he asked.

"Logistics," said Eberl. "We have separate structures for undressing and processing. In fact, we don't have room for the men to undress indoors. They disrobe in between the barracks."

The male Jews moved quickly into the barnlike structure. In ten minutes, they were all inside and the doors were closed. An order from one of the men standing nearby rang out and he heard an engine rumble to life.

"That comes from a Russian tank," Eberl explained. "They used to use truck engines, but they are too small."

From the barn Klaus could hear screaming. The engine revved, partially drowning out the yelling. He checked his watch. Where was his sugar? Minutes passed and the sounds began to wane. Eventually he could hear nothing. He checked his watch again. Twenty-five minutes.

Klaus noticed a pile of bodies near the gas chamber. "What is that?" he asked, pointing toward the corpses.

"Just runoff," said Eberl. "The limiting factor isn't the chamber. The problem is disposing of the bodies."

"And you leave them out there for anyone to see?"

"By the time they get this far, it doesn't matter anymore," said Eberl, laughing. "There's no place to run."

"What happens next?" Klaus asked.

"The Jew workers will remove the bodies and take them to the structure over there for burial."

"How many can you handle a day?" Klaus asked.

"Three thousand," said Eberl.

"But not without this mess?" he said, gesturing to the stacks of bodies outside.

"We are doing our best. Each week we come up with new procedures. Would you like to stay to watch the disposal process?"

"No, thank you," said Klaus. He rose. "I've seen everything I need to see."

Eberl stood with him, extending his hand. "I hope you will give my superiors a favorable report."

"I certainly have much to tell them. Thank you again, Doctor, this has been an illuminating day."

He turned to leave. The soldier/servant was just rushing up with a small cup, full of sugar. "I'm sorry, sir," he said. "I just found this and came right back. Can I bring you a cup for the train?"

"No, thank you," said Klaus. "Don't worry about it. You're learning more every week." He turned and walked back toward the train. Peter was there, sweating in his uniform, still looking ill.

"I'm sorry, sir," he said. "Please forgive me. I don't know what got into me. I wasn't expecting this."

Klaus took his hand. "Don't you worry, Peter. This is a regrettable process with a noble purpose."

"Did you learn anything?" he asked.

"Yes. Eberl is a pig. This whole camp is a sloppy mess. I'll be giving a full report immediately when we get back. This will be changed."

"You're going to shut down the camp?" said Peter.

"No. But the process will be made more efficient." He took his friend's hands. "The war will be over soon. All of this will be over."

"If we win," said Peter.

Klaus looked back at the camp. "We must win. If we lose, the world will make us pay."

Chapter 22
The End

August 1942
Warsaw, Poland

"Irena?" She heard her mother's voice through the fog of her mind. She didn't react, didn't move.

"Please, you have to answer me. You've been here for two days. At least drink a little water and eat something."

She didn't want to eat or drink. The searing burning in her throat could draw her away from her pain at least for a little while.

Kaji, Ewa, Dr. Korczak, the children. They were gone. All of them. Forever. She'd let it happen. She was a day too late. Why hadn't she pushed them all faster? All she'd needed was a few hours. If Jan had worked a little harder. If Julian had pulled his resources together faster, they could have saved them all.

Kaji hurt the most of all. She was her little girl. Irena was going to adopt her. After the war Adam and she would marry, and Kaji would be the first child in their family. She would have raised her as a Jew, in honor of her murdered mother and father.

In the socialist world Irena and Adam had dreamt of, religion wouldn't matter.

All of that was gone now. Everything she'd worked for these many months was finished forever, and there was nothing she could do about it. All her bravery, her risks, the danger and the death, had come to nothing. The Germans had beaten her again. As they always did.

She'd done much of this for her own pride, she realized. She was going to show the fascists that socialism would prevail. That she would prevail. She'd done it for her friends and for the children, but perhaps even more so, she'd done it for herself. Since the Germans invaded, the only things she could control were operations with her job, in defiance of the Nazis.

Peter. She saw his smiling face again as he blocked their exit at the church. If he hadn't been there, Kaji would have come out with her at the same moment as Adam. She would be alive. If it wasn't for that bizarre coincidence, she would have saved *her child*.

"Irena." She heard the words again, closer this time. She felt a hand on her back. "Please, dear, just have a little drink of water."

"I can't do it, Mother. I don't want it."

"You have to. Just a little."

"No!" Irena screamed. She twisted hard in the bed and grabbed the glass out of her mother's hand. She threw the cup against the wall and it shattered. Glass and water exploded all over the wall. "Get out!" she screamed. "Get out, out, out!"

"You're mad!" her mother shouted. "I'm going for help."

Her mother left the room and Irena rolled back over, alone again with her agony. She closed her eyes and slept for a while, her only escape from hell.

She was awakened sometime later. She felt someone sitting by her on the bed, hands feeling her forehead. "I told you to leave me alone, Mother," she whispered.

"I'm not your mother," said a man's voice.

She opened her eyes. A middle-aged gentleman sat over her, his kind eyes looking her over with deep concern. "You're badly dehydrated," he said. "I'm going to give you something for your hysteria," he said. "Then I need to get you to the hospital. You need fluids immediately."

"I'm not hysterical," said Irena, starting to pull away. "I don't need anything. Leave me alone."

"This is a little shot," he said. "Then you'll relax."

"I said I don't want it!" she shouted, jerking her arm away.

"Hold her down," the doctor said. She felt other hands on her, and in her weakened condition she couldn't resist. She felt a painful stab in her arm, and then an overwhelming warmth washed over her before she fell unconscious.

She woke in a strange bed. There was an IV hooked up to her arm. She felt like her mind was surrounded by cotton. She couldn't focus, but at least the terrible pain was gone. As the images around her came into sharper view, she saw a face materialize above her. It was her mother. She was smiling down at her in obvious relief.

"You're awake," she said.

"What time is it?" Irena asked.

"More accurately you should ask what day it is," said a voice she recognized as the doctor from the apartment. She turned her head to the left and he was there, looking down at her again with his kind, understanding eyes. "You've been unconscious for three days. We've had quite a scare, young lady. Another few hours unattended and you might not have made it. But the worst is over now and you're on the mend."

Irena was surprised to hear that. But as she regained consciousness, her sadness returned as well. The sharp agony was gone, at least for now, but she felt the despair beginning to weigh her down again. "It would have been best if I'd died," she said at last.

"I disagree entirely," the doctor said. "Your mother told me all the things you've done. The risks you've taken. You're a hero, do you know that?"

Irena shook her head. "I lost them. I lost them all."

"You did not lose them," he said, running his hand by her cheek. "The Germans took them. As they've taken so many of us. No, my dear, you've done things I wouldn't have believed the bravest person in the world would do. You fed thousands of families, and then when the ghetto went up, you kept all those children alive for months on end. You kept hope alive."

"She did all of that and more," said a new voice. Irena looked at the foot of the bed. She was shocked to see Jan standing there, flowers in hand, wearing the familiar rumpled and worn gray suit. "She inspired me to take a stand for Poland as well. And many others."

"Why are you here?" she whispered.

"I came to make sure you were okay. And to tell you it is time to lay down your burdens."

"What do you mean?" she asked.

"You've done enough," he said. "Risked enough. I spoke with Maria. She believes the Germans know who you are now. She spoke with the resistance. They agreed. It's time for you to retire. Maria is willing to take your job in the ghetto. I've arranged for you to resume your old position with food distribution. It's important work," he said, seeing her expression. "There are thousands of families out there that need you, Irena. You're an expert at gleaning every calorie from those farmers on behalf of the poor."

She shook her head. "No, I can't. Please don't do that."

"The decision is already made," said Jan. "It's for the best. If you're arrested, you put all our operations in danger. You know too much. Everyone is agreed."

Her mother reached down, taking Irena's hands in hers. "I'm

so proud of you, my dear. We all are. You've done so much. But it's time to let someone else carry the burden for a while. You can work regular hours. You'll be home for dinner every night. I'm stronger now. It's time you let me take care of you for a change."

Irena was overwhelmed and couldn't think. She tried to fight through the fog in her mind, but it surrounded her, embraced her, beckoned her to more sleep. She closed her eyes.

"That's right," said Jan. "You need your sleep. You come back to the department when you're ready. You'll have your old job back. You'll be safe and sound—like you deserve."

She wanted to say more but she was exhausted.

"It's time for another shot," said the doctor.

"No," she whispered, but she felt the light prick in her arm and soon the medicine was overwhelming her with euphoria and sleep.

When she woke again, she felt much better. Her mind was clear. She noticed the IV was missing. The room was empty. She must be nearly recovered. She wondered how much more time had passed. A day? More? Perhaps it didn't matter.

Her job. Jan's visit hit her again. They were going to take her job away. They might have done it already. They thought she might be compromised by the Germans. At least that's what they'd said. Perhaps they simply had decided she'd done enough. That her luck had run out.

Perhaps it was for the best. She'd risked her life for so long now that a part of her yearned to step away. She could go to work each morning at a regular time and return at night. She'd have weekends to visit Adam. No matter what else happened, she'd saved his life. Maria could keep an eye on Ala and Rami. She had almost no one left in the ghetto at this point.

The next morning, she was released from the hospital. Her mother helped her home and she lay in bed for the next few days, reading and sleeping. Her mother did the little things for her: making sure she had fresh water and that her meals were brought to her bedside. She felt more relaxed and at peace than she could remember since the war began. She still felt the loss of her child, of Ewa, but the sadness had spread out and become part of her, a familiar melancholy replacing the stabbing agony.

On Monday she returned to work. She found a stack of documents on her desk detailing the condition of various food distribution centers throughout the city, along with applications for welfare from new families. She ran her fingers over the paperwork. She'd hadn't dealt with this aspect of the department for such a long time, but reviewing the familiar paperwork was like visiting an old friend.

"Irena, you're back," said Jan, appearing at her doorway. He smiled down at her. "I'm so glad you're all right. We all are. We are going to have a little luncheon for you later today." He stepped toward her desk. "I see you've already got your paperwork. That's wonderful. If you could review everything this morning, and then this afternoon I'd like to have a meeting. I have an idea for one or two new—"

"I have to go back." The words left her mouth before she was even aware of them. She was as surprised as he was. She thought she was ready to leave all the pain behind.

"I'm sorry, Irena. I told you. We think you're compromised. You can't go back. One more wrong move on your part and they'll kill you."

"I know you want to protect me, Jan, and I appreciate it. But I'm going back."

"Maria has already taken your place. The resistance . . ."

"The resistance trusts me, and they'll want me there if I'm willing."

He shook his head. "I'm sorry, Irena, I can't let you."

"We've been through this before, Jan. Whether you give me permission or not, I'm going. If you take my pass away, I'll find some other way to sneak into the ghetto. But then my life will certainly be in danger."

He stared at her, exasperated. "It's a death sentence," he said at last.

"It's my life to give, Jan. I don't want Maria risking hers. If they are going to arrest someone, let it be me." She didn't want to tell Jan there was another reason she didn't want Maria arrested. For that would certainly end Adam's life as well.

He threw his arms up. "Fine. As you say, it's your life." He looked down at her with sadness in his eyes. "I hope I'm wrong, Irena. I hope they don't know who you are and what you're doing." He reached into his jacket and pulled out a paper. "Your pass."

"You knew I'd want it back?"

"I'm no fool." He stepped forward and took her hand. "Be careful, Irena. We can't afford to lose you."

"So it's set," said Ala, looking over the documents.

Irena rose, stepping over to pour herself some tea from the counter in the hospital cafeteria. "Yes. We can take out all thirty."

Ala scanned the documents again. "I don't know how you've managed to pull this off."

"There's still room for Rami on that list," said Irena.

Ala looked up. She started to say something and then shook her head. "Not yet."

"Someday it will be too late, Ala. Think of the orphanage."

"You are right, Irena, and I am wrong. But I need a little more time. I know when I let her go, I'll never see her again."

"You can come with her."

Ala smiled. "We've been through that before as well. I'm not coming out of here."

"I don't understand you."

"Yes, you do. Perfectly well. We're both fighting. You from

the outside, and me from within. We both have our roles to play. Mine is in the ghetto."

"Do think about Rami at least. She could come with this group, if you let me."

Ala hesitated. "I'll consider it. But you'll have your hands full as it is. Some of these children have been here for a month or more. Two or three are too sick to walk very far."

"My contacts say they'll have a half dozen escorts to help us. They are going to come out by the sewer."

Ala paled. "My God."

"It's the safest way now. The gates are all heavily guarded. They've shut up the courthouse and the church."

"When are they coming?"

"I don't know. In the next week though. The fifth or sixth at the latest."

"I'll get them ready."

"I'm sorry about the clinic." The Germans had shut down Ala's impromptu medical clinic at the Umschlagplatz, and forbidden her on pain of death from returning there.

"It was only a matter of time. I want to go back. Defy them."

"They'll kill you, Ala. They told you they would if you returned. Besides, you saved hundreds."

"For now. When will you know?" Ala asked. "The date, I mean?"

"I'm meeting with the resistance later today. They should be able to give me the day."

Ala raised her teacup. "To safety for these little ones."

Irena clanked her cup. "And to Dr. Korczak, Kaji, and all those who didn't make it."

The meeting with Żegota took place at the same headquarters building as before. At least they didn't abduct her anymore, she thought with amusement. She was able to communicate through Maria now, and when a meeting was set, they would pick her up a few blocks from her office. Julian was present, along with a couple of other operatives.

The leader of Żegota reviewed the documents she'd put together. They were all signed by Jan, this time with his knowledge and approval. "They are perfect," he said finally. "Truly, Irena, you're a genius."

"I couldn't do anything without the safe houses and a way out," she said. "You're allowing this to happen."

"Let's call it a team effort," he said, lifting a glass of vodka and quaffing the contents. "How soon can you be ready?"

"I could go tomorrow. I told Ala it would be the fifth or sixth at the latest."

"It's going to be a little longer than that," said Julian.

"Why?" Irena asked, feeling a flicker of panic.

"The sewers are getting tricky," said one of the men. "The Germans have figured out we are sneaking people out that way. They've started sending patrols down and booby-trapping some of the entrances."

"Then we can't go that way," said Irena.

"No," said Julian. "It's not that bad. Not yet, at least. But we're having to learn some new routes. There are lesser branches that wander this way and that. We need a little time to make sure we have a secure trail before we bring them out. With children, we can't afford to make a mistake."

"When then?"

"The seventh."

"I'll let Ala know and we'll be waiting."

The next few days passed without event. Irena briefed Jan and Maria and visited Ala each day to make sure everything was ready. Wiera was there now too, volunteering at the hospital. Ala and her cousin were reconciled. The singer had turned out to be an invaluable volunteer.

The day before the escape, Irena stayed at the hospital, working with Ala to make sure the final preparations were made.

"What time are they coming?" her friend asked her, as she was getting ready to depart.

"They should be here in the morning, no later than nine."

"Thank you, Irena. Thank you so much."

"Have you thought any more about Rami?"

"I have," she said. Her eyes filled with tears. "I want you to take her."

Irena felt joy surging through her, but at the same time she shared the terrible sadness of her friend. She stepped forward and held Ala. The nurse buried her head into Irena's shoulder and wept.

"I know it's an impossible decision, but it's the right one," said Irena.

"You have to promise you will watch over her."

"I will. You have my word."

Irena heard feet rapidly thumping on the tiles outside the cafeteria door. The door was flung open and a nurse was standing there, face pale and eyes wide. "The Germans are here!" she screamed.

Ala turned to Irena. "It's too late," she said. "We are betrayed."

"Let's get to the children now!" Irena shouted.

"We can't—"

"Now!"

Ala rose and sprinted down the back hallway with Irena following closely behind. Behind them they could hear the clipped barking of German voices, followed by gunfire.

"They're shooting the patients!" screamed Ala. "I have to go back!"

"Get me to the children!" shouted Irena.

Ala pushed through another set of double doors into the children's ward. Thirty children sat or lay on cots, lined up in a single row on both sides of a bare concrete room. Irena scanned the room quickly, noticing another door at the far end.

"Where does that lead?" she asked.

"Outside," said Ala.

"Get them up!" she shouted as she broke into a run. "We're leaving!"

"They have nowhere to go!" protested Ala.

"Just get them!" Irena sprinted the length of the room and pushed the door open. Late afternoon sunshine spilled into the room. The door led onto a small concrete platform and then down a short flight of stairs to the left and onto the sidewalk. She looked up and down the street frantically. There were no Germans there, but that wasn't what she was looking for. Finally, she saw what she was seeking. A man stood at the end of the block, leaning against the wall. She screamed in his direction and he stood up. The man turned and whistled. Three more figures joined him, and they all broke into a run toward the hospital.

By now the first children were reaching her on the landing. Ala appeared, frantic at the doorway. "Who are those men?" she demanded, spotting the group that was just now arriving at the foot of the stairs.

"They are with me."

"But you said they were taking the children tomorrow?"

"We've been betrayed too many times, so I prepared for the worst."

Ala stared at her in surprise and then threw her arms around her. "Thank you! Thank you!" she said, the tears running down her cheeks. A thought seemed to fill her mind suddenly. "What about Rami?"

"Don't worry," said Irena. "I'll get her out soon."

Ala nodded as the children rushed past her, Irena helping

them down the stairs as two of the men rushed inside to carry out those too ill to walk.

Irena could hear the screaming and the shots. They were coming closer, but they would be too late.

The Germans had been tipped off again, and they were here to spoil her plan. But she'd been prepared, and she was going to beat them. She promised herself they would never win again.

Chapter 23
Empty Jaws

September 6, 1942
Warsaw, Poland

"You've done well," said Colonel Wagner, reviewing the records. "Two hundred thousand units shipped out of the Jewish Quarter in only seven weeks."

"Everything is proceeding according to plan on our end. It's the other part of the operation I'm concerned about."

"Yes," said the colonel, shaking his head. "We read your report. We've conducted our own surprise visit. It was worse than you suspected. Don't worry. We are replacing him with a true professional. Treblinka will run like a factory from now on."

"That's excellent news."

"How much longer will your operation last?" the colonel asked.

"If we could take six thousand a day every day without any issues, we'd be done in two more months at the most. But you must anticipate that things will get harder. Rumors have hit the ghetto about Treblinka, about what is really happening. We do everything we can to dispel this information, but not everyone believes us. However, we have other incentives. We are just starting a new program to offer jam and bread to everyone who will show up at the platform for relocation. The response so far has been tremendous. We had to turn people away. So many of them are starving."

The colonel selected a pastry from a plate at the table and took a bite. "I wonder what it's like to go without food."

"Hunger is a powerful motivator."

The colonel nodded. "So, two months then?"

Klaus shook his head. "Better figure more like four. There will remain a hard core of people who will not come voluntarily. The smugglers, their little resistance movement. They will take a little more time to ferret out."

"I suppose that's to be expected." He rose and shook Klaus's hand. "Everything looks good," he said. "I'll report back to Herr Frank." The colonel turned to leave. Klaus moved back toward the mound of paperwork on his desk. "Just one more thing," the colonel said.

Klaus turned back. The colonel stood at the door. "What are you doing about all these Jews escaping into Aryan Warsaw?"

"I don't know what you mean by *all these Jews*. A handful have made it out. That's to be expected."

"Our intelligence tells us it is quite a few more than that."

Klaus was furious, but he held his emotions in check. Where was the colonel getting his information? Who was the leak? "We're aware of the situation and taking steps."

"What steps?"

"We conducted a raid tonight. There was a plot to take some children out of the hospital on Leszno Street. The escape was planned for tomorrow. Even as we speak, my men are at the hospital. We will resettle these children to the east tonight. They will never see Aryan Warsaw."

"I'd like to see that," said the colonel.

"We are getting ready to go there now. The children should already be rounded up. If you'd like, I can show you the rest of the operation, and we could tour the Umschlagplatz."

The colonel nodded. "I would enjoy that immensely."

An hour later, Klaus stood in the wreckage of the hospital with Peter and the colonel. Screams echoed down the hallway from the wounded. The soldiers were wrapping up the operation. There were blood and bodies everywhere.

"Where are the children?" the colonel asked.

"We're still looking for them," said Klaus. "My men are combing the hospital."

Another hour passed. Report after report returned. The children were missing.

"They are probably hiding somewhere," said Klaus.

"Sick children?" said the colonel with sarcasm in his voice. "Who didn't know you were coming? Let's face it, your operation was compromised, Klaus. The children are gone." The colonel scribbled notes into his notebook, shaking his head as he did so. "This is precisely what we've been concerned about. It looks like you not only have a Jewish escape problem, but you have a spy in your own department working for the Poles! And you were concerned about the problems in Treblinka."

Klaus turned to Peter. "Collect the staff. I want them all questioned until we know what happened."

"What do we do with the rest of the patients?" Peter asked.

"Liquidate them." Klaus turned back to the colonel. "Don't worry. We will get to the bottom of this."

"You had better. And quick."

Chapter 24
Rise Up

April 1943
Warsaw, Poland

The truck sat in the darkness near the ghetto wall. Irena took a long pull on a cigarette. She checked her watch; it was nearly midnight.

"Where are they?" asked the driver. "We've been here far too long."

"Another few minutes," she insisted. "They'll make it."

"We're going to be arrested," he protested.

"One of these days. But perhaps not tonight."

"You're mad," he said, only half joking.

"Look, just ahead," she said, gesturing toward the wall. A column of two dozen children were walking down the street, led by a woman in her early twenties. Irena opened the door and moved quickly to meet them. She embraced the woman, ignoring the stench that emanated off her clothing.

"Don't touch me!" said the woman. "I've been in the sewer for a day."

"I don't care, Sasha," said Irena, holding the young Jewish resistance member. "You're precious to me, whatever your scent."

"You're crazy, Irena," Sasha said.

"That's what I told her," said the driver.

Irena looked around. "We don't have much time. Let's get the children to the back of the truck."

Sasha nodded and led the group toward the rear of the vehicle. The driver removed the latch and swung the back gate down. Irena and Sasha lifted the children one by one into the covered bed.

"You must stay quiet now," warned Sasha to the children. "This is my friend Irena. She will help you from here. Remember what I told you, you cannot speak Yiddish anymore. Ever. You must memorize the new names that Irena gives you."

Several of the children hugged Sasha and then they pulled the gate back up.

"How will you avoid the Germans?" she asked Irena.

"Żegota has taken care of everything. We have a safe route."

"When will you need me again?" she asked.

"I don't know," said Irena. "We have to get more documents together and another couple safe houses. It may be a week, perhaps two."

"We may not have much more time," said Sasha.

"What do you mean?"

"There are rumors flying all over that the Germans are going to liquidate the ghetto."

"Why would they?" asked Irena. "All that's left are the workers at their factories, besides the few thousand in hiding. They would hurt themselves if they shut down Többens and Schultz."

"I'd like to shut down those bastards myself, with a knife," said Sasha, spitting on the pavement.

"They've saved thousands of people."

"By creating factories in the ghetto to profit from their slave labor. I won't give them any praise."

"But now you say they may shut down the factories?"

"That's what I've heard. We are preparing for the worst, and you should too."

"Thank you, Sasha," said Irena. "I'll consider your words and get back to you. Is there anything I can do for you?"

"Bring us some tanks," Sasha said, laughing.

"I would if I could." She pulled Sasha in, holding her for a few moments. "You must take care of yourself," she said. "The future needs women like you."

"The future needs women like both of us," said Sasha, smiling. "You take your own advice too, Irena. They have to be closing in on you."

Sasha turned and moved quickly away, disappearing within moments into the darkness. "Let's go," said Irena.

The truck roared to life and lurched forward. Irena held a handwritten map, giving directions to the driver as they maneuvered through the streets of Warsaw, lights out. Julian had assured her the route would be safe, but there were no guarantees. She was risking everything again, as she had so many times these last few months. She thought of the orphanage, of her precious Kaji. She could not bring them back, but she'd brought out so many since then.

They arrived a half hour later in the Praga district, on the opposite side of the Vistula. The truck backed into a warehouse where several men and women waited, helping the children down. Each child was given a little bread, and then they were separated by name into smaller groups. Irena watched as the children were handed packets of paperwork: their new identities.

"Another success, Irena." She heard the voice and turned. Julian was there, holding up a bottle of vodka and two glasses.

He poured the clear liquid into one of the glasses and handed it to her. "To Irena Sendler. The Moses of the ghetto."

Irena drank the bitter liquid quickly. "Don't call me that," she said. "Moses didn't lose half his flock."

Julian's eyes darkened. "Don't think about that. We are human. You've done your best. More than anyone else I know."

"That won't bring her back. Won't return their lives."

"You're right. But look at these ones," he said, gesturing behind him. "Twenty-five more who live because of you. You've given them a chance when all they faced was a bullet in the ghetto or the gas chambers in Treblinka."

Irena smiled. "Yes. We are helping these ones. But not me alone. All of us. You and Żegota, all the social workers, the resistance in the ghetto. I'm just a little cog in the wheel."

"You are the wheel," he said, patting her on the shoulder. He poured himself another shot, quaffed it, and walked away to tend to the children.

"Do you need a lift?" the driver asked her.

"It's too dangerous," she said.

"You're going to spend the night here?" he asked.

"No, I have a friend who lives nearby. I'm going to try to make it to her flat."

"Be careful," he said, winking at her.

"I always am."

She arrived a few minutes later at Maria's apartment, letting herself in with a key. She fumbled her way through the darkness and made her way into Adam's room. She climbed gently into bed with him.

"Irena, is that you?" he asked sleepily.

"Yes, my dear," she said, kissing his cheek. "Go back to sleep."

She felt his arms on her and he pulled her head down, kissing her on the lips. "Not just yet," he whispered.

The next morning, they sat at the kitchen table, sipping tea and eating toast. Adam was poring over a ledger.

"We need another hundred thousand zlotys," he said. "The cost of food is rising everywhere. We have to increase the stipends to these families hiding the children."

"I'll talk to Julian," she said. "Just get me the names." She was busy filling in small scraps of paper. On each one she wrote down the full name of one of the children from last night's escape. She then wrote down the new name the child had received in their paperwork, and the name and address of the family who was taking them in. This was dangerous; if the Germans ever came across these lists, they could trace each child to their new Polish family in hiding. She kept the scraps of paper in jars that were buried in a garden just outside her apartment. The risk was necessary. After the war, the Jewish parents might return, and they would be looking for their children. Without Irena's lists, they would never find their children again. She finished the last one. Taking a sip of tea, she folded up the paper and dropped it into a jar. She screwed on the lid. She would bury the container in the garden tonight after midnight, when there would be no prying eyes from neighbors.

"How many is it now?" Adam asked.

"I don't have an accurate count."

"Guess?"

"Several thousand."

The door swung open. Maria had returned. She dropped her purse on the counter and removed two cigarettes. She lit one for herself and stepped over to the table, handing the second one to Irena.

"It's official," she said. "The Germans are going to liquidate the rest of the ghetto."

"How much time do we have?"

"Nobody knows. But it's coming soon."

Irena shook her head. "I still don't understand why they would destroy their own factories."

"Rumor has it they plan to relocate the workers to another camp."

Irena nodded. "That would explain it."

"What are you going to do?" Maria asked.

"We have to move fast," said Irena. "I want to get as many children out as we can, along with Ala and Rami."

"Do you think she'd come?" Adam asked.

"She will now," said Irena. "There's nothing left to save."

"What do you want from us?" asked Maria.

Irena thought things over for a few minutes. "Go to Julian. And this is what I want him to do . . ."

For the next week Irena hardly slept. She had multiple meetings a day with Julian and Maria. She pressed Jan, forcing him to work long hours overtime to sign hundreds of additional documents. She met with Jewish resistance leaders, and delegates from the workers at the Többens and Schultz factories, who had heard the rumors of the imminent closure of the factories as well. These families had received special permits allowing them to remain in the ghetto. They had avoided the fall relocations and the Umschlagplatz. They'd believed they were essential, that the Germans would never come for them. Now they'd learned differently, and they were scrambling to save their children.

Irena met with these leaders patiently. She'd talked with them periodically for many months, always receiving the same smug answers. *We don't need your help*, they'd told her. *We are immune.* Now she would have every right to turn her back on them. But she never considered it. How could she condemn people for clinging to hope, no matter how misguided? One of the cruel tricks of the Germans was to divide the Jewish community among those who had privilege and protection, and those who did not.

Now they had to get them out as quickly as possible. It would be no easy operation. Her plan was for one massive operation. They would need most of Żegota's strength and that of the Jewish resistance as well. She hoped to take out as many as five hundred children at one time. She would also finally rescue her friend Ala and Ala's daughter, Rami. Ala, resistant for these many months for entirely different reasons—for the heroic purpose of serving and saving her people—had also agreed to finally come out.

The plan was the boldest she'd ever attempted. They would attack and take over one of the gates into the ghetto. After overwhelming the guards, they would drive a convoy of trucks into the Jewish Quarter, load the children up, and drive them back out again. The convoy would be protected by a hundred resistance fighters, armed with machine pistols and rifles.

Finally, everything was prepared. She met Julian at a café in Aryan Warsaw. She'd never seen him in public before, and she wasn't sure if this was an illustration of his confidence in her, or proof of the growing strength of the Polish resistance.

"Where are the documents?" he asked, sitting down and ordering some tea.

"Maria has them. They are hidden in her office. She can bring them to you, or you can send somebody to pick them up."

"I'll send someone. Are you ready for this?" he asked.

"Are you?" She noticed a nervousness about Julian she'd never seen before.

"This is the biggest operation we've ever tried," he admitted. "If we fail . . ."

"If we fail then we will lose some people, and we will rebuild. We have to try, Julian; we are talking about hundreds of children."

"I agree entirely," he said. "I only wish we'd had longer to plan. I'm not worried about getting in, I'm worried about getting back out. After we take the gate, the Germans will respond. The question will be whether they can seal off the ghetto before we can escape. If they do, then we'll have a hell of a fight to escape."

"You just be there with the trucks on time. I'll get us back out again, one way or another."

He laughed. "I knew you'd tell me something like that." His face turned serious. "When are we going?"

"Tonight," she said. "At midnight. I want to catch them sleeping."

He nodded. "And there's enough paperwork?"

"Yes. There should be ample. I've kept Jan busy for days now."

"I bet he enjoyed that. I still don't know how you turned him. A right-wing heel-clicker like that. I thought he was a spy for the Germans for the longest time."

"I had my own reservations. But he's done as much as anyone to help our cause."

Julian finished his tea and rose. "I'll see you tonight, Irena. We'll pick you up in front of the department."

Irena returned to her office and spent a restless rest of the day. She tried to sort out some paperwork but finally gave up. She couldn't concentrate. There was too much at stake tonight.

"Why bother," said a voice from the hallway. She looked up and saw Jan there, smiling. "Are we still on for tonight?" he asked.

"Jan!" she protested. "Not so loud."

"What difference does it make?" he asked, shrugging. "The whole building is in on our operation by this time."

"There are still things we should not say out loud."

"Fine," he said. "Have it your way." He whistled. Putting his hand in his pocket, he drew out a pipe and lit some tobacco, taking a few deep puffs. "Five hundred," he said to himself. "That's really something."

"They aren't out yet," she said.

"You're in charge," said Jan, turning away. "They'll get out."

Another couple of hours passed. She checked her watch. It was nearly five. She reached into her drawer to retrieve the dinner she'd packed. She still had another six hours to wait before Julian would be here with the trucks.

She took her first bite when she heard it, a rumble, then another. She rushed out into the street, sprinting to an intersection so she could have a proper view. Another thunderous explosion rocked the air. She turned, and her worst fears were confirmed. Smoke billowed out of the ghetto. She was too late. The Germans were already there.

Chapter 25
The Bright Light

April 1943
Warsaw Ghetto, Poland

Klaus stood in the middle of Zamenhofa Street with SS General Stroop and Colonel Wagner. As they watched, a Panzer IV tank rolled down the avenue a few hundred meters in front of them. A platoon of soldiers followed close behind, spraying the windows on either side of the street with machine gun fire.

A man appeared in one of the windows and hurled a fiery bottle down toward the pavement. He was shot immediately from below, but the Molotov cocktail exploded in the middle of a group of German soldiers, spraying them with burning liquid. Two soldiers writhed in fiery pain, screaming as their comrades tried in vain to save them.

"That's what we've been facing for a week now," said Stroop. "These bastards have no fear. They are more than happy to trade their own lives for one or more of us. What I'd like to understand," said the general, with a glance toward Klaus, "is how they were allowed to arm so heavily right under your nose."

The colonel looked at Klaus. "Yes, we all want to know that."

"What were we supposed to do?" asked Peter, standing behind his commander. "Five hundred thousand people and seventeen blocks of ghetto. You can't watch all of them with a few hundred men. They were bound to get in and out, some with food, some with weapons."

"Peter, be quiet," Klaus ordered. He appreciated his assistant's loyalty, but he knew that nothing they said right now would make any difference.

"Excuses," said the colonel. "For months now that's all we've had. This is a bunch of civilians. Unarmed, and starved. How they got one gun under your watch is a mystery to me. We've had no problems in Kraków or Lwów. Why are all the issues with *your* ghetto?"

"We had the biggest to deal with," said Klaus. "You have to expect more complications."

The colonel gestured at the burning bodies. "These are more than complications. I've been recommending a change in this department for months now," he said. "Unless you can get this situation under control in the next day or two, I am confident you will be relieved."

"Why wait," said General Stroop. "He should be replaced right now."

"It's not my decision," said the colonel. "Otherwise I'd make the call immediately." He turned to Klaus. "I'm going to remain here with the general and coordinate operations. You may return to your office and map out what you're going to do to fix this. I want an action plan by eight o'clock tonight. Is that understood?"

"*Jawohl*," said Klaus, giving the Hitler salute. The colonel turned, failing to give the return gesture. Klaus stormed off, followed closely by Peter. They didn't speak until they were in the staff car and driving out of the ghetto toward headquarters.

"The bastard!" shouted Klaus finally. "He's been after my hide all this time."

"You couldn't have done anything better," said Peter. "You're the most diligent, organized man I've ever known. Let them come and take your job. They'll find out soon enough how badly you'll be missed."

"It may well come to that," said Klaus. "But we must try to avoid it."

"How?" Peter asked. "You don't have control over the military units. We can't make the battle go faster. They're telling you to fix the problem, but they've taken all your power away."

"Not everything," said Klaus, musing. "We have to think about these resistance fighters. Where are they weak?"

"We've identified several of their bunkers," Peter said. "But we don't have the weapons to attack them. That's what Stroop is here for."

"The forces under *our* control are not meant for combat," said Klaus. "That's not what I meant by weakness. What would make these men and women put down their arms?"

"I don't know," said Peter. "They don't have anything left to lose, do they?"

"That's it," said Klaus, snapping his fingers. "That's the key."

"What do you mean?" Peter asked.

"Hurry up," said Klaus, "let's get back to the office. I'll explain on the way . . ."

An hour later Peter interrupted Klaus, who was poring over a map of the ghetto in his office.

"The informer is here," he said.

Klaus looked up and nodded. In this context, there was only one informer. "Bring them in," he said.

Peter led the informer in and gestured to a seat in front of Klaus.

"Now," Klaus said, "I need to know how I get to Żegota."

"I've never heard of Żegota."

"Don't lie to me," said Klaus. "I know you've been with-holding information."

"Why do you want to know?"

"In order to stop the resistance, I need to find out where Że-gota has hidden all of these children in Aryan Warsaw." He leaned forward. "You know how to lead me to them, don't you?"

The informer hesitated. "What difference would that make? Most of their parents are dead. They won't stop fighting just because you uncover another few thousand Jews who they aren't related to."

"I disagree." Klaus hoped he was right, and the informer was wrong. Otherwise, he was already doomed. "You let me worry about what will happen when we apprehend them. You just tell me how to get to them."

"I'm not certain I know."

"Like I said, don't lie to me. I want all your information and I want it now."

The informer was quiet for a long time.

"I guess you're not going to tell me. Well, in that case, I'll have to adopt more direct methods. Peter!" he yelled, calling for his assistant.

"Wait!" said the informer. "I do have one name."

"That's a Jew," Klaus said when he heard the suggestion. "I don't want Jews. I want Poles."

"That name will lead you to Żegota."

"You better be correct."

"I'll bet my life on it."

Klaus leaned forward. "You just did."

Chapter 26
A Desperate Plan

April 1943
Warsaw Ghetto, Poland

Irena stood across the street from the ghetto wall. She could
see the smoke billowing up from several directions. In the distance she could hear the staccato barking of machine gun fire.
She breathed the acrid smell of gunpowder. As she held her
vigil, she kept looking up and down the street. There were
plenty of bystanders, spectators who'd come down to gawk at
the last gasp of the Jews. However, it wasn't entirely safe here.
German soldiers periodically accosted pedestrians, demanding
their papers and what their business was this close to the wall.
They even made some arrests.

Irena desperately wanted to get inside the ghetto. She'd been
unable to enter the Jewish Quarter since the fighting began, a
few days ago. She'd attempted on the second day to walk inside, but she'd been stopped at the gate. She showed her documents, but the guard shook his head. She'd threatened. She'd
tried other gates, but the answer was the same: The old passes
were no longer valid. The ghetto was sealed, permanently it

seemed. There was nothing she could do. At least by conventional means.

She returned to the office. Maria was there, as was Jan. She huddled up with them in Maria's office. She couldn't take her eyes off the stack of boxes. The paperwork meant for five hundred children who they'd intended to remove from the ghetto less than a week ago. Now, these children were stranded, perhaps forever, as were her friend Ala and Ala's daughter, Rami. After months of success Irena felt the old failure haunting her again. Would she lose these five hundred as she'd lost Dr. Korczak's orphans? She didn't think she could bear another failure of that magnitude. There had to be something they could do.

"Why can't we still use the trucks?" Jan asked, as they debated alternative rescue plans. "We could still overwhelm a gate easy enough, even if the Germans have had some reinforcements."

"That's not the problem," said Maria. "Those bastards have tanks in the ghetto now. Once they had word a rescue was underway, they'd turn those monsters on us, and carve us up like a Christmas feast."

"She's right," said Irena. "The trucks were our best option for a mass breakout, but we can't use them now. Not until the Germans remove the tanks, at least."

"That might never happen," said Jan.

"Agreed. So, it's not an option. We're going to have to look at getting the kids out in smaller numbers."

"I don't think there's time," said Maria.

"I don't mean in waves," said Irena. "I mean all at once, but fragmented. Smaller teams, with a set number of children, escaping in different directions to designated points."

Jan whistled. "That's going to take a lot of coordination and there's not much time to make it happen."

Irena nodded. "We'll need fifty guides through the sewers. Ten kids to each."

"Where are you going to find fifty guides?" asked Maria. "Will you grow them in your garden?"

"The Jewish resistance can furnish them," she said.

Maria shook her head. "They're fighting for their lives. You'll never convince them to set aside operations—even for some children. They're trying to keep fifty thousand people alive, not five hundred."

Maria was right. She'd counted on the cooperation of the Jews, but right now that was impossible. "What about Żegota?" she asked.

"We don't have a half dozen people qualified to get through those sewers into the ghetto. It's not possible."

"What if those few could train others?" asked Irena. "Couldn't we spend a day or two getting more Poles acclimated to the routes?"

"They'll never agree to it," said Maria. "Too fast, and too risky."

"Let's go and find out," said Irena.

A few hours later she received the same answer from Julian. "That's not possible," he said.

"Why not?" Irena responded. "If they have a day to learn and another day to practice, they'd be ready."

"Have you been down there?" Julian asked.

Irena shook her head.

"There is an endless maze of passages. It takes weeks to learn even a couple of them. Worse, the Germans have booby-trapped the main routes, and they're pumping poison gas down inside. They have patrols too. There's no way we can send a bunch of newly trained men and women down there. Half won't make it into the ghetto, and the other half will be caught on the way out. I won't be responsible for losing fifty of my people."

"And what will happen to those five hundred children if we save fifty of *your* people?" she demanded. He didn't answer.

"They'll die," she said. "Can you live with that? We've sat back while the Germans exterminated half a million Jews. There aren't many left. We have a chance to save a few of them. But we don't have long. The Germans will conquer the ghetto any day now. Our friends are fighting bravely but they've hardly any arms or ammunition. And they can't fight an army of professional soldiers with tanks. We have to do something, and we have to do it now!"

Julian hesitated. "I'll have to run this by the council. You want fifty of our fighters involved in this suicide mission. This is bigger than me."

"I understand. How soon can you have an answer for me?"

"We have a meeting tonight." It would mean another day of delay, but Irena knew there was nothing she could do about it. She spent a long and anxious afternoon at the office, trying to focus on her paperwork. Maria stopped by periodically, trying to lend a supporting hand. Irena went home and spent the evening with her mother, trying to make small talk and wind the long hours down. As she was getting ready for bed there was a knock at her door. She opened it to a young man. "Your plan is approved," he said. "Meet Julian tomorrow at headquarters to begin operations."

"Stop!" the man whispered. They were in almost total darkness. Irena had her hand on the leader's shoulder. She felt a firm grip behind her neck. Behind her, she heard gagging and someone retched into the foul liquid that lapped at her waist. Another person vomited, and another.

"Pull yourselves together," their leader, Moczar, demanded in a quiet but harsh tone. "I need absolute silence."

Irena saw a flicker of light as their guide turned on his flashlight. They were at an intersection of two sewer lines. Moczar whipped the light to his right and his left. Satisfied there were no Germans waiting to ambush them in the side passages, he moved the light up and down the walls of the sewer. Irena looked up. The ceiling here was barely above her head. She could easily reach out and touch the slimy stone above her. The walls on either side of her were close, with barely room for the party to squeeze through in single file. She fought down a fit of panic as everything seemed to close in on her.

"There!" Moczar said, pointing.

Irena looked along the line of his finger. She saw nothing at first and then realized there was a thin wire stretched about halfway between the waterline and the ceiling. He ran the light toward the wall and she saw that the wire was connected to a grenade on both sides, the ends of the wire wrapped around the pins. "We have to move slowly, one at a time. Don't touch the wire! Even a tremor and it might pull loose."

"Can't we go back?" asked Irena.

Moczar turned, staring at her for a moment. "Do you want to find a passage in, or don't you?"

"I do," she said, feeling ashamed. She'd never expected this. The stench was unbearable. Every moment she fought back the nausea. The thick sewage lapped at her stomach and her chest. They'd seen rats and heard other ominous noises in the darkness. She'd insisted on coming on this training exercise. She wanted to see how the preparations were coming along and, perhaps more importantly, she didn't want to go into the sewers for the first time during the upcoming operation. For she had decided, against Julian's wishes, to personally accompany the Polish men and women involved in the operation.

A few hours later and they were back in Aryan Warsaw. They had reached the ghetto, although they did not attempt to open one of the coverings and reach the street level. Irena was relieved to step back out onto the street, and even more so when she was able to bathe and wipe away the filth she'd walked through for hours.

Julian found her as she was recovering. He held his nose in

an exaggerated expression of disgust, although she was now clean and had changed clothes. He laughed.

"Are you sure you want to go back in there?" he asked.

She wasn't, but she was determined she would see it through. She nodded.

He shook his head. "You're the most stubborn woman I've ever met, Irena."

"When are we leaving?" she asked.

"Tonight. After curfew."

"Are they ready for us?"

He nodded. "They've sent one of their best out to help us. All they could spare. You know her."

Just then Sasha came around the corner. Irena smiled as the young woman flew into her arms.

"You're coming with us?" Irena asked.

Sasha nodded, a grin covering her entire face. "I wouldn't miss this for anything. Besides, they've assigned me to you."

"What?"

"Żegota and our organization decided together. You're too important to risk. I'm taking you in and out again. We'll get Rami and Ala. The Poles will get the rest."

Irena wanted to protest. She didn't want special treatment, but she admitted to herself she was glad. Sasha was an expert. She'd been smuggling goods and people back and forth in the sewers for several years now. If anyone could bring her in and back again, it would be Sasha. "I'm glad," she said finally.

"I thought that was going to be harder," said Julian.

"What would be?"

"Getting you to agree. I was expecting an argument—and since I haven't won one of those with you yet, I had feared the worst."

Irena laughed. "I'm not that difficult."

"You're every bit that difficult," said Julian, smiling. "But that's what makes you effective."

The sun was already sinking behind the buildings and the resistance members sat around headquarters, going through maps they had drawn of the routes, taking a little cold cheese and bread. The room was quiet, each person alone with their thoughts as they prepared mentally for the dangerous operation.

Finally, it was time. Sasha found Irena, who was sitting in a corner, eyes closed, thinking about entering the sewers again. "It's time," the young woman said.

Irena nodded and accepted a hand as Sasha pulled her to her feet. She looked up into the smuggler's eyes, smiling. "I know we're going to make it tonight," she said.

"Just another trip under the wall," said Sasha. Her face grew grave. "Stay close to me," she said. "No matter what."

"I will."

They stepped into the darkness, heading on foot toward the ghetto. The resistance fighters spread out, moving in groups of two or three, some taking turns down streets to their right and left as they moved away from the headquarters. This was part of the plan. If someone had the misfortune of coming across a German patrol, the entire operation would not be compromised. Irena followed Sasha as she dashed down a side street, moving a few blocks away from the group and then turning again to her left and back toward the ghetto.

"How close will we get before we enter the sewers?" Irena whispered.

"We can't risk closer than three blocks," Sasha responded. "Too many eyes on the nearer streets."

"Do you know the route we're using?" Irena asked.

Sasha nodded. "I've been down it many times."

They traveled for another half hour in silence. Irena had a difficult time keeping up with Sasha. She was still young, a little over thirty, but Sasha was sixteen and used to physical endurance. Fortunately, her friend seemed aware of the situation, and she slowed down periodically to allow Irena to catch up.

She felt the excitement course through her as they neared the ghetto. She'd planned the removal of these children for weeks now. She'd thought the operation was hopeless after the fighting started, but she'd persisted and now all the moving parts were coming together. If she succeeded, they would take another five hundred children out of the ghetto tonight. She felt in a small way this would help make up for the terrible failure at the orphanage. Best of all, she would be bringing Ala and Rami out. Her friend had done enough. More than almost anyone. She deserved to rest, to survive the war and with luck, to be reunited with her husband, who had spent the war outside of Warsaw with his resistance group.

Sasha stopped them abruptly as they reached the corner of a street. She looked up and down the side street and then led Irena to the right. Halfway down the block she angled out from the sidewalk and approached a manhole cover that lay in the middle of the street. She stopped over it and retrieved a small metal tool from her pocket. Looking up and down the road again, she inserted a hook fashioned on the end into one of the holes in the cover. She stepped back and pulled, grunting for a moment before the cover pulled loose on one end. She kept tugging until the entire edge was over the pavement, and she rotated, pulling the cover to the side. The metal clanged loudly, and Irena started, looking around and expecting lights in windows and heads looking out. But nobody seemed to have heard anything.

"I'm going down," said Sasha. "Cover me."

Irena kept watch while Sasha climbed the iron rungs fastened in the concrete below the street level. She stepped carefully down, turning on a flashlight and examining the lower steps for any wires or other booby traps the Germans might have placed there. "It's clear," she whispered. "Let's go." Sasha descended the rest of the way down and then lowered herself onto a ledge next to the river of sewage. Irena followed her, relieved to see that this route, at least at this point in their journey, did not require her to wade through the foul liquid itself.

The journey into the ghetto lasted about two hours. The entire time Irena fought back the bile in her throat. She kept her focus on Sasha in front of her, barely perceptible in the darkness. Her guide turned this way and that, seemingly at random, but she never hesitated. Irena was impressed by Sasha's knowledge and bravery. She was a true hero of the ghetto.

Finally, she stopped underneath a circular well and put her hands to the ladder leading out. "We have to go quickly and quietly," she whispered. "When we get to the top, do not hesitate. Stay low and follow me immediately."

Irena nodded and Sasha moved forward, climbing the steps rapidly. She followed her guide, not as nimbly. Sasha reached up with both hands and pushed as hard as she could. The cover would not move, and Irena was afraid for a moment that she would not be able to open it. She heard the metal wrench and the left side of the cover jerked up. She rotated and pushed, sliding the cover out onto the street. "Now!" she whispered.

Sasha moved quickly. Irena followed as fast as she could. She climbed out of the manhole and onto the street. She looked around, shocked at the piles of rubble and the fires illuminating the night. Whole blocks were destroyed around her. "Get down!" Sasha shouted. Irena bent down low and waited anxiously for Sasha to move the cover back into place. "This way," she said, scuffling forward low and into one of the buildings across the street that was still partially intact.

Irena followed Sasha doorway by doorway, street by street. She could hear the staccato cracking of machine gun fire in the distance. The sky was orange and the air thick with dust and the acrid smell of burning buildings.

They made their way in the next half hour to Ala's apartment building. Irena was relieved to see it was still intact, as was the entire block. The Germans hadn't cleared out this section yet.

They moved quickly inside and up the stairs, brushing past dark figures huddling in the corridors. They made it to Ala's apartment and Irena banged on the door. They heard a voice inside asking who was there. It was Rami.

"Irena and Sasha," Irena answered. The door opened and Rami was there, thin and dirty, her clothes tattered. "Where's your mother?" Irena asked.

"She had to go to the hospital."

Irena was surprised. That was not part of the plan. What should they do? Should they wait for her here?

"I thought she was going to be waiting for us," said Sasha, looking at her watch.

"That was what we agreed on," said Irena. "But it's Ala. She won't go until she feels she's done everything she can."

"What should we do?" asked Sasha.

"I don't know," said Irena. "Maybe we should go get her. The hospital is only a few blocks away."

Sasha hesitated as if making up her own mind. "That's fine, but let's leave the girl behind. It will be safer."

"No!" said Rami. "Take me with you. I don't want to stay here anymore."

"She'll be fine," said Irena. "Look at her. She's young and fast. You can keep up? Can't you, Rami?"

The girl nodded.

"And you must be very quiet."

"I know how to hide," she said. "All I do is hide."

Irena realized that was likely true. For years now Rami had stayed for hours at a time in this little apartment. During the relocation, she was probably hiding for days and days. What a terrible and sad life. But all of that would change tonight.

Sasha assented, and they made their way back down and out of the building. Rami walked next to Irena, clutching her hand.

"Do you know where the hospital is?" Irena asked Sasha.

"Of course." Their guide moved off and Irena followed

closely behind. They rushed again from door to door, moving ever closer to the hospital block. They reached the corner and turned toward the structure. Irena stared in horror. The building was surrounded by trucks. A tank stood directly out front; the turret aimed at the entrance. Germans were leading a trail of people out of the hospital. Irena saw a familiar figure standing out front, directing the traffic. The tall, overweight form of Peter was unmistakable in the harsh light created by the truck headlights. He was joking with another officer as they watched the Jewish workers being loaded into the back of the vehicles.

There she was. She saw Ala stepping out, her eyes blinking in the bright lights. She was looking around as if expecting to find Irena there, saving her at last. A soldier moved forward, grabbing her arm. She was pulled from the group and whisked over toward Peter. He said something to her, as did the man next to him. She was sure it was Klaus. Ala was pulled past them and placed in a separate car. A second woman was pulled out and taken to Klaus. It was Wiera. The raid on the hospital had targeted them, Irena realized. Someone had tipped them off. She'd been betrayed again.

"Where's my mother?" asked Rami, standing next to her. "Why are the Germans here?"

"It's all right," said Irena. "Everything will be all right." She knew the lie in her words, even as she said them.

Chapter 27

A Flight in Darkness

April 1943
Warsaw Ghetto, Poland

Irena stood stunned, unable to move as she watched the scene unfolding around her.

She felt a sharp jerk on her arm. "We have to go," whispered Sasha.

"I can't," she said. "I can't leave without her."

"We have to. We can't stay here long. We'll be caught. Do you want Rami to be arrested too?"

Sasha was right. She shook her head, trying to drive the agony out of her mind. "All right," she said. "Let's go."

"What about my mother?" asked Rami. "I'm not leaving without her."

Irena didn't know what to say.

"Don't worry about your mother," said Sasha. "She's going to meet us outside the ghetto. We are going to go ahead of her."

"I don't want to leave her!" said Rami, her voice rising. "Why can't she come now!"

"Quiet!" whispered Sasha. "Now listen to me. You must be a good girl now. You must do everything I tell you. Otherwise, the Germans will catch us, and you'll never see your mother again. Do you understand?"

Rami nodded without answering. Irena was grateful that Sasha had taken over and talked to the girl. She didn't have the heart to tell her the awful truth.

"Let's go," said Sasha. "Irena, you keep close to Rami. I'm in the lead."

They moved cautiously away from the hospital. Sasha led them in a new direction. Irena was confused at first but then realized her guide must be taking them out from another route. She wondered why but finally it occurred to her that the location of Ala's apartment might have influenced how Sasha brought her in, and now she was taking a more direct route out.

They moved again in the same pattern. Rushing from door to door. Pausing for long moments at each intersection before they scrambled across to the next hiding spot. After what seemed an eternity, they made it to a street where Sasha halted them.

"We're here," she whispered. "I'm going to go open the cover. You two stay here."

Sasha crouched down and scurried forward, staying low, her eyes darting this way and that. Her figure was illuminated dimly by the orange glow of the sky. She reached the center of the street and kneeled, reaching out with her metal prybar to hook the top of the cover. She pulled and wrenched the cover open.

A shot rang out, startling Irena. Her heart jumped out of her throat. Sasha looked this way and that and then raised a hand to her head. She toppled over, her body shaking violently for a few moments before it lay still. A dark pool of liquid formed on the pavement near her head, expanding every moment. Irena watched, unable to move, horror overcoming her.

She heard the scream as if from a distance. A high-pitched shriek. She realized with horror that it was Rami, shouting in terror. Another shot. The wall to her left exploded in dust. She had to do something. But what?

She grabbed Rami's hand and took off, sprinting down the street. Another shot and another explosion directly behind her. She kept running, Rami barely keeping up. She expected any moment for the fiery pain of a bullet to erupt between her shoulder blades. Another shot rang out and another. They reached the corner and turned sharply, continuing down another street, and another. She turned left and jogged halfway down the block. She was huffing loudly now, out of breath, ready to pass out from the pain in her lungs. She pulled Rami into an alley and stopped, leaning against the wall, trying to catch her breath.

"What happened to Sasha?" Rami whispered.

"She's gone," said Irena, trying to process those words.

"Did the Germans get her?"

Irena nodded.

"What are we going to do?"

Irena wondered that herself. There was no way she could lead Rami through the sewers herself. Her hope was that they might run across one of the other guides and she could join the escape. She just had to find a manhole and then a good hiding space. Her breath gradually eased, and she could think straight again.

"Irena. What are we to do?" Rami repeated.

"We're going to find a hiding place and wait for help," said Irena. "Hold my hand and come with me."

Irena led her cautiously back out onto the street. She didn't know where they were, so she moved to the end of the block and stood, staring at the wall across the road. Miła Street. She recognized the name. They were only a few blocks from the ghetto wall. There was a good chance someone would come along near here and she could flag them down. She strained her eyes, staring into the middle of the intersection. Luck was with her; there was a manhole cover in the middle of the street. She looked around and found a set of stairs rising to a doorway. The base of the stairs offered at least a little cover for hiding. She led Rami over to the wall and pulled her down. Crouching together against the wall in their dark clothes, there was every chance they would be able to hide and wait for another group to come by.

They sat that way for hours. Irena kept checking her watch. It was four in the morning now. As the minutes ticked mercilessly by, she felt her hope slipping away. All the escapes were to take place simultaneously. Unless another group had been seriously delayed, they should all be in the sewers by now, if not already back in Aryan Warsaw. What was she going to do? She would have to make her way to one of the resistance bunkers and find another guide to get them out. The problem was she didn't know the locations. Sasha could have told her easily and led them to safety. She only had another couple of hours before daylight.

She realized she could not risk it. She could not simply wander around the ghetto, hoping to find someone to help her. They would be arrested or shot. She had no chance on the streets. The only possibility, she realized, was the one option she feared the most.

Steeling herself, she made her decision. She took Rami by the hand and led her into the middle of the street. Reaching down, she hooked her finger into one of the holes in the sewer cover and pulled. The metal disk didn't budge. She pulled again, harder this time. Nothing. She wished she'd been able to pick up Sasha's tool, but she'd have been killed if she'd tried to run out and retrieve it. She pulled Rami back to the stairs. "Stay here," she whispered. She moved away and walked along the street, moving until she found what she was looking for: a building that was partially collapsed and full of rubble.

Irena clambered up onto a pile of the bricks and began digging around in the darkness. She had her flashlight with her, but she dared not turn it on out here in the open. She moved brick after brick, desperately searching for something to help her. She'd almost given up hope when her hands came across what she was looking for, a ribbed metal bar about half a meter long. The iron rod was thick, about a centimeter in diameter. She pulled, and it came loose from the pile. She picked her way back down from the brick mound and hurried to the stairway. She checked her watch. Another half hour had passed. She had to get them underground soon or the dawn light would expose them to eyes in every direction.

She led Rami back out into the street. Squatting down, Irena wedged the iron rod into one of the holes in the cover. She twisted the bar and pulled down, trying to move the heavy cover. She felt the metal tearing at her skin and the grating shriek of metal on metal. At first the object would not move but she pushed harder, pressing all her weight down and pulling to her left at the same time. At once the cover gave, coming up at first a centimeter, then another. Finally, it rose above the street and she pulled hard, moving her feet against the street as she shoved the cover away from the hole. Three more times she had to begin again, but finally she had a large enough hole that she would be able to squeeze down into the darkness.

"I'll go first," she whispered to Rami. "If you hear anything happen to me, I want you to run and hide, anywhere you can. Wait until dark again and then go and try to find someone to help you."

"I don't want to leave you," she said, her voice trembling. "I want to leave here. I want my mother."

"I know, dear. I'm going to get you to safety. But you must promise if anything happens to me, you'll run and hide."

"I promise."

Irena took a step down into the darkness, her foot groping around until she located a rung. She turned her body into the hole and took another step down and another, lowering herself slowly into the abyss. Halfway down she remembered there could be traps set inside. She retrieved her flashlight and flicked it on, running it along the interior of the hole and along the rungs. There was nothing. Breathing a sigh of relief, she pulled herself farther down until she could feel her feet hit the stone below. She was fortunate, there was no sewage here at all. The corridor could have been nothing more than an underground hallway if not for the overwhelming stench that already threatened to suffocate her. She turned her light back on and illuminated the rungs.

"Climb down now," she ordered. Rami obeyed, pulling herself down rapidly until Irena could take her by the waist and lift her gently to the ground.

Irena considered returning the cover to its place, but she decided against it. She was too exhausted. The Germans might find the cover and investigate, but amongst the myriad of problems she faced, the risk seemed small. Flicking her light on again, she examined the corridor in both directions. It led in a straight line as far as she could see both ways. To her right, there appeared to be a passageway about a hundred meters away. Orienting herself as best she could in her mind to the streets above, this passage seemed to her to lead toward the ghetto wall. She took Rami's hand and they walked toward this opening. Irena desperately wanted to keep the light on, but she knew she couldn't risk it for long. Shutting the flashlight off, she felt her way along the wall, seeking out the passageway. Finally, they reached it and Irena prepared to take her first step into the unknown. She had no knowledge of the sewers, no guide. She knew there were dozens of branches down here, and that the Germans patrolled the corridors frequently. It would take a miracle for her to survive here. For the first time since she was a little girl, she bent her head and prayed, asking for guidance and a shepherd to lead them away.

They walked down the new corridor for some distance. Irena risked a little light. Another fifty meters ahead, the corridor ran into a "T." The new passage must be part of the main sewage system because it sunk down into a river of sludge. Irena considered going back but she was sure she was headed the right direction. They continued until they reached the stream of refuse. The smell was overwhelming, and she heard Rami choke and gag behind her.

"We are going to have to get into the water," Irena said. She heard Rami gasp.

"I can't," she whispered in horror.

"We have to," Irena said. "Don't worry, I've done this before, it's only bad for a little bit."

"No. Please," Rami pleaded. "Can't we go back?"

Irena shook her head, although she desperately wanted to agree with her. "No, we have to move forward. I'll go first."

Squatting down, she dipped her foot in and then her leg. Her toes searched for the bottom as she lowered her second leg in. She found the stone beneath her and stepped all the way in, the sludge lapping around her waist. "See," she said, trying to be brave. "It's not so bad."

She reached out and took Rami's hand and helped lower her into the sewage. The thick, putrid water reached up to the middle of the girl's ribcage. Rami gagged again and vomited, liquid spilling out of her mouth and down her chest into the foul water.

"It will be all right," Irena assured her. "We are going to be out of this and to safety before you know it."

Irena turned and flicked the light on again, searching both

directions. She wasn't sure which way was best to go. She ultimately picked her left. "Hold on to me," she said, and waded forward, into the muck, the water freezing her legs. Her eyes stung from the foul stench and every step she choked back the nausea. After a few meters she retched, holding on to the wall for a few seconds until the heaving passed. Then she continued.

On and on they went. Irena would turn on the flashlight every few minutes, trying to keep her orientation. She passed a turn to her left and then another. She kept moving, looking for a passage that would lead to her right again. She checked her watch; it was nearly seven. They'd been wading through the foul water for more than an hour. Finally, she saw a passage opening to her right in the distance.

"That's what we want," she said in relief. "We will take that and soon we can climb out." She hoped that was true, but in reality she had no idea where they were.

They moved on and finally reached the passage that opened to the left and the right. She turned her flashlight on and examined the entranceway. She was ready to turn it off when she spotted a wire a few centimeters above the waterline, extending the full length of the right passageway. In order to enter this way, they would have to swim under. She shook her head. She couldn't do that. They would have to keep going.

"Halt!" She heard the deep, violent voice ricocheting down the stone corridor. She turned her light to the left and saw a German there, waist deep in the sewage, his rifle in both hands aiming at her. She flicked off her light and she heard a sharp report. He'd fired at her.

She felt the panic scorching through her. She had an instant to decide what to do. Grabbing Rami, she dove her head under the filth, pulling the child down with her. She felt her way with her eyes closed, turning the corner and swimming through the thick muck, feeling her way along the walls as far as she could away from the entrance. Her lungs felt like they would explode but she swam on, pushing beyond her endurance to try to move as far away as she could before she surfaced. She reached her limit and pushed with her feet, driving her head above water and pulling Rami up at the same time. She gasped for breath, some of the liquid in her mouth. She tasted the bitter flavor as she gasped for breath. Her nostrils and mouth were full of the foulness. She retched again and behind her she heard Rami doing the same. She opened her eyes. They stung like fire, but she blinked over and over until she could see. A light flicked up and down the corridor. She turned back; the soldier was still there. He spotted them and screamed again, firing another shot and moving toward them.

Irena turned and swam away as fast as she could, pulling Rami with her. A second passed and another. The corridor erupted like the sun. Her ears filled with a crushing explosion and she was blown down the passage, crashing hard against the wall. She groped out in the chaos for Rami. She found an arm and pulled, bringing the girl next to her. She held her close until the brightness died down. *A grenade,* she realized.

"Are you hit?" she screamed. Her voice was distant and dull, traveling through a screaming ring in her ears. She couldn't hear the reply. She opened her eyes. There was fire burning the top of the water behind her. They were thirty meters or so away from the intersection. The German was nowhere to be seen but he could return any second. She looked at Rami, turning her this way and that. She seemed to be okay, although she was covered in filth and it was difficult to tell. She would have to trust that she was all right to move on. She could check for injuries later.

For now, they had to get away. The explosion would certainly draw more Germans soon. Turning, she pulled Rami forward and they moved on, traveling three or four hundred meters. She noticed the stream became shallower. Soon the sludge was only calf deep. They reached a turn to the right and there were steps leading up into a passageway. She lifted Rami up and they fell against the floor.

"Are you all right?" she asked again. The ringing had lessened a fraction and she could hear Rami now.

"I think so."

Irena turned on her light and examined the girl up and down, checking her arms and legs, her front and her back. She had a nasty cut on her forehead and her knees were scuffed and bloody. But she had no real wounds. Irena checked herself next. Miraculously, neither of them was badly hurt. She turned off the light again and lay her head down. Rami lay down next to her and they stayed that way for a long time, catching their breath and trying to recover from the horrible journey they'd just experienced.

Long they lay there. Irena floated between consciousness and dreams. She knew they should flee this area, that there was still danger, but she was exhausted. Finally, she opened her eyes and flicked on her flashlight, checking her watch. It was nine in the morning. She roused Rami, who was also asleep. They struggled to their feet. Irena could barely move. Every part of her body screamed with soreness and fatigue. Her clothes were caked with muck and they dragged her down, making it difficult to move. She took a step forward, and then another. Rami held tightly to her arm and the two used each other to move forward.

Eventually they reached an opening. Irena looked up. Light poked through the holes of the cover, illuminating the ground. She pulled herself up on a rung, barely able to climb. She raised herself up one step at a time, reaching the top. She placed both hands against the bottom of the cover, balancing herself so she didn't fall. She pushed with all her might. The cover moved a little, then gave way. She screamed as with a final effort she shoved the cover to the side, pushing it until half of the hole was uncovered. She pressed her head against the wall, resting for a moment. She knew she had to hurry. There was danger here again. She wasn't even sure where she was. She stepped up again and poked her head above the street level. A man and woman stood a few feet away. They were dressed nicely, and the woman was holding the man's arm, both staring in surprise at Irena. They looked at her for a few more moments and then hurried off, obviously wanting to get away from the scene as quickly as possible.

Irena looked around. There was nobody else on the street. She recognized a small hardware store across the way. She'd been here before. She was in Aryan Warsaw. They'd made it. The nightmare was over.

Chapter 28
Peter

April 1943
Warsaw, Poland

Irena sat at the table at Maria's. Adam stood behind her, rubbing her shoulders. Rami was there too, munching on some bread and talking to Adam. He was teasing her, and she kept laughing.

Irena wished they would go in the other room. She was trying to concentrate. She was working from two long lists as she wrote down the names of the children that were hidden and their new names and addresses in Aryan Warsaw. She was amazed the operation had been a resounding success. Virtually every child had come out safely. Except for Sasha, who was more qualified than all the rest, the guides had made their way in and out of the ghetto without incident. A few of the children had not come to the gathering places, either because the Germans had already reached them or perhaps because the parents did not have the heart to let them go. But notwithstanding these few exceptions, more than four hundred children had made it out.

Four days had passed. Irena had spent most of that time consolidating her lists. She would spend the day at Maria's, enjoying time with Adam and Rami while she worked on her scraps of paper. In the evenings she would take a jarful of the papers home, make dinner for her mother, and then bury the names in the garden after midnight.

She felt rested. She'd rarely had this much time in comparative peace. Still, the time was heavy on her. They'd had no word of Ala in all this time. Rami, who was for the most part in good spirits, would occasionally ask for her mother and break down when they didn't have any news. If she'd known even a little of the truth, the young girl would have been inconsolable. Irena did not give up hope. She'd learned long ago that while tragedy surprised her again and again, there were unexpected miracles that appeared just when she had given up.

She heard a jangle of keys in the hallway and then a fumbling at the door. Maria entered, rushing inside and slamming the door closed. "We've found her!" she exclaimed.

Irena rose. "Where is she?"

Maria glanced down at Rami. "We should talk in the other room."

"Adam, why don't you play a game with Rami. Maria and I need to talk for a minute."

Adam nodded and sat down at the table. He pulled a blank piece of paper out and a pencil. "Let's play the picture game," he said. "You can tell me anything in the world you want me to draw, and I'll do my best to make it."

"Draw a lion!" Rami shouted, giggling. She leaned over the table and watched closely, and Adam began sketching. Irena watched for a moment, a smile on her face. When she was sure that Rami was fully engaged, she turned and led Maria into Adam's bedroom.

"Where is she?" Irena repeated when they'd closed the door.

Maria's face darkened. "She's in Szucha Street."

Gestapo headquarters. Irena knew that meant only one thing: Ala was being tortured, likely with the intent of revealing what she knew about Irena and Żegota. She shivered, imagining what was happening to her friend. How long would they have before she broke? Would Ala be able to keep quiet?

"We have to do something," she said at last.

"Agreed. But what?"

"I don't know," said Irena. It was one thing to attack a gate with a couple of guards in the ghetto. The Gestapo headquarters would be heavily guarded. There was no way they could mount a raid on the facility with any hope of success. She tried to think of what they could do, but she didn't come up with anything. "We need to talk to Julian."

Maria nodded. "That's what I think."

Irena checked her watch. It was three o'clock. They could make it if they left now. "I'll go see him," she said.

"I'm coming with you," said Maria.

They walked the long distance from her apartment in the Praga district, over the Vistula and toward Julian's headquarters.

They were led into Julian's presence as soon as they arrived. They explained the situation to him. He listened with rapt attention, but when they were finished, he shook his head. "It's impossible," he said, taking a puff from his cigarette. "She might as well be on the moon. We can't touch her there."

"Surely there is something we can do?" Irena asked.

"I don't see what. You go into Szucha Street but you don't come back out again."

"Don't we have anyone on the inside?"

Julian looked down. He didn't answer.

"You do have someone," said Irena.

"Perhaps. Perhaps not. If I did have someone, I would have to save them for a higher-value mission."

"A higher-value mission?" Irena asked incredulously. "Who

is higher value than Ala? She was the chief nurse of the ghetto. She's been fighting the Germans out in the open, without a rest, for years. Nobody has taken more risks, or done more to defy them, than she has."

Julian shrugged. "She's not Polish, Irena. She's a Jew. Now don't get me wrong," he said, as Irena started to protest. "I'm not an anti-Semite. I know how important she is to you, and what she's done for the ghetto. But the Jewish story in Warsaw is ending. The resistance is wrapping up. The ghetto is a pile of rubble. We've got to think about the future. Our future. We will be fighting the Germans ourselves soon enough. And we intend to win. When we do, we may need our theoretical informant in the Gestapo. I can't play that card prematurely."

"I don't care what you want," said Irena, taking a step forward. "She's fought them with her bare hands. She trusted us to get her out and she's been betrayed. Possibly by someone in our very organization. Worse, she knows about me. If she gives me up, they'll arrest me. Once they are torturing me, who will I have to give up to save my life?"

His face paled. He knew the answer to that question. He took another deep drag on his cigarette. "Fine," he said at last. "I'll see what I can do. But don't get your hopes up. She could be dead already."

"I know you'll do everything you can," said Irena. She and Maria left and went on to the office. Jan was still there, and they filled him in on what was happening. He hadn't heard about Ala and she saw the sadness on his face.

"Do you think Julian can get her out?" he asked.

Irena shook her head. "There is no way to know. But if anyone can, he will. I just hope we can get her in time. I don't know what I will say to Rami if something happens. I keep putting off her questions, but she's growing more insistent every day."

"She won't be the first child without her parents," said Maria. "It's a lucky one who will leave this war with a mother or a father."

They spent the next several days waiting impatiently for word. Finally, a messenger arrived and told them that Julian was summoning Maria and her to headquarters. Irena was excited. She held hope that Ala might already be there when they arrived. He wouldn't send word unless he had significant news.

When they arrived she knew immediately that something was wrong.

"Your informant betrayed us," she said.

He shook his head. "No, he's turned out to be as reliable as I could possibly have hoped."

"What then?"

"We asked him to sneak her out. He said he could do it. He's waited the last couple of days, trying to find the right opportunity. This morning, he thought he would have a chance. But when he went to her cell, she was gone. He's tried to find out where, but so far, he doesn't know anything. Ala has disappeared."

Irena wanted to argue with him, to beat her arms against his chest or fall to the ground and collapse. Instead she stood there, stony faced, and absorbed this newest failure as she had the others. Ala was gone. Probably forever. She was helpless again and there was nothing she could do about it.

They walked back to Maria's apartment in silence. Her friend tried to engage her in conversation, but she refused. When they arrived home she barely spoke to Adam. She went directly to his bedroom where she kept a few things and changed into her newer dress. She stood at a mirror that rested over his dresser and adjusted her hair, applying makeup and making sure she looked her best.

"What are you doing?" Adam asked, concern in his voice.

"Take care of Rami," she said, turning to walk past him.

He took her wrist, holding her back.

"Where are you going?"

"I have something I must do."

"Irena. Maria told me what's going on. You're not in your right mind." She tried to move past him, but he maintained his grip.

"Let me go!" she shouted, her eyes flashing fire. "I know what I'm doing."

He took a step back, his hands raised as if in surrender. "I'm just trying to help," he said angrily.

She walked to the door. "I'll be back," she said.

The restaurant on Wilcza Street was a simple one. A long walnut bar on the right held a dozen stools. There were six or seven tables scattered around. A woman sat in the corner, facing away from the crowd, playing a stand-up piano. Irena perched at the end of the bar, a cigarette in her mouth. She'd been approached twice already by men eager to speak with her, but she'd politely declined. She wasn't here for the attention of random males.

She'd heard of this restaurant before but never been here. She'd avoided the place until tonight. She really wasn't sure whether she was wasting her time, but she couldn't think of anywhere else to go. She kept an eye on the door as she sipped some vodka, watching people come and go. This was a place to meet people. A special kind of person in fact.

The door jangled open again. He was here. He filled the doorway as he blinked, his eyes adjusting to the light. Someone shouted for him to get in or get out and he laughed, stepping in and clumsily shoving the door closed behind him. His shirttail was sticking out of the back of his tunic. He probably didn't know or care. He turned, scanning the room. A hawk seeking his prey. His eyes fixed on Irena and she saw the surprise and recognition. A flicker of a smile lit up his face and he headed toward her.

"Fräulein Sendler, to what do we owe the pleasure?"

"It's *Frau*, as you know," she said, not unpleasantly.

"That's right. You have some husband or other, don't you?" said Peter, looking her up and down. "What are you doing in here then?"

"I needed a drink."

"Don't we all," he said. He turned and loudly ordered a vodka. The barkeeper hastened to pour a double and bring it to him. He bowed his head slightly to Peter. He obviously knew who he was. Peter took the vodka and tipped the glass back, draining the contents in a flick of his wrist. He sighed in satisfaction. "I needed that." He turned back to Irena. "We were discussing your presence in this bar. It has the worst reputation, you know."

"For what?" Irena asked innocently.

"For Polish women coming to meet German men." His eyes bored into her. "Surely you know that." He waved at the bartender and directed more vodka for himself and for Irena.

"I've heard the rumors," Irena admitted. "I guess I was curious after all these years to see what goes on in here."

"Curious, were you?" Peter laughed. "I didn't think anything pulled your attention away from your duties."

"It's been a long war."

Peter raised his glass. "To an end of this beastly war."

She clinked his glass, smiling up at him. "Finally, something we can agree on."

"Perhaps we have more in common than that," he said.

"Like?"

"I don't know for sure," he said, his eyes twinkling. "But perhaps there is an opportunity to find out."

She stared back at him for long moments. "Perhaps," she said finally, her eyes darting downward.

Peter quaffed his second shot. "No reason to stay here longer, is there?"

"I don't know what you mean," she said shyly.

"Yes, you do. Let's go."

"Peter, I couldn't."

He took her arm, pulling her toward the door. She resisted for a moment and then relented. "You already have," he said.

Chapter 29

Anguish

April 1943
Gestapo Headquarters, Warsaw, Poland

Klaus sat with Colonel Wagner, going over the reports from the past few weeks. The news was mostly good. The ghetto was hardly more than a memory. Most of the resistance fighters had been killed or had surrendered. The workers at the Többens and Schultz factories had been relocated to a new camp at Poniatowa near Lublin.

"What about these reports of all the escaped children?" the colonel asked.

"Rumors at best," said Klaus. "Of course, a few people got out of the ghetto, but there couldn't be more than a couple of dozen at the most."

"That's not what my people tell me."

"And who are *your* people?"

The colonel smiled. "We have our watchers, as you know." He shrugged. "It doesn't matter. Governor Frank is satisfied with the conclusion of this project. Even if it wasn't the best example of liquidating a ghetto." The colonel leaned across the desk. "What he's not satisfied about, is your failure to find Żegota."

Klaus stared across the desk, battling down his anger. "What more could I do? I have five men assigned to this duty alone. They're working day and night. We'll crack into the group. Don't you worry."

"What about the vaunted arrest you made? You promised answers from her."

"She obviously didn't know anything."

"What makes you think that?"

"Because after what we put her through, anyone would talk. Anyone. And she had nothing to say. I think she was just what she said she was. A nurse in the ghetto. An important person among the Jews, I suppose, but she apparently didn't dabble with the resistance movement."

"What did you do with her?" the colonel asked.

"I didn't have any further use for her," said Klaus. "But no matter. We are days away from infiltrating Żegota or finding Żegota. Hell, I still don't even know if it's a person or a thing."

"We want a solution in the next week."

"Or what?"

The colonel raised his eyebrows. "I don't think you're going to want to find out." He rose, giving the Hitler salute. He started for the door when there was a knock.

"What is it?" asked Klaus.

"An urgent message sir," came a voice from outside the door.

"Come."

The soldier stepped inside. He had a document in his hand. He glanced at the colonel. "Sorry, sir. I didn't realize you were in a conference. This can wait until—"

"Whatever it is, it can't wait," said the colonel. "Hand him the message."

What now? Klaus thought. Reaching out he took the paper and read it. He felt the blood run out of his face. *Not this.*

"What is it?" asked the colonel.

Why couldn't his man have waited a few more minutes? There was nothing he could do about it. "Bad news," he said.

He could see the anticipation in the colonel's face. Almost glee. "What kind of news?"

"They have Peter."

"Your assistant? Who has him?"

"Żegota."

"How did they capture—"

"It doesn't say," said Klaus.

"What do they want?"

Klaus hesitated. *His failure would be complete.* "They want a trade for the nurse."

The colonel's face lit up with triumph. "Oh, they do, do they? The nurse that doesn't know anything about Żegota? What are your men doing downstairs? Tickling them?" He started for the door again. "Governor Frank will be very interested in this." He turned back to Klaus. "Seven days. I suggest you use it. Don't bring me bad news again." The colonel strolled out of the office like a man who'd just won a significant wager.

Klaus sank into his chair. They had Peter. What might be happening to his friend? He felt his breath speeding up as panic overran him. What was he going to do?

They wanted Ala. What did he care about her? Still, could he pull off a trade and keep his job? Did it matter? He sat there for a long time going over the alternatives. He could ignore the message and allow the consequences to play out as they might. He was sure he knew how that would end. He could also turn Ala over immediately and Peter would be safe—whatever the consequences to his own future. As he turned these questions over in his mind a third option came to light. *Yes,* that would work.

He scrawled a hasty note on the back of the letter and then called the soldier back. "This message is a response to the resistance."

"What do you want me to do with it, sir?" the soldier asked. "They didn't leave a way to contact them."

"Don't worry," said Klaus. "They'll be in contact soon. Give them the message when they do."

This was perfect. He would agree to the exchange but set the time for tomorrow night. In the meantime, he would bring Ala back and his men would have an entire night and day to work on her for information. If she gave up Żegota, he could send his men in and rescue Peter, along with taking down the organization, or person, or whatever it was. Now that he knew she had knowledge, all the remaining restraint would come off. She would sing. He would personally take part in the interview. He had to make this work.

He gathered his coat and left his office, arranging for a car. He had to retrieve Ala and he wasn't going to trust this to just anyone. He had to wait a half hour for a driver to be located, but soon he was motoring through the streets of Warsaw. An hour later he'd left the suburbs and was heading southeast toward Lublin. He'd had Ala sent to the camp there as well. He'd considered simply executing her, but something had held him back. She'd been too important in the ghetto. She might prove useful in the future as an informant, or a bargaining chip. He was relieved he'd made this decision. It was about to pay off.

They arrived at the camp two hours later. He was ushered into the office of the Kommandant, who was surprised to see a Gestapo major from Warsaw at his threshold. He was more surprised when Klaus handed him orders for a transfer of an individual Jew into his custody.

"How are things in the city?" the Kommandant asked Klaus as they waited for Ala to be brought to him.

"They are fine," said Klaus. "The Jewish problem is wrapping up. Although the Poles are a bigger nuisance now than ever. There is never any rest."

The Kommandant laughed. "Tell me about it. These Jews are getting feisty. There was a rumor in one of the sections that we might liquidate the camp." He wagged his finger. "Just a rumor, mind you, and it resulted in an insurrection. Two of my guards were killed and we had to eradicate the whole batch of them. Good workers too, and there was nothing to the story. They weren't going to be touched. Well . . . at least not yet."

Klaus shook his head. "Thank *Gott* they waited until now. Could you imagine millions of them fighting us? We'd have had our hands full, all right."

"What do you want with this one?" the Kommandant asked. "We don't usually get requests for someone by name. Mostly just the number of units around here. She must be someone important. Knows something, does she?"

Klaus ignored the question. He checked his watch. "How much longer?" he asked.

"It shouldn't be much. Our camp isn't so big. My man just had to check the records and then go locate her."

Klaus accepted some tea and took a sip. He was impatient to get out of here. He'd have limited time tonight and he wanted to get back to Warsaw and get started. A thought occurred to him. Perhaps it would all be unnecessary. If he revealed to Ala that he already knew something, she might talk on the way back. The chance was small, but perhaps she would crack under the pressure. That would save him time and effort, and he could move up the exchange for Peter. He thought of his friend again. They better not have harmed him. If they had, he would ruthlessly weed out the responsible parties and make sure they suffered like they couldn't possibly imagine. He felt fiery anger and he was surprised by the intensity of his response. *Those bastards.*

A guard knocked at the door and entered on the Kommandant's request. He was by himself and Klaus could tell immediately that something had gone wrong.

The guard looked at Klaus and then turned to the Kommandant. "What is it?" Klaus asked.

"Out with it!" shouted the camp commander.

"I'm sorry, sir, but she is . . . she was in the barracks that was part of the incident."

"What incident?" Klaus snapped.

"The uprising, sir."

Klaus nodded. "Your commander told me about it. Well, where is she then?"

"She's . . . she's gone, sir. All of them are."

Klaus couldn't believe it. He turned furiously on the commander. "How could you have let this happen!" he demanded.

The Kommandant sputtered for a moment and then became defensive. "I'm sorry, sir, but you didn't give us any special instructions when she was delivered here. If we'd known she was a special guest, we would have taken precautions to protect her. You must understand!"

Klaus rose from his seat and took a step toward the commander, but he stopped himself. The man was right. He'd made no special arrangements for Ala because he'd only kept her alive as an afterthought. She'd been sent to this labor camp and he'd assumed she would be just fine in the general population. He wasn't sure he'd ever need her again, so why arrange for anything more significant? Now he didn't know what to do. He walked out of the office without another word and stormed to his car. On the trip back to Warsaw he was silent, staring out the window, trying to determine what he should do next.

He would lie to them, he decided finally. He would take another woman out of custody and deliver her with a hood over her head at the same time he took Peter. He would bring a platoon of guards and have his agents case out the exchange point ahead of time. If they tried to pull back after realizing he didn't have Ala, he would shoot them down and take his friend back. He would instruct his men to take a few hostages after he had Peter. He might still be able to break into Żegota, regardless of Ala's death.

He arrived back at Szucha Street and set his plan into immediate operation. He stayed the night at his office, taking calls and receiving updates. He was going to make sure this plan operated without any problems. About midnight he was informed his message had been received by the resistance. He smiled to himself. This plan was going to work. In the morning he went over a briefing with one of his assistants. They'd located several vantage points above the exchange point, for snipers. There was a garage nearby and they had confiscated the structure temporarily. A full platoon of SS would be brought into stage from this room. They would attack and overwhelm the Żegota operatives at the moment of the exchange. He went over the details again and again, making sure each of the commanders understood their orders. When he was satisfied, he finally allowed himself to be driven home for some rest.

He awoke late in the afternoon. He checked his watch. The exchange would take place in about three hours. Perfect. He rose and came down for a late lunch with his daughter and wife. He was in a good mood, excited to secure the release of his friend and potentially to crack open the Żegota mystery. There was a knock at the door. A servant scurried off to answer. He came back a few moments later.

"A package for you," the servant announced.

Klaus looked up. The servant held a square wrapped package. He took it and pulled out his service dagger, slicing through the paper and tearing open the box. He stared down in shock and horror at the contents. Peter's decapitated head was inside, staring grimly up at him. He dropped the box and the head rolled out and onto the floor. He heard his daughter's screams, but he couldn't move. They'd killed his friend. Somehow, they'd known. They were going to pay.

Chapter 30
Revenge

October 1943
Gestapo Headquarters, Warsaw, Poland

Klaus sat at his cramped desk in the basement of the Szucha Street headquarters. He stared blankly at a line of names on a paper. They were possible black marketeers. A group of Poles who would end up with broken fingers or worse because they were trying to sell a little bacon or a piece of fruit on the street.

What difference did it make? He thought about the war. The newspaper and radio continued to declare victory after victory, but maps never lied. The cities named were getting closer and closer to Poland. In the west, the Germans had lost Africa, Sicily, and a chunk of Italy. The Italians, perhaps wiser than they were, had quit the war. Nobody would talk about the obvious truth: they were losing.

What was going to happen to them? He'd already sent his wife and child back to their hometown. He couldn't afford to keep them here any longer anyway, on his reduced salary. He'd lost his position, his friend, and he feared he would lose far more than that before this was done.

There was a knock at the door. A guard was standing in the doorway. "The colonel wants to see you."

He sighed, nodding without a response. He stood, brushed himself off, and walked up the multiple flights of stairs to the commander's office. *His old office.* He entered the room. Colonel Wagner was there shuffling some papers. He cleared his throat, but the commander did not look up for several minutes. Finally, he set the papers aside and motioned for Klaus to have a seat.

"Well, Rein, I've been reviewing your performance these past few months. I told the governor when I took over that I thought it was a mistake to keep you on at all, but he insisted that you still had value to us. I believe he was wrong." The colonel traced his finger down a page. "Fourteen arrests in all these months? What have you been doing? Picking your arse?"

"You took me off Żegota," said Klaus. "That's what I had put my resources into. There was a certain amount of time needed to get up to speed on my new, and *important*, targets. By the way," he said, leaning forward. "How is the hunt for Żegota going?" He knew the answer and relished the response.

The colonel's face flushed. "We're making progress," he responded finally.

"I'm sure you are, Colonel. It's not as easy when you're in charge, is it?"

"You worry about your assignments and I'll worry about mine," the colonel snapped.

"Of course," said Klaus. "Is that all?"

"Yes," said the colonel, waving his hand and returning to his paperwork. "You're dismissed."

Klaus stormed out of the office. *The bastard*, he thought. *He'd been after my job the whole time. Now that he has it, he's not getting a damned thing done.* Klaus had been so close to cracking the Żegota group wide open. After Peter's death, he'd tripled the number of men investigating the resistance group. Then word had come down from the governor that he was relieved from his command and demoted in rank. He still remembered the triumphal entrance of the colonel and his followers.

Klaus returned to his office. His one assistant was there, crammed into a seat between the wall and Klaus's metal desk. He had a look of excitement on his face.

"What is it?" Klaus asked.

"We've caught the informant," he said.

"Which one?" Klaus asked, bored already with the discussion.

"The Żegota one. The big one."

Klaus couldn't believe it. "Where are they?" he asked.

"In a cell less than fifty meters from here."

"Let's go!" He turned and, with the assistant right behind him, he stormed down the corridor.

A half hour later he was back in the colonel's office, laying out his information.

"You obtained all this in the past half hour?" the colonel asked. "How reliable is this person?"

"They've been entirely reliable in the past."

The colonel shook his head. "Well, give me what you have, and I'll look into it."

Klaus couldn't believe his ears. "You're taking this away from me?"

"You're not on Żegota. You know that. Thank you for the information. Please get back to work and I'll look into this—if we have time."

"But, sir. We have everything we need. We can move instantly. I can be ready in an hour."

The colonel's face flushed red. "Was I unclear, Rein? You don't have any authority here anymore. Now get out of my office and for once try to do your job. And let me tell you something else. This is going in my report along with a recommendation that you be relieved of all duties and sent back to Germany."

"Do what you will, Colonel," said Klaus, turning to leave.

"I didn't tell you you're dismissed."

Klaus turned, staring into the colonel's eyes.

The colonel returned the look for long moments, but then glanced down at his documents. "That's all."

Klaus left and returned to his office. He sat at his desk for a long time, fuming. His assistant returned and he passed on the news.

"What are you going to do?" the agent asked.

"I'm going forward, without orders." He looked at the young man. "If you don't want to be involved, I understand."

His assistant hesitated for a few moments, then nodded. "No, sir. I'm with you."

"Good," said Klaus. "Then here's what we are going to do."

Irena walked with Adam and Rami in the gardens near the Vistula. They were taking a little bit of a risk. Adam had Jewish features and they might be stopped at any point. But they had their papers with them, and the documents were flawless.

She couldn't resist. The day had dawned beautiful, with the sun rising above the buildings into a clear blue sky. The air was crisp but not cold, and there was a rich warmth emanating from the direct sunshine. Irena strolled between them, holding Adam's hand with her left and Rami's with her right.

"We have much to be thankful for," Adam said.

He was right. They were alive. Their operation was still thriving. There were no more children to rescue, but they were keeping twenty-five hundred little ones throughout the city. Żegota paid vast sums of zlotys per month for food and support of these families. Adam, ever the intellect, kept the books, and made sure the resources were allocated and that each payment was precisely accounted for.

Better yet, the end of the war was on the horizon. The Germans did their best to hide the truth, but the rumors came through from many sources. The Nazis were falling back in

Russia and in Europe. They'd lost a terrible battle at Stalingrad and another massive engagement at Kursk. The Soviets had started another offensive and were threatening to drive their enemy entirely out of Russia. Poland would not be far beyond.

"What will we do when it's all over?" she asked.

"We will live," he said simply.

"What about us? You and me?"

He stopped and looked at her. "That is up to you, my dear. The Germans have taken care of my marriage. But yours is still intact."

"I will remedy that," she said. "If you want me to."

He smiled. "Of course, I do. We will marry one day, and then we will build our socialist Poland. The fascists and the capitalists will be driven out of our nation, and the people will rise under Russian tutelage and carve out a workers' and farmers' nation, devoted to the people."

"What if the Germans stop them?" she asked. "What if they turn things around and win?"

He shook his head. "I don't think they have it in them. Look at our own city. They've pulled half the soldiers out and sent them to fight. When is the last time you saw a tank or an airplane? I think they're scraping the bottom of the barrel now."

"I hope you're right," she said. She looked around. They had to be careful discussing this in public. "Let's hope and pray that this is the end."

"Pray?" he asked, laughing. "Don't talk about praying when the Russians get here. You need to repress your Catholic background, or you'll get yourself in trouble."

Rami had stood quietly this whole time. "What about my mother?" she asked. "My father?"

"Your dad has been in the woods this whole time," Irena explained again. "He should be back when the fighting is over." She hoped this was true. "For your mother, I hope she will be too." This was a lie. She knew what had happened to Ala. Julian's inside person had told them, along with the planned ambush. Thus Peter. She hated to tell Rami this, but she had not been able to bring herself to share the truth yet. She hoped when the war was over that Rami's father would reappear. Then she could bear to tell her about her mother.

Adam frowned. He didn't approve of this. He thought they should tell her now. "Let's go," said Irena, starting to walk again. This was certainly not the place to have that argument again.

They continued their stroll, enjoying the trees and the bushes. The garden was not as beautiful as it was in the spring and summer, but just the opportunity to walk here as if the war had never happened was a wonderful salve to their spirits.

They returned to Maria's an hour later. Her friend was there, setting out some bread and cheese for an afternoon meal. They sat around the table, sipping a little vodka, laughing and teasing each other. Even Maria joined in. At the end of the meal Irena rose to leave.

"Why can't you stay?" Rami asked.

"I have to look in on my mother," she responded.

"Wouldn't she be all right for a day?" Adam asked. "You could spend the night?" He winked at her and she felt the warmth inside her. Perhaps she could spend the night here and check in on her mother in the morning. No, she'd come down with a cold and Irena wanted to look in on her to make sure she was all right.

"Tomorrow night," she promised. "As long as she's on the mend."

"Fine," said Adam, pretending he was offended. "I'll just stay here with the other women in my life." He made a playful grab at Maria's arm. She slapped him away.

"Stop that nonsense," she protested.

"Well," said Irena, checking her watch. "I'm off."

Adam rose and walked her to the door. He unlatched it and

they stepped outside. "Are you sure you can't stay?" he whispered, kissing her neck. "I'll make it worth your while."

She moved in closer, putting her arms around him and reaching up to kiss him on the lips. "I'd love to," she said, still struggling with the decision. "But I have to go check on her."

He kissed her back, holding her tight. "Did you mean what you said today?"

"About what?" she asked.

"About the divorce. The marriage."

She looked up at him intently. "I wouldn't want anything else more in the world."

He smiled, kissing her again on the forehead. "Go to your mother and hurry back tomorrow. You've promised me a night together and I intend to collect on it."

She kissed him again and left. She had a long walk ahead of her. She hardly noticed the passing of the streets and time as she headed back to her apartment. She fantasized about the end of the war. A flat of their own. Children. They would both return to meaningful work, her in social work for the new Polish socialist regime, and Adam as an attorney, or working for the government. She thought about the day, perhaps not too far in the future now, when the Germans would evacuate Warsaw. She smiled to herself. There was a future now. Something to live for after all this struggle and death.

She arrived at her building and hurried up to the apartment. She opened the door and immediately knew that something was wrong. She called for her mother but there was no answer. She rushed to the bedroom. She was there, in bed, but she wasn't answering. Her hair and forehead were soaking wet. Irena touched her head. She was on fire.

"Mother!" she called. "Mother, can you hear me?"

Her mother's face tensed, and she opened her mouth, as if she had heard her and was trying to respond. But the words would not form in her mouth. Irena rushed to the kitchen sink, pouring water into a cup. She brought the water in and tried to pour some of the liquid down her mother's throat, a few drops at a time. Her mother sputtered and coughed. Her eyes opened wide, but she stared past Irena as if she didn't see her.

"Don't worry, Mother, I'm going to get you some help." Irena turned and rushed toward the door.

Halfway across the threshold the door ripped open. Torn nearly off its hinges, the door buckled at an odd angle. She screamed. There were men there. Soldiers and two young men in long leather trench coats. They rushed forward and seized her arms.

"My mother!" she screamed. "My mother is sick! She needs my help."

One of the men held a cloth to her mouth. "Don't worry about your mother," he said. "Worry about yourself."

She struggled against the rag, barely able to breathe. She felt dizzy and the lights above her shrunk down as if she were in a tunnel. She felt herself falling forward and the hands seized her harder. She fell into darkness and remembered no more.

Chapter 31
The Dark Dance

October 1943
Gestapo Headquarters, Warsaw, Poland

"Irena." Klaus said the words in a gentle whisper. He stood over the Polish woman, who was still passed out. She was tied ankles and wrists to a chair. Her head was slumped to the side. She was starting to grimace, starting to come to.

It had been Irena all this time. How had he missed this? He remembered the investigation at the office. He recalled pulling her out of the line at the Umschlagplatz. He thought she'd just been concerned about a Jew or two that she had known, but now he realized it was so much more than that. He shook his head. He normally saw things so clearly, but for this woman he'd seemed to have a blind spot. He wondered why. Perhaps it was because he saw something of himself in her. She was strong, persistent, fanatical about her duties. While he could never understand her socialist leanings, he had sacrificed everything for his own ideological beliefs. Only to be betrayed by his own people. The same was happening to Irena now. One of her own had given her up to save themselves. To make their own life a little easier. Such was the way of the world.

He nudged her ankle. "Irena," he repeated. She opened her eyes halfway and slurred some words in reply. He touched her leg, giving it a gentle squeeze. "Irena. I need you to wake up."

Her eyelids fluttered and opened. She stared out with a glazed expression for long moments, but finally focused on Klaus. He saw the shock and surprise as she realized who she was looking at, where she was. Her body jerked as she tried to rise. Her body dragged to the left and the chair toppled over. She hit the concrete floor hard.

Klaus nodded his head and a guard ran forward, seizing her and bringing her chair back up with her in it. She looked at him again, eyes full of terror.

"Irena. What on earth am I going to do with you?"

"My mother," she managed to whisper. "She's ill. She needs a doctor."

Klaus shook his head. "No sense in worrying about her now." He tapped his cheek with his index finger. "Unless you are willing to tell me everything I want to know. Yes, that would be a solution," he said finally. "And a wise one for you." He took a step and loomed over her. Her head arched back, struggling to meet his eyes.

"Yes, you know what's coming, don't you Irena? But no matter what you've feared, what you've dreaded, you cannot imagine what it is really going to be like. Your mother is ill, you say? If you tell me what I want to know, she'll get assistance today. What's more, you won't be touched. You'll be released and you can go on with your life with that Jew lover you have in hiding."

He saw her eyes widen. "Oh yes, we know about him too. We know much already, Irena. I'm only asking you to tell me a little more." He saw the struggle in her eyes. He smiled to himself. She was going to break, perhaps without him having to apply any pressure. This was surprising, and so much more than he'd hoped for.

He motioned for the guard, who brought him a chair. He sat down in front of her and put his hand on her leg again. "Irena," he whispered. "I can see it in your eyes. You don't want to go through this." He leaned forward. "The war is almost over," he said. "You can live out the rest of it in peace and quiet. You can save your mother, your lover, anyone you name—within reason. But I need something from you. I need Żegota. Give me Żegota and a hundred children you're hiding, and you'll walk out of here today, intact. We'll take care of your mother and we'll leave you alone for the rest of the war."

He squeezed her leg again, gently. "We know you're hiding hundreds of children, Irena. I don't need all of them. Just a few. I need some arrests, and I need Żegota. You can play the rest of your game. You can save most of them."

She stared at him, her face still full of fear and indecision.

"I'll give you an hour," he said. "Then we must begin."

He stepped out of the room and returned to his office. His tea was laid out on his desk just the way he liked it. He poured himself a cup and measured out his sugar. Closing his eyes, he took a sip and allowed himself to relax. This was going to be far easier than he'd feared. Now he just had to consider what to do with the information. If he gave it directly to the colonel, Wagner would assuredly take credit. He was going to have to do something he'd never done before: He would go out of channels and send the information to Hans Frank through some of his contacts in Kraków. He could imagine the colonel's face when he realized that Klaus had ignored his orders, gone around him, but was protected because of the victory he had achieved. He smiled to himself. Perhaps he would get his old position back. He could imagine the colonel standing by, furious, while his things were gathered up and Klaus moved back into the office. That would be sweet revenge indeed.

He checked his watch. The hour had passed. He returned to the cell. He knew immediately that there would be a delay. Irena's face was stony and full of defiance. She'd reached some sort of conclusion. The wrong one. He shrugged. No matter, whether early or late, she would come around.

"Are you ready to tell me what I've asked?" He already knew what her answer would be.

She stared at him for long moments. There was just a hint of indecision in her eyes. This was the last moment she could make a deal without any physical consequences to herself. Finally, she closed her eyes and shook her head.

"That's too bad," Klaus said. He removed his service dagger and bent down. He slashed the knife across the back of her hand. A thin line formed. She gave out a scream, and struggled in her chair, but her wrists were firmly tied and there was nowhere she could go. The cut was deep, and it quickly filled with blood, the liquid dripping out onto the floor until it made a small pool below her. He stood up. There were tears in her eyes and she gasped at the pain.

"So it begins," said Klaus. "I'll let you think about that and we can chat again this evening." He turned and walked out of the room. She'd chosen badly. No matter. She would talk. He'd seen it in her eyes.

Chapter 32

A Woman's Strength

January 1944
Gestapo Headquarters, Warsaw, Poland

Irena woke. Her eyes were puffed, and she could feel the pain in her cheeks. The fire in her leg was worse. She lay on the floor of her cell, her clothes in rags. She remembered last night's nightmare. A terror among terrors. She looked down and saw that they'd set the bone in her leg. There was a dirty bandage wrapped tightly around her upper thigh. She wished they'd left it alone. If she had an infection she might die. She wanted death more than anything.

How long had she endured his torture? She couldn't keep track of the time. Months had passed, that was certain. She had no idea how she had endured. At first, she thought she would expire from the pain, or worse, that she would talk. But she'd fought down the words and by concentrating on each day, moment by moment, she'd somehow managed to hold her tongue.

Why didn't they shoot her? Klaus had threatened to kill her so many times now. He'd held a gun to her head a dozen times, even pulling the trigger. But the chamber was empty. He must have thought he was motivating her, but he didn't realize, she *wanted* the gun to be loaded.

Her mother. She was gone. He'd described her arrest, torture, and murder. Had he taken Adam and Rami too? He hadn't said anything yet, but she knew that didn't mean anything. Klaus liked to dish out his terror, course by exquisite course. He might be holding it back for just the right emotional moment. Did he know how close she'd been to talking last night? If he had, he wouldn't have let her go. He would have kept her there, kept her awake, and played his last cards. She would have talked. She was desperate to talk. She didn't know how much more she could resist. She was starving, exhausted, the pain had stacked on, brick by brick, until the weight of it threatened to crush her soul.

But he'd given her a break. He'd patched up her wounds and let her sleep. She had a sliver of resistance left. Perhaps enough to hold him off for another day. Every day was a miracle from God.

God. Was there a God? The Russians didn't think so. Her socialist friends were sure it was a myth. But here in this cell, where every moment was agony, she wasn't sure. She knew one thing for sure: There might not be a heaven but assuredly there was a hell.

There was a knock on the door. She felt the fear course through her. Why did he bother knocking?

The latch moved and the door opened. Klaus was there. He smiled down at her. "How is our little patient today?"

She spat on the pavement, unwilling to answer.

"Ungrateful as ever, I see," he said. "I've kept you alive all this time and yet you don't thank me for my efforts." He stepped in and lowered himself to the pavement, leaning his back against the wall. "Ahh," he said. "It feels good to rest for just a minute." He looked at her, his face full of concern. "Honestly, Irena, I wish you would just tell me what I want to know. If you believe I've enjoyed this, you are entirely wrong. The same truth exists that I presented to you on the first day of your visit. I don't want to harm you; I just want some answers."

"You want names so you can torture and kill others. So you can send those poor little children up the chimney," she hissed. "I'll never give them to you."

He looked at her intensely for a moment. "It's the children that really bother you, isn't it? I'll tell you what, Irena. I don't want them anymore. You can keep the little ones safe. I just want Żegota. Just give me the names I need, and once I verify things you can walk out of here."

She was shocked. He didn't want the children anymore. Just Żegota. She could save them if she just told him what he wanted. She thought of Julian, of her friends in the resistance. She would mourn their loss. But she knew she wasn't going to last much longer. Could she pass up this chance to save the children, even if it meant betraying her cause? Did she have a choice? She saw the grin on his face. She was struggling with this decision and he knew she was.

She ran the issue through her mind. What was she going to do? "Can I have a little time to think?" she asked.

He pulled himself up. "Of course, you can. And let me give you something else to help your decision." He opened the door and a guard brought in a platter with bread, sausage, cheese, and some grapes. He lowered the tray down to her. "Here's something for your information. A little appreciation in advance." He stood and bowed his head slightly. "I hope you'll now see reason," he said. He turned and left the cell.

She couldn't believe it. They'd only given her a little bread and water each day. She was starving. She ripped off some of the sausage and shoved it into her mouth. She'd never tasted anything better in her entire life. She gorged on the cheese and grapes and then wolfed down the bread. She felt sick from the influx of food and she threw up on the pavement. She didn't care. Her stomach felt better than it had all these months.

Klaus returned sometime later. He looked at the mess she'd made, shaking his head. "I should have warned you," he said. "Too much too quickly is a bad thing. After we've had our little talk you can have a shower and we'll get you some new clothing."

She hung on his words. She couldn't imagine the feeling of warm water on her skin. Of being clean. Of having new clothing brought to her. She wanted desperately to tell him what he wanted, but she couldn't bring herself to do so. She shook her head, the tears welling up in her eyes. "I'm sorry. I can't. I just can't."

He stood over her for long minutes. Finally, she heard him scoff audibly and he opened the door, letting himself out. She laid her head back on the concrete and erupted in sobs. He would be back, she knew, and soon. The terror would begin anew.

Chapter 33
New Horizons

January 1944
Gestapo Headquarters, Warsaw, Poland

Klaus walked down the hallway and opened a cell door. Another woman was there. She was sitting in a chair, her eyes full of fear. She'd just arrived.

"Hello, my dear," said Klaus. "I hope we haven't disturbed your schedule."

"Why am I here?" she asked. "You promised me protection."

"I have protected you these many months," said Klaus. "But I need more information from you."

"I've told you everything I know," she said. "And you said you were done with me."

"You don't want me to be *done with you*," he said, taking a step toward her. "Be happy you still have something to tell me."

"What do you want?" she asked.

"I want you to tell me where Irena's lover is. What is his name? Where is he living?"

The woman looked at him with surprise. "I told you, I don't know that."

Klaus stepped closer to her. "Come on, now. You certainly do know where to find him. Look, we've played this game for years now. You always hold something back. Something in reserve. Today is your lucky day. Your strategy has paid off. I only want one more thing from you."

She shook her head. "I don't know. I told you, I haven't any idea."

"I'm sorry, but I'm going to have to be sure." He removed his dagger and pulled her hand up. He looked at the fingers, so long and slim. There were no wrinkles on the hand. It was perfect. He held the knife up to her little finger.

"What are you going to do?" she asked, her eyes lighting with fear.

"I'm going to cut your finger off," he said. "One finger a minute until you tell me what you know."

She stared at him in horror. "You promised," she said.

"I lied. I do that when I need to. Now don't be stupid," he admonished. "You've never played the hero, and now isn't the time to start." He placed the knife against the finger, sliding it gently until it made the slightest cut. The woman gasped.

"Tell me," he whispered.

"I don't know."

"Very well then," he said. "Let us begin."

"Wait!" the woman yelled. "Wait. I might have some idea."

"I knew you would be reasonable, Wiera," he said, sliding his knife back into its sheath. "You always have been."

Ten minutes later he was on his way back to Irena's cell. He had everything he needed now. She was exhausted and he'd offered her a compromise. He was sure he had the last component to get her to talk. She might have let her mother die, but she'd never let Adam. *Adam.* He'd know immediately if that slut had lied to him. If she had, he'd cut off more than a finger.

He put his hand on the door, starting to turn the handle. He felt the triumph in his heart.

"Lieutenant." He heard the voice of his assistant. He looked up in annoyance. "What is it?"

"The colonel wants to see you."

"Tell him I'll be up in an hour or so."

"He said immediately."

Klaus thought about ignoring the order. He was so close. Still, the last thing he wanted was for the colonel to come looking for him. Not when he was so close to getting what he wanted. He sighed. "Fine, I'll be right up."

He opened the door. Irena was there, still lying on the floor, amidst a torn-up tray of food and a pool of vomit. "I've had some new information," he said.

She looked up.

"I know about your Adam."

Wiera had told the truth. He saw it in Irena's eyes. He smiled. "I have a couple of issues to attend to, but when I'm back, we are going to discuss your lover. Or perhaps I'll just have him rounded up and we can all visit together. Why don't you think about what I want from you, and when I get back, we'll have a nice little chat. Is there anything I can get you in the meantime?"

She turned away, her face flushed, refusing to answer.

"Very well then. Think long and hard on this one, Irena. I can't hold back the future any longer."

He turned and went through the door. He felt the elation coursing through him. He'd seen the look in her eyes when he mentioned Adam. She was going to turn. This was the last straw and it was more than she could sacrifice.

He arrived at the colonel's office a few minutes later. He was summoned inside immediately, and the door was closed.

"You've ignored my orders, Rein," said the colonel, looking up.

"What are you talking about, sir?"

"You know exactly what I'm talking about!" the colonel screamed. "I told you to leave off on Żegota, but you went out and arrested this Sendler woman, and you've been interrogating her for months under my nose? Do you take me for an utter idiot? In my own building!"

"I don't know what you're talking about." He knew there was small chance a denial would work, but he had to try something.

"Who do you think you're dealing with!" the colonel demanded.

A fool, Klaus thought.

"I know Sendler is here. Do you want to take me to her, or shall we go and tour the cells together?"

"I don't know what you're talking about."

The colonel turned to Klaus's assistant. "Take me to her."

"*Jawohl.*" The assistant gave a meaningful look to Klaus, and then turned, leading the colonel down a hallway—in the opposite direction of Irena's cell.

Klaus rushed the other direction. He tried to clear his head. He knew he only had a few minutes. What was he going to do with Irena? If he was caught with her, in direct violation of the colonel's orders, he would be court-martialed, even shot. He rushed down the stairs to the basement, shouting at a guard to follow him. He reached her cell a few moments later and stood impatiently while the soldier fumbled with the keys. He tore the door open. Irena was there, crumpled against the wall. She was passed out or asleep.

He moved to her quickly, seizing her arms and dragging her toward the doorway. She woke up, screaming in pain as he pulled her broken leg along the concrete floor.

"Shut your mouth!" he ordered. Klaus turned to the guard. "Give me a hand, you fool!"

The soldier moved to assist him and together they pulled

Irena out the door and down the hallway. Klaus led the way, dragging her to the end of the corridor where he located an empty cell. "Put her in here!" he demanded. He stood waiting for the door to open, his eyes staring down the passage, waiting for the colonel to appear. A minute passed while the guard looked for the correct key. Finally, he found it and opened the door. Klaus pulled Irena in and slid her against the wall. She looked up at him with terror in her eyes. "Adam," she whispered.

"Shut your damned mouth!" he shouted. They moved out of the cell and he slammed the door shut. He turned to the guard. "You are to make sure nobody enters or leaves this cell. This prisoner is an enemy of the state and has invaluable information. You are not to reveal where she is to anyone, do you understand?"

The guard nodded and returned to his position at the end of the hallway. Klaus rushed up the stairs, not wanting to run into the colonel in the cell area. His heart raced. He was safe for now, but he knew it wouldn't last. He would be caught, unless he could figure out some way to rid himself of Irena. He reached his office and set himself at his desk, trying to calm his breathing and appear to be working. He was there for less than five minutes when the colonel appeared, his face a fierce scarlet.

"What have you done with her?" the colonel demanded.

Klaus looked up, assuming his most arrogant and disdainful expression. "I told you, there is no Irena Sendler here. You've been lied to."

"I don't know how you managed to hide her, but you'll never reach her again. I've posted guards all over this headquarters. You are barred from entering the cell area as of this moment. Do you understand? I'm going to sort this out, and when I find her, I'm placing you under immediate arrest. You will answer to Hans Frank for your insolence!"

"Do what you will," said Klaus. "There's nobody to find.

Besides, you can't even locate Żegota, how will you find a phantom woman?"

That statement told. The colonel shook with anger.

"Is there anything else?" Klaus asked, looking down.

"You will stand and salute me!" the colonel demanded.

Klaus kept his eyes on his paperwork. "I don't think so," he replied.

The colonel sputtered. "Enjoy your last day of freedom, Rein." He stormed off.

His assistant appeared a few minutes later. "What are we going to do?" he demanded of Klaus.

"I don't know," he said. He was frustrated. He had everything he wanted now. Irena was broken, ready to talk, but he couldn't reach her. He closed his eyes, letting that go. That didn't matter anymore. He had to save himself. Then it occurred to him. He could get rid of her; it was so easy. Nobody would ever know the difference. But he had to clean up other things as well.

"Release Wiera," he said.

The assistant's eyes widened. "You're letting her go?"

"I have to. The colonel cannot know she's here."

"But she's the last link to finding Żegota, unless that resistance group . . ."

"That was a dead end," said Klaus. "They were some nowhere right-wing group. They had nothing."

"Then you're giving up?" his assistant asked.

"I'm surviving. I'm saving myself, and you too. Don't forget," he said, eyeing the man sharply, "you're in this as deep as I am. If you don't want to be lined up against a wall, I suggest you do as I say, and keep your mouth shut."

The assistant nodded and then turned to follow his commands. Klaus rubbed his hands together. He might not win this game after all, but he had no intention of losing either . . .

*   *   *

There was a knock at the cell. The door opened and an SS guard appeared. He looked down at Irena, assessing her condition. He noted the bandage on her leg.

"Do you need assistance walking?" he asked her brusquely.

She nodded.

The soldier reached down with rough hands. He pulled her to her feet and held her arm tightly with his. "Let's go," he said.

She'd waited all day and night for Klaus to return. She knew she couldn't hold back any longer. She was going to have to tell everything. The hours had ticked by, but he'd never appeared. And now, here was this other soldier, someone she'd never seen before. "Where are you taking me?" she asked.

He looked at her for a moment, as if debating his answer. "I'm sorry," he said. "You're slated for execution."

So, this was it, she thought. She'd known this day might come. She felt the elation that she hadn't broken, that her friends and family were protected, that her Jewish children were safe in hiding. At the same time, she experienced overwhelming sadness. She wanted to live. There was so much she'd wanted to do. More than anything, she'd wanted a baby. Adam's baby, growing inside her. Now she would have nothing. Her mother was gone. He would be dead soon as well. Everything would be finished.

The soldier drew her to her feet. She was pulled through the door and down the hallway. The guard was rough. She wondered where he was taking her. They reached the end of the corridor and he pulled open the door. Outside it was freezing. They were in a small courtyard. There was snow on the ground and her bare feet stung against the cold. He pulled her across the space and toward the wall. Of course, this must be where they conducted the executions. She looked around for a firing squad, but they were alone. The soldier wrenched open another door at the far end of the space and pushed her toward it.

"Go," he said.

"What do you mean?" She was disoriented. She looked through the opening. She could see a sidewalk beyond, and the street.

"Go," he repeated.

"I don't understand. I can't walk. What are you saying?"

"I'm saying that Żegota has taken care of things," he whispered. "Now get out of here."

She couldn't believe it. She felt herself coming back from the brink. *Żegota*. The word filled her ears. She wasn't going to die after all. But she looked again to the street. He must be kidding.

"I can't walk," she said. "I'm injured. I have no shoes, no papers."

He pulled her through the door. "You have to go now! Get out while you're still alive!" He threw her down on the pavement, wrenching his arm away from her. He slammed the door behind him. She was alone, sprawled out on the sidewalk in the snow.

She had to live. She had to make it to Adam and Rami somehow, before Klaus got there. She knew it was probably too late, but she had to try. She pulled herself to her feet, grasping at the wall for balance. She turned and stumbled into the snow, crossing the street. Her leg was on fire. She could barely move. Her clothes were in tatters and she had no shoes. She was kilometers from the Praga district. She knew she would likely be arrested before she'd shambled a hundred meters, but she had to try. She continued, stumbling step by step. A pedestrian passed her, staring at her in amazement. She kept walking, knowing it was a matter of minutes before she ran into a German.

There was a whisper to her right. A man stood in a doorway, motioning for her to come to him. She hobbled through the threshold. He was a Pole. She was standing in a small hardware store. There were a few tools and some bags of nails for sale. The man gestured for her to sit down on a chair. He left quickly, perhaps to betray her. She didn't care. She was already exhausted. He returned a few minutes later with hot tea. She took a couple of sips gratefully as he scurried around. He returned with a shawl that he placed over her shoulders. He had shoes in his hands, and socks. He reached down, wiping her feet clean and then placing the socks on her feet. He worked her good leg into a shoe. It was too large, but he laced it up tight.

"My wife's," he whispered.

"You can't give me these," Irena responded.

"She doesn't need them anymore," he said through choked words.

He now worked on her hurt leg, more slowly and gingerly. She winced at the pain but didn't stop him. He tied up the shoe and then helped her to stand. He brought her an overcoat and helped her put her arms through the sleeves. Finally, he handed her a cane. "My own," he explained. "But I have a spare."

"Thank you," she said. "How can I ever thank you?"

"Don't worry," he said. "We must help each other. But you must go," he said, his eyes apologizing. "They are always watching."

She finished her tea and hobbled to the door. She was able to move much more quickly with the cane. More importantly, she now looked like a regular Pole, at least if someone did not look too closely. She had a fighting chance to make it, with some luck.

She thanked him and stepped back into the cold. She expected the Germans to be waiting for her. Perhaps they'd seen her step into the store. But they were not there. The street was empty.

She hobbled out, each step agony. She walked east and north, passing the rubble and ruins of the ghetto. She tried to keep her bearing, just another crippled Pole making her way through Warsaw. She reached the Vistula, crossing to the Praga district. She passed the deserted market square and continued, finally reaching Maria's apartment complex. She thought she would find cars there, the Gestapo waiting to scoop her up, but the street was empty. Perhaps they'd already come and gone. Or they could be waiting upstairs for her. She didn't care. This was in God's hands. She felt God now, walking next to her. Whatever was going to happen.

She hobbled up to the front door and placed her hand on the handle. She drew a deep breath and opened the door. She expected a hallway full of Gestapo, but nobody was there. She stepped in and made her way toward Maria's apartment. A middle-aged man passed her in the corridor. She stiffened, expecting him to seize her, but he didn't even glance in her direction. Finally, she was standing in front of Maria's door. She knocked, waiting for the door to open, for Germans to rush in from every direction.

The door opened. Maria was there. She stared at Irena for a moment in shock, then she rushed forward, throwing her arms around her.

"You're alive!" she screamed. "Adam! She's alive."

She looked up. There was Adam, sprinting toward her. They all held each other. He was here, alive, the Germans hadn't taken him. Life began again.

Chapter 34
Checkmate

January 1944
Warsaw, Poland

Klaus checked his watch. It was midday. He had stayed the night at the office, expecting to be arrested at any moment. Morning had broken. The soldiers never came. The execution hour came and went. The condemned prisoners would have been collected at about eight. The routine was the same every day. He had ordered Irena to be added to the execution list. He'd given the cell, not the name. He still felt anger and frustration that he hadn't gleaned the location of Żegota out of her, but at least she was dead now, and the colonel would never be the wiser.

His assistant appeared. Finally. "Is it done?" he asked.

The soldier's face was white. Something was wrong.

"They found her before she was killed?" he asked. Of course. That was just his luck.

"No, sir."

"What then?"

"She's gone."

"What do you mean?" he asked.

"She isn't in her cell and she was not brought to the execution ground. I wanted to pull aside the guards for questioning, but how could I? There are eyes watching everywhere."

Klaus felt his anger rising. She'd escaped? How could that be? He would get to the bottom of this. He rose and started toward the door. Before he made the entrance, the colonel appeared.

"Where is she?" he asked again.

Klaus laughed, confident now. "I told you, there is no *her*. You'll never find her because she doesn't exist here."

The colonel stared at him in stunned silence for a moment. "I'll tell you what else doesn't exist, Rein: your future. As of this moment you are dismissed from your post. You are to report to Hans Frank within the next twenty-four hours in Kraków. He will decide your fate."

Klaus thought of Wiera Gran, still lying in a cell below. He hadn't had time to release her. There was still a possibility . . . "But sir," he protested. "I have things to—"

"You're done, Rein. Get out of my sight. I want you out of this building in the next half hour."

Klaus knew there was nothing he could do to stop this. He wasn't going to have his revenge after all. Well, he thought philosophically, at least he was leaving alive. He nodded and the colonel stormed off.

"Sir, I'm sorry," started his assistant.

Klaus waved him off with a hand. Soon he was alone, staring at his small office, smiling to himself at the ruin of his personal empire. He whispered the name: "Irena."

Irena sat on the sofa in Maria's apartment as her friend worked to remove the bandages and tried to clean her wounds. Adam sat next to her, holding her hand. They were peppering her with questions as she explained what had happened in the past few months.

"How did you arrange for my escape?" Irena asked through clenched teeth, trying to talk to keep her mind off the searing pain.

"Żegota had a contact in the SS," Maria said. "You remember he was holding it back for something important? You were that something. Julian has been working with that soldier for months, waiting for the right moment to get you out. But you were too closely watched. Finally, he was on duty when Klaus had you moved to another cell. He learned you were on the list for execution the next day and he arranged to escort you out. It's a miracle he was at the right place at the right time, or you would have perished."

Irena couldn't believe her good fortune. "But we're in terrible danger," she said. She explained her last interactions with Klaus.

"How could he know about Adam?" Maria asked.

"I don't know. Someone has betrayed us."

Maria raised her hand to her chin, considering the situation for a few moments. "You're not safe here," she concluded. "Neither is Adam."

"I know," Irena said. "None of us are. We all have to go into hiding."

"Your mother too," said Adam.

Irena turned to Adam, her eyes filling with tears. "You haven't heard. They killed her."

"What are you talking about?" he asked.

"Months ago. It was Klaus."

"Nonsense," he said. "I saw her yesterday. She's ill, she's grown worse since you were captured, but I assure you she's very much alive."

Irena couldn't believe it. Klaus had lied to her. Of course, why would he be honest? If he'd lied about her mother, perhaps he didn't know where Adam was? No, they couldn't risk it. "What are we going to do?" she asked.

"We're going to disappear," said Maria. "Today. All of us. Julian will hide us. We've dozens of safe houses." She turned to Irena, a wry smile on her face. "We'll finally be able to try out some of that paperwork on you. You deserve it."

There was a knock at the door. Irena froze but Maria put a hand on her leg. "Don't worry," she said. "It's Julian. I put out word the moment you got here."

She moved to the door and opened it. Julian was there, looking thin and ill himself. He had a half dozen men with him and they rushed in, checking all the bedrooms and forming a protective circle around them.

"Irena," Julian said, moving to kneel in front of her.

"Hello, Julian."

He took her hands. "Months of torture and you held your tongue." He smiled. "I knew I was right about you. Don't you worry now, we've already picked up your mother. We're going to move you into hiding."

"How long until I can return to work?" she asked.

His eyes widened and he shook his head. "You've done enough," he said. "Too much. Let us take care of you now."

"Perhaps for a little while," she relented. "But not forever."

He laughed. "You're impossible. But all right. If you insist, we'll find something for you."

"Something for both of us," said Adam, taking her arm. "And you must keep us together. We've been apart far too long."

Julian nodded. "That can be arranged."

Another man entered the room. "It's clear," he said. "We can go."

Julian turned to Irena. "Can you walk?"

"I'll manage," she said.

"Let's go then," he said. He drew her up and then put his arms around her, holding her for a moment. "For Poland," he whispered.

She whispered back, "For the children."

Chapter 35
Bitter Endings

April 1945
Böhlen, Germany

Klaus sat at the dinner table with his family. He looked around at his humble flat. He was back where they had started. Briggita reached out, taking his hand, as if understanding his thoughts.

"It will be all right," she said. "We had a wonderful time in Warsaw. Thank you for that. But this is where we started. We'll make do. Perhaps you can get your old job back." She smiled with encouragement.

Klaus looked at her and at their little girl. He smiled. She was so beautiful and so encouraging. She'd believed in him and supported him in every way. Now, when their world was falling apart, she was still here for him, no matter what.

She was so innocent. She had no idea what was coming. She did not know the Russians. He did. He'd reviewed the intelligence reports from East Prussia. The rapes, the murders. He looked at his beautiful wife and his heart broke. She didn't know the suffering they were about to endure. And that was just for the general population. When they discovered he was in the SS—worse yet, when they learned of his role in Poland—their fate would be even worse.

How had everything gone so wrong? The Nazis had brought him out of dire poverty. They'd promised a new world of order and truth. He'd believed in everything they promised, even if he detested the actions that were required to get them there. He'd performed those duties. He had the lives of half a million Jews on his hands. He could have lived with that somehow, for the future of his family, of his child. But the dream had turned into a nightmare. The promises were shallow lies. There would be no Greater Germany to last a thousand years. Instead the Russians had won. Communism would rule here, and there was no place for Klaus in that future.

He heard the sharp footsteps on the stairway. His wife looked up in alarm, her eyes full of fear. "What is it?" she asked.

"It is nothing," he lied. His final lie. His final protection. There was a sharp rapping on the door. He stepped up and moved from the table. At the door he paused, turning to look at his family. "I love you," he whispered.

He opened the latch with one hand while with the other he removed the pins from the two grenades in his pocket and took a few steps toward his family. The Russians were there, charging him, seizing him by the arms. He heard Briggita scream. His heart wrenched with pain. He closed his eyes. There was a flash, and all was darkness.

Irena and Adam sat at the kitchen table of their flat, sipping tea. Adam flipped through the paper, shaking his head. "It's as bad as when the fascists were here," he said. "All lies. Look at this," he said, pointing to an article. "They claim that food and fuel production is up forty-five percent from last year at this time." Adam laughed, glancing over at their empty stove. "I guess it could be true. What is forty-five percent more of nothing?"

"They are doing their best, my dear," said Irena. "The Nazis set the world on fire and burned it to the ground. It will take some time to rebuild."

"Look at us," Adam observed. "I was always the communist and you were the socialist. Now our roles are reversed. I hate the Russians and you're encouraging me to accept them."

"What choice do we have?" she asked. "What should we do? Pack up and move to the west? With what money? What language skills? Besides, it would be the same as the old Poland. A bunch of nationalist capitalists who hate us. No, we need to give the Russians time. They will build a new nation for all of our people."

She rose and moved toward the sink, taking their dishes. She ambled slowly. Her back hurt and she ran her hand over her stomach, feeling the new life in there. She smiled to herself. Adam was right, the times were still terrible, but when their little one had grown, he would have a different life. Besides, no matter what their child faced, it could never be as bad as the Nazis.

There was a sharp knock at the door. Irena looked up in surprise. Who could it be? She stepped over and opened the latch. A uniformed Polish soldier stood at the door.

"Irena Sendler?" the soldier asked.

"Yes. That's me."

"You are to come with me immediately."

"What's the meaning of this?" asked Adam, rising from the table.

The soldier took a step into the apartment, his hand moving to a pistol at his side.

"Don't, Adam!" Irena shouted. "Stay here. Don't worry. I'll be back soon."

Irena followed the soldier out of the apartment building and into a waiting car. She sat in the back as the vehicle sputtered off into the ruined streets of Warsaw. She looked around for a moment. Most of the blocks were still just mounds of rubble, with an occasional burned-out structure maintaining a little of its previous form but utterly unusable.

She stared out the window as if in a dream. She remembered the last time she'd been whisked away to an unknown location. Would this be the same? She wanted to believe that the Soviets were not capable of the same conduct as the Germans, but she knew better. She tried to understand why they had appeared at her door. Had she done something wrong? She'd resumed her old duties in the social welfare department of the new government a few months ago. She was enthusiastic about her work. She'd never been critical out loud to anyone. *Thank God they couldn't hear what Adam said*, she thought. She ran through all the conversations she'd had at her office and she could think of nothing she had said. Still, she knew. In this system, as with the Germans, sometimes it didn't matter if you were innocent.

The car stopped outside a large building on the edge of the city. A Soviet flag fluttered in the wind from a flagpole jutting out above the entranceway. Russian guards stood on either side of the double doors leading into the building. They were at attention with rifles shouldered. She didn't recognize their location but assumed it must be some kind of government headquarters for the Soviets.

Her door was opened and the man who had appeared at her door was there, gesturing for her to get out. "Why am I here?" she asked.

"That's not for me to say," the soldier responded. She hadn't expected an answer. He led her up the stairs and through the doors. The guards on either side stared forward, not acknowledging them.

She followed him down a long corridor, dimly lit. It reminded her so much of her old welfare office on Złota Street. She smiled to herself. Perhaps all government structures had the same oppressive, sterile feel.

The soldier stopped midway down the hall and opened a door to his right. He gestured for her to enter the office. Irena stepped in to find a middle-aged man in a Russian uniform with green trimming on his collar sitting at a desk. The office was well appointed, with wood paneling and a fine mahogany desk. An enormous painting of Stalin peered down from behind his leather chair. She recognized the collar. He was a member of the NKVD, the Russian secret police. *First the Gestapo, now this.*

The gentleman rose, gesturing for her to sit down. She felt a fraction of her fear subsiding. If they were going to torture her, they would have taken her to a cell, not an office.

The soldier sat back down and then opened a file, thumbing through it for a few minutes. She was reminded strongly of her first interview with Klaus, all those years ago. She searched the man's face, looking for any clue of what he might be thinking, why she was here, but his features were an impenetrable mask.

"You've been working for us for about three months now," he said finally in Polish with a thick Russian accent.

"Yes. At the department."

"But it says here you have extensive experience in social welfare, dating back from before the war. Is that correct?"

"Yes, sir. What is the meaning of this?"

"Have you always worked with food distribution?"

"Most of the time," she answered. "Except for a period in '41 and '42 when I worked in disease control."

"Ah yes," he noted, scanning a page from the file. "You worked in the Jewish Quarter."

"I did."

The man looked up. "That's the time frame we are particularly interested in. Stop me if I'm wrong, Mrs. Sendler, but it appears that your activities in the ghetto went well beyond your official duties. Isn't that correct?"

"I don't know what you mean."

"Let's not play games. We know you were a major player in getting children out of the ghetto. You were an operative with

Żegota, correct? How many Jewish children did you manage to evacuate?"

"I'm not sure exactly."

He looked over his glasses at her. "I hardly believe that. How many?"

"Approximately twenty-five hundred."

She saw his surprised reaction. *You don't know everything.*

"That's very impressive. Do you have the names and locations now?"

She shook her head. "They were gone when I was released. I know a few locations from memory, but almost everything is missing."

"Your release?" He looked down. "Ah yes, you were captured and held for four months. Is that correct?"

She nodded, not wanting to think about that time.

"Did they torture you?"

"Every day," she managed to respond.

"And you never revealed your organization? You gave no names?"

She shook her head. "I almost did," she admitted truthfully. "They took me beyond what I was able to endure. But in the end, I got away before it was too late."

"Yes, I see here that you were slated for execution, but you escaped. How did you manage that?"

She told him the story of Żegota's involvement and the harrowing escape from Szucha Street.

"Finally, I see you and your live-in companion, Adam, fought with the Polish resistance during the Warsaw uprising?"

She nodded again.

He sat back, staring at her for a long time. "I don't quite know what to say. I've seen a lot of things the past six years, as I'm sure you can imagine. But your story might be the most remarkable of all. You are a hero," he said. "One of the great Polish heroes of the war."

She felt hot embarrassment. She looked up. He was smiling

now. She wondered what all this meant. "Thank you," she said finally.

"My department has been studying you for some time now. There's been much debate about your future in the new government."

What did that mean? Were they thinking of promoting her? She felt her excitement rising.

"I have many ideas," she said. "It's always been my dream to serve in a socialist state. My father attended university in Kiev. He taught me from a little girl that—"

"We concluded you will stay where you are," he said.

"What?" she asked incredulously. "But surely with my record, I have so much to offer."

"The plain facts are you collaborated with the Polish government-in-exile in London throughout the war," he said. "Żegota was a branch of that government, as you know."

"Yes, but—"

"There are no excuses, Mrs. Sendler. The London exiles have been proven traitors to Poland, traitors to socialism. And you were a primary officer here during the war." He leaned forward. "I have to tell you that there has been a great push for your arrest and trial."

"Arrest? How can that—"

"I, for one, resisted that position. I have the good news to tell you that the conclusion was to leave you alone, provided that you keep your mouth shut."

"What?" she asked.

"You will not talk about your activities during the war again. To anyone. You will stay in your current position. You will follow the rules and you will forget Żegota, and the ghetto, and those children. Do you understand me?"

She couldn't believe his words. Everything she'd done during the war was to be ignored and forgotten? She was to remain silent forever, or face more arrests, torture, and likely death.

This was the world she'd fought for? A socialist paradise? How could she have defied the Germans, put her life on the line, saved all those children, only to be told that everything she'd done was a betrayal of socialism. "You can't ask that of me," she said.

"I have to," he responded. "Listen to me, Mrs. Sendler, because this is the last time you will ever hear this. You either follow my directions, to the letter, or you and Adam, and that bastard child you carry in your belly, will disappear forever. I'm doing this for your own good. You've done great things for Poland. Great things for the Jews. But you made the wrong friends during the war. Because of your service I've convinced the other investigators to let you go. But they won't give me a second chance. You must agree now, and you must follow this order for the rest of your life. Can you make that commitment to me?"

She realized she had no choice. She had to forget the war. In her mind she saw Dr. Korczak, Ewa, Kaji, the orphanage children playing at the center and then marching hand in hand to the Umschlagplatz. She saw Ala, the Jewish resistance fighters. She remembered her arrest and torture. Lastly, she thought of the lists. The thin little papers where thousands of lives were recorded—and now lost. One by one she burned these memories in her mind. If she was to survive now and have the family she'd dreamed of, she must deny that any of it had ever happened. She looked up and nodded.

"You've made the right decision, Mrs. Sendler. Thank you for coming." He stood and extended his hand. She rose, not taking it.

"You won't see me again," he said. "Unless you break the rules. In which case, we will meet in very different circumstances."

The door opened behind her and the soldier was there again, motioning for her to follow. Soon she was back in the vehicle and riding through the broken streets of Warsaw. They arrived back in front of her apartment building a half hour later. The soldier helped her out of the car and then drove off without saying a word.

Irena walked upstairs to her apartment and into Adam's arms.

"I was so worried," he said. "What did they want of you?"

She buried her head in his chest, letting the tears flow, sobbing for the loss of all she'd fought for and sacrificed for.

As they stood there, she reached down and touched her stomach, thinking of the life that was growing inside her, of her future with Adam, with Poland. She didn't need the past, she realized. Everything she'd ever wanted was here.

Author's Note

Information About Characters

Irena Sendler

Irena Sendler grew up southwest of Warsaw in the resort town of Otwock. Her father, a founding socialist and doctor, died when she was twelve years old. He served the Jewish community selflessly in Otwock, often working for free.

Moving to Warsaw with her mother, Irena attended the University of Warsaw. She became associated with a group of radical thinkers coming out of the Polish Free University. She married Mietek Sendler in 1931, at age twenty-one, but their marriage ended in separation several years before the beginning of World War II. Irena developed a relationship with a Jewish intellectual and attorney, Adam Celnikier, who she became romantically involved with.

Irena began the war working in food distribution. She forged documents for Jewish families so that they could continue to receive food and other social welfare. After the ghetto was sealed off, Irena obtained a permanent pass into the Jewish Quarter to inspect for communicable diseases. She met considerable initial resistance from Jan Dobraczyński, her supervisor, who was a member of the conservative party. He ultimately agreed to assist her but created additional controversy by pushing for Jewish children hiding in Warsaw to be baptized as Catholic.

Irena joined the Polish resistance. She worked with the Jewish community to smuggle children out of the ghetto and hide them in Aryan safe houses with new identifications. Her work was greatly expanded when she was recruited by Żegota, a resistance branch of the Polish government-in-exile (in London), to run the social welfare section, working with the Jewish community.

Irena, code-named "Jolanta," worked with a cell of Poles and Jews to smuggle 2,500 Jewish children out of the ghetto. To compare, Oskar Schindler saved approximately 1,200 Jews. She was arrested by the Gestapo in October 1943. Despite months of intense torture, she did not give up any contact information. She was scheduled to be executed in January 1944, but Żegota managed to bribe a guard and she escaped. She and Adam went into hiding under assumed names but remained actively involved in the resistance movement. They took part in the Polish uprising in Warsaw in 1944.

After the war, Mietek returned from captivity to find Irena five months pregnant with Adam's child. They divorced shortly thereafter, and Irena and Adam were married. Irena went to work again as a social worker within the Polish government. She was discriminated against by the Soviets and forbidden to tell her experiences from World War II. As time passed, Irena was promoted to more important positions in Poland, and her achievements during the war were increasingly brought to light.

In 1965, Yad Vashem in Israel recognized Irena as one of the Righteous Among the Nations. In 1999, a group of students in Uniontown, Kansas, discovered her story and created a play titled *Life in a Jar*. This initial movement led to a book and an organization that promotes education related to the Holocaust throughout the world. In 2007 and 2008 she was nominated for the Nobel Peace Prize. She passed away on May 12, 2008.

Irena had a difficult personal life after the war. She divorced Adam in 1957 and remarried Mietek in 1961. They divorced again in 1971. Her children expressed mixed feelings about her as a parent. Despite all of this, 2,500 children survived the war thanks to her direct efforts. Irena is a beautiful hero because she was a real human, with flaws, problems, and failures. We want our heroes to be perfect, but each person we look up to suffers from their own shortcomings, their own warts. The complexity of Irena's personality is much richer than a two-dimensional heroine.

Dr. Janusz Korczak

Dr. Korczak was born in 1878 or 1879. He was a pediatrician who focused his career on the humane treatment of orphans and on children's rights. He was a well-known individual in Poland before World War II.

When the Warsaw ghetto was formed, he moved his orphanage inside the walls, eventually to Sienna Street. He kept about two hundred children at the orphanage along with a dozen staff. Because of his advocacy and reputation, the orphanage received significant donations of food, money, and resources, despite the desperate conditions within the orphanage itself.

In early August 1942, the Germans marched the children of the orphanage off to the Umschlagplatz. Dr. Korczak had opportunities to escape into hiding prior to the evacuation but refused to do this. Many people witnessed his conduct on the hours-long march from the orphanage to the train embarkation. He was calm, in charge, and encouraging to the children and those around him. He assuredly knew his fate, and the fate of the children, but he acted with incredible bravery to keep the children as calm and reassured as possible. It is said that at the train platform there were additional efforts to save him, but he refused, staying with his children to the end.

Ewa Rechtman

One of Irena's pre-war friends and social workers. Ewa lost her job early in the German occupation of Poland, as did all Jewish professionals. Ewa lived in the ghetto from fall 1940 until the summer of 1942, assisting Irena and Dr. Korczak. Irena attempted to save her, but Ewa refused to leave her work in the ghetto. She died in Treblinka in the summer of 1942.

Ala Golab-Grynberg

Ala was a close friend of Irena's. She was appointed the head nurse in the ghetto by the Judenrat, the Jewish council in charge of the ghetto. She worked tirelessly to help the population of the Jewish Quarter. She refused Irena's efforts to save her life, but her daughter, Rami, was brought out into hiding and ultimate safety. She was transferred to work in one of the factories late in the life of the ghetto, and ultimately moved to a labor camp outside Warsaw where, defiant as ever, she was killed in an uprising. Her daughter, Rami, survived the war.

Wiera Gran

Wiera Gran, the stage name for Dwojra Grynberg, was a well-known singer and actress in Poland before World War II. During the ghetto period, she sang in the cafés, sometimes with composer and musician Władysław Szpilman of *The Pianist* fame. Wiera escaped from the ghetto and went into hiding. She survived the war.

She was arrested and tried after the war as a German collaborator, with many prominent Poles testifying against her, including Szpilman. She was found not guilty in 1949 and released. She spent the rest of her life attempting to clear her name. Her innocence or guilt is still shrouded in mystery to this day.

Klaus Rein

Klaus Rein is a fictional character. However, his story is not unusual in Nazi Germany and typifies how easy it was to commit atrocities. Klaus came from a poor family and he became an adult during the troubled economic and political times in Germany between the world wars.

Klaus lost his job during the depression in the early 1930s and, like millions of people worldwide during this time, would have sunk to the depths of despair. His fortunes change when Adolf Hitler rises to power in 1933. This new leader takes over Germany, promising new jobs and a bright future. Germany begins a massive rearmament. The economy recovers, there are new jobs, new opportunities. Perhaps more important, he tells this generation that grew up after Germany's defeat in World War I that their nation is a great one, that it's not their fault that they lost the last war. He promises a future where Germany will be the first nation on the earth. There will be jobs, money, family, arts, culture, everything anyone would want.

Klaus finds new employment as a policeman. He is married and starts a family. Everything that has gone well in his life has happened thanks to Hitler and the Nazi party. When the war starts, everything Hitler promised is coming to pass. They defeat Poland, France, they have England on the ropes. Klaus finds new opportunities in Poland, he has a better job, house, and social structure than he's ever dreamt of. He may struggle with his conscience now, as certain regrettable things are happening in Warsaw, but he's been taught for a decade that Germans are better than other people, particularly Slavs like the Poles. What he's doing is a necessary short-term evil. After all, didn't millions perish in the last world war?

As the war turns against them, he sees his world start to crumble. His own fortunes begin to fall. He must send his family home to safety as the Russians approach. As Germany begins to lose the war, everyone is pointing fingers. His loss of stature is not surprising. He becomes increasingly desperate, taking greater and greater risks to protect himself.

Finally, he loses everything in Poland, as does Germany. Klaus retreats to his hometown and waits for the inevitable. He may not have the resources or connections to escape to the west, where the Americans or British might be gentler with his family. He can only await the awful vengeance of the Russians. When they arrive in Poland, he knows he will be found out. He will be tried and killed. His wife and daughter will likely face rape and perhaps murder. Such was the life of a good many Germans in the SS during World War II. Klaus's actions and life are not defensible. But it is terribly important to understand just how easily one can walk down this road. Whether in ancient Rome, with the Mongolian hordes of Genghis Khan, or in Rwanda, Sudan, or Bosnia, genocide comes all too easily to humankind.

Peter Schwarzmann

Also a fictional character. Peter represents the double standard Klaus could apply to those he cared about. Klaus followed a strict code of conduct through the war. He was fastidious and a rule follower. However, he turned a blind eye to Peter's drinking, gluttony, and womanizing, because he was family.

This is yet another example of the complexity of humans. Just as Irena, the heroine, carried on an affair throughout the war and had a difficult relationship with her husbands, mother, and children, so is Klaus, the Gestapo murderer, a wonderful husband, father, and boss.

Hermann Göring, the number-two Nazi directly below Adolf Hitler, was a passionate advocate for animal rights. During the Nazi regime, with his encouragement, Germany passed the widest ranging and forward-thinking animal rights laws of any nation on earth at that time.

Irena's Children

The legacy of the 2,500 children secreted to safety cannot be measured. Almost all of the children's parents were killed in the death camp at Treblinka or died in other camps or by starvation or murder within the ghetto.

The jars where all the children's names were hidden were never recovered, but Irena and some of her friends were able to re-create much of the information from memory. Irena was a tireless advocate after the war for assisting these children to return to their roots, although with most of their families eradicated by the Nazis, this was a difficult if not impossible task.

In any event, there are generations of families now who owe their existence to Irena and her associates. She is a true heroine.

Further Reading

Because of the realities of a novel, the author was forced to pare down the number of individuals mentioned in the story. Irena's network of friends and associates was extensive. A fantastic and detailed nonfiction book written about Irena Sendler's life is *Irena's Children*, by Tilar J. Mazzeo.

Another interesting read is *Life in a Jar: The Irena Sendler Project*, by Jack Mayer, which covers both Irena's life and the story of the Kansas high school children who discovered her story and brought it widespread knowledge in the United States. This group continues to fund educational programs through their website: www.irenasendler.org.

Acknowledgments

I want to thank my agent, Evan Marshall, and editor, John Scognamiglio, at Kensington Books, for all their support and work in putting together this novel. Special thanks to my wife, Becky, and Mr. P., Ken, Jan (Mom), Cynthia, and Darren, who read through my drafts. Thank you also to Grace, who helped with first draft proofreading.

IRENA'S WAR

James D. Shipman

ABOUT THIS GUIDE

The suggested questions are included to enhance your group's
reading of James D. Shipman's *Irena's War*!

DISCUSSION QUESTIONS

1. The Soviets and the Germans were ideological enemies on the extreme left and the extreme right. Why did they ally themselves and attack Poland?

2. Was it unethical/immoral for Irena to continue working in the Polish government after the Germans took over?

3. Irena's actions put the lives of her fellow social workers at risk. Did she owe any duty of safety to those in her department who were not involved, and potentially unaware of her actions?

4. What motivated Irena? Was she truly motivated to help these children or was this a selfish action on her part to resist the Germans and maintain an important role during the war?

5. There is a scene in the story when Klaus overeats at his daughter's birthday party. At the same time, he comes up with the solution to cut the calories of the ghetto inhabitants from 600 to 300 per day. Members of the Nazi party were capable of strong family connections and other noble traits while also able to perpetuate incredible atrocities. How does this happen?

6. Irena did not give up the names of any of her contacts during months of torture. There are other documented instances during World War II of women handling torture more effectively than men (such as four women conspirators caught during a revolt in Auschwitz). Why might this be the case?

7. Who was the most heroic person in the book and why?

8. Why did the Soviets, after the war was over, suppress Irena's role in helping Jewish children?

9. Irena had a complicated relationship with her mother, carried on an affair during the war, had a difficult relationship with her children, and was divorced three times. Do those personal issues change the way you view her wartime heroics?

10. If you put yourself in Irena's shoes, could you do what she did? Would you have escaped Warsaw early in the war, as her mother desired? Would you stick to your duties in the department? Is Irena extraordinary, or would many people in her position do the same?